SPARE ME THE TRUTH

CJ Carver is a half-English, half-Kiwi author living just outside Bath. CJ lived in Australia for ten years before taking up long-distance rallies, including London to Saigon, London to Cape Town and 14,000 miles on the Inca Trail. CJ's books have been published in the UK and the USA and have been translated into several languages. CJ's first novel, *Blood Junction*, won the CWA Debut Dagger Award and was voted as one of the best mystery books of the year by *Publisher's Weekly*.

www.cjcarver.com / @C_J_Carver

By the same author

The Indian Kane series

Blood Junction

Black Tide

The Jay McCaulay series

Gone Without Trace

Back with Vengeance

The Honest Assassin

Other novels

Dead Heat

Beneath the Snow

SPARE ME THE TRUTH

CJ CARVER

ZAFFRE

First published in Great Britain in 2016 by

Zaffre Publishing
80-81 Wimpole St, London W1G 9RE
www.zaffrebooks.co.uk

A CIP catalogue record for this book is available from the British Library.

ISBN: 978-1-7857-6033-4
Trade Paperback ISBN: 978-1-7857-6211-6

Also available as an ebook

3 5 7 9 10 8 6 4 2

Typeset by IDSUK (Data Connection) Ltd

Printed and bound by Clays Ltd, St Ives Plc

Zaffre Publishing is an imprint of Bonnier Publishing Fiction, a Bonnier Publishing company
www.bonnierpublishingfiction.co.uk
www.bonnierpublishing.co.uk

For Vic and Jean Ayres

PROLOGUE

Three weeks ago, Saturday 3 November

She steps into a corridor. She is behind Peter Miller and Suzie Lui who are chatting excitedly, seemingly oblivious of any danger, but Stella takes one look at the four men and knows things have gone terribly wrong.

She is already bending forward, reaching to grab the case from Suzie, planting her weight on her right foot to spin round, make a run for it, but the men are fast. Much faster than her. She has barely moved and they've drawn their guns. A Glock, an Uzi and two MAC-10 auto sub-machine pistols which are immediately trained on her. The Uzi is on Peter, the Glock on Suzie. The men's hands are steady, their eyes hard and cold. They've done this before. They're pros.

Suzie gives a little scream. Peter goes as white as chalk and makes a soft whimpering sound.

There are places Stella will remember all her life – a shabby house in the East End, the hospital room where she gave birth to her daughter, a serene Mayfair street with rows of glossy black railings – but there will be nothing branded more deeply in her memory than this moment.

How had Cedric found out?

Nobody knew about this. Not even Bernard.

Had Peter or Suzie let something slip?

She suddenly sees how stupid she's been. She thinks she's so *clever*, but he's always been one step ahead. Was it the arrogance of age? The fact she thought she'd had a lifetime's experience? She's due to retire next year – perhaps she thought she'd go out in a spectacular shower of success but instead she's facing monumental dishonour and disgrace. Something that the office will whisper about in decades to come. How Stella Reavey, one of the so-called best, brought not just ignominy and humiliation to their front door, but how she risked their families, their friends, and their country. All through hubris.

The man with the Glock moves to take the case from Suzie. The young woman recoils.

'No!' she protests violently. '*No!*'

In one smooth movement the man raises his pistol, aims it between the young woman's eyes and pulls the trigger.

The bullet enters Suzie's skull, leaving a neat hole the size of a pebble in her forehead, but the back of her head is a mess of blood and bone, brain matter.

The woman's body drops into a soft crumple of slender limbs and cloth.

Peter is trembling from head to toe. A keening sound comes involuntarily from his throat.

'You didn't need to kill her,' Stella says. She is glad her tone is authoritative and doesn't reveal her fear.

The man doesn't answer. He grabs the case.

The weapons remain trained on her and Peter as the man steps backwards down the corridor. He vanishes through the door. She watches his men leave. The instant they are out of view she races after them but the door is locked. She spins round and tears to the other end of the corridor to find that door is locked too. By the time she summons help, it is too late. The men and the case are gone.

It is after midnight and Stella stands quietly and alone, wondering how to salvage the situation. She needs something from left field that can't implicate her, something unpredictable, something *random*, as her daughter might say. When an idea comes to her, she closes her eyes and wonders whether her conscience will ever forgive her for entering Dan's life again.

CHAPTER ONE

Thursday 22 November, 10.04 a.m.

Dan Forrester was in aisle five of his local Tesco supermarket, struggling to decide whether Jenny wanted a well-known branded packet of noodles or the cheaper generic version, blissfully unaware that in the next few minutes his life would be ripped to pieces.

It wouldn't be the first time.

He already knew how fragile life could be. That the wall between sanity and insanity, life and death, was paper-thin. One moment, life was mundane and ordinary, even boring, the next it tilted on its axis and plunged into chaos. Dan had survived the chaos before and was now in a place of harmony where the most stressful thing he had to think about was which type of noodles to buy.

'Daddydaddydaddy!'

Aimee tore down the aisle towards him like a sparkling Catherine wheel, a blur of white-blond hair and pink tinsel yelling at the top of her voice.

'I found it, foundit foundit!'

She narrowly missed his trolley and smacked into his shins, triumphantly waving a packet of chicken stock cubes in one hand while grabbing a fold in his jeans to stop herself from falling over with the other. Her face was flung back, her beaming smile like a laser straight to his heart.

'Well done, pumpkin.'

'I'm *not* a pumpkin. Pumpkins are *fat*.'

'OK. Well done, carrot.'

'Carrot?!' Her screech of indignation made several shoppers nearby flinch and give him stares of disapproval, but he was too old to be bothered by what other people thought. He was forty in two weeks' time. What was that all about? He'd been sixteen when his father turned forty – *ancient* – but here he was with flecks of grey growing through his hair just like Dad.

'OK,' he said. 'Celery.'

'Daddy, I'm not a *vegetable*.'

'Really?' He affected surprise. 'Not even an avocado? I love avocados.'

Aimee did a twirl, arms outstretched. 'Avocado, avocado, avocado,' she sang. 'I'm an avocaaado.'

Dan went back to his inspection of noodles satisfied he'd distracted her nicely from the subject of *fat*, which her best friend Tara had introduced her to at the weekend. Before her sleepover Aimee had had no idea what a calorie was, but now she was picking up cereal boxes trying to read the sides, determined to find out how many calories were in a Cheerio, whether she was having too many and if she should go on a diet. Apparently Tara's mother was obsessed with her weight and Aimee wanted to know if she should be too. Jenny had had to restrain Dan from marching over the road and jamming Tara's mother's head inside a cereal packet.

'What else can I get, Daddy?' She was still twirling.

He pretended to think. 'Hmm. Well, one thing we really need is a reindeer for the hall table. I don't know which sort, though. They come in all colours. Gold, pink, silver or just plain brown.'

Her eyes brightened. 'You mean a *chocolate* reindeer?'

'Do you think you'll be able to find one?'

Aimee scampered away, heading for the aisle-end display of Christmas chocolates. He could keep an eye on her there. Without consciously making a decision, he put the cheaper noodles in his trolley and began to head for the spice rack further down. His mind was on nothing but ground ginger and dried chillies when he felt a familiar tell-tale prickle at the back of his neck.

Someone was watching him.

He didn't swing round to see who it might be, but maintained his inspection of condiments. After ten seconds or so, he turned to his trolley and dropped in a small bottle of ground ginger. At the same time, he took in the woman out of the corner of his eye. She was still watching him. This time, a small smile curved on her lips, as though she knew he was observing her.

Late fifties, she had glossy waves of dark hair threaded with silver. Strong jaw, cut glass cheekbones. Slender, wiry body. Understated trouser suit. Still smiling, expression warm, she stepped towards him.

'Dan,' she said.

Something hitched in his chest at the sound of her voice.

'I'm sorry?' he said. He didn't recognise her.

She came to stand in front of him. Her eyes were clear and candid, the colour of burnt hazelnuts. She carried no shopping. A plain leather satchel hung from her shoulder.

'You don't remember me.' She stated it as a fact.

Her clothes weren't cheap, but they weren't expensive either. Middle of the road. Bland. The same couldn't be said for her shoes, however, which were sleek high-heeled black leather with a patent finish. Smart and sexy. She could be a secretary or a barrister.

'I'm Stella. Stella Reavey.'

As she said her name, he felt a lightness enter him. Perhaps he *did* know her after all. She put out her hand. It seemed churlish not to take it. Her skin was warm and smooth, her grip strong.

'We used to work together,' she said.

'Er . . .' He wished Jenny was here instead of getting her hair cut across the road. After his breakdown five years ago he struggled to remember a lot of things. Some were small, like not remembering a favourite café or meeting an old friend for a pub lunch one Sunday, but others were huge, like not remembering anything about the office job he'd had before Luke and Aimee were born.

'Interesting how some things have stayed with you,' she told him, moving briefly to give some space to a blowsy woman walking past with her toddler in the trolley child seat. 'You knew I was watching you but you didn't give anything away. I guess it shows that our training sticks with us even if we don't realise it.'

She'd used the word *training*. He said, 'Are you a driving instructor too?'

For a moment she looked as though she was unsure how to react, whether to laugh or cry. 'No.' She cleared her throat. Glanced over her shoulder, then back. 'I'm something entirely different. So are you, although you don't know it.'

His patience thinned the moment she began talking in riddles. Some people thought it amusing to play games with an amnesiac but joking around with someone who had suffered memory loss due to a colossal personal trauma was insupportable as far as he was concerned. His psychiatrist, Dr Orvis Fatik, told him people played tricks on him because they enjoyed the sense of control they wielded, especially if, before his memory was damaged, he had been the more dominant in the relationship. But, whatever the explanation, Dan rarely forgave them for making him feel stupid.

'I knew this wasn't going to be easy,' she continued, 'but I couldn't see any other way.' Her eyes were on his, frank and sincere. 'We're out of options. We need your help, Dan . . .'

He flicked a glance past Stella Reavey and down the aisle to see Aimee waving at him. She was holding a toy, an oversized white puppy, complete with red matching collar and lead. Her expression was pleading. He shook his head at her, making a pair of antlers with his fingers. *Reindeer*, he mouthed. She pouted in return but nodded.

'We need to find someone called Cedric. It isn't his real name, but a code name. CEDRIC.'

She was looking at him expectantly, as though he might suddenly clap his hands to his head and shout, 'Cedric! Of course!' but instead, Dan looked pointedly around the supermarket. 'Is there a hidden camera here somewhere?' he asked. His tone was biting. 'Did Matt put you up to this? Are he and his buddies cracking up in the car park?'

Last Christmas Matt had hired a stripper to approach Dan in a pub, pretending she was his ex-girlfriend. It had been embarrassing and humiliating and, although Dan had laughed it off, inside he had been seething. This time, however, he wasn't going to roll over and play nice and he changed his body language to exude aggression. To his surprise, Stella didn't back down. She lifted her chin and held his gaze, showing she wasn't easily intimidated.

'Matt?' she queried.

'An old school friend. He's renowned for his sick sense of humour.'

'God, no.' She looked shocked. 'It's not like that at *all*. Please believe me, Dan. Just listen to me for a moment.'

There was something so urgent about her, so intense – as though she longed to plunge her arms inside him and touch his inner core and connect with him – that he briefly overrode his instinct to turn his back on her.

'Thank you,' she breathed. 'Look, I'm sorry to drop in Cedric's name like that, but a professor of neurology at a brain research institute told me recently that sometimes memories can break through, even in the toughest cases of dissociative amnesia.

It all depends on whether the biochemical pathways allow a particular memory to be recalled. Obviously Cedric has been blocked or disrupted . . .' She ran a hand distractedly through her hair. 'I know this is difficult, but you need to know we used to work together before your breakdown. For the government, where –'

'In the Immigration Department?' he cut in, his interest piqued. He'd been told this was where he used to work when he and Jenny had lived in London. Perhaps he *did* know her.

Stella blinked. 'Not exactly.'

'Where was the office?' he asked, deciding to test her.

'Westminster.'

Correct.

'Who was my boss?' he asked.

'I was. But the person we reported to . . . I'm afraid I can't tell you who he is. Not yet.'

Wrong answer. His boss hadn't been a woman but a tall man with spectacles and untidy red hair. Jenny had shown him a photograph of him taken at an office Christmas party eight years ago.

Stella nibbled her lip. 'It's maddening that I'm not authorised to tell you much, but you have to trust me when I say a situation has arisen that is extremely urgent. It's a security issue, hence the need for discretion but –'

'I think you ought to stop right now,' Dan said stiffly. He should have ignored her from the start and he was angry at himself for not trusting his instincts. It had to be another prank of Matt's. He couldn't think what else she was doing here. His attention flashed to check on Aimee and when he couldn't see her his blood pressure spiked only to fall a second later when she suddenly reappeared.

'Dan. Listen, *please.*' Stella's tone was earnest. 'We used to work closely together, OK? And when I say closely, I don't mean sharing an office, although we did do that too. I mean we depended on each other, *really* depended . . .' She paused as though struggling to find the right words.

To his relief, Aimee began walking down the aisle towards them. The quicker they got out of here the better, but Aimee was taking it slowly, her tongue pressed against her lower lip as she concentrated on not dropping the large gold-foil wrapped reindeer.

Stella's gaze clicked straight to Aimee and then straight back to him. His heart went cold. She knew Aimee?

'We depended upon each other in the field,' Stella went on, her words coming faster. 'We were a team. I saved your life once. You saved mine too.'

He stared at her. *What?*

'Look . . .' She turned her neck and pulled down her jacket collar. 'See this?'

He stared. The scar was the length of his thumb and crawled like a grey worm across her neck muscles, puckering at each end.

'You know the scar on your abdomen?' Stella said. 'You got it in the same firefight.'

No way. He'd had enough of this. He was out of here. He didn't care if Matt was involved or not. She was creeping him out big time.

'Daddy . . .' Aimee was standing expectantly in front of him, holding out the golden reindeer, waiting for him to take it and put it in the trolley.

'Hi, Aimee,' Stella said.

'Hi.'

Dan didn't hesitate. He whipped round to Stella. Gripped her upper arm and swung her around so they faced away from Aimee. 'How the fuck do you know my daughter's name?' he hissed.

'Hey, steady on, Dan.' She looked alarmed. 'You're hurting me.'

He didn't relax his grip. He pushed his face close to hers. His tone was ice-cold. 'You say another word to my daughter, and I will kill you.'

Stella fixed him with a clear gaze but as he stared her down he saw a flicker of uncertainty.

'Christ,' she murmured. 'You're bloody scary when you want to be. No wonder Bernard warned me to be careful, but I honestly thought that when you saw me something in your memory might –'

'Stop,' he hissed. 'Not another word. My daughter and I are leaving now. I don't want to see you again. Got it?'

He turned to Aimee and put her reindeer in the trolley. 'Time to go, sweet pea.' Holding Aimee's hand in his, he started to wheel the trolley towards the exit.

'Daddy, slow down!'

'Sorry, sweetie, but I'm in a hurry.'

He glanced over his shoulder but Stella seemed to have vanished. Grabbing his phone he rang his old school buddy.

'Yo, Dan the Man,' Matt answered. 'What can I do you for?'

'Have you just sent a woman called Stella Reavey to wind me up?'

'What? Stella *who*?'

Matt's bafflement sounded genuine but Dan pushed on.

'Some woman in the supermarket is claiming to be from my past.'

'Is she attractive?' Matt brightened. 'If she is, hang on to her until I get there, OK? You're married, remember?'

'She wasn't picking me up, you idiot. She . . .' – he paused briefly to amend what he'd been about to say – '. . . obviously made a mistake.'

He hung up, wondering if Stella Reavey was some kind of stalker. She looked so *normal* – sounded sane too – but she'd been way off the wall. Had he overreacted? Not as far as protecting Aimee was concerned. The woman knew enough about him to get him interested but then things had started to unravel. Him, caught in a firefight? His scar was from an accident in his workshop when he'd been repairing the back door of their old home and the chisel slipped. Jenny had rushed him to hospital where he'd had six stitches. Apparently the blood stain on the workshop floor had still been there when they'd sold the house a year later.

Was the woman on drugs? He drove cars for a living for Chrissakes. He didn't get involved in gun battles. He used to be a civil servant, a paper pusher, and the closest he would have got to any weaponry was watching a cop show on TV. The most excitement he got in life was when the lawnmower refused to start. Well, that wasn't quite true, considering yesterday one of his clients had decided to overtake when specifically asked not to do so, narrowly escaping a head-on collision. What was it with some men that they wouldn't listen? They had to show they knew better, he guessed, especially when behind the wheel of a Porsche 911. Dan far preferred teaching women high performance driving because they didn't have the same type of ego and tended to brake when he told them to.

He made his way past a short queue of people at the 'cash only' checkout, wondering whether he should report Stella to the police. Ditching the trolley at the far end of the supermarket he headed for the exit. Aimee glanced up at him then back at the trolley. 'Daddy, you've forgotten the shopping.'

'I've got to make a phone call,' he told her. 'We'll get another reindeer when I'm through.'

'But we won't have anything to eat tonight.'

'We'll eat out.'

Her expression lifted. 'Can we go to Candy's?'

Candy's was her favourite café, which was currently decked out in carpets of fake snow and sleigh bells. The staff wore elves' outfits.

'Candy's it is.'

'Yay!' Aimee was leaping with excitement as they walked outside into a light drizzle. He helped put Aimee's hood up, and at the same time he heard Stella's voice, soft but insistent as she fell into step with them. Gritting his teeth, he tried to ignore her.

'Haven't you ever wondered why you're so secretive?' she asked. 'Why you have a great memory for faces? Why you can listen to three conversations at once without appearing to do so? Tell me, Dan, why do you always look for the exits when you enter a room? Why do you hate sitting with your back to the window? And what about your job? Why do you think you chose performance driving? Not for the money, I'm sure. My guess is because it's the most exciting thing you could find to do.'

She glanced across at him but he refused to look at her. 'Tell me if I'm wrong,' she said. 'You like the flexibility of doing free-lance work. You like not knowing what next week might bring. You also like being in demand and although you don't earn huge amounts of money, you don't earn peanuts either. But still. My bet would be that after five years of doing pretty much the same thing, you're bored rigid but daren't admit it. Least of all to your wife.'

Dan was gritting his teeth so hard he wondered why they didn't shatter. Keeping himself between Stella and Aimee, he said to his daughter, 'Keep hold of my hand, no matter what.'

'Yes, Daddy.' Aimee was staring across at Stella, wide-eyed.

'But should anything happen,' he continued, 'you run to Mummy at the hairdressers. You know where it is?'

'Yes.'

Reaching into his fleece pocket he brought out his mobile phone. Dialled 999.

'Which service do you require?' A woman answered promptly.

'Police,' Dan said.

'Putting you through.'

There was a click, then another woman said, 'Police. What is your emergency?'

'I have a woman here who is threatening me and my daughter, and I believe she is dangerous. I need the police immediately.'

'Where are you?'

Dan gave the dispatcher the details. Stella had fallen silent, but she was still walking alongside. Christ, he thought. She is definitely a hamper short of a picnic. He thought she'd vanish the second he called the police.

The dispatcher continued to ask questions.

'Has she hurt either of you?'

'Not yet.'

'Is she armed?'

'I think I saw a knife,' Dan said.

He hadn't seen anything of the sort but he wasn't going to mess around with Aimee here. He knew the police would prioritise his call now.

'I'm sending a car to you immediately. Please stay on the line.'

Dan strode out, wanting to get to Jenny, who would keep Aimee safe while he dealt with Stella.

'I know you want me out of here, Dan,' Stella said, 'but I can't leave. I'm sorry. This is bigger than both of us.'

Keeping the phone against his ear, Dan took a route through the car park that didn't go past his car. He didn't want Aimee to pick it out, show it to Stella.

'We just want to borrow you,' Stella said. 'For a day, maybe two. But no more, I promise. We simply want you to pretend your memory's coming back. That's all. I wish I could brief you properly, but I wasn't allowed to. Not until you're on board. All I can say is it's a black file.'

A minnow of memory darted through his mind but it was so fast he failed to catch it.

'Which means it's top-secret as well as extremely urgent. I'm truly sorry for being so cryptic but we couldn't think of another way. We'll pay you, of course, but then you're not particularly turned on by money, are you? And once we've completed the mission, you can go back to your normal life.' He felt more than saw her gaze intensify. 'But only if you want to, that is. You might find yourself tempted to do something a little more out of the ordinary afterwards.'

He led Aimee around the car park barrier. Jenny's hairdresser's was two hundred yards away, on the opposite side of the road. He didn't like bringing Stella into Jenny's proximity, but he didn't see he had a choice. Aimee was his priority.

Mr Forrester?

It was the dispatcher.

'Yes,' he said. 'Please tell the police to hurry.'

'They will be with you in two minutes.'

At the same moment, he heard a siren in the distance. Stella did nothing to indicate she heard it.

'Dan,' she said. 'You're not giving me anything to work with here. You're not giving me a chance. You're blocking me off. I can't let you do that.'

He kept his teeth gritted and didn't respond.

'You give me no choice.' Frustration laced her voice. 'I wasn't going to tell you this because I didn't want to destabilise you or cause you more pain. I was hoping you'd be intrigued enough to want to know more but it's obviously not enough. I know you won't believe what I'm going to say, but trust me, every word is true. It's up to you what you do with it.'

He tightened his hold on Aimee's hand. He was sweating, his heart knocking. Thank God, the siren was closing in. The police couldn't get here fast enough as far as he was concerned.

'Your son,' she said. 'Luke. He didn't die in a hit-and-run. Yes, he died in your arms, but he didn't die on Brick Lane as you've been told.'

His heart stopped.

Liquid ice poured through his veins.

She knew about Luke.

'You're not who you think you are, Dan. Your identity, your past, is a lie. Your entire family has been lying to you.'

CHAPTER TWO

'Paperwork,' said Grace, scrabbling in her handbag for her purse, 'should be abolished.'

She was in her local deli, getting supplies to sustain her through the usual mountain of paperwork that blighted every GP's life: a holiday cancellation form followed by a referral; a medical report for an insurance company; a fitness to work document. To complete even the simplest form she had to check the patient's entire record. Carelessness or an inaccurate report could have serious consequences down the line, so she liked to make sure every 't' was crossed, every 'i' dotted.

'I'll get a box of matches if you like. We can have a bonfire. Toast some marshmallows.'

Jamie gave a smile – genuinely warm and friendly and utterly uncomplicated – and, as usual, she couldn't help but smile back.

Younger than her, with dreadlocks and a Celtic cross with feathered wings tattooed on the nape of his neck, Jamie had been the first person to welcome her into the village six months previously. Although Ross had helped her with the main move at a weekend, she'd still had a handful of items to shift, and on the Monday she'd been struggling to lift a pot plant from the back of her car when

Jamie had appeared and given her a hand. He'd helped unload the rest of the car, and when he'd seen the jars of honey she'd collected from Devon, Scotland and France, had asked if she was going to keep a beehive. Her garden was, apparently, perfect for bees and if she was interested he'd be happy to introduce her to the art of beekeeping. Grace had been enchanted by the idea, especially when she learned he helped look after several beehives for people he did odd jobs for in the village, including the surgery. Today he was helping out at the deli, making sandwiches.

'That advice you gave me,' he said cheerfully as he handed her an egg mayo on granary. 'Fantastic.'

'What advice?' She was baffled.

'You encouraged me to start masturbating.'

'Jamie, I never said that,' she scolded, pretending she couldn't see the disconcerted glances of the other customers.

'You did! You told me that men who ejaculated more than five times each week in their twenties, thirties and forties, reduced their risk of getting prostate cancer by a third.'

He was right. They'd been sitting in her kitchen one evening when she'd told him about a report from the *British Journal of Urology* which said just that. She couldn't remember how their discussion had been initiated – he'd probably heard something about the subject on the radio – and although she couldn't remember discussing masturbation with him, she supposed it was the same thing. Ejaculating was ejaculating, after all.

'My mates and I were talking about it,' he went on. 'We thought we should take this information to a wider audience. Help advertise prostate cancer awareness. So we've started a

Twitter campaign and we're going to climb Mount Kilimanjaro to raise funds.'

'Well done you,' she said.

'Dr Grace . . .' He came round the side of the counter and lowered his voice, suddenly looking serious. 'Can I come and see you privately? I want to talk to you about something.' A sudden look of distress crossed his face, so intense, she felt a moment's alarm.

'What is it?' she asked.

He looked away. 'It's just that someone I know . . . well, I don't know her. Not really. I only met Bella once. But she was really nice. I just heard that she's gone missing and it's made me feel . . . I don't know . . .' His voice trailed off. He looked at her miserably.

'Oh, Jamie.' Her heart went out to him. 'That's really tough.'

'Yeah.'

'Look, I should finish work around seven or so. Do you want to come over and talk about it? And if you could check whether I've insulated the bees properly for winter I'd be eternally grateful.'

He bit his lip. 'I can't do tonight. I've got to meet some friends at the pub.'

'Tomorrow?'

Another smile, but this one was authentic and tinged with relief. 'Yeah, that would be great. I'll bring an entrance reducer for your hive too.'

Grace paid him for her sandwich and coffee, then headed to the surgery. As she stepped into her office, her phone rang – the landline – and she prayed it wasn't an emergency that she'd have to leave the surgery for or she'd never complete her paperwork. But it wasn't an emergency; it was her mother.

Grace nearly fell over in surprise.

'Mum?' She couldn't remember a single time when her mother had rung her at work. She never rang Grace simply for a chat, either. The call always had a reason behind it – like plans for Christmas and birthdays – and she suddenly saw how very self-contained they both were.

'Darling, have you got a moment?' Her mother's voice was brisk.

'Of course.'

'I need some advice.'

Grace blinked. 'What about?'

Her mother didn't say anything for a moment. Grace heard a hollow *shhh* on the line, indicating her mother might be outside, and then she heard the faint sound of a siren coming through the receiver.

'Where are you?' Grace asked.

Her mother didn't answer. She said, 'I've just met an old friend.'

'Oh?' Grace was curious. 'Who's that?'

'Nobody you know. But the thing is, he doesn't remember me.'

'How come?'

Another silence, which was most unlike her mother. It was as though she was trying to work out what to say. Either she was being ultra-cautious or she was finding the conversation difficult.

Finally, her mother said, 'He's suffering from dissociative amnesia.'

'Oh. I'm sorry.'

'Is there *anything* I can do right now to jog his memory? It's really . . . quite important. I have to talk to him, make him listen to me, but he refuses.'

Grace heard the frustration in her mother's voice, but there was also something more – a tremor of emotional pain.

'I'm not sure what to suggest,' Grace said honestly. She didn't know the person or their medical history or how he might react to her mother trying to jog his memory. 'Have you tried his GP?'

'No time.'

'What's the urgency?'

'Later, Grace.'

Although she was surprised at the uncharacteristic call and the even more uncommon request, Grace trusted her mother and decided not to waste time demanding answers to the questions crowding her mind.

'If he's suffered a high-level, stress-induced trauma –'

'Yes.'

'It could take years before something triggers his recollection.'

'I know that, darling,' her mother said, and although her voice was even, Grace felt the reprimand and guessed her mother had already done her research. She probably knew as much if not more about her friend's condition than Grace did. 'But I hoped you might have had someone in your surgery . . . or heard about someone's memory suddenly returning. Something that I might be able to use.'

Grace put her hand over her eyes to intensify her concentration. 'The only case I know of personally was when a young girl watched her father rape and kill her mother. She had no memory of it until twenty years later when she saw certain facial expressions of her son, which triggered her recollection. I know you want your friend to remember you now, but you can't rush these things. I'd suggest you simply be yourself. Don't be someone you're not by pushing him because he may not recognise that behaviour . . .'

Silence. Grace heard the siren growing louder.

'Mum?'

'I'm sorry,' her mother said. 'I shouldn't have bothered you. I just hoped you might . . . create a miracle.' She gave a soft bark of laughter but it wasn't humorous. It was the sound of despair.

'Mum, where are you?'

'Darling, I must go.'

'What's with the siren?' Grace asked. She felt a surge of alarm as she recognised it as a police siren, not an ambulance. 'Is everything OK?'

'Love you.'

Grace was about to say *love you too*, but the line went dead. Her mother had hung up.

CHAPTER THREE

Dan watched a police car appear at the end of the street, fluorescent stripes gleaming through the rain.

He stepped out and beckoned urgently. His ears were ringing, his mouth dry.

Stella Reavey pocketed her mobile phone. He'd heard every word of her conversation to someone she'd called *darling* – her husband? her psychiatrist? – and didn't discount the likelihood she'd staged it for his benefit. As if one overheard conversation would convince him she wasn't lying.

The car switched off its siren and came to a halt. Two officers climbed out. One was in his thirties, male, close-cropped dark hair, the other younger, female, with acne scars on her cheeks. Both had epaulettes embroidered with their names and collar numbers, a new initiative by the Gwent police to try to make their officers more approachable. Jim Parsons and Vicky Cross.

'Mr Forrester?' Jim Parsons asked.

'Yes. This is the woman who's been harassing us.' Dan pointed at Stella, who was standing there looking about as dangerous as a day-old kitten. 'If you wouldn't mind keeping her here, I'd like to take my daughter to my wife. She's having her hair cut.'

He indicated the Loose Ends salon across the road. 'I'll come back immediately.'

'Are you OK?' Vicky Cross ducked down to ask Aimee, who nodded. She'd put her thumb in her mouth and her eyes were as wide as dinner plates. 'Great,' said the PC. 'Let's get you to your mum, shall we?' She held out her hand but Aimee ducked behind Dan, clutching his knees. 'OK,' she said, glancing at Dan. 'Let's all go together. Jim can stay and talk with . . .' She looked pointedly at Stella.

'Stella Reavey,' said Stella and to Dan's disbelief, she reached into her bag, brought out a business card and handed it to Jim Parsons as though they were all networking at some high-flying corporate event.

'Let's go.' Dan's voice was brusque.

Vicky Cross walked with him and Aimee to the salon. When he opened the door, he saw Jenny at the far end with Stacey the hairdresser. The two women were chatting. Jenny was laughing, giving a funny little snort in the middle – almost a snigger – that meant they were talking about something personal, probably rude. Her hair was dampened flat against her neck, the colour of wet straw, but when it was dry it would lighten into pale yellow waves. Long limbed with blue eyes and a mischievous sense of humour, all she had to do was twitch her little finger and he came running. Jenny and Aimee. His two girls, the centre of his world. His *raison d'être.*

Jenny gave another snort but then her eyes went to the mirror and the reflected image of Dan, Aimee, and a uniformed officer. She froze for a moment, her face draining of colour. Then she exploded from her chair. Stacey's scissors went flying and she stumbled backwards 'What the . . .'

'It's OK, sweetheart,' Dan told his wife, soothingly. 'Everything's fine. Aimee's fine. I promise.'

But Jenny was already on her knees and holding Aimee, checking her face, running her hands over her body. 'Honey, what happened?' Her voice was urgent. 'Are you OK? Please God, tell me you're OK. Tell me . . .'

Aimee's face began to crumple under her mother's panic.

'Jen, she's fine.' Dan squatted next to them. 'Aren't you, celery?' He gave Aimee a wink.

'Avocado,' Aimee managed to whisper.

'Not now, Dan.' Jenny rounded on him. 'Tell me what this policewoman's doing here.'

Dan rose to his feet. Jenny stayed with Aimee, stroking her head rhythmically, making crooning noises under her breath.

'A woman harassed us in the supermarket, that's all.' Dan automatically tried to downplay it. 'She wouldn't go away. So I called the police. I wanted to –'

'What woman?'

'She's with my colleague,' the PC said. 'Your husband thought it best that you look after Aimee while we talk to her and your husband about the incident.'

Jenny scrambled to her feet. One side of her hair had been cut and her fringe stuck up in an odd little quiff Dan hadn't seen before.

'Where is she?' Her eyes were wild. She seemed to have forgotten about Aimee and as she began to move to the window

Dan pulled her back and out of sight. She was trembling, her hands fluttering like birds.

'I don't want her to see you,' he said. 'I don't want to give her any more ammunition before –'

'Ammunition?'

'She claimed to know me. But she doesn't.'

'Claimed?' Her voice began to rise. 'What does that mean?'

Aimee's lips were wobbling. Tears starting to form. He said quietly, 'You're scaring Aimee.'

'Christ.' She put a hand briefly over her eyes. 'Sorry. It's just that you're scaring the crap out of me.'

'We're fine,' he said. 'Honestly.'

She looked at him for a moment and then, before he could stop her, she was at the window, looking out. She went quite still. Dan sensed a heightening of tension, like an animal catching sight of a predator.

All the hairs rose along his forearms. 'You recognise her?'

Jenny's mouth opened but no sound came out.

'Jenny?' When he touched her arm she jumped as though electrified. 'Do you know her?'

She swung her head to look at him. Worked her mouth before she spoke. 'No.' Her voice was steady. 'I've never seen her before.'

'Are you sure?' He was frowning.

'I'm sure.' She moved away from the window, her movements slow, her gaze unfocused. 'For a moment . . . I thought it was someone else . . . An old school friend. But it's not. What does she want?'

He didn't think he'd tell her that it was to find someone called Cedric. That would really freak her out. Keeping his voice low, he said, 'The best thing for Aimee right now is that you get on with your day as usual. Finish getting your hair cut. I don't want this to get blown into anything it isn't, OK? Can you do that for her?' *And for you*, he wanted to add, but didn't.

Jenny looked at Dan, straight into his eyes, but he wasn't sure if she was seeing him. She said, 'Of course. Aimee comes first.' Her tone held no inflection.

Dan watched Jenny turn and give the policewoman a nod. 'Thank you.' She was stiffly polite. Then she ducked down to Aimee and said, 'Time to finish my haircut, don't you think?'

Aimee looked anxiously at Dan. He said, 'I'll be back soon, hunny bunny, then we'll go home, maybe watch a movie before we go to Candy's later. How does that sound?'

'Can we watch *How to Train Your Dragon*?'

Aimee's favourite movie of the moment.

'Yup.'

The anxiety vanished beneath a brilliant smile.

As Dan left the salon, Stacey settled Jenny back into her chair. Aimee was chatting brightly to Stacey. As he glanced back, Dan noticed how pale and quiet Jenny seemed. He put it down to the shock of seeing a police officer with Aimee. The last time she had received a personal visit from a PC was when she'd been informed of Luke's death. No wonder Jenny had reacted the way she had.

As he stepped outside, Dan's pulse rate increased. Stella Reavey was standing by the patrol car, but PC Jim Parsons wasn't with her, questioning her, or even looking at her. He was leaning his hip against the boot of his car, talking on his mobile and holding up what looked like Stella Reavey's business card.

He seemed to be reading from it. Dan walked quickly across the road, PC Cross thudding alongside. As he neared, Jim Parsons nodded a few times before putting his phone into his pocket. Walking to Stella, the police officer returned her business card. Dan swept the card from her fingers but she didn't protest.

Stella Reavey. DCA & Co.

Aside from a landline telephone number, that was all that the card showed. Nothing else. No address, no email, no website.

'Very minimal,' he remarked acidly. And pocketed it.

Again, Stella didn't protest. Instead, she reached into her handbag and brought out another card. 'I'd like you to have this one as well.'

It was an identical card but on the reverse side it showed a handwritten address and mobile number. The writing was small and neat, very precise.

'My home details,' she said.

Dan looked at Jim Parsons. 'I'd like to get a restraining order against this woman. Make sure she never comes near me or my family again.'

'You have my word that I won't,' Stella said.

'Shut up.' His voice was flat. 'I'm talking to the police.'

'And the police,' the PC said with a sigh, 'need a moment. Sorry, sir, if you don't mind . . .' Parsons took his colleague aside and started talking. Dan watched their body language. He saw the female PC's eyes widen slightly then flick to Stella Reavey with an expression of . . . what? Surprise? He couldn't be certain, but then she began to look interested, even intrigued. The policewoman's gaze swept over Stella Reavey, taking in her apparel, her shoes, her bag, absorbing every detail of her appearance. Why?

PC Parsons brought out his phone and dialled. He spoke briefly before passing it to his colleague who didn't say much, mostly listened. All the while, her gaze remained on Stella Reavey. Finally, she hung up. Gave a nod to Jim Parsons. Both police officers came and stood with Dan.

Parsons cleared his throat and fixed his gaze on a space past Dan's shoulder, clearly uncomfortable. He said, 'I'm sorry, sir, but we have to return to the station.' To Stella Reavey, he said, 'I'd rather you didn't do this again.'

'Sorry for the inconvenience,' she said smoothly.

Both officers gave a nod and moved towards their patrol car.

'Hey! Wait!' Dan strode after them. 'This woman harassed me and my daughter. I want her dealt with. I want her *warned off*, and if you won't help me I won't be responsible for my actions . . .'

Jim Parsons glanced at Stella who shook her head briefly. Neither officer looked at Dan as they climbed inside their car, buckled up.

'What the hell is going on?!' Dan yelled.

Jim Parsons buzzed down his window. Jerked his chin at Stella. 'Ask her.'

With that, Parsons started the engine, shoved the stick into gear and drove away.

Dan felt a wave of anger and frustration so strong he felt sick.

'You . . .' He spun round to see Stella was walking away. He jogged after her.

She said, 'Dan, you've got to calm down.'

'Don't you dare tell me what to do.'

'Come and see me when you're calmer. I'll be at home all day tomorrow.'

She turned towards the road. It was only then that he took in the black Jaguar with darkened windows pulling up next to the pavement. Stella moved to the passenger door, her hand reaching for the handle.

'Hey,' he said.

She didn't respond. Opening the door, she slipped inside. The car was still moving.

'Wait!' he called.

But the door was already closed and the car was accelerating away. Dan stood in the street with her card in his hand, watching it go.

CHAPTER FOUR

Stella leaned back in her seat and closed her eyes.

'How was it?' Bernard asked. She could sense him studying her but she kept her eyes shut. She felt strangely grey, as though the meeting with Dan had drained her of energy.

'Not as well as I'd hoped.'

'No recognition at all?' he probed.

'Nothing.'

'You approached him as we discussed?'

'Pretty much.'

'Do you think he believed you?'

'Not a word.' She sighed. 'But I know one thing. He won't be able to resist following it up. Too many questions unanswered.'

'You laid the bait well enough?'

'Oh, yes.' She forced herself to open her eyes. 'But still, there could be a fly in the ointment.'

Bernard's head turned briefly to look at the side of her face. 'What's that?'

'His wife.'

'You think she'll be a problem?'

'We have to hope not.'

The last remnants of Chepstow slid away as Bernard accelerated east and on to the M48. Rain spattered against the windscreen.

'Have you told Grace yet?' he asked.

'No.'

She didn't want to admit she'd just spoken to Grace, albeit about Dan, and was thankful when Bernard didn't say any more but concentrated on his driving. He stayed in the outside lane as they crossed the Severn Road Bridge, windscreen wipers working to clear the spray thrown up by three lanes of traffic.

'It's got to be done,' he said.

So, he wasn't going to let it drop. She turned her gaze to the River Severn below, oozing smooth and brown.

'I know,' she murmured.

Bernard gave a sigh of exasperation.

'I'll do it,' she said quickly. 'I'll call her the minute I get home.'

'If you say so.' His tone suggested that he didn't believe her but she didn't pursue it. Grace must already be surprised that she had called up out of the blue – and with such an odd request – but she'd be even more shocked at the next topic of conversation. How would Grace react? All she had to do was think of the bombshell she was about to drop and Stella's mouth turned dry. She couldn't believe she was feeling so apprehensive and she had to remind herself that she wasn't going to confess everything over the phone. All she had to do was get Grace to see her, which sounded simple but – knowing Grace – it might prove impossible to do this without giving something away.

She closed her eyes again. With the steady *shhhush* of the Jaguar's tyres on the wet road, and the way the leather cradled her, she felt as though she could drop off to sleep at any second. Talk about unnerving. She'd never napped during the day.

'Are you OK?' Bernard asked.

'I'm fine,' she said, irritated by his anxious tone. 'Just a bit tired, that's all.' She hated the feeling. She only used to feel like this when she was jet-lagged.

'You need a holiday.' He smiled at her and she knew he was trying to lift her mood. 'Somewhere nice and warm.'

'I've heard the British Virgin Islands are nice at this time of year.' She smiled back, suddenly feeling better.

By the time Bernard dropped her off at home, darkness had fallen. 6.30. Both her neighbours had their lights burning and their TVs on, indicating they were home. Stella unlocked her outer door and stepped into the tiny porch before unlocking the front door and punching in her alarm code. Normally she didn't get home until after eight and the heating had yet to come on. Dropping her bag on the hall table, she went into the kitchen and pressed the override button on the boiler. Seconds later it kicked in with a comforting *whoosh.*

For the next hour or so she pottered, checking her emails, half-watching the news, putting on some washing. Yet all the time at the corner of her vision stood Suzie Lui protesting: *No!* The young woman would stay there, haunting her soul until Stella died – a constant reminder of her appalling miscalculation.

Stella was ironing a shirt for the next morning when the phone rang. She looked at the display.

Grace.

Her stomach hollowed.

Did she have to do this now? Bernard thought so, but she'd been dreading it, putting it off, hoping for a stay of execution . . .

The phone continued to ring.

She didn't have to tell Grace tonight, Stella told herself. She could do it tomorrow. But she'd been using that excuse for the past three weeks and time was running out. *She had to see her daughter.*

The phone clicked to the answer machine and at the same time, Stella snatched up the phone.

'Gracie,' she said.

'Hi Mum.' Grace sounded surprised. 'For a moment I thought you weren't there.'

Stella muted the TV.

'Is everything OK?' Grace asked.

This was the perfect opening, but she didn't have the courage to take it. Instead she said, 'Absolutely.'

There was a brief silence.

Stella opened her mouth to say something, she wasn't sure what, but Grace spoke first.

'I've been thinking about you and your friend all day. How did he lose his memory? Do you know?'

Should she tell the truth? Or should she lie? She was so used to living in a shadow world that the truth had become an elastic thing, twisting and stretching over the years until . . . well. One day, obviously, it broke. For the first time she could remember in years, she spoke the truth without pausing to weigh her words.

She said, 'I rather suspect he was given an amnesia drug.'

A brief silence.

'A *what?*'

'It was probably for his own good. His three-year-old son was killed in front of him and his mind snapped. He was locked up in a mental institution.'

Stella could picture Dan from that time as if it were yesterday. Unshaven, eyes rimmed with red, angry and bloodshot. His hair a matted tangle. When he spoke there had been no sound; his throat had been made raw from screaming. She closed her eyes, praying she hadn't tripped him back into that world of insanity. The last thing she wanted was to affect his mental health now, when he appeared so stable.

'Who on earth would dispense an amnesia drug?' asked Grace.

'A private hospital, probably.'

Another silence.

'I've never heard of an amnesia drug being used in any hospital, private or not,' Grace said. 'As far as I'm aware, that sort of thing is still very much in the research phase. Which hospital?'

Of course Grace, being a GP, would want to know.

'I wouldn't know,' Stella sighed. 'I'm only hypothesising.'

Grace snorted. 'Nice try, Mum. Come on, you can't dangle something so juicy in front of me and then play coy.'

'It's true!' Stella protested, half laughing. 'I only have a suspicion it may have been used.'

'So what's the story?'

Stella hadn't planned it like this, but it suddenly seemed incredibly simple. She said, 'Come and see me and I'll tell you. Face-to-face. I'm at home right now.'

'Seriously?'

'Yes. I'd love to see you.'

'Mum, I'm really sorry, but I'm on call tonight.'

This meant Grace couldn't leave the area, let alone drive an hour and a half to get to her. Stella lived in Tring, one of the most efficient commuting satellites into the West End of London, while Grace was near Basingstoke; also in the London commuter belt but on the southerly side.

'When can you come?' Stella asked.

'Er, I'm not sure . . .'

Stella considered Dan and what time he'd turn up the following day. He'd come early, she decided. He wouldn't be able to wait any longer. They'd be done by the time Grace arrived. She said, 'I'm at home all day tomorrow.'

'You are?' Grace sounded surprised.

'Working.' Her tone was dry.

'Of course.' Grace's tone was just as dry. Both of them could be called workaholics but it wasn't because they were obsessed with their jobs or had their egos tied into them; it was simply the nature of the work they did.

'The weekend would be easier,' Grace began, 'I can make –'

'Please, Grace,' Stella interrupted. 'Come tomorrow. We have to talk.'

'About your amnesiac?'

Stella swallowed. Closed her eyes. 'No. Something else.'

She could almost see Grace taking the phone away from her head and staring at it.

'Like what?'

'Not on the phone.'

'Oh.'

Stella waited for a barrage of questions but, surprisingly, none came. 'Of course I'll come tomorrow, Mum. Are you all right?'

'Yes,' Stella lied. 'But I do need to see you.'

'I'll come as soon as I can. Get to you, say, early afternoon or so. I'll bring something from the deli for a late lunch. OK?'

'Lovely.'

As she got ready for bed, Stella listened to the news. The headline story was about a pretty young university student who'd been missing for two days. Bella Frances. Disappeared from her shared flat in Stockton-on-Tees. The police hadn't found a single clue, forensic or otherwise, that might explain what had happened. She left behind her keys and handbag, and police admitted they had no idea what had happened to her. Her family were distraught.

Two days missing. The girl was probably dead. What a waste of a young life.

Suddenly Stella felt close to tears, which was most peculiar. She couldn't think when she had last cried.

CHAPTER FIVE

PC Lucy Davies glanced at the photo of Bella Frances stuck on the board. Glossy dark hair framed a heart-shaped face with a generous mouth and bright, laughing blue eyes. Eighteen years old, slim and vivacious, she'd been missing since Tuesday. And now another time-waster had called in claiming to know where Bella was.

'Rio de Janeiro?' Lucy repeated. Since Bella didn't have a passport, Lucy knew that the idea of her travelling to Brazil was highly unlikely, if not impossible. 'Are you sure?'

The caller sounded as though he was in his teens and, when she heard a snigger in the background, a flicker of crimson shimmered in her mind.

'Oh, yes,' the boy replied, obviously trying to stifle a laugh. 'She was wearing a bikini and a sunhat.'

'Hoax calls to the police will be investigated and dealt with by the courts,' Lucy intoned. 'You can be imprisoned for six months with a fine of five thousand pounds.'

'Filth,' he sneered.

'I need to make you aware this phone call is being traced,' Lucy stated in the same emotionless tone. 'And that we already have your location. Two officers have been alerted and are on their –'

Clunk.

Lucy grinned as she put her phone back down. Little shits. She hoped she'd given them a scare that would make them think twice before they pissed the police around in the future.

'Another joker, I take it?'

She looked across to see Howard devouring his third Lion bar. *Blobby on the beat.* That's what a kid had called him this morning but he'd pretended he hadn't heard and despite desperately wanting to bring the subject up – Howard was so fat his stab vest didn't meet at the side – Lucy had kept her mouth shut. She hadn't wanted to antagonise him. She'd been in the job less than five weeks.

'Kids,' she said.

'I got one too,' he said. 'Could be the same ones. They were winding me up, saying she was in some container park.'

Something scurried across the back of Lucy's neck, like an invisible spider. She paid attention to that scurry: it had alerted her to vital strands of investigations on plenty of occasions and she'd learned to ignore it at her peril.

'What if they're not winding you up?' Lucy said, and at the same time, her brain suddenly lit up with flashes of colour, electricity humming. She felt a sudden elation. Perhaps she was meant to be in this place at this moment, even though it was a shit-hole and she didn't want to be here at all but back in London. (Note to self: find missing girl, get promoted and return to London in a blaze of glory.)

Howard just looked at her.

'Seriously,' she said. 'Shouldn't we check it out?'

He kept looking at her.

'OK, OK,' she relented, but she knew she wouldn't let it drop. Not until she'd satisfied herself that Howard's call really had been a hoax. Just in case.

CHAPTER SIX

It was 6 p.m. and Candy's was packed. Families and kids. *Lots* of kids. Everyone had obviously decided to start celebrating Christmas early. At least half the tables held a bottle of wine – parents obviously feeling the need for a drink – and suddenly Dan felt like joining them. When the waitress, a large sausage-shaped girl who could take the prize for Most Miserable Elf in the World – next came by, he ordered some of the house red.

Jenny raised her eyebrows.

'You like red,' he said, trying not to sound defensive.

'Um . . .' She frowned. 'Are you driving? Or would you like me to?'

'It's OK,' he said. 'I won't go over the limit.'

Aimee was colouring in her place mat, a festive scene of Santa's sleigh porpoising through the sky. Her cheek was almost touching the table and her tongue pressed against her lower lip in her usual 'I'm concentrating' pose. She didn't look up as the wine was poured.

Jenny said, 'We could always get a taxi and collect the car tomorrow.'

'We could,' he agreed, relieved she was making a concerted effort to be pleasant. She'd gone berserk when he hadn't returned to the salon straight away, but taken the car and driven to the police station. She'd had to take a taxi home with Aimee and had nearly slapped him when he'd finally got home. It had taken him ten minutes of apologising before he could explain and another ten before she finally calmed down.

'So where the hell were you?' she'd demanded, her eyes blazing blue.

'I wanted to know why they let Stella Reavey go.'

'And?' Jenny prompted.

'No luck.'

A flash of what could have been relief crossed her face but she raised a hand to her eyes so quickly he wasn't sure if he'd imagined it. Was he getting paranoid after Stella's mental jabbing?

You're not who you think you are, Dan. Your identity, your past, is a lie. Your entire family has been lying to you.

He pushed Stella's voice firmly out of his mind. He wasn't going to let her come between him and Jenny. Jenny had already proven herself. She'd stood by him through the roughest of the rough, watching him lose his mind then moving them lock, stock and barrel across the country to live somewhere she considered restorative. He wasn't going to start believing some mad woman over his wife. But a small worm of anxiety wouldn't go away: what if Stella Reavey was telling the truth?

He recalled what the policeman had said to Stella before he'd climbed into his patrol car and driven away.

I'd rather you didn't do this again.

Dan had had little joy getting any answers from the police. At Chepstow Police Station, the duty sergeant had been sympathetic until he'd made a handful of phone calls. Then he'd shut down and wouldn't listen to Dan any more. He'd been polite but adamant on the phone. 'You need to talk to Ms Reavey about this. We can't help you. You have her details?'

'I'd like to speak to PC Jim Parsons.'

'I'm sorry, that's not possible. I suggest you contact Ms Reavey. She'll explain.'

'OK. I'd like to talk to PC Vicky Cross.'

'Please, sir. Just call Ms Reavey. She'll explain everything.'

'Who's your boss?'

The duty sergeant, a grizzled and experienced-looking man in his fifties, considered Dan for a moment, then said, 'I think it'll save us all a lot of time if you have a word with the Chair of Gwent Police Authority.'

The top dog. Who in fact turned out to be a woman, who politely but firmly repeated what the other officers had told him.

'Please, Mr Forrester,' she said. 'Contact Ms Reavey. If you have trouble getting in touch with her, let me know. But in the meantime, it is in your best interests to speak to her directly.'

'But she harassed me and my daughter,' he said, feeling oddly ashamed, as though he was bleating on about something that didn't concern the police, like reporting that his heating wasn't working.

'Should you have trouble contacting Ms Reavey . . .'

'I'll let you know,' Dan finished for her, and hung up.

He hadn't bothered going any higher. It was a whitewash job that painted him into a corner with Stella Reavey. Part of him wanted to ring the woman now. Drive to her home and demand answers. But the other part was sick with apprehension. For some reason, Stella's words had dislodged something deep inside him. He felt as though she'd lifted the lid off the top of a volcano and he was waiting for a gigantic rock to explode into the air.

Haven't you ever wondered why you're so secretive?

Which drove Jenny mad, he had to admit. But weren't most men guarded about their jobs? He hated talking out of turn about anybody, and that included his clients as well as the postman. He didn't see why a husband should divulge every second of his day either, even if it was to his wife of thirteen years.

And yes, he had a great memory for faces and could listen to three conversations at once, but he could also read upside down and bake a loaf of walnut and raisin bread, no problem.

Stella was right that he enjoyed the flexibility of freelance work, choosing when and where to see his clients, be they the police in Lincolnshire or ambulance trainees in Kent. Yes, he enjoyed a good wage. And yes, he enjoyed being at the top of his profession and, strangely, he even enjoyed turning work away. It made him feel in control. But anyone could guess these things. It wasn't rocket science.

And she could easily guess he was bored. Who wouldn't be, after doing the same job for over five years?

But how did she, how *could* she know that he daren't admit it to his wife?

He looked at Jenny, toying with her Rudolph Special Steak and Chips. Then he looked down at his Comet Classic Burger. He hadn't realised they'd been served. He had to get a grip. There was a reasonable explanation, he was sure. He just had to find out what it was. Meantime, he was having supper with his family, and the irony was that it was only thanks to Stella they were at Candy's and not eating fried chicken and noodles at home.

'Here's to Christmas.' He raised his glass. Aimee immediately responded, 'Happy Christmas!' and plunged into her Blitzen Mini-Burger.

'Christmas,' echoed Jenny but there was something sad in her eyes, something that immediately reminded him of Stella.

You saved my life once . . .

Damn it. He had to stop thinking about that woman.

He took a mouthful of burger but couldn't taste anything. He continued to chew and swallow, and smile and chat, but he wasn't really there. He was inside his mind, turning things over.

Why do you always look for the exits when you enter a room?

Didn't everyone do that? It seemed stupid not to, in case there was a fire or other emergency. Knowing where to head immediately and without having to search for the stairs or a back door could save lives. Carefully, he took each thing Stella had said and studied it. He resolutely refused to think about what she'd told him about Luke.

'Dan?'

He looked up to see Jenny watching him expectantly. The sausage-shaped elf waitress hovered. 'Have you finished?'

He'd barely eaten half of his meal. And Jenny, he saw, had hardly touched hers. His heart clenched. She normally had the appetite of a horse. That was one of the things he loved about her, that she loved her food. Her weight would go up and down but she always looked great, and if her clothes started to get tight she'd join a gym, and drink nothing but vegetable juices for a week until the pounds fell off. He'd never known her not to eat all her chips.

'I'm sorry,' he said.

She looked at him, then away. 'I hate it when you're like this.'

He stared. He hadn't realised he was repeating past behaviour. 'Like what?'

She fluttered her hands. 'Absent. In another world.'

'I used to do this?'

'All the time.' She gave a rueful smile. 'That's probably why I flew off the handle earlier. It reminded me of how you used to be. Doing things without telling me. Never really explaining. You were quite self-centred, you know. But that was before . . .' She glanced at Aimee, then back to Dan. 'You know.'

Before his breakdown. Before Luke was killed. Before his mind decided it was best to forget, and obliterated half his history practically overnight. Before and After. That was how he saw his life. Before Luke died. And after.

'I don't sound particularly nice,' he offered uncertainly. They hadn't touched upon his change of personality much before. Wary of opening old wounds, perhaps, or creating new ones.

'I don't think it was that as much as you were . . .' She shrugged, looking slightly uncomfortable. 'Well, just different.'

Friends of theirs had said the same. Matt was a classic example. According to him Dan used to be a bit of a live wire – *work hard, play hard* – but today's Dan was quiet and sober, contemplative, and according to Matt, much less fun.

'Do you miss the old me?' he asked.

Jenny's eyes widened. 'Good God, no!' She leaned forward, expression earnest. 'It wasn't that I didn't love you to bits before, but I love you even more now. I love the fact that you're not wedded to work anymore. I love having you home before midnight. I love having you around at weekends. I love that I'm an integral part of your life . . .'

'I'm not boring?'

'No, my love.' She looked at him quite seriously. 'Stripping wallpaper is boring. You are absolutely not in the same league as DIY.'

He realised she was trying to lighten the mood. Even Aimee appeared subdued, or perhaps she was just tired after the weird events of the day.

'I'm sorry for who I used to be,' he said. 'I sound like a bit of a nightmare, really.'

'You were,' Jenny admitted gently. 'But that's a long time ago now.'

Jenny drove them home when it transpired she'd only had one glass of wine and Dan had polished off the rest of the bottle. Oddly, he didn't feel particularly inebriated and if it hadn't been for the evidence of the empty Rioja bottle, he would have thought he was sober.

He let Jenny put Aimee to bed. He could tell she was trying not to be clingy with Aimee but their daughter knew something was amiss because when he ducked in to kiss her goodnight, she was unusually teary and fretful.

'Everything's fine, sweet pea,' he reassured her. Thanks to Dr Orvis Fatik, the shrink he'd seen subsequent to Luke's death, he'd learned to make sure she felt assured that her needs for care and protection were being looked after. 'I'm here, and Mummy will feel better in the morning.'

'Is she missing Luke?' Aimee asked. She couldn't remember her elder brother – she'd barely been a year old when he died – but she knew all about him and that he and Jenny occasionally grew sad or angry that he was dead.

'Yes, she is.'

'But he died *ages* ago.'

'I know. But it doesn't stop Mummy from missing him.'

'I hate him,' she announced angrily.

'Sometimes I hate him too.' He echoed her sentiment to show he understood how she felt, another trick learned from Orvis.

Aimee blinked a couple of times. 'You do?'

'Yup.'

'Why?'

'Because although he's not here anymore, he still has a big impact on our lives, and that can make me angry.'

'Like us having to visit his grave.' She picked at a loose thread on her duvet cover. 'We go *all the time*. It's boring. I don't want to go any more.'

'Don't exaggerate. We don't go all the time,' he chided gently.

'Well, *nearly* all the time.'

In fact, they went as a family twice a year, once on Luke's birthday, 2 December, and then on 16 June, the day he'd died. Dan guessed Jenny had brought up the subject to prepare Aimee for their trip to Brompton Cemetery next weekend.

'Do I have to go?' she pouted.

Yes, he thought, but there was no point in saying so and creating a fight. His mind flipped through a variety of London attractions from Madame Tussauds, which he considered too grisly and death-like after visiting the cemetery, to Sea Life, and then out of nowhere a flash of memory came.

He and Luke ice skating. Luke's fair hair – as white as Aimee's – his blue puffa jacket and red woolly hat. His cheeks were pink, his eyes bright. Dan could see the plane trees arcing high, dancing with fairy lights, and behind his son loomed the great façade of the Natural History Museum. He heard Luke yell, 'Dad! Watch me!'

Dan felt as though a giant hand had plunged into his chest and gripped his heart.

'Daddy?'

'Yes, avocado?' He responded without a beat. His emotions might have been rioting inside but he kept his expression perfectly still, his voice steady. He didn't know where it came from, this ability to hide his feelings no matter how passionate or excited he became, but it could be incredibly useful. The downside was that it drove Jenny crazy.

'Seriously.' Aimee sighed dramatically. 'Do I have to go?'

'If you'd rather not, we'll have to talk it through with Mum.' Then he put a finger on his lips in a studied frown. 'But if you don't come, who will be my partner on ice?'

Aimee blinked. 'What partner?'

'Well, after visiting Luke's grave, I was going ice skating. It's something your brother and I did once, maybe a couple of times, in Kensington. But I need someone to partner me.'

The rest of the conversation went exactly as Dan had planned. He was aware that some might call him manipulative, others calculating or devious, but all Dan knew was that his machinations usually meshed nicely with the path of least resistance. It wasn't long before Aimee's eyelids drooped and she allowed him to tuck her arms beneath the duvet and kiss her goodnight.

Dan watched the ten o'clock news with Jenny and, as usual at around 10.30, she snuggled close and he put his arm around her, making a pillow for her with his chest. Instead of falling asleep, however, she wriggled closer, sliding her leg over his thigh, slipping her fingers between his shirt buttons and lightly stroking his chest. He was pretty sure it had to be the emotional stress of the day – because his body reacted fast.

He looked down at her. 'You're not tired?'

She looked up, a twinkle in her eye. 'Why, are you?'

'It's been one hell of a day.' He gave her the opportunity to back out if she wanted.

The twinkle deepened. 'Let's finish it with a bang, then.'

CHAPTER SEVEN

Dan could hear a woman's laughter, joyful and carefree. Strangely, it only seemed to increase his disquiet. He was looking for something, but he didn't know what, and he didn't want the woman to know. He opened a drawer to find stacks of beige manila files. None were labelled and each one was empty. In the next drawer he found nothing but piles and piles of blank paper. The woman was standing beside him. She was tanned. She had long, elegant feet. Dark hair, blue-black as a raven's wing, tumbled at the edges of his vision, but he couldn't see her face. He felt suffused with anxiety.

The feeling remained when he awoke and for a moment he wondered where he was. He didn't feel concerned, though – he knew he was somewhere safe from the soft sounds of someone sleeping nearby.

Jenny.

Gradually his senses came awake.

But with them came the voices.

I'm so sorry, Dan, said a man's voice. *Luke's dead.*

You've had a breakdown. Another man spoke. *We had to section you for your own safety.*

Then a woman's voice. Stella Reavey. *Your son Luke didn't die in a hit-and-run.*

He couldn't remember the accident, or the events leading up to it, but he'd been told so many times what had happened that it felt perfectly real. One Sunday, he'd taken Luke to Brick Lane Market. He and Jenny had planned to go together as a family and have lunch at one of their favourite food stalls. But that morning Jenny had felt exhausted, run ragged looking after baby Aimee as well as boisterous three-year-old Luke all week, and he'd suggested he take Luke on his own to give her a break. Jenny had agreed with alacrity, and by the time they left the house, she was back in bed, fast asleep.

Dan and Luke took the Tube to Aldgate East. Walked hand-in-hand along the chaotic, graffiti-daubed streets looking at the leather and vintage goods for sale, the street artists and a wild-haired guitarist playing Hendrix at full volume.

Nobody knew how Dan had lost Luke. Maybe Dan had been distracted, let go of Luke's hand to pay for something, nobody knew. Whatever happened, Luke had vanished.

Apparently Dan had searched for his son with increasing desperation. He had finally found him standing on the edge of the road, and although he had shouted, *screamed* at Luke to stop, Luke hadn't heard him and had stepped out into the path of a blue van.

He had died in Dan's arms with a broken back, a three-inch gash on his forehead, a seven-inch gash in his scalp, a skull fracture, brain swelling, a lacerated liver, a fractured pelvis and a broken leg.

Dan knew the details because he'd insisted on reading the post-mortem report, followed by the coroner's report which held a single witness statement from Anne Saber, a nurse at A & E. She said the blue van hadn't stopped but the man driving the car behind it had. The man said he didn't think of taking down the van's number; he'd been more preoccupied with bundling Dan and Luke into his vehicle and driving them to Mile End Hospital A & E.

The man then vanished. He didn't leave his name or an address. Dan couldn't remember what he looked like, or what type of car he drove and, despite police appeals, he never came forward. The police also appealed throughout Brick Lane for witnesses to the hit-and-run, without any luck. The only witness remained Anne Saber, who simply repeated what the man had told her, and described what she'd seen: Dan running down the corridor clutching his son's broken body and screaming.

With insufficient evidence to support the story of the hit-and-run, the coroner returned an open verdict. Jenny attended the inquest. She told Dan that thanks to advice from a barrister, the verdict was what she'd expected.

He was still amazed that she didn't blame him and that, despite such a trauma, their marriage had survived. The fact they'd both had counselling must have had a big impact but Dan thought it was probably Aimee that made the difference, forcing them to concentrate on being there for *her*, and not looking inward and blaming themselves. Because Jenny blamed herself too.

If I hadn't been so stroppy that morning, we would have spent the day together. You would never have gone to Brick Lane without me. We would have left later and the blue van would have been long gone.

If Dan had gone to the local park and kicked around a football with Luke instead of heading to Brick Lane.

If, if, if.

Orvis had taught Dan not to look back and play the 'if' game, because that way lay madness. As Dan knew only too well.

Dan lay next to his wife in the dead of night, listening to Stella Reavey's voice slowly increasing in volume and power.

You're not who you think you are . . .

After an hour or so, he slipped out of bed. Jenny's breathing didn't falter. She remained deeply asleep. As quietly as a cat, he retrieved some underwear and socks and crept into the bathroom for a quick wash before getting dressed in the spare room, where they both kept an overspill of clothing.

Downstairs, he wrote a brief note. He made sure it was light, nothing to worry Jenny. He said he hadn't been able to sleep – which was true – and was going for a dawn raid. Jenny knew he did this from time to time – going for a performance drive before the world woke up, when the roads were empty and he could drive the cabriolet as it was meant to be driven – fast and with the rev needle hovering between four thousand and five. She would understand that, but she wouldn't understand him going to see Stella Reavey.

His headlights cut through the night, pale white swords shearing through black. He let his driving ebb and flow with the conditions. Wet leaves on the side of the road. Sharp corners and steep inclines, the occasional stretch of straight tarmac. Brake and release, turning the wheel smoothly and without pause before stepping back on the gas and pushing through the turn. The rhythm of the drive soothed him, taking away the tendrils of unease that still clung to him from the woman in his dream. Each time she appeared she brought with her a sense of fun, but the underlying emotion he felt was always anxiety. He supposed she could be an ex-girlfriend but despite trawling through his old photographs nobody seemed to fit. Not wanting to ask anyone out of respect for Jenny, he guessed he'd never know if she was a real memory or simply a slightly disturbing fantasy.

The night was dark, no moon. There were no lights out here. It still surprised him that they lived somewhere so remote. Though it was near Chepstow, it felt secluded, almost isolated thanks to the fact they lived halfway up a hill with moorland all around.

Jenny had moved them out of London after his breakdown. He'd been too much of a mess to question things much, but even he couldn't deny the convenience of having Aimee's school within walking distance. And being just six miles from the M48, another eight to the M5, it was relatively easy for Dan to travel around the country to meet his clients.

Jenny was an accountant and worked part-time from home doing personal tax, VAT and audit work. She said she loved it thanks to her regulars, like the farmer who gave her fresh eggs every other week and the Ultralight pilot who flew her over the Black Mountains each summer. Was Jenny bored? She didn't appear to be, but then neither did he. Dear Lord, what if they were *both* bored out of their minds but were too frightened to admit it?

When he arrived outside Stella Reavey's house it was three minutes past six. The street was quiet, still asleep, lit orange by the streetlights. He parked two houses down on the opposite side of the road, where he could watch unobtrusively. He studied her house curiously. He wasn't sure what he'd expected, but it wasn't this: a middle-of-the-road suburban property with a tiny front garden. He'd pictured her in something larger, more powerful.

The house was neat, the garden immaculate. Did she sweep the flagstones and prune the small pear tree herself, or pay someone to do it for her? His mind hopped forward a couple more steps. Did she live with anyone? Was she married? He hadn't seen any engagement or wedding ring. No rings on any of her fingers, he recalled. Just a simple silver Saint Christopher pendant at her throat.

Dan watched the house, listening to the radio. The heat in the car dissipated but he took no notice. He didn't know where it came from, but he'd always had the ability to wait patiently, without getting bored or irritable. At ten minutes past seven, a car drove down the street. He watched it gradually slow until it was almost outside Stella Reavey's house, then it cruised to the end of the road, where it parked. A man climbed out and stood on the pavement. When he looked around the street, Dan instinctively hunkered down in his seat, melting into the dimness of his car.

He watched the man walk along the pavement. In his fifties, dressed in a double-breasted camel coat with a fedora, leather gloves, and an umbrella hooked over his arm, he looked like a city businessman. He stopped by Stella's gate. Leaned down and unlatched it. He was about to step on to her garden path when he suddenly froze. Slowly, he turned his head until he was looking directly at Dan.

It can't be a coincidence, Dan thought. *He's seen me.*

For a few seconds, both men stared at one another. Then the man in the fedora carefully closed Stella's gate, and walked back to his car. Before he climbed inside, he tipped his hat at Dan in a faintly old-fashioned gesture of acknowledgement.

Puzzled and not a little disturbed, Dan watched him drive away.

CHAPTER EIGHT

Friday 23 November, 7.15 a.m.

Stella dressed and slipped downstairs, where she made coffee: a long, strong espresso with a rich and foamy head. As she sipped, she looked outside. A man sat in his car on the opposite side of the road, five cars down from her front gate.

Dan.

She couldn't make out his features but it had to be him since he was sitting in Dan's car with Dan's number plate. She wondered what time he'd arrived and guessed sometime in the middle of the night. She doubted he'd slept much. Too many questions needed answering.

Putting down her coffee cup, Stella turned back to the kitchen where she put the oven on low before extracting a packet of bacon from her freezer and defrosting it in the microwave. Then she cut four thick slices from a cottage loaf and lavishly buttered them. She fried the bacon until crisp and sandwiched the rashers between the bread, set the butties to keep warm in the oven. She made another coffee – a double espresso with a dash of milk – shrugged on her winter coat and put on her shoes. She wrapped the butties in a couple of napkins and took them and the coffee across the road to Dan.

The air was raw and nipped at her cheeks and fingers. She'd have to make sure the heating remained on all day or the house would turn into a fridge. As she approached, Dan wound down his window. Looked at her cautiously.

'Your usual,' she said, holding them out. 'Coffee, white, no sugar. Bacon butty made with white bread and oozing with butter, no ketchup, no brown sauce.'

He continued looking at her.

'If I wanted to kill you,' she said, 'I can think of far better ways than poisoning you after the whole street has seen me deliver you breakfast.'

A ghost of a smile played on his face. He took the butties and the coffee. He didn't say anything, and she didn't expect him to. Not yet. Give him another hour or so, and he'd knock on her door. She turned to cross the road when to her astonishment, she saw Grace climbing out of her car, clutching her little leather backpack. As Grace beeped her car shut, Stella hastened to greet her.

'Gosh,' she exclaimed. 'You're early!'

'I switched shifts.' Grace looked her up and down. 'I know you'll hate me for saying it, but I was worried about you. And with good reason. You look dreadful.'

'And you look fabulous,' Stella remarked dryly.

Grace snorted. 'I look a mess. I literally fell out of bed and into my car this morning. I wanted to miss the traffic. Can I have a shower?'

'Of course.'

'Great.' Grace's eyes went to Dan sitting in his car. 'Why the breakfast delivery?'

'He's been up all night,' Stella replied. 'He's hungry.'

'Why doesn't he come in?'

Stella looked over at Dan, who was watching them. 'He probably will in a couple of hours.'

Grace frowned. 'Why not now?'

'Let's talk about it inside. It's far too cold out here.'

In the kitchen, Stella looked through the window at Dan who appeared to have been spooked by Grace's arrival. He was putting on his seatbelt and yes, his indicator was on and he was pulling out.

Damn.

She had to hope he'd return once Grace had gone.

'Who is he?' Grace stood beside her, watching him go.

'Dan Forrester,' she said. 'I saw him yesterday.'

'What?' Grace glanced round. 'Your amnesiac?'

'Yes.' She put her head on one side and surveyed her daughter. 'He still doesn't remember me, but he's curious. Which is why he came here. He doesn't know how his son died, you see, and I need to tell him. It's pretty traumatic. Any ideas how to break it gently?'

'Loads. Like starting with giving the poor sod a stiff drink of some sort. Look, can we do this in a mo? I'm desperate for a shower and then a coffee and maybe a croissant. Do you have any in the freezer? I won't be able to concentrate until I've had some breakfast. You know what I'm like . . . '

Stella watched her daughter hare up the stairs. Grace might think she looked a mess with her curly hair uncombed and her clothes crumpled, but to Stella she looked perfect. She rarely gave compliments and as she moved back into the kitchen to see if she could unearth a couple of croissants from the freezer, she made a mental promise to tell her only daughter not just how much she loved her, but how proud she was of her.

Out of nowhere a wave of weakness swept over her and she had to grip the worktop to stop herself from falling. She started to sweat. It was infuriating, she thought, this sensation. It would come and go without warning, and where it used to occur every week or so, it had increased to a worrisome once or twice a day.

She heard the shower running upstairs and decided to take the opportunity to email Grace the information she'd wanted to impart for ages, but hadn't been able to without speaking to her first. If she received it without knowing Stella's history, or her future plans, Grace would simply be bemused. But once they'd spoken, all would become clear. What a relief to know everything would be in the open at last, and even better that Grace had taken the day off. It would take at least half of that to explain why she'd lied to her daughter for so long.

Stella switched on her laptop and typed in her password. It didn't take long to collate the information. Most of it Stella knew by heart, but not the address in the British Virgin Islands. She had to look that one up.

The grey feeling intensified, forcing her to pause. *It'll go away in a minute*, she told herself. She pressed SEND. Then, ever security conscious, she logged out of her computer.

The energy that had propelled her to set up the meeting with Grace, the carefully orchestrated meeting with Dan, trickled away. She didn't think she'd ever felt so leaden. She closed her eyes. She couldn't hear the shower any more. Grace would be down shortly. Even as a teenager, she never took long to get ready but since she could be easily distracted, she invariably ran late.

Stella smiled.

She was so glad Grace was here.

CHAPTER NINE

Grace entered her old room and immediately her eyes went to the photograph of Simon on her chest of drawers. Actually, it was of the two of them, taken at the top of Snowdon, but she never looked at herself in the picture. Just at Simon – his bright brown eyes and messy hair – and as usual she felt a weight press on her heart, the burden of grief.

Would it ever go, she wondered? And what about her guilt? She'd never told anyone what had happened. Her culpability was her cross to bear. Only Martin, a fellow GP, knew what she'd done but he hadn't reported her, thank God. And ever since he'd moved out of the area, sometimes a whole week could go by without her thinking of Simon and the consequence of her actions. But when she was reminded – like now – the heaviness returned.

Turning away, she rummaged in her rucksack for some fresh underwear and came up with a purple satin bra that Ross had bought her last Christmas. Unfortunately the pair of matching knickers hadn't made it in her rush out of the house this morning, and she ended up pulling on an old cotton pair that she'd thought she'd thrown out ages ago. They used to be a buttery cream but were now a hideous ashen colour. She really should clear out her underwear drawer. A tidy underwear drawer showed a tidy . . . what? Tidy mind?

Ross's underwear drawer was immaculate, every item neatly stacked, his socks put together and folded inside out so they resembled a single flat sausage. Was Ross's mind particularly tidy? Perhaps it was, compared to hers. He seemed to know what he was doing and when, whereas she led a more chaotic life, always arriving everywhere slightly out of breath and slightly dishevelled. Luckily, he didn't seem to mind. Like last Thursday, at his office Christmas party. She'd careered into the gallery – TDK Investment Bank had requisitioned an exhibition space at Tate Britain for the evening – alternately trying to drag her fingers through her unruly hair and hopping on one foot in an attempt to keep her slingbacks in place. Ross had simply wrapped his arm around her waist, drawn her close and kissed her, murmuring, 'God, woman. Are you worth the wait, or what?'

She could say the same about him. She'd been single for three years while she'd completed her foundation training attached to Winchester Hospital and then *bang!* There he was. And two years later she couldn't believe how she'd survived without him. He was gorgeous. He was generous. He was kind. He listened when she moaned about her workload. He spoiled her. He dropped everything to be there when she needed him. And he did DIY. When her best friend Sally heard that he could wire a house, tile a bathroom and sent her flowers every week, she'd said if Grace didn't marry the man, she would.

'What if I told you he can't cook?' Grace said.

'What are takeaways for?!'

Where was the nearest takeaway to Lone Pine Farm? Grace wondered. *Was* there even a takeaway restaurant in Duncaid? She'd never worried about not being able to cook before and now she wondered if she should do a cookery course. Oh, God. She still couldn't believe he wanted to move to Scotland. *Scotland!* And he wanted her to move up there with him. She'd only just moved to Ellisfield. She'd done barely six months of her salaried position, with a view to eventual partnership. If she even hinted she might be moving, they wouldn't be best pleased. Not that she'd said as much to Ross right then because she'd been so shocked she couldn't have vocalised a single thought if she'd tried.

'You know I've wanted to do something different for ages,' he had told her. They were sitting at her kitchen table in her cottage, sharing a bottle of red wine and waiting for the beef and onion pie she'd bought from the local butcher to heat in the oven. 'Investment management is all very well, but it's not *me*. Yes, I like the client contact, that's the best bit in all honesty, getting their objectives and strategies absolutely right, but the rest of it . . . well, it's become a bit of a slog. I don't want to wear a suit anymore.'

'Yes,' she had said cautiously. 'You have mentioned it.'

But she hadn't taken him seriously. She thought everyone who worked in the city had dreams of moving to the country but never acted upon them. They'd played what she thought was a game when they were lying in bed, picturing her jumping into her four-wheel-drive with her doctor's bag to do some house calls and Ross coming home with a freshly caught trout and pan frying it for supper on their wood-burning Aga.

But it wasn't a game any longer.

Ross looked at her, seeming to pick up on her reticence. 'I thought you said you were getting frustrated with townie-style patients? That you found them excessively demanding?'

True. She'd been attracted to the thought of treating rural people whom she assumed were more robust and self-reliant. Only last week she'd had a phone call from a woman demanding a house call for a common head cold.

'But what about my patients?' she said. 'The last doctor was only here for a year, and now I have to tell them I'm doing the same? Abandoning them after a few months? I'm only just getting to know them . . .' *And their likes and dislikes*, she added silently, *their husbands and wives, their children and their pets.*

'By moving now,' Ross said reasonably, 'it won't be half as hard a wrench as it would be in another year or more.'

Don't you understand? I don't want to go! she shouted inside. *But I don't want to lose you!*

She licked her lips. 'I'm not sure if it's financially viable. Is it? I mean, I'm not earning enough to –'

'Look.' He leaned forward, expression deepening. 'You don't have to put anything in. This is my project, but of course I want to share it with you. My finances are OK, I can buy the farm twice over with what I can get for my apartment. I can then plough the remaining money into renovating the outbuildings. I can easily swap my car for a second-hand Land Rover . . .'

He went on to outline his plans. He'd found the perfect farm near the Cairngorms, beautiful and wild with a trout-fishing stream as well as a small loch. Trails led from the farmhouse over rugged moorland that was home to red grouse and deer. The fact the place was almost in ruins, the cottages dilapidated, wasn't a drawback because he was *dying* to do them up and turn the place into a highland adventure holiday destination: horse riding, mountain biking, hiking, shooting, stalking and fishing.

'I didn't think you rode,' she said. She was glad her tone was relatively light and didn't reflect how she felt; bewildered and increasingly panicky.

'I'm going to learn.'

'I didn't realise you were so . . . ' She took a breath. 'Serious about this.'

He frowned and she knew she was on dangerous ground.

'So soon,' she added swiftly. 'I didn't think you'd find anywhere for at least a couple of years.'

His brow cleared. 'Neither did I. But it's *perfect*.' He leaned forward, his eyes alight. 'You're going to love it, Gracie!'

Although she knew it was childish, already part of her hated the place for upsetting what had been, for her, a perfect couple of years that she'd assumed were going to stretch into a perfect couple of decades. Lone Pine Farm. God, even the name gave her the creeps.

Slicking on some mascara and a sweep of blusher – any tan she'd caught during the summer was long gone – she wondered what her mother would think. Mum had only met Ross a few times but she was a great judge of character and would give a balanced, impartial view on the situation. It wasn't often Grace needed her mother's advice, always dispensed perfectly objectively and without favouring her daughter, but today it would be welcome.

Dressed in jeans and a stripy woolly jumper she'd bought in Cornwall years ago, Grace legged it to the kitchen, but her mother wasn't there. No smell of croissant either, or coffee.

'Mum!' she called. 'Where are you? I need your advice!'

Normally this would have had her mother appear by her side in a flash – Grace could count on one hand the amount of times she'd asked her mother for help and vice versa – but the house remained silent.

'Mum?'

She didn't bother checking the sitting room or downstairs bathroom but went straight to her mother's office. The door was ajar. She could hear the fan of a computer humming.

'Mum?'

Grace pushed open the door and peered inside. It took a moment for her brain to process what she was seeing.

Her mother was sprawled on the floor. She appeared to be unconscious. Her lips were blue. The fingers of her right hand had spasmed into a claw.

Grace stumbled across the room, fell to her knees.

Her mother wasn't breathing. She couldn't feel her heartbeat, or a pulse.

For a moment she went lightheaded.

Then her training kicked in.

Forget she's your mother. She's a patient. Save her.

She scrambled up and grabbed the phone. Dialled 999. Asked for an ambulance, paramedics. Told them she was a doctor and that it was a blue light case. Gave the operator the address.

Inside, she was screaming and cursing herself for not keeping a defibrillator in her car. She had a first-aid kit, but not a goddamn defib!

Working fast, she found the lower end of her mother's breastbone. Found the midline. Placing the heel of her left hand on her mother's chest and interlocking the fingers of both hands, she began compressions, counting out loud.

'One, two, three, four, five . . .'

Current protocol – if you were trained in CPR – stated that you should give thirty chest compressions before giving two breaths, and you keep going until the ambulance arrived.

'Come on, Mum! Don't give up!'

Thirty compressions. Two breaths.

CPR took an enormous amount of energy and already she was tiring but she kept going, kept up the pressure.

'Sixteen, seventeen, eighteen . . .'

The doorbell rang. Grace turned her head and yelled, 'Come in!' but nothing happened. Her mother would have locked the door.

The doorbell rang again.

'Oh, God God God . . .' Grace leaped up and tore along the corridor, feet flying. She flung open the front door and when she saw it wasn't a paramedic but Dan Forrester, her mother's amnesiac friend, she panted, 'I'm waiting for the ambulance, show them in when they get here, would you?'

She didn't explain any further but raced back inside.

Every minute her mother remained like this was another minute of sustained brain damage.

She'd barely started the compressions again when Dan came to squat opposite her. 'Let me,' he said. 'I know what to do.'

Grace ignored him.

'You're tiring,' he said. 'I'll compress, you breathe. More efficient.'

She waited until she'd completed thirty compressions and finished her second breath into her mother's lungs. Gasped, 'Go.'

'I left the front door open,' he told her as he pulsed the heels of his hands on her mother's chest. 'They'll find us, no problem.'

'OK.'

They didn't stop until the paramedics drew them aside. One started trying an IV line. The other exposed her mother's chest, attached sticky pads and started defibrillating.

No response.

They worked fast, rolling her mother onto a stretcher and hastening her outside, into the ambulance. Grace hurried after them. She sat to one side, holding her mother's hand while they continued CPR. Her mother's hand was warm, but lifeless.

She said, 'Come on, Mum. Make an effort!' Her voice was trembling. 'You're too young to die!'

Siren blazing, the ambulance accelerated down the street. Grace clutched her mother's hand, begging, pleading for her to fight back and *not die*, dammit!

But Stella Reavey couldn't hear her daughter's pleas, or see the pain and panic in her eyes, because when they arrived at Stoke Mandeville Hospital, nine miles away, she was pronounced DOA. Dead on arrival.

CHAPTER TEN

Friday 23 November, 9.10 a.m.

Bella was naked. Lying on a cold floor.

Pitch dark, black black black.

Pain. Great waves of pain. Nausea.

Dark.

Thirsty.

She needed water. She tried to move but it was impossible. Her limbs refused to budge. They were shrieking endlessly. Pain pain pain.

Wet sticky stuff everywhere. Her blood.

She'd thought she was dead.

But she wasn't.

She was alive.

Help!

Her mouth was gummed with blood. Pieces of tooth. She wanted to scream and shout but all that came from her throat was a dry rasping sound.

Please, can anyone hear me?

More rasping.

Nobody was going to hear. She had to make more noise.

The next thought sent panic racing: what if the man heard her? The man who'd done this to her? The man she'd laughed at when he'd brought out a pistol and pointed it at her. She'd thought it was a joke until he pulled the trigger. A fizzing, crackling sound and then the most indescribable pain shot through her body and she fell to the floor, unable to move, unable even to shout.

He'd stepped over her. Pushed some cloth into her mouth. The gun had fine leads hanging from it. Leads that were attached to her body. She'd never seen a weapon like that in real life before, but she'd heard about them.

A taser.

He'd used it on her twice. Agony. But then he'd given her an injection. Whatever it was made her feel wobbly, and then the space behind her eyes began to change and she felt as though she'd been thrown outside herself and into a strange new kind of reality. Nothing could touch her there, nothing hurt. Not like now.

She wasn't sure what he'd done to her but it was bad. She kept fainting. Retching before passing out again. The atmosphere was dense, airless. She was gasping for oxygen. Was she going to suffocate? She managed to roll her head to the side and felt a tiny trickle of cold air on her cheek. Fresh air. But what about her thirst? How long could a person live without water? Days? Or less? She knew it wasn't long. She had to *do something.*

Bella lifted her head a fraction and let it fall to the floor. She barely made any sound. She tried harder.

Thud.

That was better. She did it again.

Thud.

And again, and again.

She had no idea how much time was passing. After a while her head felt as though it was swelling. About to explode. She knew she was bleeding profusely. Losing blood. She had to make more noise. Get help.

She tried to raise her arm. She could feel something metal on her left wrist. It wasn't a watch, more like a big, chunky bracelet. She didn't wear bracelets like that. What was it?

An immense pain swept her in and out of consciousness.

Tears streamed down her face.

'No,' she mumbled.

She didn't want to die. She was only eighteen. She had her whole life ahead of her. She wanted to travel the world. See the pyramids. Go shopping in New York. Swim with dolphins.

And then she heard footsteps approaching. *Crunch, crunch.* Shoes walking on what sounded like gravel. She began to whimper. *Please God it wasn't him.* She didn't want to die.

CHAPTER ELEVEN

Friday 23 November, 9.30 a.m.

Lucy stepped over an oil-smeared puddle, her boots crunching on grit. Howard walked beside her. He hadn't wanted to come but when Lucy persisted he'd caved in with a roll of the eyes. *Anything for a quiet life.*

The container park was quiet, and thick mist rolled in from the North Sea, cloaking the city in a chill blanket. God, it was cold, and as damp and gloomy as hell. Her uniform felt damp, her bones felt damp, and she could feel the beginnings of a headache that had been dogging her since she'd come up here. Why did she have to be banished up north? Why not somewhere warmer down south, like Devon? It had to have been Magellan's idea. Everyone knew she hated the cold.

Footsteps muffled by fog, they approached two security guards standing next to a lone shipping container that looked as though it was awaiting collection. One was smoking a cigarette, the other rolling a pebble beneath his shoe. Both looked indescribably bored.

'Hi guys,' Howard greeted them.

Both guards were in their mid-thirties and wore black trousers, black shoes and socks, a blue company shirt, a blue company tie and sported three tin stars on their shoulder tabs that meant absolutely nothing except to try and make them look like policemen. Their customised patches announced the name of the security firm, *ZF Services*, with *Integrity & Proficiency* embroidered below. One name tag read: *Ralph Duggan*. The other, *Bill Grant*.

'Some kids reported . . .' Howard wiped chocolate from the corner of his mouth before reaching for his notebook and reading from it: 'Strange noises coming from one of the containers. A green one. Marked RFC, they said.'

Although Howard had shared this information with her earlier, Lucy's mind suddenly flared with colour as it spun over the initials, RFC. Rainforest Concern, Rangers Football Club, Rockefeller Centre . . .

'Yeah,' Duggan said. 'We checked it out. But we didn't hear anything.' He was still looking at Lucy. He did a man scan, sweeping his eyes from her sturdy black boots up her uniform to her breasts, then her mop of brown hair forced into submission beneath her cap. As usual, she didn't blink an eye but stared back, expressionless. Men found it confusing if you didn't react.

'It's a hoax,' Duggan added.

'What if it's not?' Lucy said.

'Oh, come on,' Duggan snorted, 'you said some kids rang you, what do you expect?'

'Haven't you been listening to the news?' she said. 'Or perhaps you're not aware that a university student went missing in this city just *three days ago.*'

'And don't they know it. The little bastards are always winding us up.'

'That may be so,' Lucy responded, pleased with her self-control when she wanted to clip him behind the ear for being pig-headed. 'But we still need to check it out.'

He snorted. 'You can't believe she's here or you'd have the entire force with you. What did they tell you they heard anyway?'

Howard checked his notebook. 'A kind of whimpering. An animal, maybe.'

'Could an animal have got trapped inside the container?' asked Lucy.

'Unlikely,' said Duggan.

'You didn't open it to check inside? You do have the authority to do that, don't you?'

'Er . . . Well, yes. But what if it was something dangerous? Like a rabid dog or something?'

It took all of her self-control not to roll her eyes at him. *For God's sake. Security guards are such wimps.*

'And we didn't want to damage anything,' Duggan added with a self-righteous air. 'We're very conscious of our insurance obligations to our clients.'

Which meant she and Howard would be breaking open the container and covering the guards' backs. 'OK,' she said. 'Show us.'

'You must be kidding,' said Duggan, blinking. 'There's no point. It's a *hoax*, get it? A total waste of time.'

Cherry red splashed at the corners of her mind. 'Just show us, would you?'

'But there's no –'

'Show. Us.'

He stared. 'Persistent little girlie, aren't you?'

Lucy straightened her shoulders so that she was standing at her full five foot four. 'If you don't show us the container *now*, I will charge you with wilful obstruction of justice.'

'Ooooooh,' he flung up his hands in mock surrender. 'I *am* scared.'

'Right.' She brought out her notebook. 'Ralph Duggan, ZF Services, you have the right to remain silent –'

'OK, OK!' he exclaimed. 'Jesus Christ, keep your hair on. I'll show you, OK?!'

'Thank you.' She put her book away and gave him her most brilliant smile.

The security guard stared at her. She could see the word *psycho* forming in his mind. Her smile broadened. Duggan glanced at Howard, checking to see if he could garner some sympathy there, but Howard was gazing into the middle distance, seemingly oblivious.

Watching her warily, the security guards led them to the container in question. Sludge-green with dents and scars all over it. Rust streaked its sides. RFC was stamped in faded white letters on both doors. Lucy put her head against the metal and listened. Nothing.

'Hello?' Lucy knocked her fist against the metal. 'Hello?'

Nothing responded. No clatter of paws on metal, no whimpering. She banged her fist harder. Still nothing. Perhaps the dog, or whatever it was, had died.

'If anything's in there, it'll be rats,' Howard said. 'Got trapped by accident.'

She had to hope not. She hated rats. She tried to hide her shudder; she didn't want Howard to think she was a wuss.

Lucy banged on the metal some more. She yelled, 'Police!' then, 'here, doggy, doggy!' but nothing responded.

'Come on,' she said, 'let's get it open.'

'No way,' Duggan protested.

'Who's got a crowbar?' she said in reply.

Groaning and muttering about slave drivers, Duggan and Grant wandered off and eventually returned with a breaker bar, a steel chisel and a hammer, all of which were useless. The container had a system that secured both the left and right door while also incorporating a high security seal within its locking mechanism. To remove the steel locking bar they needed a power-cutting tool. Which, it transpired, Duggan and Grant didn't have.

Howard took Lucy aside. He spoke in an undertone. 'You really want to keep going with this?'

'Yup.'

'Look, I know you probably did things differently in the Met, but don't you think you could cut us some slack from time to time? It's different up here. We're not quite as . . .' He glanced up at the sky as he searched for the right word.

'Professional?' she said, and immediately cringed. When would she learn to bloody *think* before she spoke?

Howard raised his eyebrows. 'You're not likely to make many friends with that sort of attitude.'

'I'm not here to make friends.' She was brittle. 'I'm here to do my job.'

'Which didn't stop you getting chucked out of the Met, if I heard right,' he said.

Lucy wanted to tell him he hadn't heard right, but she couldn't because officially she'd resigned, but unofficially the Met had indeed chucked her out. Sent her up here to this godforsaken dump whose greatest claim to fame was inventing the match-stick. That said it all really. She held Howard's eyes, hoping her humiliation wasn't draped around her shoulders like some sort of shawl.

'OK,' he said with a sigh. 'Let's do it.' He turned to the guards. 'We'll wait in the car until you've got the right equipment.'

Both Duggan and Grant groaned audibly.

'No need to rush,' Lucy said brightly. 'We've got all day.'

The guards didn't say any more, but trudged off to their van, climbed in and drove away.

As they walked to their car, Howard said, 'Are you normally like this?'

Instantly she was on her guard. 'Like what?'

'Kind of . . .' He appeared to be searching for the right word. 'Lively.'

She'd been called overexcited, weird, manic, mad, bonkers and everything in between but never *lively*. Lively she could live with. She decided not to take the conversation further in case it made him ponder her behaviour any more.

In the patrol car, Lucy was glad Howard agreed to run the engine to power up the heating. It had started to sleet and it was now officially freezing because when it hit the ground, it didn't melt. While they waited, Howard ate a jumbo Snickers bar. Lucy picked up her phone. Usually she'd text Nathan to give her a boost but she couldn't. Not any more. Not since he'd betrayed her.

But I love you, he'd begged as she'd packed her car. *I don't understand. We're getting on so well at the moment. Everything's perfect. I was going to ask you to marry me!*

Suddenly she felt as though she had a sock stuck in her throat and, to her horror, she felt tears begin to surface. Blinking rapidly, holding her breath, she forced them down. She didn't want to cry. Nate had broken her trust and she was angry at him, *furious.* She didn't want to waste her tears, but the fact was she missed him dreadfully.

She'd met Nate not long after she'd left school (at the pub, through friends). They'd gone on their first date two days later (to the movies, they were both addicted to action thrillers) and slept with each other the week before her eighteenth birthday (in her bedroom when her mother had gone out for the evening). They'd moved in together three years later (top floor flat of a Victorian terrace) and had started saving to buy a house. Nathan had been her only lover. Well, aside from one slip that she never, *ever* thought about . . .

Had Nate ever been unfaithful? He'd said not, but she wasn't sure whether to believe him. Didn't most men lie? Look at her father. When he'd left her mum he'd sworn there was no one else involved, and the next minute he was on a plane to Australia with a neighbour of theirs, a yoga teacher called Tina, who he'd been carrying on with for over a year. He never returned. It was as though he'd died. It had been awful but after a while the pain lessened and she learned to live without him. Her mum had done a fantastic job bringing her up, proving that you could do pretty well with only a mother.

She gazed glumly through the windscreen at the gravel slimed with pollution and moss, the weeds climbing the fence. A faint aroma of sewage seeped into the car from the works near Portrack Marsh. Perhaps it was a good thing she'd been sent to live somewhere she'd never been before, where there was nothing to remind her of Nate. No memories to distress her, or comfort her.

She put her phone away.

Duggan and Grant finally returned with an angle grinder, apparently borrowed from a pal. Maglite in hand, Lucy stood in the sleet while Grant wrestled with the machine, grinding through the locking bar and leaving a fine pile of metal filings on the ground. Finally the bar was released, and Duggan pulled open the door, stepping back quickly in case a wild animal burst out. Lucy looked at Howard, who looked back placidly. 'Ladies first,' he said.

Lucy swung the door open. A mattress toppled out. She peered past it to see a motorbike, a freezer and several fridges. Second-hand white goods, she guessed, possibly destined for third world countries. The rainbow in her mind shimmered. This may not be a waste of time after all. If the items weren't fully workable, were they being disposed of illegally?

Lucy had worked on a similar case – Operation Orchid – with the National Environmental Crime Unit last July. She'd stuck her neck out and persuaded her boss, Superintendent Magellan, to order the return from Mumbai of eighty-two shipping containers, supposedly filled with recyclable plastics. The Indian Institute for the Environment and Renewable Resources had told Lucy at least half of them carried a mix of household and clinical waste, including syringes and condoms. On their enforced return to the UK, three men were arrested in Crawley, starting the investigation of a huge crossover crime industry masquerading as a legitimate business. It had been a bit of a bugger when – during the celebrations at their local pub – she'd blown her potential promotion by telling Magellan that it was his fault they'd missed catching the Mr Big because he hadn't acted on her request soon enough, giving Mr Big ample time to vanish.

Lucy cautiously opened the left door and stepped inside the container.

'Here, ratty ratty ratty,' she called.

'Very funny,' Howard remarked.

She squeezed past the mattress to see more fridges and maybe a dozen or so washing machines. Switching on her Maglite, Lucy continued to force her way through the container. TVs, a Coca-Cola vending machine. A crate of computers and another of keyboards. She was checking out a stack of microwaves when she thought she heard a noise, but it was so faint, she wasn't sure if she'd imagined it. She cocked her head to try to catch it again but she couldn't hear anything above Duggan and Grant's conversation about Aston Villa's chances against Arsenal at the weekend.

'Quiet!' she called.

Immediately the men fell silent.

She heard Howard make his way into the container behind her. 'What is it?' he whispered. She held up a hand and he paused, silent.

Then it came again. A faint thud, followed by a kind of whimpering bleat. Lucy crept forward, past a fridge and a chest freezer. The noise turned into mewling, like a wounded cat. Lucy knelt down, trying to pinpoint the noise. At the same time, she smelled something bad. Something *really* bad. Maybe the cat was nearly dead.

'Hello?' she said.

The noise turned into words.

Help help help.

They were coming from the chest freezer just behind her. All the hairs on Lucy's body bolted upright.

'Christ,' she said. 'Someone's in here.'

Lucy glanced back at Howard to make sure he was ready, then she gripped the lid of the freezer and tried to raise it, but it was locked. There was no key.

'Duggan, Grant!' she yelled. 'Chisel, hammer, *now*!'

Howard grabbed the tools from the guards. He set the chisel against the lock and cracked it open with a single strike. Lucy flung open the freezer lid.

The smell hit them like a physical blow. Trying not to retch, Lucy swung her torch beam inside.

A girl was lying on her side. She was naked. She wore a handcuff on her left wrist which didn't appear to be secured to anything. A hood was tied over her head. Her legs had been broken. Each finger had also been broken, and all of her toes, which lay at odd angles and were bruised blue and purple and horribly swollen. Blood, shit, urine and vomit were everywhere.

Breathing shallowly, Lucy bent down. 'I'm Lucy Davies. I'm a police officer. My partner, Howard Miller is calling for an ambulance *now*.' She swung to Howard, gesticulating urgently. His eyes were wide with shock, his mouth open, but he rallied quickly, grabbing his radio and thumbing the transmit button. When he spoke, his voice was thick with horror but it soon firmed as he gave the dispatcher the details.

'Help . . . help . . .' the girl murmured.

'You're safe now,' Lucy said. 'Nobody can harm you. I will stay with you until the ambulance arrives. You're safe,' she repeated again, wanting to reassure the girl. 'I'm Lucy, I'm a police officer . . .'

The girl's arms were covered in bruises, as though she'd been beaten with a cricket bat. She'd been hit so hard on her right elbow that the bone had broken through the skin.

'Help . . . help . . .'

Lucy bent into the freezer and said to the girl, 'I'm going to take the hood off, OK? So that you can see me, see my uniform, and know you're safe.' Lucy picked at the knot but she was trembling so hard her fingers slipped. She had to force herself to step aside and take a couple of deep breaths to steady herself.

'You OK?' Howard asked.

'Yup.'

She turned back, working as fast as she could, grateful she had strong fingernails and fingers small enough to slip through the loops and force the knot free. As gently as she could, she brought her hands beneath the girl's head, talking all the time, telling the girl what she was doing, that the ambulance was on the way, that she was safe now, she was easing off the hood . . .

The girl's eyes were open. They were a bright, vivid blue.

Her mouth was also open, her lips cut and swollen, clotted with blood.

She had no teeth. They'd been pulled out.

Lucy felt panic rising, forced it down. 'Hi,' she choked. 'I'm Lucy. You're safe now . . .' She gulped back a sob.

The girl's eyes were on hers, pleading. Lucy worked her mouth.

I must not show my horror. I must remain professional.

She said, 'The ambulance is on its way.' She glanced over her shoulder at Howard, who was staring at the girl, white-faced. 'It'll be here in . . . *Howard*,' she snapped. 'When?'

He jerked visibly. 'Three minutes.'

'Any time now,' she told the girl, trying to keep the atmosphere from erupting into hysteria. 'Before it gets here, I need to know your name. As I said, mine's Lucy. What's yours?'

'Ell . . . ella . . .'

Although she'd already guessed, she still felt a rush of horror. The missing girl, Bella Frances.

'You're Bella Frances, aren't you?' she said. 'Blink once if I'm right.'

The girl blinked once.

'Bella,' she said. 'Oh Bella, Bella. Thank God we've found you.'

CHAPTER TWELVE

Lucy sat on a plastic chair in the hospital corridor. She didn't think she'd ever felt so emotionally wrecked. She wasn't sure whether it was the stress or if she was dehydrated, but her head was aching badly. She should have been at the station, being debriefed, writing up her report, but she'd ended up accompanying Bella to the hospital. The girl had panicked, almost hysterical when the paramedics had made to leave Lucy behind, so she'd joined them in the ambulance. She had kept her hand on Bella's forehead, stroking back her hair and murmuring to her softly.

She'd stayed with the girl while she underwent X-ray and was prepped for the operating theatre. In short, she did everything Bella's family would have, if they'd been there, but they'd been away on holiday and only arrived half an hour ago.

Now Lucy saw Dr Chris Cobern, Bella's surgeon, approach. He looked as exhausted as she felt. He said, 'She's in the recovery ward. I had to pin both her legs, and her right elbow. She's in plaster up to her hips. I couldn't do anything about her broken ribs but I strapped her fingers and toes and they should heal

OK. The dentist did some good work, readying her mouth for implants. She'll be OK, Lucy. It'll take time, but she'll be OK.'

'Thank God.' A tremor of tension released itself in her shoulders.

'I also found some tiny wounds on her neck and upper chest. It's my guess they're burns from a taser.'

Lucy's fingers clenched. Some days she wished stun guns had never been invented, but at least they now knew how Bella had been overcome. Tasered and handcuffed, she wouldn't have stood a chance.

'Another thing,' he went on. 'A toxicology report came back saying she had traces of ketamine in her system.'

Ketamine was a powerful general anaesthetic that Lucy knew was used not just recreationally, but for operations on humans and animals.

'There's some bruising on her hip,' he added. 'I'd say it was injected several times, to keep her under.'

She gazed at a mark on the wall. 'Thanks,' she said.

'No problem.'

'Can I see her?'

'I'd come in the morning. She won't surface from the anaesthetic for a while yet. Besides, her family are with her now.'

Lucy headed for the station where she was debriefed, asked if she wanted a counsellor – no, thank you – and after she'd typed up her report she was ordered home even though it was barely three in the afternoon. The second she walked through her door she downed two painkillers with a glass of water. She'd never suffered headaches before but over the past couple of weeks she'd been dogged by them. She put it down to stress. Stress of being busted to this rat-hole. Stress of moving home, stress of splitting up with Nate. She wished he was here to give her a hug. She needed one after today. She couldn't get rid of the vision of Bella's broken body, the stench of blood and shit.

A fist of anguish gripped her heart and she had an overwhelming urge to cry. She felt so *alone*. She had to get out of here. Get back to London where her mum was, where her friends were. She stared out of the window, but she didn't see anything. She was picturing Superintendent Magellan's face when she walked back into his sector office. What had he said when he'd told her it would be in her best interests to resign?

It has been brought to my attention that you're not the easiest person to work with.

Apparently this had been a massive understatement. Magellan had been too much of a wimp to say as much to her face, and had left it to her sarge, Baz Lewis, to run through her imperfections.

'I can't complain about your work,' Baz had said. He wouldn't meet her eye as he continued. 'None of us can. It's the way you, er . . . interact with people. You can be a bit, ah . . . temperamental.'

One colleague apparently called her *irritable*, another *obsessive*. Someone called her an *Energiser Bunny on speed* and that they couldn't keep up with her and found her exhausting. Another complained she never slept (how did they know? It wasn't like they lived with her for God's sake) and that she was *unpredictable.*

She had listened to the litany of her faults with her chin raised and her gaze level. She would cry later, she told herself: bottle it up, don't show you're hurt, rise above it all . . . And then Baz said, 'Look, none of us are perfect, but if you hadn't yelled at Magellan last week, we wouldn't be sitting here now.'

She opened her mouth to protest but he held up a hand. 'It doesn't matter if he deserved it or not, your behaviour was inexcusable. You made him look stupid and –'

'I didn't know a journalist was there!'

'You were in a fucking *pub*, Lucy. You can't let rip in public like that. Christ, the press had a field day thanks to you. "Top Cop Is Left Flat-Footed" is not a headline we wish to see again.'

'But –'

'It's not the first time you've embarrassed him, remember.'

She raised her eyes to the ceiling in a parody of exasperation. *So what? He's a prat of the highest order.*

'Look . . .' He took a breath. 'I know it's not my job to do this, but I wanted to give you a heads-up before you go and see HR.'

She snapped her gaze back to Baz. Her spine tingled in alarm.

'I'm sorry, Lucy.' His gaze was fixed over her left shoulder. He looked as though he was facing a firing squad. 'But it's been decided you're to be transferred. Voluntarily, of course. It's best for everyone all round.'

She stared at him. The Met never transferred anyone, not *ever*. It just didn't happen. If you'd made a mistake, you were fired. And if you were fired, you couldn't work for another force. Your career was over. Full stop. The only way for someone to legitimately leave the Met and work as a cop elsewhere in the country was for them to resign.

'The Cleveland Police,' he went on, 'have confirmed they're currently recruiting and – please don't tell anyone this – I pulled several strings to get you jumped to the top of the list.'

'What?' She honestly thought she'd misheard him. Had he said *Cleveland Police*?

'They have a position open for you and expect to see you at the end of the month,' Baz sped on. 'I know it'll be a rush as you'll need to be fitness and medically tested as well as interviewed but if you don't get up there quick smart, you'll struggle to find a position elsewhere for at least six months. And by that time Magellan may well do something really serious and scupper your career permanently.'

She could feel her eyes bug. This had to be a joke.

'You can work out the rest of the week but I suggest you take it as leave, so you can organise yourself.' He picked up a pen and put it back down. 'Look, if you prove yourself up there, we'll welcome you back, I'll make sure of it.'

Confusion turned to horror. 'But I haven't done anything wrong!'

'I'm sorry, Lucy.' He swallowed. He still wouldn't meet her eye. 'It's not my decision.'

At that point she'd totally lost it, but she didn't want to think about the past – it still made her cringe – she wanted to think about the future. Getting herself back to where she belonged. Pulling on a pair of sweats and a fleece, she settled at her kitchen table with her laptop. First, she checked out RFC's website – Recycling For Charity – which looked genuine enough. Apparently their charity counterparts in India snapped up each and every workable second-hand fridge, steam iron, cooker, monitor and TV they could send over there. The charity's trustee board members were listed, and she jotted them down.

Lucy then considered the container, which had been full, its steel locking bar in place, and turned her efforts to finding out when it had been due for export. Because she knew the shipping system from Operation Orchid, it only took three phone calls to get hold of the right person. In this case, RFC's shipping agent was a man called Lewis Cunningham of Weald Logistics who, according to their website, provided *Affordable Shipping Solutions*.

Lewis Cunningham said, 'I've already spoken to the police.' He sounded tired and not a little shell-shocked. She guessed it wasn't every day he learned that one of his clients had a badly beaten girl locked in amongst their goods.

'I'm sorry if it appears we're doubling up,' she apologised, 'but with a case like this I'm afraid it's inevitable. I'm sure you'll appreciate we have to move fast, and what I need to know is whether this container was on your radar.'

'Our driver was due to pick it up tomorrow,' he told her, 'for delivery to Liverpool docks and loading on to the *Raipur* to Chennai. She was due to sail on Monday but she's been delayed for repairs. I expect her to sail later in the week, maybe Wednesday or Thursday.'

Chennai, Lucy knew, used to be known as Madras. On the east coast of India, it was an enormous, teeming city with a huge port to match.

'Is this a port-to-port service?' she asked. 'Or door-to-door?'

'Port-to-port,' he said.

Which would make the container that much harder to track once it left Chennai docks.

'Do you offer customs brokerage?' she asked.

'The other policeman didn't ask that.' He made it sound as though she'd stepped over some invisible line.

'Do you?' she insisted.

It transpired they did. They had direct links to Customs at Liverpool and prepared RFC's documents and electronic submissions, sorting out any taxes, duties and excises due. They also collected RFC's containers from three other recycling centres: Reading, Birmingham and Stirling, and shipped a container or two at a time, every two months or so, via Liverpool.

When she couldn't think of any more questions Lucy asked for Cunningham's mobile number – she always took a note of everyone's mobile number in an investigation – before thanking him and hanging up. She checked her watch. Seven o'clock. Had she really been working for eleven hours? It felt more like eleven minutes. She was definitely *lively* today. She liked Howard's expression. It certainly beat being called manic. She had to hope her elevated mood continued and that her despondency over Nate wouldn't lead to a crash. She'd struggled with her 'moods', as her mum used to call them, ever since she was a kid, but luckily they didn't interfere with her work. *Well, not that much*, she amended guiltily. And usually only when a particular event triggered her into plunging down the slippery black slope. She dreaded that happening up here. Without Nate to cover for her she was going to have to be incredibly careful nobody found out.

Wanting to check whether the charity RFC was legitimate, she dashed off an email to her old contact at the CBI in Mumbai. He responded quickly, apologising that although he couldn't help, a colleague of his in Chennai might be able to. When she eventually got through, the contact sounded so uninterested, she requested someone else but they didn't do handsprings either. They put her on hold for so long she reckoned they'd gone to lunch so she hung up.

On the CBI website, she did some digging. Checked her watch. Chennai was five and a half hours ahead. Past 9 p.m., their time. Nobody would be there, but still, Lucy picked up the phone. May as well test the number to see if it connected.

Yup. It worked all right. It rang and rang. Rang and rang.

She pictured an old-fashioned black telephone ringing on an empty desk in the middle of a vast office with walls coloured tobacco-brown. She could see windows hanging open to the sultry night air. Palm trees swaying beneath the city lights. The occasional horn beeping outside, people calling. Lucy was so deep in her fantasy that she nearly dropped the phone when it was answered.

'Namaste,' a boy answered. He sounded weary.

'Hello?' She wondered if she'd got the number wrong.

'Hello,' he responded a little more brightly.

'Er . . . I'm from England. Do you speak English?'

'Oh, yes. I am very good speaking with your country.'

'Am I through to Chennai CID?'

'Oh, yes,' he answered. 'This is the right place you are talking to.'

'OK. Well, I'm a policewoman from Stockton –'

'A policewoman?'

'Yes. My name is Constable Lucy Davies and –'

'Please, you will be giving me your telephone number.'

Lucy rattled it off. 'I just need some information,' she said. 'Who am I speaking with?'

Short silence, then he said, 'Junior Constable Chitta.'

'Nice to meet you, Chitta. Now, this morning we found a girl who was very badly beaten and left for dead. She was locked in a freezer inside a shipping container due to be transported to Liverpool, and then on to a ship to Chennai –'

'I am very sorry, but I cannot be speaking with you. Niket will be very angry.'

'Please, it's very important . . .' Lucy scrambled to persuade him not to hang up, and failed. The line buzzed in her ear.

She put down her phone, baffled as to why she'd bothered in the first place. God alone knew what ringing India had cost her.

She pinched the bridge of her nose between her fingers. What had Magellan said about her in her forwarding report? Oh, yes.

Lucy could be an exemplary officer, but unfortunately she jumps in with both feet without thinking things through. She calls this 'instinct' but in police terms this type of impetuousness is simply unacceptable and irresponsible behaviour.

Lucy sat looking at her phone and wondering, not for the first time, if she'd chosen the wrong career.

CHAPTER THIRTEEN

Saturday 24 November, 9.12 p.m., Chennai local time

Chitta looked at his handwritten notes. He'd been so excited he could barely read his own scrawls. Painstakingly, he re-wrote every word while the conversation was still fresh in his mind.

An English police officer. Constable Lucy Davies. She found a girl locked in a freezer due to be shipped to Chennai.

Could it be a case of trafficking? But why was she badly beaten? It would make her worthless when she arrived. He wished he'd been able to ask some questions, like whether the girl had any food and water with her, but Niket had been absolutely definite about taking phone calls.

'The number *only*, Chitta. Do *not* engage in conversation with *anyone*. If you do, you will lose your job and be rag-picking the city's rubbish dumps before the day is out.'

Chitta copied the Constable's telephone number in extra-large letters so there would be no mistake. Carefully, he re-read the note. It was good, he thought. It was clear and concise and professional, written just like a real policeman.

Chitta propped it next to Senior Constable Niket's phone, where he wouldn't miss it in the morning, then he picked up his mop and continued to clean the office.

CHAPTER FOURTEEN

Friday 23 November, 6.07 p.m.

Dan arrived home just after six and poured himself a finger of scotch. Downed it in one gulp.

He saw Jenny open her mouth to say something then close it, obviously deciding to keep quiet. Dan rarely drank spirits. The last time he had a whisky was when their cat died three years ago. The vet had come out and put the ageing tabby to sleep but when he'd offered to take the body to the pet crematorium Dan demurred; the family had already decided they wanted Gibson buried in the back garden. Dan had been fine until Jenny left him to dig the grave. With the dead cat lying beside him, he'd begun digging and, out of nowhere, found himself sobbing like a child.

He'd wept non-stop until Gibson was buried and he'd returned to the house, where he'd drunk two huge whiskies in an attempt to gain control. Dr Orvis told Dan it wasn't uncommon for men to be almost debilitated when someone in the family died. Apparently sorrow over smaller things that were not grieved over at the time built up so that when the tears finally fell, they came as a storm of pent-up anguish. But, Orvis added, Dan's reaction could have been triggered by something he was unconscious of, something that his memory couldn't bring to the surface.

Like now. He'd tried to save Stella Reavey, resuscitate her, and when he'd stood on the pavement, watching her being loaded into the ambulance, he'd felt a thick rope of grief knot itself around his windpipe. Why? He didn't remember knowing her. But now he'd thought it over, he wondered if it was his body responding to something subconscious. He felt strangely bereft and close to tears.

'Dan.'

He saw Jenny watching him anxiously.

She said, 'Are you OK?'

He pressed the glass against his forehead and closed his eyes. 'Not really.'

He felt her move closer, but she didn't touch him. 'Want to talk about it?'

'Promise you won't shout at me?' He opened his eyes and gave her a sad smile.

Her responding smile was tense and didn't reach her eyes. 'As bad as that?'

'I don't know.' He was tempted to pour himself another drink, but he didn't want any more alcohol in his system. He felt as though he should be ready to jump in the car at a moment's notice, fit and able to deal with anything that might be thrown at him.

'Tell me.' Her eyes remained on his, wary.

'OK.' He took a breath. 'I went and saw Stella Reavey today.'

Jenny didn't move, but he knew every nerve, every cell in her body had tautened. 'Why?'

'I was curious,' he said. Which was truthful enough. But there was no way he was going to tell her that Stella had said Luke hadn't died in a hit-and-run.

'What did she want?'

He pictured Stella stepping across the road, as neat as a pin, and handing him his breakfast. His *favourite* breakfast. She knew him. He could admit that now. But somehow she'd been lost with a host of other memories when Luke died.

'I don't know,' he said.

'Don't be evasive, Dan.' The colour began to rise in Jenny's cheeks. 'Either you saw her or you didn't.'

'She gave me breakfast.'

Jenny gritted her teeth so hard the muscles in her cheeks stood out like rocks. 'You said she was a stalker. A crazy woman. You wanted to keep her away from Aimee and then there you are, leaping into your car before dawn and –'

'She died,' he said.

'What?' Jenny's face went blank.

'She had a massive heart attack. I tried to resuscitate her with her daughter, but it was too late.' He'd followed the ambulance to Stoke Mandeville. He'd stood with Grace when she was given the news that her mother was DOA. Grace seemed to accept his presence without any trouble, and he wondered what Stella had told her. He'd desperately wanted to ask, but it hadn't been appropriate.

The doctor who broke the news was in his twenties and had swallowed reflexively, showing his nerves. He'd jerkily explained that Stella's medical notes showed that she had recently been diagnosed with aortic stenosis. When he'd started to elucidate, Grace had jumped in, telling Dan it was a heart valve problem, when a valve opening was smaller than normal due to stiff or fused leaflets. The narrowed opening made the heart work extra hard to pump blood through it.

'Her arteries had hardened,' she told Dan. 'Restricting blood flow.'

'Correct,' the doctor said. 'She was due to have heart valve surgery next week, but . . .'

'It wasn't soon enough,' Grace said woodenly.

'I'm sorry.'

Grace was sheet white, but she hadn't cried. Dan guessed that would happen later. She let him drive her back to her mother's house. He'd asked if he could call a relative for her, or maybe a doctor.

'I am a doctor,' she'd said, without any irony.

'A friend, then.'

She thought about it. 'Ross,' she said. She brought out her mobile phone. 'I'll ring him now.'

Ross said he'd be there within the hour. Dan offered to wait until he arrived, but Grace said no, she'd be OK.

'Can I help with letting people know what happened?' Dan suggested. 'Like her work colleagues?' He was hoping Grace might give him an address for DCA & Co.

'I'll do it.'

It wasn't the right time, but he couldn't let it go without making another effort. 'Where did she work?'

It was as though he hadn't spoken. She climbed out of his car and walked into her mother's house without looking back.

Jenny was looking at him as though he'd sprouted horns and a tail. 'Stella Reavey is *dead*?'

'Yes.'

'A heart attack?'

'Yes.'

'Jesus Christ.' She put a hand on the back of the sofa as though to steady herself.

'Daddy!' Aimee's voice trailed from upstairs. 'I know you're back! Come up, come up here! Bring a carrot with you. Please! Neddy's being really naughty and I can't catch him. I need you to help me because . . .' A stream of nonsensical chatter followed.

'I'll go up,' he told Jenny.

He was halfway up the stairs when he thought that he might surprise Aimee and actually bring a carrot with him to help 'catch' her stuffed horse. Footsteps muffled by the carpet, he padded towards the kitchen. He could hear someone murmuring and for a moment he thought it was the radio, but then he realised it was Jenny. She must be on the phone. He was about to step on to the stone floor when he heard her say, 'Stella Reavey's dead. What the *hell* is going on?'

He froze.

'No, he's upstairs with Aimee. But I've got to be quick . . .' Her tone was low and urgent. 'Yes, she's *dead.* A heart attack, apparently . . . What do you mean, you didn't know?'

Dan remained as still and silent as a tomb.

'No, Dan doesn't remember her. But she obviously said something because he went to see her this morning . . . No, he didn't tell me what . . . OK, I'll try and find out. Yes . . . Yes, yes. OK. Bye.'

Dan backed into the corridor. He had to act fast. He didn't want her to wipe the last number called. He coughed and cleared his throat. He heard the tiny beep as she replaced the phone in its cradle.

'Who was that?' he asked as he entered the kitchen.

'What?' Jenny looked round.

'On the phone.'

'Oh, just Ali. We were talking about having a coffee in town tomorrow.'

The lie tripped off her tongue so easily that he had to force himself not to stare at her. 'Ali?' he repeated.

'Yes. I've got to see the bank as I've been locked out of my Internet banking account.' She rolled her eyes. 'I can't believe they want me to bring my passport and a utility bill. They *know* me but they still need to do their checks.'

He felt a moment's bewilderment as though he'd imagined her conversation only seconds ago. A cold finger touched his spine as he recalled Jenny looking through the window at the hairdresser's, her pallor, her assurance she didn't know Stella . . . What else had she lied about?

'I see,' he said. 'Say hi from me.'

Ducking into the fridge, he brought out a carrot. Jenny looked startled. 'For Neddy,' he said. 'Would you mind doing the honours? I need to ring Tommo. He rang me this morning and I completely forgot to ring him back.'

'Sure.' She took the carrot. As she turned away he thought he saw her eyes flicker over the phone. Or had he imagined it?

Jenny left. He moved quietly to the kitchen doorway. He knew she was upstairs because he heard Aimee say, 'Mummy, that's *brilliant*. Neddy, look what Mummy's brought for you!'

With Jenny occupied with Aimee, Dan swiftly crossed the kitchen and checked the last number dialled. A mobile. Highlighting the number, he pressed *call*. Almost immediately, it started to ring. A man answered.

He said, 'Jenny?'

Dan didn't say anything.

'Jenny?' the man repeated. 'Are you there?'

'Tommo?' Dan said, filling his tone with puzzlement. 'Is that you?'

'No.' The man's tone was smooth. 'You've obviously got the wrong number.'

'Oh, I'm sorry,' said Dan. 'I must have pressed the wrong . . .'

The man hung up.

To add a layer to his subterfuge, Dan called Tommo, who was another high performance instructor. 'Any overspill?' he asked. Occasionally, when one of them was too busy to take on new clients, they'd recommend the other.

'I thought you were busy,' said Tommo.

'I am. But I could do better.'

'Try Porsche, Swindon. I heard their in-house driver might be stepping down.'

'Thanks. I'll do that. How's Sara?'

'Oh, muddling along.'

When they hung up, Dan picked out Stella's business card from his wallet, turned it over between his fingers. He'd searched DCA & Co. on the Internet to no avail. The only company with the same initials was DCA Ltd, a hydraulic specialist in Southampton who, when he rang, said they'd never heard of Stella Reavey. Dan checked his watch. Six thirty. Would anyone answer? He took his mobile outside and into the car. Rang the number.

'DCA,' a man said.

'I was given your number by Stella Reavey,' Dan said.

'Your name, sir?'

'Dan Forrester.'

'I will get Stella to call you tomorrow, would that be all right? She's usually in by eight.'

It looked as though the man didn't know Stella had died.

'I want to drop something off to Stella before we speak,' Dan said, frantically thinking of a way to get the address without setting off alarm bells. 'What's the address there?'

The man ignored his question. He said, 'Mr Forrester, if you wouldn't mind giving me the best number for her to reach you in the morning?'

Dan gave his mobile number. The man hung up. Dan sat in his car staring into the darkness outside.

Stella's voice.

We want to borrow you for a day, maybe two . . . pretend your memory's coming back. You see, we need to find someone . . . Cedric.

And what about Luke? He rested his forehead on the steering wheel. Had Stella been telling the truth about his death? Or was it simply a way of getting his attention? As he pictured Stella's small, still body lying on the stretcher, her face bloodless and still, tears streamed down his face.

CHAPTER FIFTEEN

Friday 23 November, 6.15 p.m.

Grace was wearing one of her mother's soft cashmere sweaters. The garment smelt so like her – coffee, burnt sugar, pomegranate – that when she held it under Ross's nose and asked him what it reminded him of, he said, 'Stella.'

It was like being wrapped in her mother's hug and she already dreaded the day when it no longer smelt of her.

She'd been crying for most of the day and her face was swollen and red, her eyes sore. Ross had coaxed her outside for a walk late afternoon, but they hadn't gone far before it began to pour with rain and they were forced back inside. As she took off her coat, her mobile rang.

'The surgery,' she told Ross. He nodded, indicated that he was going to put the kettle on, then disappeared.

Grace hung her coat over the banister as she answered her phone. 'Hello?'

'Grace, I know this is a really bad time, but both partners are out and there's no one else I can ring.' It was Amanda, their super-efficient receptionist, sounding harassed. 'I'm sorry, but something's happened.'

'What is it?'

'Jamie Hudson's gone missing. The police want a word with his GP but Dr Smith's in Budapest on that conference.'

Grace's mind stalled.

Jamie, missing? She'd only seen him yesterday, at the deli. And then she remembered. She was supposed to be seeing him this evening but with everything that had happened, she'd forgotten.

'When did he go missing?' she asked.

'Last night. The policeman's on the other line. Can you have a quick word with him? Please?'

'OK.'

According to the officer, Jamie – who liked sparrows, bees and butterflies and drank tea with loads of milk and ate as many biscuits as you offered – had vanished off the face of the earth. He had left the pub to walk home, and hadn't been seen since.

'He mentioned someone he knew had gone missing,' Grace told the officer. 'He was quite upset over it. You don't think it could be connected, do you?'

'Who was that?'

Grace racked her brains but couldn't remember. 'It was a girl,' she said. 'He only met her once but he said she was nice.'

'And you can't remember her name.'

He made it sound as though she was being purposely stupid, but she couldn't even remember that girl's name, the one who'd gone missing up north and had, according to the news this morning, been found in a container park.

'No, sorry.'

The policeman gave a grunt.

Because Jamie was adult, and male, and no foul play was suspected, the police were never going to press the panic button unless he was vulnerable in some way. Which was why the police officer was calling, to check and make sure Jamie didn't need to be found fast for his own safety.

'I'm not his GP,' she told the officer. 'You really need to talk to Dr Smith about this. He looks after Jamie.'

'Would you consider Jamie high risk?'

'Well, no. Not offhand. But it's not for me to say. Nor do I have his file to hand as I'm out of the –'

'Would you consider him a threat to himself or others?'

She sighed. 'No. But you really need to talk to someone who can check his file. I suggest you –'

'Low risk, then. Would you agree?'

'I can't say. You need to –'

'OK, OK. I'll call Dr Smith.' He sounded irritated.

'Good,' she said, relieved.

'Thanks,' he said, not sounding particularly grateful. He was obviously about to hang up.

'Please,' she said quickly, 'could you make a note on the file to let me know the instant you have any news?'

'Of course. But I wouldn't be too concerned. I'm sure he'll return home by the weekend.'

Grace wasn't comforted by the officer's platitude. In her job she'd seen several people voluntarily walk away from their established lives and relationships, and now she wondered if that's what Jamie had done. Walked out on his long-term girl-friend to start a new life elsewhere. Which promptly reminded her of Ross and his new life in Scotland. Which in turn made her think of her mother and the fact that she'd never asked her what she thought of his idea of moving to Scotland.

Grace raised the cuff of her mother's sweater to her nose and breathed deeply. Coffee, burnt sugar, pomegranate. Tears filled her eyes. She wished she'd told her mother she loved her when she'd arrived at her house instead of demanding a croissant and legging it upstairs.

CHAPTER SIXTEEN

Jamie Hudson had no idea where he was but he wasn't worried about it; he didn't think he'd ever felt so happy. Which was odd, because usually he felt happiest when the sun was shining and he was working in a garden or tending bees, and right now he wasn't outside. He was somewhere dark and damp and cold. He could be in a cave or a dungeon. What would grow here? Nothing with colour. Not even snowdrops or Lily of the Valley would thrive. It wasn't just dark but *black*. Not a pinprick of light.

He knew he should be worried, terrified. He should be trying to find a way out. Escape. But he couldn't harness his mind. His thoughts danced like sunbeams through a canopy of leaves. He was eight years old again, capturing crickets and putting them in a jar with a lid in which he'd punched holes. His mother was smoothing back his hair and kissing him. Then he was swimming naked with Gemma, her hair trailing behind her like water serpents. She looked so beautiful, her skin pale and smooth as marble. He started to cry. He loved Gemma *so much*.

They'd moved in together six months ago. They were saving up to get married. Have loads of children. They were going to call their first girl Heather, their first boy, Birch. Dr Grace Reavey was going to be their GP and watch over each pregnancy. They'd decided last weekend. They were with Dr Smith at the moment but he was a grumpy old sod and they both much preferred Dr Grace who was sunny and kind and smelled of bluebells.

He had to get to Gemma. Make sure she was all right. Make sure the man who'd attacked him hadn't gone after her. The man with the taser. The guy who'd pushed him in the back of a van. Who had tasered him again and again before injecting him with something that took hold of his senses and sent him to another realm.

Was this what had happened to Bella? Pretty Bella who he'd met in London last month, who was doing a Bachelor of Science course in Sport and Exercise and who he'd thought would be interested in what he had to say but she'd ignored him, telling him he was paranoid. He couldn't blame her. If someone banged on like he had he'd think they were paranoid too, but what if the same person who'd kidnapped him had also kidnapped Bella?

What about Gemma?

Was she safe?

He rolled on to his side and tried to push himself upright but his wrist wouldn't support him. It felt floppy, as though it had been broken, but there was no pain. He tried to use his elbow but something gave with a sickening sucking sound and he fell back.

He strained to control his mind. He knew he was in immense danger but he could do nothing about it. His reality melded and blended from his childhood to his teens and beyond. He couldn't help being absorbed by the scenes playing inside his head. He had no sense of time passing.

Until the pain started.

He'd thought getting his tattoos was painful, especially on the inside of his arms, but this was something else.

It began slowly, a dull sense of unease in his muscles. At the same time, his mind began to clear.

Then a small garden rake was in his veins, digging and scraping away. His brain was shouting at him. *Get out of here!*

He tried to raise himself but the rake grew into a spade, slicing and burrowing deep inside, smashing against the surface of his skin, the back of his skull. Red and black, billowing pain erupted in every part of his body and he collapsed, a scream in his throat.

Suddenly a light went on. Jamie forgot about the pain as the man stepped inside.

Please, help me, Jamie begged.

He saw the syringe in the man's hand, tried to wriggle away but it was no use. The man simply bent over him and stuck the needle into his hip, squeezed the plunger, and left.

The light was still on.

What did it mean? Had the man left the door open?

Jamie attempted to crawl across the floor. He battled through the pain, fighting to push himself along with his feet, elbows and knees. Why didn't his limbs work? And why was he wearing a handcuff on his left wrist? He took in the baton hanging from a hook on the back of the door. It reminded him of a police truncheon, something he'd only seen on TV. Was he in a police station? Out of nowhere the question expanded then contracted. A floating sensation began to drift like a bank of fog across his mind. The pain began to dissipate.

It was his twenty-first birthday and he was in Wales driving his camper van, his mates in the back, Gemma in the passenger seat, bicycles on the rear rack, surf boards on the roof. Laughter and beer and salt on their skin. Sunshine, friendship and love.

He no longer saw the bare brick walls covered in damp. The concrete floor. He was overlooking Freshwater Beach, watching his friends launch themselves into the surf.

He cried from the beauty of it all.

CHAPTER SEVENTEEN

Saturday 24 November, 6.30 a.m.

Bella should have come round from the anaesthetic by now, but when Lucy visited her before she headed to work, the on-duty nurse told her she was still unconscious.

'It could be Bella's way of starting to heal,' the nurse said.

Personally Lucy thought it could also be Bella's way of hiding from the hideous reality she'd suffered.

Asleep in a chair next to Bella was Bella's mother, snoring lightly. She was what Lucy's mother would call 'big-boned', a large brown-haired woman with a double chin that had the unfortunate effect of making her look fatter than she was.

Lucy crept across the room – always difficult in a pair of heavy-duty black shoes – and put her hand gently over Bella's, careful not to touch the splints on the girl's fingers. 'It's only me,' she whispered. 'Lucy Davies. I'm the policewoman who found you, remember? I just wanted to check up on you. Dr Cobern did a great job. And don't worry, your bones will heal, your scars will fade . . . not the mental ones, sure, but there's loads of help if you want it. Oh, and you'll have teeth that will be as real as your own. The dentist did some work so he could put in some implants. I looked them up on the 'net. They look incredible. Nobody will know they're not real, not even you. Amazing, huh? Look, I can't stay for long as I've got to go to work, but I'll drop by when my shift finishes. Keep getting better, OK? Don't let the bastard that did this get the better of you.'

Before she left, Lucy read Bella's get-well cards to check for anyone they didn't already know about. Then she looked through Bella's chart. She had to squint to decipher the doctor's handwritten notes about Bella's previous medication. She was on the Pill, which wasn't much of a surprise for an attractive eighteen-year-old, but the Zidazapine made Lucy blink.

Lucy tracked down a staff nurse who was wading through a morass of paperwork in the Intensive Care Unit. Machines and monitors hummed and beeped, doctors and nurses moving between patients. The hospital smell seemed to increase here, heavy with antiseptic.

'Sorry to interrupt . . .' Knowing how annoying it was being disturbed when you were in the middle of filling in a report, Lucy waited until the nurse had finished scribbling and raised her eyes. Lucy said, 'I want to double-check Bella Frances's prescription for Zidazapine.'

The nurse put down her pen. 'It's an antipsychotic drug. Bella's bipolar. She's suffered massive mood swings for years, manic highs and extreme lows. She developed psychotic symptoms during her manic episodes – hallucinations, hearing voices – hence the drug, which enables her to live a pretty normal life.'

There were moods, like Lucy had, and then there were *moods*. 'How come it's the first I've heard of it?' she asked. Usually when a person went missing, the first thing the police did was check with their GP whether they were mentally or physically vulnerable.

'Administrative stuff up,' the nurse said cheerfully.

Lucy was appalled. Someone's head would roll when this came out. Or had it already rolled? In the station, Lucy hunted down Jacko, who she found concentrating on a beef and horseradish sandwich in front of his computer.

'Bella's on a drug called Zidazapine,' she told him.

'Yup.' He nodded. 'She's bipolar.'

Lucy felt like grinding her teeth. 'Is this common knowledge or am I the only one who didn't know?'

Jacko sighed. 'The family hid it from us. They thought if the media got hold of it they'd paint her as a schizophrenic lunatic and there'd be no sympathy, and that nobody would bother looking for her.' He brushed breadcrumbs from his desk top and got to his feet, brushing down his trousers as well. 'I told everyone at Wednesday's briefing.'

Her day off. She'd missed it. She had to stop shift work, become a detective and then this kind of thing wouldn't happen.

'Boss?' she asked. 'Can I keep Bella's case? After all, I found her.'

'I know you did, Lucy, but I'm sorry.' He shook his head. 'It's not my decision. It's the DI's.'

'Can't you persuade him?' she wheedled.

'We've a new DI, don't forget.'

'Ah, shit.' She had forgotten. She just had to hope the new guy was amenable to having an inferior foot-soldier muscling in on his case.

'Look, I'll try and put in a good word for you, OK?'

'Thanks, sarge.'

Lucy walked to the beat office barely taking in anything around her. She could see the pink and blue pack of Zidazapine hidden in the back of her bathroom cabinet. She could hear Baz's voice, and she was back in his office, listening to him tell her she was to resign from the Met. She hadn't reacted very well to the news. In fact, she'd reacted rather badly. She remembered staring at Baz, his short-cropped brown hair and steady brown eyes that were unable to meet hers. It was the realisation that if she didn't resign from the Met she'd get kicked out and never work as a police officer again that made her snap.

'Fuck,' she'd said.

'I'm sorry, Lucy,' Baz had repeated. 'It's not my decision.'

It was like a geyser exploding inside her chest, erupting into a great cloud of rage. She was on her feet screaming and Baz's voice was calm and controlled and she was yelling at him and the rage expanded so far it made her head swell until she thought it would burst. She slammed out of his office, still yelling. The whole sector office fell silent as she stormed across the room. Twenty pairs of wide, shocked eyes stared at her. She yelled at them too, feeling her face twist, hating them for conspiring against her, hating herself for losing control. *Fuck the lot of you!*

How she got outside she couldn't remember. The next thing she knew she was in a pub. She didn't recognise it. She was downing vodkas. Ignoring the stares. She was in uniform. Against the rules. Rules rules rules made to be broken, *fuck them.*

'Are you OK?' the barman asked.

Shit day. Shit shit shit.

When she stumbled outside, it was pouring with rain, bucketing down, but she couldn't feel it. She had too much energy to expel, too much anger, so she broke into a run. People glanced at her and then around, looking to see who she was chasing.

I am not a failure, I'll show them.

Neon signs fizzled all around. She hadn't realised evening had fallen. Cars and buses swept past, throwing up spray and water and making the neon shimmer. She increased her pace, *I'll run until I can't feel any more* – but something rolled beneath her foot – maybe a can, a stone – and she lost her balance, teetered wildly on the kerb and then –

Nothing.

She awoke in hospital.

Mum crying.

She hated herself for making her cry.

A man she'd never seen before was standing nearby. He looked as though he might cry too.

I'm fine, I promise.

Her mouth was dry, her skin taut and hot, her head pounding. Familiar sensations of a hangover. How much had she drunk? She couldn't remember.

Her mother held her hand.

'Lucy, love. This is Marc Davey.' She introduced the man. He'd been driving his car when she'd appeared from nowhere. How he didn't hit her, he doesn't know. He must have missed her by millimetres. He jumped out of his car to find her in the gutter staring up at him. She hadn't said a word. She appeared to be in some kind of shock, so he took her to hospital.

'I didn't hit you,' he said. His hands were spread, begging her to believe him.

How long have I been here?

'Overnight,' said her mother.

'Were you chasing someone?' the man asked.

Yes. Sorry I gave you a fright.

'So you won't press any charges?' the man said. 'I mean, I didn't hit you . . .'

No charges.

The man hesitated a second, then scarpered, quick smart.

Who knows I'm here?

Her mother looked blank. 'Everybody,' she says. 'I mean, Nate. Your boss, Baz. I rang him. He came by earlier but you were asleep.' Her mother studied her carefully. 'Lucy, what happened?'

She nibbled the inside of her mouth as she prepared to lie. *I was chasing someone. A young guy who'd snatched a woman's bag, right in front of me.*

She stuck to her story through thick and thin. All she could think was that she had to stop anyone knowing what really happened. That she'd lost it. She would never tell anyone the truth. Thank God the barman of whatever pub she'd ended up in seemed to have kept quiet. Everyone appeared to believe what she told them. That she'd been chasing a criminal.

Nate took her home to their flat. 'Don't go to work,' he said. 'Not until you feel better.'

Lucy hadn't argued. She was exhausted, utterly spent. She went to their bedroom and drew the curtains. Lay on the bed, staring at the ceiling. She crept to the tiny dark cave inside her skull and curled up inside it. She didn't want to eat or drink. She was numb, she had no interest in the world. No energy. Nothing.

Nate came and sat with her for a while. 'It's a bad one, isn't it, Luce? I'm sorry.'

She didn't say anything. She couldn't. She let him hold her hand until he got bored and went away.

She heard car engines outside occasionally, the sound of a telephone ringing, the radio. Nate went to work and came home around six. He tried to reach her, but her mind was slow, her thoughts sticky. It was oddly peaceful, being alone with the hum in her head.

When he came to bed she turned away and faced the wall. Slept.

'Baz told me about you having to resign,' Nate said the next morning. It was a Saturday. He was drinking tea in bed next to her. He sighed. 'What a bugger.'

He didn't say any more because that was his way. He didn't need to say anything more. It was indeed a bugger. She reached across and touched his face with her fingers. 'Thanks,' she said.

'Welcome back.' He smiled.

She'd got up then and had a shower. Re-entered the world feeling fragile, slightly shaky, but soon her strength began to return and she knew she was on the uphill slope once more. Nate made her scrambled eggs and bacon, and gave her the newspaper to read.

Late morning, she was at the kitchen table, drinking tea, when she heard the doorbell chime. She heard Nate answer it and the next instant their GP, Dr Mike Adamson, walked inside. Mike was also an old school buddy of Nate's and the two men saw one another every other week or so, meeting up for a beer, playing football, the odd game of poker. Lucy had seen Dr Mike – as she called him – professionally once, to get a prescription for the Pill. Standing before her in a jacket and tie, with his medical bag, he looked ten years older than he did when he was kicking back in jeans and trainers.

She glanced past him. 'Where's Nate?'

'He's stepped out for a bit, to give us some privacy.'

Alarm bells began to ring, but she leaned back. Circled her mug with her hands.

'Privacy?' she repeated.

'Nate wanted us to have a chat.'

'What about?'

'I hear you had a bit of a close shave . . .'

'Yes. But I'm fine.'

'Perhaps I could take your blood pressure.'

'But –'

'Indulge me.' He smiled gently.

She tried not to sigh dramatically as she stuck out an arm. While he checked her out, they talked about nothing in particular. He told her about Chelsea's game against Liverpool. She told him about arresting two football hooligans last Saturday. Once he'd put away his equipment he calmly looked at her and, out of the blue, asked if she'd ever considered she might be bipolar.

'I'm sorry?' Her mind went perfectly blank.

'Bipolar. It describes a variety of mood disorders, defined by mood swings, from excessive energetic highs to depressive lows.'

She stared at him. 'I don't get depressed.'

'Nate said you have bouts of excessive happiness, hopefulness and excitement. Increased energy and less need for sleep –'

'I was only in the hospital because I was chasing a criminal down the street and ended up nearly getting run over.' Her voice was flat. What was going on? Jesus, if she had some mental problem she'd be thrown out of the police faster than Magellan could say *good riddance.*

'There's nothing wrong with me,' she added tightly.

He looked at her for a while. 'It's not something to be ashamed of.'

'I'm not ashamed, OK? I get a bit excited sometimes, that's all. And I get tired. Like most people do.'

'Nate says it's a bit more than that.'

'He would.' Lucy flung up her hands. 'He hates it when I get emotional. And it's not just Nate either. Everyone gets uptight as soon as someone shakes the box. We live in an emotionally repressed society where anyone who's not a stuffed shirt, all bottled up and inhibited, is considered a freak.'

'Do you consider yourself a freak?' he asked.

'Of course not!' Her cheeks started to heat. 'I just get more emotional than other people, a bit headstrong, and people find it difficult to cope with because they're so dull and *boring*.'

A long silence followed.

Lucy looked away.

'Nate's concerned, that's all,' he said softly. 'So am I, especially considering the job you do.'

Her stomach lurched. If he wanted to, he could end her career with a single phone call. So she fixed her gaze on the footy calendar stuck on the wall and concentrated on turning her mind away from her anxiety and relaxing the tension in her shoulders, her belly. When she looked back at him, she was pretty certain she appeared calm and that she'd hidden her fear successfully, caught it like a slippery eel in her fist.

'You're both really kind.' Lucy was pleased she sounded relatively genuine even though she detested them for talking about her behind her back. 'But I'm OK. Seriously.'

'I'd like you to consider taking something that might help balance the more extreme spectrums of the condition.'

She stared at him, shocked. Suddenly she wasn't just a young woman being forced to resign from a high-pressure job she loved, she was a patient with a mental disorder.

'Like what?' she managed.

'Zidazapine. It's very effective at smoothing out excessive mood swings. It also helps you sleep, and you will probably find your relationships improve, both at work and at home.'

Her mouth turned dry. He was serious? He really believed there was something wrong with her?

He gave another gentle smile. 'I gather things have been a bit tough lately.'

A chill swept through her. He knew about her situation with the Met?

They were silent for a minute. Then he said carefully, 'I think you should consider trying it, at least.'

The first clear thought arrived: *No one must know*.

'OK,' she said.

He brought out a prescription and five small boxes containing samples of Zidazapine. Each box was stamped with the name 'PepsBeevers'.

'I will ring you at the end of the month . . .' He checked the date on his phone. 'And you can tell me how it's going. Not everyone necessarily responds the same way.'

She managed a nod.

'If it works for you, I'll monitor you.'

'OK.'

She hadn't seemed to have a choice. He'd know if she didn't try it. She only had to take the stuff until she knew what effect it had, and then she could, if necessary, lie and say she was still taking it. Anything to prevent her from getting chucked out of the police.

*

When Nate asked how the visit had gone, she locked her emotions down tight. 'Fine,' she said. She wanted to slap him for going behind her back and jeopardising her career, but didn't dare do anything overdramatic that might get reported to Dr Mike. So she swallowed her anger along with the pills.

When she'd gone back to the sector office she was as calm and cool as a glass of freshly poured spring water. She worked her final shifts without raising her voice once, without being *irritable* or *unpredictable*. She apologised to everyone for being so indefensibly rude and bought them all cakes and doughnuts and although nobody cheered that she was going, nobody said they'd miss her. Except for Baz.

'It's going to be very dull without you,' he sighed.

At first it was OK, she found she had more self-control, but soon she started feeling odd. Yes, she slept like a log, but her thoughts and responses slowed to such a level that if she hadn't known differently, she'd think she had flu. Her thoughts were grey. She had to drag herself out of bed in the morning and sat through every briefing as though poleaxed.

'You're so much better I can't tell you,' said Nate one evening. He hugged her happily.

She drew back, looked at him. 'What do you mean?'

'You're not as volatile. You're calmer, easier to deal with.' He grinned. 'You haven't yelled at the TV once.'

'We haven't had sex since I've been taking them either.' A high-pitched hum started in her ears. 'Anything else?'

He shrugged. 'You're a lot easier, I guess. Less combative. I don't have to worry about how you're going to react to anything.'

'You prefer me like this?' *Half dead, comatose, unfeeling and with the emotions of a fish that's been filleted?*

'Why?' He looked puzzled. 'Don't you?'

She'd ditched the pills the day she'd left him. The same day she'd left for Stockton. She couldn't risk him telling Dr Mike she wasn't taking them anymore. Within a week she was back on form, sparky and alive, her mind flourishing with colours. The relief of having reclaimed her own emotions and energy was indescribable.

When Dr Mike called, she lied. She told him she found the drug helpful and that she'd get another prescription from her next GP in Stockton. He said, 'I'm so glad, Lucy. I was really worried that I might have to report this, but if you continue being monitored, we'll be fine.'

Yeah, right.

The morning briefing had just finished when Lucy's mobile rang. She checked the display.

Blocked.

Puzzled, she answered. 'Hello?'

'Ah.' A man's voice. 'Is this the police officer who will be ringing the CID in Chennai?'

'Er, yes, this is she.'

'Good evening, madam. My name is Senior Constable Niket. I have been hearing you were ringing our department last night. How may I help?'

Quickly, she grabbed a pad of paper and a pen and scribbled down Niket's name.

'It's regarding a girl we found,' she told him. 'She was badly beaten and mutilated, and dumped in a shipping container, nearly dead.'

'A girl?'

'Yes. Bella Frances. She is eighteen years old. You can check the story on the BBC website immediately, if you like.'

A brief silence. 'I am having the BBC site in front of me. The girl is in hospital now, am I being correct?'

'Yes.' Lucy talked him through the case. At first she'd thought he was an older detective, but as they spoke further, she realised he was in his twenties like herself. Apparently, a boy called Chitta had answered the phone. Chitta cleaned their offices every night and was always answering the phone and pretending to be a police officer.

'We have been telling Chitta he will be losing his job if he does not stop his pretending,' Niket said.

'Please thank him for taking my message.'

'We must not be encouraging him.' Niket's voice was tinged with amusement. 'He might be thinking he is a real policeman and taking over my job. Please, tell me what I can be doing to help you.'

Lucy asked him to check what happened to RFC's containers when they arrived in Chennai. 'I want to make sure that the charity is legitimate. That nothing illegal is going on with the organisation in your country.'

'Of course I will be looking into this for you straight away.'

After they'd hung up, Lucy began making notes to share with Bella's case team, so they could see her thread of investigation.

'Lucy,' said Jacko. 'I'd like you to meet DI MacDonald.'

She looked up expecting to see her new DI but instead she saw Sergeant Faris MacDonald.

'Hello, Lucy,' he said.

A kaleidoscope of memories tumbled: his hands, square-tipped, broad and masculine, on her body; his mouth on hers (much softer than she'd imagined); his bare skin beneath her fingertips (smooth and firm and sunbaked warm and smelling of suncream); sand gritting against her shoulders; his chest above her (broad, strong and immense like a statue); his head haloed by blue sky and two soft white puffy clouds; the faint sound of seagulls, *kyow kyow.*

She realised she was staring at him and jerked her gaze aside. What the *fuck* was Mac doing here? She was trembling inside, her cheeks aflame. Cool it, she told herself. You're a single woman now. It's OK. *Calm down.*

He was saying something but it sounded as though he was underwater so she looked back. *Sharpen up for God's sake!* She tried to concentrate. He was broader than she remembered but the curly brown hair was the same, as were the mismatched grey eyes. Then she took in the two pips on his epaulettes. He wasn't a sergeant any longer. She tried not to show her shock. Fucksake. He was her new DI, and the Senior Investigating Officer into Bella's case.

CHAPTER EIGHTEEN

Mac put out a hand. She had no choice but to shake it with Jacko watching them. His grip was as warm and dry and strong as she remembered (his hands on her naked waist, lifting her up to meet him before slipping them round to support her backside).

'Hello,' she said. Her voice was raspy, her heart galloping away.

'Nice to see you again.' His face was neutral.

'You know each other?' Jacko looked between them.

'Er . . .' said Lucy.

'Oh, yes,' said Mac. The neutral expression remained but his eyes began to dance. 'Lucy and I met on a team-building exercise in Wales for new recruits. We found we had a mutual passion for coasteering.'

At the words *new recruits* Jacko lost interest but Lucy could feel her cheeks beginning to heat. She fixed her gaze on Jacko's shoes, wishing, *longing* for them to both go away.

'I gather it's thanks to you that Bella was found,' Mac said. 'Well done.' The amusement was gone. He was all business, expression attentive. 'Jacko tells me you want to be involved on the case. And that you're keen to join CID.'

'Yeees.' The word drew out slowly, indicating her caution.

'How would you like a support role on my team?' He turned to Jacko. 'That OK with you, sergeant?'

Jacko nodded, looking pleased with himself at orchestrating the offer.

Mac looked enquiringly at Lucy. When she didn't respond immediately, Jacko also looked at her, eyebrows practically in his hairline and obviously mystified that she wasn't leaping at the chance. She couldn't refuse to join now. Not unless she wanted to appear totally fickle.

'It would be a great opportunity,' she said stiffly. 'Thank you.'

'Good,' Mac said. 'I'm going to the halls of residence to double check Bella's room this morning. I'd like you to come with me. In half an hour, OK? I can brief you en route.'

She opened and closed her mouth. Managed to say, 'OK.'

'If you do well, it'll look good for your career.'

'Thank you, sir.' She sat down and picked up her pen, writing a sentence of complete gibberish on the back of an arrest form and, to her relief, when she glanced up both men had gone.

Lucy went limp. Perspiration dampened her neck and forehead. Of all the police stations in all the world, why had he been transferred to hers? She'd been unfaithful to Nate once. *Once!* And here she was, being faced with her living, breathing misdemeanour as though she had to be reminded what a terrible person she was.

She hadn't been engaged to Nate back then, but even so, her behaviour had been unforgiveable. And it wasn't just because she'd been going out with Nate either. Having a sexual relationship with a superior officer wasn't forbidden but it wasn't exactly encouraged either. Why had she slept with Mac? Why, *why?* Yes, he'd looked good, but it was more than that. She could remember standing in the car park when they first met and staring at his hands and wanting to feel them on her body. She'd been aflame for him the second their eyes had met. She had looked up at him longing, *yearning* to kiss him. It was as though he wore an invisible magnetic cloak that had pulled her straight against his chest.

She felt like tearing out her hair. An invisible cloak! As if that was any kind of excuse! She'd practically dragged him to the beach that Sunday and ripped off his clothes. And it had been fantastic. Seriously incredibly fantastic. But when Mac had asked for her phone number later, she'd panicked. She hadn't told him about Nate.

She'd left the course early. She'd made up some ridiculous excuse about forgetting a meeting and raced back to London. Mac had rung her at the Met a couple of times but stopped when she didn't return his calls. She put him firmly in the past and whenever she thought about him, the memory felt like nothing more than an extremely sexy dream she'd once had.

And now here he was, in the same cop shop, under the same roof. Faris MacDonald. Her DI.

Before she joined Mac, Lucy hastily read up on the case. Motive, means and opportunity. Motive was anger, she reckoned. Anger and fear. There was rage in the attack. Raw brutality. Personally,

Lucy didn't think Bella was meant to survive. The only reason why the girl hadn't suffocated in the freezer was because the seal had perished. Plus the fact that the drain hole at the bottom hadn't been bunged up.

Means? Bella had been tasered. The taser, however, could have come from anywhere. Lucy had recently arrested a teenager who had zapped his maths teacher as he'd stood outside the school gates. The kid had purchased the taser over the Internet for less than fifty pounds, delivered by post. The Internet had made it far too easy for arms dealers to circumvent the law. No clues there.

Opportunity? Bella had been taken from or near her accommodation. There was no evidence of a struggle. Her handbag, purse and keys were still in her room. If he'd tasered her there, how would he have got her outside without being spotted? Or did he lure her to his car and taser her once she was inside? If so, it would mean he was either incredibly persuasive or she'd known him. What about fingerprints? Lucy checked the file and saw that there were no matches, and no evidence that Bella had been sexually assaulted. Nothing was missing, which pointed to the possibility that he wasn't a sexual predator or a thief, which Lucy found extremely odd. No clues with the ketamine either, she saw. It wasn't particularly difficult to get hold of. He probably administered it to keep her quiet. It created a dissociative state that would have made her malleable and it was also a painkiller. If he was moving her around it would stop her moaning or screaming.

'Lucy?'

She scrambled to her feet and joined Mac outside. As they walked to his car she surreptitiously studied his profile, wondering why he'd moved from Bristol, but not daring to ask. She didn't want to get on to anything personal. If anyone found out she'd slept with a colleague – a superior officer at that – it would totally undermine her.

He beeped open an unmarked Vauxhall. They climbed inside.

She expected him to start talking straight away, but unnervingly, he didn't. He drove the car in silence, his brow furrowed, obviously deep in thought, and it wasn't until they were over the River Tees – its water the colour of dull pewter – that he finally spoke. 'Why did you run away?'

She closed her eyes. *Here we go.*

'Lucy?'

'I heard you.'

'Why?' he pressed.

'I don't want to talk about it.'

Silence.

Lucy chewed her lip. *Please let it go. Please.*

'Hmmm,' he said. The frown was still there. 'But what if I do?'

No way. She had to put a stop to this. And right away. She said, 'Do we have a psych on the case?' Her voice was stiff.

It started to rain. Mac switched on the wipers.

'I'd like their view on the handcuffs,' she added.

He turned in the direction of the University of Durham and accelerated past a white van. He heaved a sigh. 'No psych,' he said. 'They can't help until they've cleared three cases. How's Nate?' he added without missing a beat.

She would rather cut off her own arm than have him know Nate was no longer around.

'Nathan,' she said coldly, 'is fine. How's your girlfriend?'

'Cleo's fine, thank you.'

She blinked. Had he been seeing this Cleo back then? Had they *both* been unfaithful at the time? If so, how did she feel about it? Not great, she decided. How she wished she could take back every step, every touch, every kiss . . . to her horror, she started to flush. *Get a grip!*

'There's something you don't know,' Mac said.

OK, so Cleo wasn't his girlfriend. He was married. Big deal.

He said, 'Bella wasn't tortured in the container. Forensics say that would have happened elsewhere. And I split up with Cleo, by the way,' he added, suddenly looking cheerful. 'I'm currently single.'

Lucy scowled but his cheerful look remained until they arrived at the student accommodation block. She followed Mac inside, shaking water from her jacket, assailed by the palpable smell of student living. Fried food, baked beans and toast, stale coffee. Bella's room overlooked the river. A small desk stood beneath the window covered with stacks of reference books and box files, notebooks and pens. A space indicated where a computer would have sat, a computer that was now with forensics.

Posters, memorabilia and photographs adorned one wall. Happy pictures of Bella and friends. Quite a few appeared to be missing, no doubt taken by the police. Lucy stared at a photograph of Bella standing with her arms straight in the air, a wide grin lighting up her face. She was in a stadium strobed with coloured electric lights. Behind her was a gigantic hydraulic dragon on top of which was a red and gold howdah. Inside the howdah were four men, waving.

Frank, Bob, Graham and Steve.

Johnny had come on later.

'Lucy?'

She'd been at the same concert. Well, maybe not exactly the same one, but she'd policed one of them. Baz knew she was a bit of an At Risk fan and had managed to wangle her the job in her last week at the Met. 'My goodbye present for you,' he'd grinned.

Wembley. The national stadium. Seating for ninety thousand people and the second largest arena in Europe. Host to the FA Cup Final and the Horse of the Year Show, and concerts by Coldplay, Madonna and lastly, At Risk. Although Lucy knew she'd be working, she'd really looked forward to it.

She'd seen the group's grand entrance atop the dragon, heard the crowd go wild. It had looked to be a fantastic evening until for no reason whatsoever, the crowd had fallen silent. Eighty-five thousand noisy, happy people suddenly seemed to freeze. The band faltered but continued playing and soon the fans were singing along again, waving their arms, everyone acting normally except for Lucy, who remained still and quiet. Her mouth was dry, her heart beating fast. An increasing sensation of dread began to build inside her. Why had the crowd fallen silent? What was going on? Was a terrorist attack imminent? Was the stadium about to explode or burst into flames?

She became convinced something awful was about to happen. That they were all going to die. She started to head to another police officer, to talk it over, but was overcome with such a strong sensation of fear all thought fled. She simply turned for the nearest exit, and ran for her life.

She erupted outside the stadium and kept running until she reached the exterior barriers. Only then did she turn and look back, doubled over, trying to catch her breath, gasping and sweating.

Absolutely nothing happened. No disaster. Nothing.

A young man with dreadlocks had come up to her and asked if she was OK. He called her Lucy, confounding her for a moment until she remembered her name was on her epaulettes. She brushed him off before hurrying back inside. Fortunately her colleagues assumed she'd been caught short and had to rush for the loo. She hadn't corrected them. Whenever she thought back on the experience, how she'd deserted her post, her face burned with shame.

Discreetly over the next few days she'd tried to make sense of what had happened, searching the news as well as the Web, but although there were small pieces in the newspapers and some chat on social network sites, nobody else seemed to have experienced Lucy's immense dread. They didn't appear to take the strange event seriously, and most made light of it referring to *angels flying overhead.*

Looking back, she saw how stressed she'd been, not just at splitting up with Nate, but losing her job at the Met as well. And what about the damage done by being exiled up here? No wonder she'd lost control in Baz's office, and then lost it again at the concert, which had obviously triggered something in her psyche – fear of being found out, fear of failure, fear of the future. She supposed she'd had a breakdown of sorts and, as she pictured herself back then, terrified and furious all at once, she felt immeasurably sad.

'Lucy?'

'I can hear you, Mac.'

'I'm done here. You?'

'Yup.'

That night, she had the same dream that had dogged her since the concert. She was in uniform, watching the dragon sway across the stage. Everything was silent. There was no music. Nobody moved, nobody spoke. Her dread was like black treacle oozing through her veins. She wanted to flee, to run to safety, but for some reason she couldn't move. She couldn't scream, couldn't open her mouth. She was frozen with fear.

CHAPTER NINETEEN

Tuesday 27 November, 9.00 a.m.

Grace reached for a pair of bronze and pearl dangly earrings and was immediately reminded of Jamie, who'd asked where she'd bought them as he thought Gemma would like a pair. He was still missing but there was little she could do about it, especially since it was her mother's funeral today.

The autopsy had been completed, the death certificate issued, the body released to the funeral directors. She knew the system and how it worked but she'd never been part of the inexorable chain before. Now she was in the thick of it. The outpouring of sympathy. The constant act of reassuring people she was OK when she was anything but. She couldn't shake the strange breathlessness in her lungs. No matter how deeply she breathed, it never let up. She felt constantly short of oxygen, lightheaded, dizzy.

She pulled on a pair of sheer tights and slipped into a deep blue velvet skirt. A soft cherry silk blouse followed, along with a floaty multi-coloured scarf. Chunky necklace. Bracelets.

You look like a fortune-teller.

Her mother's voice. But it wasn't disapproving. When she'd worn this combination of clothes to lunch one day, Mum had looked at her with not a little approbation.

I wish I could wear what you do, she'd said wistfully. *But I seem to be welded to the dreaded suit.*

Grace touched Simon's face in the photograph that sat on her chest of drawers. 'Keep her safe,' she told him. 'Tell her I love her.'

The doorbell rang.

'I'll get it,' Ross called.

She put on some lipstick then checked her appearance in the mirror. Her face was bloodless. She looked like a vampire. She scrubbed it off.

She heard men's voices downstairs. Gradually, Ross became politely insistent, before falling silent. When she heard the front door close, she went to the window and looked outside to see a man in his fifties, dressed in a double-breasted camel coat, with a fedora and a pair of leather gloves, walking back up the path.

'Who was that?' she called.

'A friend of your mother's. He wanted to speak with you but I said he could wait until after the funeral.'

The word *funeral* was like a hammer blow in her lungs.

Oh, Mum, she thought. Why didn't you tell me earlier? Why didn't I hug you closer, press my head against your chest and *listen?* I would have heard your heart was in trouble immediately. Instead of a steady thump-thump I would have heard a thump-shoosh and I wouldn't have let you put off your operation, not even for a *day*. I would have dragged you into the operating theatre myself.

It transpired that Stella's doctor, Murray Walsh, had sent her to a specialist three weeks ago, who had immediately diagnosed aortic stenosis. Murray had talked Stella through the ramifications. Stella had appeared resolutely calm. Murray had told Stella how she should talk to her family and her work colleagues about her change in circumstance. He'd tried to persuade her to allow the cardiac specialist to make an immediate date for surgery. Stella had looked Murray straight in the eye and said calmly that she needed more time.

'She told me that she had urgent, important things to settle first,' Murray told Grace.

'What things?' Grace asked.

Murray, thickset, greying, shook his head. 'She didn't say. But from her demeanour they weren't trifles. I told her to take things easy, not to put herself under undue stress.' He scratched his cheek. 'She laughed. I mean, genuinely laughed. She said her health was the least important thing at the moment. She was still laughing like it was the greatest joke. I told her it wasn't a laughing matter and she sobered immediately. She said, "I know". And then she said again, "Seriously, Murray, I have things to do that cannot wait".'

'I don't understand.' Grace felt bewildered. It was like being shown a completed crossword puzzle with all the letters filled in but each word was gibberish. 'She put these other things before her own health? Her own *life*?'

'I'm sorry.' Murray sighed. 'I wouldn't usually . . . but you're a GP. I thought you'd understand . . .'

He thought she'd take his version of her mother's response to a life-threatening problem with more aplomb. But she couldn't. The patient had been her *mother*.

Now, Grace dithered over whether to wear a hat or not. From downstairs she heard Ross call, 'Gracie, my love. Are you OK?'

'Yes,' she called back, thinking *No, I want to rewind time and turn up at Mum's and not have a shower and this time, save her.*

She'd found a strange solace being at work over the last few days. Kerry and Hugh, the practice's partners, had told her to take time off but she found she was better at work and that the distraction helped. On her first morning back, she'd been disconcerted to find three emails from her mother, sent just minutes, maybe even seconds, before she'd died. In one, her mother had apologised for not telling her of her bad health before and then listed what appeared to be a lot of unconnected and random names, mostly from Grace's childhood.

The second email contained a list of banks, sort codes and bank account numbers. Aside from the bank addresses, all were incomplete. Oddly, one bank was in the British Virgin Islands. Also, what appeared to be an address: *Ocean View, Nail Bay.* She couldn't find any reference to Ocean View on the Internet, but Nail Bay looked spectacular; acres of white sands, tropical blue ocean rimmed with palm trees. Grace had dashed off a quick letter to Ocean View, in case it existed and someone there was connected with her mother.

The third email simply said: *Dearest Grace, If anything out of the ordinary happens, remember one thing: trust no one. Love, Mum x*

Her hair had just about stood on end when she'd read that. What in the world had she meant? What did 'out of the ordinary' mean? Was she talking about her own death? Or something else, something to do with the urgent, *important* things she wanted to settle before she had heart surgery?

'Gracie,' Ross called. 'I don't want to pressure you, but . . .'

'I'm coming,' she called.

She walked down the stairs. Ross came to her, expression sombre. He said, 'I know it's probably not the time or place, but you look beautiful.'

She managed a wan smile. 'Thanks.'

He smiled back. 'I'm sorry, my love, but it's time to go. OK?'

Which meant she was already late.

She picked up her handbag. She said, 'I'll set the alarm.'

'OK. I'll see you outside.'

Grace paused at the front door and looked back. The grey space in her chest expanded. She couldn't remember standing here without her mother. They would always leave the house together to walk to the shops or a restaurant, or her mother would stand in the doorway to kiss her goodbye. She could see her mother's clear brown eyes, her firm mouth that only smiled when she was genuinely amused, her determined chin. She'd brought Grace up on her own. No man to lean on, no husband. Grace's father had gone missing – assumed drowned while sailing off the Norfolk coast – when his daughter had been barely a year old. His body was never found. Her mother had erected a memorial headstone in the local cemetery and continued to work and bring up Grace as she'd done before he'd died.

She punched in her mother's code and pulled the door shut. As she stepped outside, she saw Dan Forrester, her mother's amnesiac friend, standing on the other side of the road, watching her. His posture was weary, as though he'd walked a long way and had further to go. He half raised a hand then let it fall. She waited for him to come across and speak to her, and when he didn't, let Ross take her hand, slip her arm through his and walk her to the church.

CHAPTER TWENTY

Dan watched Grace walk up the street. He assumed the tall, angular man in the perfectly tailored suit was Grace's partner, Ross. He liked the way they walked together. Grace was a strong woman but now she was debilitated, laid flat by the death of her mother, she leaned against Ross and Ross was supporting her. Just as it should be.

His mind switched to Jenny. Had she supported him similarly in hospital? Had he leaned against her as Grace did against Ross? He closed his eyes briefly, trying to imagine what had happened. He hated not remembering *so much.* He could stand in Starbucks and look at the drinks menu and say, *I'd like to try a Chocolate Cookie Crumble Frappuccino* and Jenny would look at him and say, *but you'd much prefer an Iced Caffe Latte.* And he'd say *but I've never had a Chocolate Cookie Crumble* and she'd get that look on her face that he now knew meant: YES YOU HAVE BUT YOU DON'T REMEMBER.

Some days he could scream with wanting his memory back. Tear the walls apart looking for snatches of Luke, glimpses of his past life, his old job that remained a perfect blank. He could remember university – Bristol, engineering – as well as school and all the holidays in between. He could remember meeting Jenny – at Glastonbury Festival along with a gang of uni friends – but thereafter his memory went awry and the job he'd had from leaving university, the one he'd stayed in until Luke died, didn't exist. Not in his mind.

Apparently he'd been a civil servant working for the Home Office in the Immigration Department. He couldn't think why he'd joined that particular section but oddly enough every time the subject of immigration popped up on the news, from illegals to terrorists to asylum seekers, he tuned in. He laid his hand over the scar on his stomach that Stella had said came from a firefight. Stella, Stella, Stella. He could see her bright hazelnut eyes, see the humour there, and the hurt when he didn't recognise her.

He wished he could have resuscitated Stella, saved her life. Saved Grace her sorrow. He'd come here today wanting to help in some way, half-thinking he might attend Stella's funeral, but seeing Grace and Ross together made him realise his presence wasn't appropriate. He didn't know them.

A loud *tchook-tchook* burst from the tree behind him, a blackbird's alarm call. He turned to see a cat prowling through the undergrowth. The hum of traffic drifted, children's voices, music from a radio. Sounds of suburbia. He felt a moment of happiness and realised it reminded him of when they'd lived in London. Now, the sounds of home were more rural; sheep bleating, tractors rumbling, the moan of the wind off the moors. He wasn't sure which he preferred. What about Jenny? Was she happier in town? Two days ago he would have said not, but things had changed and he wasn't sure he knew her any more. Last night, over a supper of fishcakes and peas, she had tried to find out what Stella had said to him.

'You didn't go for a dawn raid, then.'

'No.'

'You went to see this woman, Stella Reavey.'

'Yes.'

'Where?'

He put down his knife and fork. Looked at his wife, her glossy waves of blond hair that he loved to wind around his fingers. The lush mouth that he loved to kiss. Her high breasts and narrow waist, and those blue eyes that could twinkle with merriment but were now gazing resolutely at him.

'I'm guessing London,' she said. 'Am I right?'

He didn't respond.

'What did you talk about?'

He continued to study her. She wore a form-fitting jersey top with a silver necklace he'd bought her three birthdays ago, simple but elegant. Her skin was clear and smooth; the only giveaway that she was no longer in her twenties were the fine laughter lines etched at the corners of her eyes. Normally he'd look at her and marvel she was his, love and pride swelling, and he'd smile, but tonight he'd never felt less like smiling because whatever he said would get reported to the man she'd called. The man who had Jenny's name and number programmed into his phone.

'Dan?'

'Are you happy?' he asked.

'What?'

'Are you happy?' he repeated.

'Of course I am.' She looked bewildered. 'But I'd be happier knowing what you spoke to that woman about. She freaks me out.'

Stella's voice: *Your son Luke didn't die in a hit-and-run.*

He pushed away his plate and got to his feet. 'I'm going to read to Aimee.'

Jenny looked at his half-eaten meal. She bit her lip. 'But she's asleep.'

'I'll read very quietly, then.'

'Dan, please . . .' Her voice was gentle, pleading as he walked out of the kitchen, but he didn't turn back.

Upstairs, Aimee was sprawled half-in and half-out of her bed, Neddy squashed in the crook of one arm. He carefully drew her duvet over her shoulders and tucked her and Neddy in. She didn't wake. He kissed her cheek, inhaling her scents of soap and shampoo, something sweet and fruity that made him think of apricot jam. Carefully, he lay on top of the bedcovers next to her. She murmured and snuggled up to him. He put his arm around her. He fell asleep soon afterwards and when he awoke, it was past 2 a.m. and he was cold, but he didn't join Jenny in bed. He went and slept in the spare room.

Standing in Stella's street, Dan felt a moment's empathy for his wife. If he didn't think he knew Jenny any more, then how had she coped when he'd undergone his personality change?

She said she liked the new him, but did she really? Friends said he retained his innate caution and his analytical approach to things, but he seemed to have lost his overt charm as well as his sense of fun. He now struggled to make small talk at parties, for instance, and found being impulsive and spontaneous almost impossible.

'You were a bit of a charmer,' Jenny admitted when he'd returned to the subject in bed, after their supper at Candy's.

'And I'm not any more?' he teased gently.

'You're more genuine now,' she said, rolling over to look at him. 'You're more reserved maybe, but you're more thoughtful too.'

He quite liked the idea of the old him, charming and a bit of a party-goer, but that was all. He was content with the man he was now, and he guessed that was what mattered most.

Dan was still thinking of Jenny, her unwavering cheerfulness that morning, the way she sang to the radio, pretending, perhaps *willing* herself to believe nothing was wrong, when he became aware of a van drawing up outside Stella's house.

R.V. Carpet Cleaners.

Two men sat up front. When the van parked, one climbed outside and went to the rear of the vehicle and opened the doors, disgorging another two men. They wore matching blue trousers and blue tops; company uniforms. One man carried a stubby canister vacuum along Stella's path while another stood on the pavement glancing up and down the street.

Dan's skin tightened all over his body. His senses switched to high alert.

The men had triggered a primeval instinct in him. Dr Orvis said any response like this came from the myriad memories that weren't memories but subliminal associations of what was around him; sounds, colours, body language, actions, incidents. His instinct told him not to let the men notice him.

Dan began walking along the street, away from them. He made his steps easy, unhurried. He reached into his jacket and brought out his phone. He sauntered and pretended to be texting. Casual. Nothing for anyone to worry about.

He reached his car and climbed inside. Drove to the top of the street, turned right, and parked. Googled *R.V. Carpet Cleaners* on his phone to find a bog-standard single page website that anyone could have posted. He thought things over briefly. Even if he had Grace's mobile number, he wouldn't ring her, not when she was at her mother's funeral. Were they really carpet cleaners? Was he paranoid? Instinct said no. And Dr Orvis was all for instinct.

Each memory has an emotional core. You might find yourself instinctively responding positively or negatively to someone or something you think is new, but it may be your subconscious recognising them. I'd suggest you start trusting this instinct and let it become your guide to what you like and don't like, who you trust and who you don't.

Pulse humming, Dan returned on foot. Looked back down the street.

The man on the pavement was still checking the street. He wasn't behaving like a carpet cleaner. He was behaving more like a lookout.

The driver remained in the van with a newspaper he wasn't reading. This one was definitely a lookout.

Senses alert, Dan stayed where he was.

He watched the third man open Stella's front door and disappear inside her house, closing the door behind him.

A minute later, no more, the two men, one carrying the vacuum cleaner, joined him.

Dan watched as the curtains were drawn.

This time, he didn't call the police but walked back down the street. He kept his pace relaxed, his head down, pretending to text as he approached Stella's gate. The lookout in the van was pretending to read his newspaper but Dan knew he was watching him. At the last second, Dan swung into Stella's front yard. Immediately, the lookout was on the phone.

Dan knocked on the front door. He couldn't hear anything coming from inside. Certainly no sounds of carpets being cleaned.

He knocked again.

Finally, the door opened. 'Yes?' The man had sandy hair and pale eyes. A mole sat on his right cheekbone, another on his chin. His nose was narrow, and slightly skewed to the left. Small earlobes. Very slightly receding chin. Small mouth with a fuller upper lip.

'I'm a neighbour,' Dan said. 'I want to know what you're doing in my neighbour's house.'

The man tapped the logo on his chest where *R.V. Carpet Cleaners* was stitched in yellow. 'What do you think?'

'She died,' Dan continued. 'Her daughter's at her funeral. Which as we all know, is the perfect time to execute a burglary.'

The man raised his eyes skywards before bringing out a card. 'Ring the office and check, if you want.'

Dan pulled out his phone and dialled. A cheerful woman's voice answered. 'R.V. Cleaners, can I help you?'

'Your managing director, please.'

'I'll put you through,' she said brightly.

Another woman's voice. 'Mr Fetzer's office.' Not quite such a bright tone.

Dan said, 'Can I speak with Mr Fetzer, please.'

'I'm sorry, but he's in meetings for most of the day. Who can I say is calling?'

'How long has your company been in business for?' he asked.

'Oooh, around twenty-odd years or so.'

'Who started the company?'

'That would be Mr Fetzer's father.'

'Bill Fetzer?'

'No, Jim,' she responded without a beat. 'Can I take a message for you?'

Dan hung up.

The sandy-haired man raised his eyebrows. Dan raised his back. 'Very good,' he said. Then he turned and walked away. He heard Stella's door click shut behind him. As he turned on to the street, he looked at the man in the van, who looked straight back. Raising his hand, Dan gave him a flick-salute with his forefinger, which immediately reminded him of the man in the camel coat who'd tipped his hat to him outside Stella's. The look-out gazed back stonily.

Dan walked to the end of the street and out of sight. They were professionals, but what sort? Pulling out his phone, he called the police.

'It's an emergency,' he said calmly, a part of him amazed he was calling 999 for the second time within a week. 'I'm witnessing a break-in. Four men going into a neighbour's house. She's a single woman, who lives on her own. What should I do?'

CHAPTER TWENTY-ONE

Grace wasn't sure what she'd expected from her mother's funeral, but it wasn't this great throng of people spilling over the path and on to the grass and for a moment she thought she'd come to the wrong church. 'Who are they all?' she said, bewildered.

'I couldn't tell you,' Ross replied. 'I'll try and find out if you like.'

'No.' She gripped his arm. 'Stay with me.'

'Of course.'

As she walked up the path people came to her to express their sympathy. She knew the small handful of relatives – distant cousins on her mother's side – and perhaps a dozen or so friends from her childhood, but nobody else. She tried to place them. Some were in their fifties, others in their forties, a handful in their early thirties. Quite a few seemed to know each other. She spotted Joe Talbot, a work colleague of her mother's who she'd met a couple of times, and when he caught her eye, he came over.

Ross released her as Joe took both her hands and kissed her cheek. 'Grace, I am so sorry,' Joe said. She caught the faint scent of aftershave, something warm and spicy that reminded her of Christmas. 'We had no idea she was so ill.'

'Neither did I.' She looked around at the gathering. 'Who is everyone? I don't recognise any of them.' She wanted to exclaim, *I didn't know Mum knew so many people!* but refrained.

Joe glanced at Ross. 'Hi,' he said. He put out his hand. 'Joe Talbot. I worked with Stella for the past hundred years.'

Ross shook. 'I'm Grace's boyfriend,' he said.

A jet of panic stabbed through her grief. *Could they retain their relationship when he vanished into the Highlands?*

'I can introduce you around, if you like . . .' Joe subtly gestured for Grace to join him, letting the suggestion hang.

'I'll follow.' Ross gave a nod.

Joe waved at a fifty-something man with wispy white hair, who immediately walked across. He wore a crumpled suit and his tie was crooked. Spots of what looked suspiciously like gravy stained the front of his jacket.

'Your mum's boss,' Joe said.

'Philip Denton,' the scruffy man supplied. His voice was soft, his attitude gentle. Grace could imagine him soothing anything from a wild animal to a hysterical child without any trouble. 'I'm so sorry,' he added. 'We're going to miss Stella enormously; she was such an integral part of our team. Personally, however, I will miss her greatly. She was a very good friend to me over the years.'

Grace frowned. 'How long have you known her?'

He glanced into the sky briefly. 'Thirty years or so.'

Grace blinked. 'Nearly all my life,' she remarked. She'd turned thirty-two in October. Why hadn't she met Philip Denton before?

He gave a faint smile as though he'd heard her thoughts. 'Stella liked compartmentalising. It's usually a masculine trait, keeping people in separate boxes, but she was particularly good at it. I've never met any of her family before, or personal friends.' He glanced around as though they might suddenly make themselves known, then said vaguely, 'I mustn't hold you up . . .'

Joe took his cue and moved Grace on to meet the receptionist at Stella's office, along with two more colleagues and a personal assistant who looked after Philip and Stella's admin. Grace followed the flow of people into the church. She said, 'How many people work at DCA?'

'Oh, there are about twenty of us, spread around the place.'

She raised her hand to indicate the humanity filling the pews. 'So who are all these people?'

'From her previous jobs, probably. She hasn't worked for the one company the whole time. She had a lot of contacts, business acquaintances . . .'

On impulse, Grace walked up to a young woman in her early thirties and introduced herself. She said, 'I hope you don't mind me asking, but how do you know my mother?'

'We used to work together,' the woman replied, smoothing down her suit skirt. 'I'm really sorry she died. She was like a mentor to me.'

'Was this at DCA?'

The woman shook her head. 'We met before.'

'Where was that?'

The woman flicked a glance at Joe, then away. 'The Home Office.'

Her mother had been a civil servant for as long as Grace could remember, commuting to and from London daily, until she'd left to work for DCA & Co. – global political analysts – five years ago. She'd been a high-flying interpreter and translator for top businessmen and politicians, in great demand not just in the UK but abroad. At a moment's notice, she could find herself flying to Brussels or Budapest, Moscow or Washington. When she was a child and her mother had an important meeting in London, she sometimes took Grace with her. She could remember doing her homework upstairs in a strange house once, somewhere in the East End, while downstairs her mother talked to a stranger, a foreign man with fierce yellow eyes. Apparently he'd needed something translated urgently and at the time Grace hadn't questioned this, but now, looking at all these people, she wondered exactly what her mother had been translating.

Grace was going to ask more about her mother's job, but then the vicar appeared. He wanted her to sit at the front of the church. Joe walked her down the aisle and settled her next to Ross. The service sped past. When Grace and Ross headed outside with her mother's coffin, the congregation followed. But when Grace and Ross started to walk to the wake – being held in the pub opposite the church – only her mother's family and a handful of friends followed. All her mother's work colleagues melted away.

CHAPTER TWENTY-TWO

Tuesday 27 November, 10.35 a.m.

When the police car arrived outside Stella's house, the lookout in the van was immediately on his phone, expression urgent.

Dan could see that the cops weren't taking any chances. To combat four men potentially robbing a house, they'd sent an armed response vehicle. Two uniforms climbed out, leaving an operator to man the in-car comms and send on-the-spot information back to base in case specialist firearms officers were needed.

The uniforms didn't have to knock on the door. As they approached, it swung open. Sandy Hair was there again. He talked to the police for thirty seconds, no more. One policeman spoke into his radio, updating his comms man, and then the police entered the house. The door shut behind them. Dan counted the minutes.

At 10.45 the police stepped outside. Dan walked quickly to intercept them. He had no doubt Sandy Hair was watching.

'Yes, sir?' one asked.

'I reported the four men,' Dan said. 'I thought they were burglars.'

'Ah. You're the neighbour.' He glanced at his colleague, who gave a nod. "They're carpet cleaners all right. But thanks for ringing us. You never know about these things. Always better to call than not.'

Dan didn't stay to watch them drive away. He walked to the top of the street and ducked out of sight. Kept an eye on Stella's house. The men were inside for half an hour. Oddly, they didn't appear to take anything when they left. He'd rather thought they might have taken Stella's laptop, perhaps some files or papers, he wasn't sure, but to see them empty-handed made him frown. Maybe they'd pocketed what they needed? A computer disc or memory stick?

When the driver started up the van, he raced back to his car and climbed in.

He wanted to see where they went.

Because his was the only car following the van, he had to hang well back and change positions regularly to try and avoid being spotted. He lagged steadily behind, but when they hit the dual carriageway of the A41, he became exposed.

The van trundled along at a steady sixty miles per hour until they reached the Hemel Hempstead turn-off. As soon as they hit the second roundabout, Dan knew he was in trouble. Whether they'd designed it or not, they'd timed it perfectly to force their way across, leaving him two cars behind and struggling to make any headway. On the other side of the roundabout, he saw them swing right and out of sight. He floored the accelerator when the road was clear ahead, racing for where he'd last seen them. His senses were alive and sharp, taking in everything around him; the mother and pram on the pavement, the trees planted between parking slots, two dark-skinned men smoking and chatting by a bus stop.

He swung right. His eyes went straight to the bottom of the street, a T-junction. Traffic streamed in both directions. The van turned left.

Dan put his foot down, burning rubber, overtaking two cars, one of which blared its horn. At the junction he swung left and pushed his car hard. The van was accelerating up a hill towards a pedestrian light. When the light turned amber the van didn't slow down. The light was red when the van blasted across.

By the time Dan passed the traffic stopped at the light, the van was long gone.

Carpet cleaners or not, it was obvious they'd spotted him and hadn't wanted him to follow.

CHAPTER TWENTY-THREE

Tuesday 27 November, 11.00 a.m.

Grace stood next to the fireplace watching drizzle slide down the window. Outside, pedestrians huddled beneath umbrellas, their faces pinched with cold. But inside, everyone's expressions were expansive and rosy, no doubt helped by the copious quantities of alcohol Ross was helping to provide.

It had been his idea to hold the wake in the pub and now she applauded him for not holding it at her mother's house. Less formal and somehow more comfortable. She'd spoken to all the cousins, and was thinking it was probably time to wind things up – she felt exhausted – when the man who'd come to her mother's door earlier approached. He held his hat in his right hand but hadn't shed his camel coat or his leather gloves.

He said, 'I'm sorry for your loss.'

'Thank you.'

'My name is Sirius Thiele. I am a debt collector.'

For a moment she thought she'd misheard. 'I'm sorry?' she said.

'I appreciate this is a difficult time, but my business has become increasingly urgent. I am here on behalf of a client of mine.'

She stared at him. 'I think there must be some mistake.'

'Please, if I could trouble you to step outside.' He flicked a glance at Ross. 'I think you may prefer it if we weren't overheard.'

'I'm sorry, but –'

'A friend of yours is waiting to see you,' he cut over her. 'Someone you haven't seen in a while. His name is Martin Fairfield. He told me a very interesting story about you and your friend, Simon Granger. What a sad and touching tale it was, when poor Simon died.'

Her nerves fizzed with shocked disbelief. 'Simon?' she repeated. The pitch of her voice came out unnaturally high.

'Martin wants to see you. Privately.'

Grace didn't move. Her brain seemed to have stalled. She hadn't seen Martin in over six years. What was this?

Sirius Thiele leaned forward confidentially, his tone low. 'Does your boyfriend Ross know about you and Simon? What Martin saw?'

It was as though he'd just slapped her. She jerked visibly, her eyes wide.

'I thought not.' He smiled.

She worked her mouth. Her lips were dry, her tongue like cardboard. 'What do you want?'

'For you to follow me outside, and into the car park, where Martin is waiting. It won't take long.'

Without waiting for her response, he turned on his heels and wound his way through the mourners towards the exit.

Grace's mind churned. Was Martin really here? Why had he turned up after all these years? What was he doing with Sirius Thiele?

I am a debt collector.

Grace didn't move. She wasn't going to trust a stranger's word that Martin was outside. But how did he know about Simon? Or was he guessing?

'Are you all right, my love?' She jumped when Ross put his hand on her waist. 'You look terribly pale.'

'I'll be OK when the day's over,' she said.

'Can I get you anything?'

'A brandy would be good.' She rarely drank spirits, but she thought it might help steady her nerves. She watched Ross head for the bar and at the same time, took in the man who'd put his head around the corner and was staring at her.

He'd barely changed. Still boyishly good-looking, with a fresh complexion and a thatch of fair hair and baby blue eyes.

Martin Fairfield.

The years poured away.

She was in Simon's house. She was trying not to cry.

I can't, she told him. *What if someone finds out?*

Please, he begged.

She'd known Simon since they were toddlers. Their mothers had met at pre-natal classes and forged a bond that had remained until their children left home. They had lived two doors from each other and as Grace grew up, Simon had walked her to and from school. They learned to ride their bicycles together, helped one another with their homework.

When Simon took up judo, so did Grace. When he took up squash, so did Grace. He was active and sporty, and together they went hiking and mountain biking. She met his various girlfriends, and he'd vet her boyfriends. Simon was her big brother in everything but blood.

While Grace went to uni to study medicine, Simon joined a university air squadron. His dream was to become a fighter pilot and Grace was there to celebrate when he was accepted into the Royal Air Force, and sent to Cranwell for officer training. She sent him a bottle of champagne when he got engaged to a pretty, bubbly fitness instructor called Juliet, and put the date of his wedding in her diary.

Everything looked perfect.

Until he went skiing one day.

Black run and demanding off-piste skiing in Val d'Isère with two friends. Frequently icy, the run was littered with old stumps and fairly steep in places, around 45°. Many of the markers were becoming difficult to pick out in the flat evening light so – being the more experienced – Simon led the way, skiing fast, fuelled by adrenalin until he missed two of the markers and, caught unawares, faced an unexpected cliff. He started to make a turn away from the lip but a runnel of ice made him lose control and the next second he'd shot over the edge.

He hadn't even had time to shout.

He plummeted a hundred feet before he smashed into a boulder, then bounced a further forty feet to crash into another rock where he came to rest, unmoving, unconscious.

Two doctors and four members of the Val d'Isère rescue service raced to the accident. They took Simon to hospital where they discovered he had suffered a catastrophic high cervical spine injury.

When Grace heard, she had to go home. She cried herself to sleep.

Simon remained in a coma until he was returned to the UK, where he awoke paralysed from the neck down, and had to be ventilated in order to stay alive. The RAF began medical discharge proceedings. The wedding was postponed. After Simon's family brought him home, Grace visited him every week, each call leaving her more and more despondent as his muscles grew weaker and wasted away. He sank into depression. *Why me?*

His depression soon turned to anger. Rage at being helpless, unable to move, unable to do anything for himself. Fury that he couldn't have sex any more. He was a tactile person and now he couldn't even show physical affection, not a hug, not a cuddle.

Juliet wanted to care for him for as long as she could. She didn't want carers' working hours dictating what time he awoke or went to sleep, but Simon didn't want her wasting her active, young life on him.

If I was dead, he told Grace, *she wouldn't feel obligated to look after me.* He'd had a tracheotomy – an operation to place a tube in his neck just below his Adam's apple to ventilate his lungs – but could only speak during the exhale phase of the ventilation cycle. Even then his voice was weak and bubbly, nothing like he used to sound. Another frustration he was forced to live with. He'd also been catheterised shortly after the accident but now he had to suffer regular suppositories for bowel care which he found unbearably demeaning.

I want to be dead, he cried, sobbing in Grace's arms.

He had all his faculties, but his body was useless.

He'd been robbed of his future.

He got pressure sores. Muscle spasms. Urine and mouth infections. He began to plead for compassionate release. He wanted his family to take him to Dignitas in Switzerland, an organisation that legally assisted suicide, but they recoiled, horrified. They adored Simon. Loved every inch of him and wanted him to live for as long as possible. They didn't care he was incapacitated. They didn't want to lose him – wouldn't contemplate euthanasia. They thought his request to die meant he didn't love them.

Of course I love them, he told Grace. *I don't want to hurt them but I can't live like this anymore . . . I'm a fighter pilot, remember? Not a bloody vegetable. I hate every minute of every day. Please help release me . . .*

Grace talked to him about having ventilation withdrawn but he baulked.

They won't understand. They'll be distraught, thinking I don't care for them. There has to be another way. You're a doctor! You have to know of a way I can die without them knowing I orchestrated it. Please, Gracie!

His eyes were on hers, pleading.

Grace fell into turmoil. It wasn't just that she was terrified she might go to prison, or get struck off; it went deeper than that. She hated seeing her friend so desperately unhappy. She wanted to help him, yet this conflicted with all the reasons she had become a doctor. Life was sacred to Grace. Life was to be prolonged and protected. Revered.

I'm sorry, she told him. She was trying not to cry. *But I can't.*

The pain and disappointment in his eyes was like a scalpel slicing through her heart.

A week later, Grace visited Simon with a friend and fellow GP. Martin Fairfield. They'd met at uni and kept in touch over the years, meeting at the odd conference and sharing medical papers they thought the other might find of interest. One day he accompanied her to Simon's. He had a patient who'd suffered a similar catastrophic spine injury and he wanted to see how Simon's home care had been set up. With two of them there, Juliet took the opportunity to go shopping. Grace sat with Simon while Martin took a phone call outside.

They were listening to the radio via the Internet when suddenly, the music stopped.

Click.

Her eyes snapped to the digital display on Simon's medical equipment. Blank.

Then his ventilator stopped.

Simon couldn't breathe without it.

Her pulse went into overdrive. *Power short.*

She leaped to her feet. *Where's the trip switch?* she asked out loud.

Simon's eyes smiled, blazing with a joy she hadn't seen since before his accident. He didn't want her to trip the switch. He wanted her to ignore the power cut and *let him go.*

She stood, racked with indecision.

His eyes continued to smile. Then he gave her a wink.

Simon . . .

Slowly, he closed his eyes. It was his way of saying goodbye.

No!

Grace looked around wildly. A scream built inside her head. *Why wasn't the ventilator's back-up battery working?*

No time to think. She had to do something. She tore out of the room. Raced around the house searching for the circuit box. Kitchen, hall, hall cupboard, laundry, sitting room . . . she pelted upstairs. Nothing. She ran downstairs. Remembered the basement. Raced into the kitchen for a torch. Returned, flung open the basement door and shone the torch around.

The circuit box was at the bottom of the stairs. Not far. Just ten steps.

She glanced at her watch. At least a minute had passed since she'd started searching. It took approximately three minutes for someone without air to die. That was all. Three minutes.

Grace ran down the stairs. Shone the torch on the circuit box. Opened it. Put her fingers on the trip switch that would fire up the electricity. Force Simon to start breathing again.

The look in his eyes returned to her. His smile. His blazing joy that he would at last, die. And without hurting his family.

Grace stood motionless.

She let her hand drop. She stood staring at the circuit box.

In her mind, she started to count.

One thousand, two thousand, three . . .

Tears seeped down her cheeks.

The seconds rolled past.

'What's going on?' Martin's silhouette appeared at the top of the stairs.

She didn't respond for a moment. She only needed a few more seconds, to make sure. She'd never be able to face Simon again if he survived this, because not only would he be mentally disabled – brain damage started after sixty seconds – but he'd never forgive her.

'Grace?' he prompted.

'Power cut,' she said.

'Is that the circuit box?' he asked.

'Yes.'

'Why haven't you flipped the switch?'

Grace counted the last few seconds away. Slowly, she raised her hand and put her fingers on the switch.

Just a couple more seconds . . .

'Grace?' Martin prompted.

Two more . . .

'Grace!' Martin shouted, and at the same time, she flipped the switch.

The lights snapped on. Immediately she heard Simon's medical equipment beep and his ventilator resume its pumping.

'Jesus,' Martin said, and vanished.

She found him at Simon's side. 'He's dead,' he said. He looked shocked.

Grace checked Simon's vital signs. 'Yes,' she agreed.

'How come the back-up battery failed?'

'No idea.'

'What were you doing down there?' Martin said. 'You were standing there not doing anything . . .'

'I didn't cause his death,' she said calmly.

'But you didn't prevent it, either.' His look was accusing.

She held his gaze. She didn't say anything. Just looked at him.

Martin looked at Simon, then at the machines, steadily beeping and humming. 'You had no right.'

'There was a power short,' she said. 'I couldn't find the trip switch in time.'

'How *dare* you.' His expression turned furious. 'His family will be devastated.'

She took a breath. 'What about Simon?'

'What about the sanctity of *life*?' he spat. He stalked outside, slamming the door behind him so hard the entire building shook.

To her relief, Martin hadn't reported her, but it was obvious to everyone with half a brain cell that they'd fallen out. Luckily most people assumed he'd asked her out and she'd refused, or vice versa, and there had been no professional blowback. She'd had sleepless nights worrying he might change his mind and report her to the General Medical Council, but as the days passed she began to relax, and eventually weeks went by without her thinking of him and what she'd done to Simon.

But now Martin was here. And he was looking straight at her.

CHAPTER TWENTY-FOUR

Martin's features were pinched with tension, his expression urgent. She stared back, every hair on her body standing upright.

What do you want?

Martin jerked his head towards the exit and mouthed, *please.*

Feeling press-ganged and unsteady, she walked to Ross and collected her brandy, drank it in three swift swallows. She said, 'I'm going to the Ladies.' Her voice was hoarse from the alcohol. 'Back in a moment.'

She felt his eyes follow her as she left the room, but she didn't look back.

Outside it was misty and dank. Droplets of moisture began to collect in her hair. Cars splashed along the road that ran parallel to the car park, hidden by a stone wall, but otherwise it was quiet. She couldn't see anybody about, except for Martin and Sirius Thiele at the far end of the car park. Both were watching her expectantly.

Leave them! her instincts warned her. *There's danger here!* But what could she do? She had to know what was going on.

As she approached, Martin started to gabble. 'I'm sorry, Grace. God, sorry, I didn't want to say anything but he wouldn't –'

'Shut up.' Sirius Thiele's voice was flat.

Martin fell silent. His skin turned pale.

'I buried my mother barely an hour ago.' She held her chin high to try and hide her apprehension. 'Can't this wait until –?'

'No,' said Sirius. 'I tried to see your mother on the morning she died, but there was a man sitting in a car outside her house, watching me. Then this morning when I tried to see you instead, your boyfriend sent me away. I cannot wait any longer.'

His eyes held hers: hard, black and shiny, like wet pebbles.

'Your mother owes my client a lot of money. We are not talking about tens of thousands, but much, much more. When you find this money, you will ring me and I will arrange to have it returned to my client. Do you understand?'

Grace stared at him, her mind spinning. What money? What on earth was this? It had to be a mistake. She had to make him understand that.

'No,' she said. Her voice quavered and she cleared her throat, not wanting to appear weak. 'I'm afraid I don't understand. My mother's never been in debt. She's not like that, she's –'

'Quiet,' he said, holding up a hand.

Reaching into his breast pocket Sirius brought out a mobile phone. 'Unregistered, pay-as-you-go,' he said. 'It already has my number programmed. You will use it to call me. Should anyone decide to investigate, they will find no names, just two phones that receive and make calls to and from two unknown users. We cannot be traced.'

He held it out to her. She didn't take it.

'You're mistaken,' she said. She started to tremble. She held her hands together to try and stop it showing. 'I cannot believe my mother owes anyone anything. She's not that sort of person.'

'Perhaps you didn't know her as well as you thought.'

'If what you say is true, then why does she owe this money?'

'I'm not authorised to tell you.'

'How convenient.' Out of nowhere a welcome flare of annoyance overrode her fear, making her sarcastic.

He considered her for a moment. 'You don't need to know why. It is a private matter between your mother and my client.'

'Then how can I believe you?'

'You don't have to. You just have to do as I say. You will not talk to anyone about this. Not the police or any other establishment you think might be able to help because if you do, I will get Martin to go to the authorities and report that you caused the death of a patient and covered it up. You will be struck off.' He cocked his head to one side. 'What will you do then? Stack shelves in a supermarket, perhaps? Re-train as a hairdresser?'

For a moment, she was dumbstruck. 'You're blackmailing me?'

'And what about your family?' Sirius went on as though she hadn't spoken. 'What will they do when they find out you murdered a helpless, vulnerable patient?'

A whistling started in her ears. She suddenly felt terribly cold.

He held out the phone again. 'Take it.'

She looked wildly at Martin. He looked desperately back. 'I'm sorry,' he said. 'He gave me no choice. I have to do as he says. He's threatened to –'

In one deceptively graceful movement Sirius Thiele knocked the edge of his hand against Martin's neck, just below the angle of his jaw. It was a smoothly balletic movement, and for a moment Grace didn't understand what was happening.

Then Martin dropped to the ground as though felled.

Sirius had struck Martin's carotid artery, which supplied the brain with blood.

She knew she had to help him but she was rooted to the spot. She wasn't any kind of heroine. She was just an ordinary person, a simple GP. She wasn't about to turn into Superwoman and save the day. She was frozen with fear.

Sirius stood over Martin. 'I thought I warned you,' he said softly.

'P-please,' Martin choked. He was holding his hands to his throat. 'Please don't. Not again . . .'

'If you promise to keep quiet.'

'P-promise.'

Dear God, she thought. I can't believe this is happening. Oh God oh God oh God. She looked frantically about. *Where was everyone? Why wasn't anyone around?*

Sirius stepped back, hands raised, letting Martin stagger to his feet. 'I didn't harm him permanently,' Sirius told Grace.

Martin's face was ashen, his lips trembling.

'Now,' Sirius turned to Grace. Once again, he held out the phone.

Don't take it! her inner voice shouted. She unclenched her teeth, but they still chattered as she spoke.

'T-this is a mistake. It has to be. You've got the w-wrong person. My mother would never be in debt, let alone –'

'I will hurt him if you don't take it.' Once again he reached into his coat but this time he didn't bring out a mobile phone. He brought out what looked like a filleting knife.

Her adrenaline spiked so hard she felt a wave of nausea. No no no no no.

'Please, Grace,' Martin bleated. 'Take the fucking phone!'

Keeping her eyes on the knife, she did as he said. Her fingers felt stiff and numb.

'Good.' Sirius's voice was calm, and as she looked into his eyes, she saw no expression. Nothing but a pair of hard black pebbles.

'Now, I won't send Martin to the authorities unless I have to,' he said in the same calm, reasonable tone. 'Nor will I tell Ross, or your family, that you killed Simon. They will remain oblivious. So will Simon's family. Your godchildren will never know their godmother is a murderess. Little Alice and Oliver will be quite unaware of the fact as long as you keep our arrangement absolutely secret. Do you understand?'

How did he know so much about her?

Grace swallowed drily. Her voice was hoarse. 'Yes.'

'My client has given us until the end of the week.'

She could feel her lips quivering and pressed them together. She didn't want him to know how frightened she was but it had to be obvious.

'Call me the minute you find the money. The second it is returned to my client, your life will return to normal.' His black eyes held hers. 'If you tell anyone about this, they'll be next on the list. Understood?'

She gave a jerky nod.

He turned to Martin. 'In the back. Now.'

Martin stumbled to the back of the van, opened the doors and climbed inside. There was some old carpet on the floor, but nothing else. Before Sirius closed the door, Martin looked at her. His mouth was twisted. He was crying.

'Don't tell anyone,' he begged her. 'Just find the money he wants. Then I won't have to go public over Simon. And *he* –' Martin meant Sirius – 'won't . . .' He trailed off as his eyes went to Sirius. He scurried to crouch at the front of the van. Started to sob.

Sirius slammed the doors shut. He didn't look at her as he walked to the driver's door and climbed inside. Trembling, nauseous, Grace watched him drive to the exit, turn right, and vanish.

The moment the van was out of sight, her knees buckled. One moment she was standing paralysed in terror, the next she folded on to the ground. The sharp jags of stones against her palms and knees helped steady her and she rose to see Ross running across the car park.

'Grace.' He skidded to her side, putting an arm around her. 'What are you doing out here? You're all wet.'

'I needed some air.'

'You were ages. I'm sorry. I should have taken you home long ago.'

'It's OK,' she managed. She wanted to throw up, to curl up and die, to weep forever. But she did none of those things. She let Ross lead her back inside the pub, where he told the cousins they were leaving, initiating a round of farewells that seemed to take an eternity. Finally they were on their way home. Grace brought out Sirius Thiele's mobile phone and, with trembling fingers, checked the contacts list to find just one number.

Call me the minute you find the money. The second it is returned to my client, your life will return to normal.

She closed her eyes briefly and tried to regulate her breathing. She felt shaky and sick. How did Sirius Thiele know so much about her family? How had he found Martin? What was he threatening Martin with?

She looked across at Ross. The strength in his jaw, the steadiness in his hands on the wheel. She desperately wanted to tell him what had happened but he'd only take her to a police station to report it. And it would put him in immediate danger.

If you tell anyone about this, they'll be next on the list.

She had to protect Ross until she found out what was going on.

When he parked outside her mother's house, he turned and looked at her. 'OK?'

'OK,' she lied.

A smile ghosted across his face. 'I know it's been an awful day. But I just want you to know that I love you, Grace Reavey. One hundred per cent. And don't forget it.'

She touched his face. 'I love you too.'

She had to find the money. Make Sirius go away. It was the only solution to ensure her life would return to normal.

Back inside her mother's house, she headed straight for the study, switched on her mother's computer. Although she felt wobbly, as fragile as a baby bird, the full-blown panic had eased now she had a sense of purpose.

'Cup of tea?' Ross called. 'Or something stronger?'

'Stronger,' she called back. She began pulling open drawers, searching for bank statements but there was nothing. They'd all be online. She looked round when her mother's computer awakened with a boot-up tune.

'Brandy,' Ross announced.

'Password,' she said, staring at the screen.

'Ah.'

She sipped her brandy while she attempted to gain access, trying her name, her childhood nickname – Gracie Macie – and a variety of dates that she knew her mother knew by heart.

'Could take a while,' Ross remarked.

'Yes.' She brought out her mobile phone and scrolled to her mother's recent emails.

'Do you mind if I watch the news?'

'Of course not.' She glanced up at him. His expression was solemn. He wore a beautifully cut charcoal grey suit with a white shirt and a black tie. He'd loosened his collar which made him look almost unbearably handsome. 'Thanks for today,' she said. 'I couldn't have done it without you.'

He came and put his arms around her. Kissed the top of her head. 'I wish you hadn't had to go through it.'

She leaned against him. 'Me too.'

With BBC1 murmuring in the background, Grace tried to crack her mother's password, but nothing worked. She then searched her mother's meticulously arranged study but there wasn't much to find. A handful of household bills, insurance documents, car log book. The file marked *Financial* contained details of a fairly decent private pension but nothing else. No portfolio of investments or ISAs, or lists of stocks and shares.

Eyes aching, she finally switched off the computer and headed to the sitting room. The TV was still on but Ross wasn't watching it. He was fast asleep. Gently she woke him and they headed to bed but Grace couldn't rest. She kept seeing the filleting knife Sirius had produced. The pallor on Martin's skin, the fear in his eyes.

What if there was no money? What if Sirius was mistaken? What would happen if she told the police? At the time it hadn't crossed her mind to get the van's number plate. Should she confess about Simon and risk Ross's life? Lose her career? What about Simon's mother? His fiancée, Juliet? And how in the world had Sirius found out about Martin? Did anyone else know? Her mind went round and round at dizzying speed until finally, just before dawn, she fell into a troubled doze.

She awoke with a sour mouth. Her limbs felt lethargic, as though they'd been filled with cement.

'Let me bring you breakfast in bed,' Ross said.

'You're wonderful, but I'm not hungry.'

'Tea, then.'

'Tea would be lovely.'

She drank it while looking out of the rain-streaked window, listening to the news. Bella Frances, that was the girl's name, the one who'd been found. She was still in hospital. What about Jamie? Where was he? She hoped he was OK but she didn't have the mental capacity to worry about him at the moment. She had enough problems of her own.

Sirius's voice in her mind: *You have until the end of the week.*

She ran through her choices, and decided on the path of least resistance. If she didn't find the money by the weekend, she'd re-think her strategy. But until then, she'd better get moving.

CHAPTER TWENTY-FIVE

Wednesday 28 November, 11.00 a.m.

'Good God.' Ross stood in the doorway, looking around. 'It looks like a bomb's gone off.'

Grace leaned back on her heels, pushing a lock of stray hair out of her eyes. The bed was strewn with her mother's clothes, the carpet heaped with shoes and boots and boxes, handbags, scarves, gloves. She'd known her mother loved shoes, but she seemed to have developed a fetish. There were killer shoes, designer boots, glamorous sandals. Grace held up a fabulously sexy pair of black and white chequered high-heeled signature pumps called 'Hot to Trot' and, before she could change her mind, slipped them on.

'Wow,' he said admiringly. 'Your mum had great taste.'

They fitted perfectly. Tears rising, Grace took them off. 'Hell,' she said.

Ross crossed the room and took her in his arms. 'Would you like me to stay?'

They'd agreed he would go back to London today at lunch-time and that they'd meet up at the weekend, and if it hadn't been for the spectre of Sirius Thiele hovering, she might have changed her mind. She wanted to speak to Martin, but she didn't want to do that with Ross around. She had to keep the situation contained.

'No,' she said. She wiped her eyes. 'I need to sort the house out. Much better if I'm on my own.'

'You're sure?' He leaned back and studied her, concern in his eyes.

'I'm sure.' She gave him a wobbly smile. 'But thanks. I'll text you later.'

With Ross gone, Grace set her mind to tracking down Martin. Luckily, it didn't take long. He'd spent his first year in the same surgery as her in Reading before moving to a rural practice in Wiltshire, where he'd worked ever since. She asked to speak to him.

'Who's calling?'

'A colleague. Dr Reavey.'

Brief pause.

'I'm sorry, doctor, I just had to double-check. Dr Fairfield has taken extended leave until Christmas.'

Her stomach turned over. 'Does he have a mobile?'

'Well, yes. But apparently he's out of electronic contact. He's on a ski safari in Norway.'

Grace's hand spasmed to clench the phone. 'But I only saw him yesterday!'

'He flew there this morning.'

'Did he use a travel company? Do you have any contact details?'

'No. Sorry. He's out of touch until he returns on Christmas Eve but he won't be back at work until the new year.'

Grace swallowed the urge to scream. 'OK. I'll take his mobile number, but if you hear from him, tell him to contact me urgently.'

After she'd hung up, she tried his mobile number but it immediately switched to his answering service. She left a panicky message but she knew she wouldn't hear anything back. Martin had abandoned her. She was on her own.

Fuelled by a mixture of anger and fear, Grace attacked the house with a feverish urgency. What if her mother no longer had the money? What if she'd spent it? Loaned it? Given it away? Spent it on *shoes*?

When the doorbell rang she checked the spy hole to see her mother's amnesiac friend standing on the doorstep. With his tall frame and broad shoulders, he made the tiny porch look as though it belonged to a doll's house. What was his name? Dan something. She was usually pretty good with names – useful for a GP – but for some reason his surname eluded her. She opened the door.

'Hello,' she said.

He wore a leather jacket over a pressed blue shirt, black jeans and leather shoes. His face was drawn, his eyes bruised.

'We need to talk,' he said.

'Not now. Sorry.' She didn't give him an explanation or make any excuses.

His gaze flicked past her shoulder. Something about him stilled. 'Are you packing up or looking for something?'

'How about we talk after the weekend?' Grace suggested. Hopefully she would have resolved the Sirius issue by then.

'If you're looking for something, then you're going the wrong way about it.'

'What?' Her voice was irritated. *Why didn't he go away?*

'Don't go for the obvious places. Think laterally.'

'I'm sorry but I really don't think –'

'Let me show you.'

'Sorry,' she said again, her voice firm. 'But I really don't have time to . . .' She trailed off as he ducked down and emptied the umbrella stand, picked it up and turned it over. He rapped the bottom with his knuckles. 'See? It sounds hollow. This is the kind of place to look.' He put his other hand inside the stand. Metal screeched briefly. His hand came back into view with a circular piece of metal from the bottom of the stand. Taped beneath it was a key.

Dan stared at it for a moment. 'Christ,' he said. 'I didn't expect . . .'

He then fitted the key into the front door lock and turned it.

'Christ,' he said again. He looked shaken. 'I swear I didn't know . . . I was just messing about, to give you an example.' Hurriedly he gave her the key. 'Sorry.' His mouth trembled and she suddenly realised he was close to tears.

Her heart softened.

'Come in,' she said. 'I'll make us coffee.'

She wasn't being entirely altruistic. The thought had crossed her mind that he might be able to help her find Sirius's money. But if he had amnesia, how much help could he be? She filled the machine with water and popped the capsules. The smell of fresh coffee wafted through the room. She said, 'Thanks for trying to save Mum's life.'

'I'm sorry I didn't succeed.'

Both of them drank their espressos.

'She told me you had amnesia,' Grace said hesitantly.

'She did?' He looked surprised.

'She was really sad you couldn't remember her.'

A haunted look crossed his face. 'I had a breakdown when my son was killed. I was there, apparently, but I can't remember it. There's a lot I can't remember.'

'I'm sorry,' Grace said. Then she put her head on one side, looking at him speculatively. 'Mum said she rather suspected you were given an amnesia drug. If that's true, who administered it? I thought it was only at the research stage.'

He stared at her as though she'd suddenly started talking Urdu. '*What?*'

Her stomach swooped. Dear God, the stress must be getting to her. She should have known better than to launch in like that.

'She only *suspected*.' Grace found herself hastily backtracking. 'It doesn't mean to say it actually happened. I'm so sorry. I shouldn't have said anything. It was totally unprofessional.'

'No, no. I'm glad you did,' he assured her quickly. His eyes were alive but there was something dark and dangerous moving in their depths, like a shark cruising at the edges of a sunlit reef. 'What else did she say?'

Grace bit her lip.

'Please,' he urged. 'Tell me. I need to know.'

'She didn't say much, I'm afraid,' Grace admitted. 'Just that it was probably for your own good. She said your mind had snapped after you'd seen your son killed. You were sent to a mental hospital.'

He nodded. 'That's what I've been told.'

'That's it, really. Mum wanted my advice on how she should talk to you about your past.' She gave a rueful smile. 'I told her to give you a stiff drink.'

He drained the last of his coffee. Placed the cup by the sink. 'Can I ask a couple of questions?'

'What about?'

'How come my memories of my wife and daughter are fairly intact, but anything to do with my old job and Luke are non-existent?'

'What sort of amnesia were you diagnosed with?' she asked.

'Dissociative.'

'Well, that makes sense, because dissociative amnesia results from a psychological cause, including repressed memory – which is the inability to recall information about a stressful or traumatic event.'

He then moved on to ask her about amnesia drugs.

'In my experience,' she said, 'drug-induced amnesia is to help a patient forget any traumatic surgery or medical procedures that are undertaken without full anaesthesia. They're pre-medications, like midazolam or scopolamine, and memories of the procedure – which usually takes a short time – are permanently lost. But once the drug wears off, memory is no longer affected.'

Dan looked at her.

'But that's not what we're talking about here, is it?' She ran a hand abstractedly over her forehead. 'We're talking about deleting memories already formed.'

He nodded.

She didn't really have time for this, but the GP in her couldn't resist grabbing her iPad and having a look. With Dan hovering, she flicked quickly through the search pages until she found what she wanted. 'OK,' she said. 'As far as I can see, by injecting a particular drug at the right time, when a subject is recalling a particular thought, neuroscientists say they can disrupt the way the memory is stored . . . There's talk of potentially making it disappear but nothing definitive.'

'What sort of drug?'

She turned back to her iPad. Flipped through a couple of pages. 'Here.' She turned the iPad so they could both look at the screen. 'Researchers in the US used propranolol, a drug normally used to treat hypertension in heart disease patients. It says that propranolol breaks the link between memory and fear. Like many scientific advances it was discovered as a by-product of something else.'

She kept digging. 'There are lots of studies going on with propranolol and individuals suffering from chronic post-traumatic stress disorder, resulting in erasing human fear responses over a particular memory. My guess is that if there's an amnesia drug out there it'll be derived from propranolol but I can't find anything conclusive. There's a lot of research being undertaken by a British firm, PepsBeevers . . .'

'I've heard of them,' Dan said. 'Aren't they one of the top one hundred FTSE companies?'

'Yes. They have a brain and neurological research institute near London. They invented what's considered a bit of a miracle drug. Zidazapine. It's made them a fortune.'

'What does it do?'

'I prescribe it to bipolar sufferers. But there's no mention of an amnesia drug on their site. It's my bet it will have been developed by an organisation who aren't sharing their findings.'

From the way the research was going, Grace guessed that by the time she hung up her GP hat she may well be prescribing a memory blocker or two herself. Quite how it would be regulated was anyone's guess. The last thing doctors needed were memory-altering drugs that could be abused by healthy individuals to delete unwanted memories on a whim.

'How do I find out if it was used on me?'

She stared at him. 'You really think it was?'

'I don't know.' His gaze was distant. 'But I'd like to find out.'

'I'd start with your GP and work backwards.'

A silence fell.

Dan moved to stand by the window, looking up and down the street. He said, 'Can I ask you one last question?'

Grace raised her eyebrows. 'Which is?'

'Did you or your mother ask for the carpets to be cleaned yesterday?'

CHAPTER TWENTY-SIX

Wednesday 28 November, 6.25 a.m.

'Hi Bella. It's only me.'

Bella heard Lucy cross the room, her shoes squeaking on the floor. She could smell boiled potatoes and something like minced beef, maybe cottage pie, indicating it was time for the next meal. Not that she ate anything. She got her food through an IV of some sort.

Bella listened as Lucy talked to her. She wasn't sure why, but she paid more attention to Lucy than anyone else. She thought it was because the policewoman didn't patronise her. She told it like it was. She didn't lie, not like Mum. Mum said things like *Everything's going to be OK* and *We'll have you back to normal in no time.*

Normal? She had to be joking. She wasn't normal anyway being bipolar, but after what had happened was there any point in re-joining the world? There seemed little to live for now the man had pulled out her teeth. Who would kiss her now? Who would even *look* at her? She might as well be dead.

But then Lucy told her she'd have implants. That no one would know her teeth weren't real. Not even her. Gradually she began to wonder if things might be manageable. She'd been on the dark side before. She'd sliced open her arteries several times. She'd been sectioned. She'd spent months on the psych ward. But since they'd stuck her on Zidazapine she'd been better. So much better that people thought she was *normal.* She'd been brought out of the dark and into the light. Perhaps it could happen a second time.

Why had he pulled out her teeth? What for? Oddly, she couldn't remember him doing this. Nor could she remember him breaking her legs, or snapping the bones in her fingers and toes, which was a bit of a relief. She had to have been unconscious the whole time – until she'd come round in the container, that is, which she assumed hadn't been part of his plan. She was pretty sure she was supposed to have died.

'Your mum's gone to get a cup of tea,' Lucy said, and then she sighed. 'She's looking terrible, you know. She doesn't want to leave your side. Your dad has to drag her home just to get her to shower, let alone remind her that Patrick still exists. He's been in to see you lots, did you know?'

Bella had heard her brother flit in and out but hadn't really taken him in.

'He's a bit lost without you. Says he's got no one to annoy anymore.'

Bella felt a bubble of emotion pop inside her.

'He told me about letting your tyres down recently. You know why he did it? It wasn't to annoy you. Well, it was, but it went deeper than that. He wanted to try and keep you at home longer. That's all. Even if it was only for another half an hour while your dad fixed them. He gets bored with just your mum and dad at home. He misses you now you're at uni.'

Lucy gave another sigh.

'I wish I had a brother. It's just me, though. Me and Mum. Mum's great, but rather like Patrick, I get bored on my own. I'd love to have come from a big family. Three sisters, five brothers. Wouldn't that be great?'

Five of the suckers? Bella reeled. She had to be kidding. *Just one's enough, believe me.*

Bella felt Lucy touch the back of her hand gently. She said, 'Time for the daily report, OK? I don't want you waking up without having a clue, so here goes . . .'

Bella listened to an incredible litany of shipping details and searches, phone calls, Indian policemen and some cleaner called Chitta. She couldn't believe how amazingly complicated the whole thing was and wondered what it was all about.

Why me?

'Bella, stay with me, OK?' Lucy said. 'Don't give up. We want to know who did this to you. And we won't stop until we find him. Put him behind bars. But we need your help. And we can't get that unless you're awake. Compos mentis. AWAKE, dammit . . .'

She could hear the frustration in Lucy's voice.

'I know you don't want to surface,' Lucy went on in a gentler tone. 'I know it's too painful. I know you feel safe down there. But what if he's targeting your family? What if Patrick is in danger? What if . . .'

Lucy's voice abruptly vanished beneath a wave of sheer horror.

Patrick.

Her brother. Four years younger than her and a royal pain in the bum. He'd flour-bombed her. Super-glued her make-up to the floor. Scraped the cream out of her favourite cookies and filled them with white toothpaste.

Her baby brother.

What if the man came for Patrick?

For the first time, Bella tried to open her eyes.

CHAPTER TWENTY-SEVEN

Lucy studied the whiteboard while Mac gave the briefing. He looked to be in a foul mood, probably thanks to the fact that Bella's face was still on the front pages of the newspapers. Related articles abounded: *How students can stay safe, Five easy ways to defend yourself.* Bella's family had also rung in, demanding answers as they did every morning. As he spoke, his frustration became palpable. 'We're getting nothing. No leads. *Nothing.* Not a single new avenue of investigation has opened . . .'

Lucy stuck up a hand. Mac raised his eyebrows at her.

'What about the fact that she's bipolar?' Lucy braved the question, even though it made her feel uncomfortable. 'Do you think it had any bearing on her abduction?'

'It doesn't look like it,' he answered. 'She was taking a particular drug to control it.'

'Zidazapine.'

He gave a nod. 'Without it she was a mess, apparently, but the drug is like a miracle cure. She used to fall into a depression for weeks, tried to commit suicide, hallucinated, heard voices, the lot, but nobody would know she's bipolar any more.

None of her uni student friends had a clue she had a serious medical problem.'

Her mind splashed magenta, purple and black. How in God's name could Dr sodding Mike Adamson think *she* was bipolar? She didn't hallucinate or hear voices. Well, no more than any normal person and she'd never been remotely suicidal. She was nothing like poor Bella, thank heavens, and right now she couldn't believe she'd taken the same drug.

'How long has she been taking the Zidazapine?' she asked.

'Just over three years.'

'Side effects?'

'None that anyone's shouting about. The company that produces the drug is, apparently, thrilled with it.'

'Which company?' she asked.

'PepsBeevers.'

Now she remembered. It was the same name stamped on the sample boxes Dr Mike had given her.

'Does she have a psychiatrist?' Lucy asked. 'A bipolar support group of any sort?'

'Yes to the first, no to the second. I've interviewed her psychiatrist, who's really pleased with her. He checks out OK, if that's what you were asking. He was in Brussels when she was abducted. Anything else?' he added, looking around the office, and when nobody responded, wound up the briefing.

She was striding down the corridor when Mac caught up with her in a rush. 'Do you fancy a drink later?'

'No thank you, sir.'

'You don't have to call me sir.'

'OK, sir.'

She kept her gaze focused just past his left ear, where she wouldn't have to look into his eyes or – God forbid – at his mouth. He had a tiny kink in his upper lip that she remembered kissing before she'd slipped her fingers to the nape of his neck and . . . *Stop it!* she yelled at herself.

Still staring into the distance, Lucy cleared her throat. 'Any luck with the Indian authorities?' She still thought there might be a link between Bella's killing and the recycling charity.

'Chennai CBI have nothing on RFC,' Mac told her. 'Everything appears squeaky clean.' He ran a hand through his hair, making the curls dance. 'I won't jump on you, you know. I just want to talk through the case. See if we can find a random clue that we've missed.'

'Sorry.' She was stiff. 'I'm busy.'

He gave her a sideways look before sighing and walking away.

When Lucy called Senior Constable Niket, he answered on the tenth ring.

'Oh, yes,' he said. 'I am having many talks with the people we were speaking about. They are very nice, good people from Recycling For Charity. Everything is seeming to be very legitimate. I am not finding anything criminal.'

'Who collects the containers from Chennai Port?' she asked.

'This will be the people who are belonging to the charity.'

'And where do they take it?'

'They are taking it to their counterparts in this country. But rest assured, Madam Constable, there is nothing criminal here.'

'Counterparts?' she repeated, hoping he'd expand.

'They are charities also. They are doing good things over here.'

He was giving her nothing. He was either stonewalling for some reason – maybe he wanted to keep what he'd found close to his chest? Or maybe he was a lazy bum who'd done fuck all.

'Please could you send me a list of the counterparts?'

'Madam, of course I will. Just as soon as my team collates them, but I do not hold out much hope they will be helping you.'

He was purposely obstructing her. Dragging things out. She'd heard of foreign countries being obstructive before, but this was a serious case, dammit. Despite wanting to shout at him for being such a dick, she took a breath and made sure her tone was temperate.

'That would be great, thank you,' she said sweetly. 'And please could you email me your findings, which I will then pass on to my superiors. But before we get to that stage, Niket, could I have the name of your commanding officer and his contact details? I will have to pass this on to my boss. I will send you an email now. Can I have your email address, please? Then we can copy the right people when we need to.'

Long silence.

'Of course,' he said. His tone was stiff.

Lucy scribbled down Niket's email as he recited it. 'Thank you so much,' she said, all sweetness and light.

'Oh, I am very happy to be helping the British police,' he said. 'Very happy indeed.'

Yeah, right. Lucy hung up with a grimace. They'd have as much luck getting information from India as extracting an elephant's tooth with a pair of eyebrow tweezers. No cops liked foreign cops on their turf and invariably dealt with foreign requests at a snail's pace. Niket was a case in point. She had to hope her threat of copying in his superiors would act like a stick of dynamite under his arse or she'd never get a decent break.

CHAPTER TWENTY-EIGHT

Wednesday 28 November, 1 p.m., Chennai local time

Chitta stuck his mop in the bucket and watched Niket stare into space. He'd lost colour and looked faintly ill.

'Shit,' he whispered.

Chitta knew better than to say anything because Niket would just bite his head off. He couldn't work out why the police officer had been so rude to Lucy Davies in England. Nor could he understand why Niket wasn't in the thick of helping her solve this case. Surely having an international assignment on his books would help further his career? Niket was as sharp as a thicket thorn and twice as ambitious, but he hadn't lifted a finger. He'd been acting oddly too, jumpy and nervous. Maybe he was coming down with another bout of stomach trouble? He'd eaten something bad on Sunday and taken time off work on Monday because of it. It was the first time Chitta had known him to take sick leave.

Chitta's mind drifted. If *he* was a police officer, he would have found something out by now. He would have emailed Constable Lucy Davies with his findings and be up for a promotion. What had happened with the girl found in the freezer?

Was she still alive? Was it was possible that the freezer had been left on? If so, the girl would eventually have frozen. Had that been the intention?

'Shit!' whispered Niket again. He closed his eyes.

They were outside Inspector Chakyar's office on the third floor of the CBI offices in Besant Nagar, sweating profusely thanks to the air-conditioning breaking down the previous day. The air was choked with cigarette smoke and reverberated with the sounds of phones ringing and voices yelling, bicycle bells and car horns sounding through the open window. It was noisy, crowded and frenetic, but Chitta didn't notice. He was used to it.

'She only fucking wants Chakyar involved . . .' Niket opened his eyes and leaned against the wall, looking suddenly exhausted.

Chitta kept silent.

'How can I do this?' Niket muttered. 'How the hell do I find out where the goods go without –?'

'I have a cousin who works at the port,' Chitta said, excitement spilling.

Niket's head switched round. 'You do?'

'Yes. She cleans for the Customs and Excise.'

'Are all your family cleaners?' Niket asked but he obviously didn't want an answer since he then said, 'Do you think she will help us?'

Us.

Chitta's spirits soared. 'I am a policeman now?'

Niket gazed at him. For the first time, Chitta felt as though the policeman was looking at him. *Really* looking at him.

'Can I trust you?' Niket asked.

'Of course.' Chitta looked insulted. 'I would never do anything to bring dishonour to your or the Police Department's door. I will commit myself to your mission with moral clarity and hard work and –'

'OK, OK, Chitta.' He held up both hands. 'But whatever you find, you bring to me. Understand? Nobody else.'

'Of course,' Chitta repeated.

'In that case,' Niket said, 'you may become an honorary assistant for the time being.'

Chitta straightened up and saluted. 'My duties?'

'To find out everything, and I mean *everything*, about this charity and its containers, what it is shipping, where and when. I want to know every detail, no matter how big or how small. *Everything*. Do you hear me?'

'Yes, sir.'

Niket reached around the back of his chair for his jacket and delved inside. He brought out his wallet and extracted a quantity of rupees that made Chitta's eyes water. Niket folded them in half, then held them up. 'I want to know how every rupee is spent. I don't want a single one wasted. There isn't any time for you to walk to the port, it will take you days. I want you to be fast, little Chitta. So use this money to expedite our investigation. Take rickshaws, boats or taxis. Bribe who you need to . . .'

Feeling as though he was in a dream, Chitta took the roll of notes and pushed it carefully into his front pocket where it would be harder to steal.

Niket held Chitta's eyes. He said, 'If you succeed, little man, I will consider your application to join the police.'

Chitta felt an emotion so intense, he nearly passed out.

'You have two days.'

Chitta opened his other hand and let the mop drop with a clatter. Niket didn't yell at him. He didn't even seem to notice. He was looking at something in his mind's eye. He flicked his hand and said, 'Go.'

Chitta ran for the door, for the street, as though his life depended on it.

The sun was already lowering in the sky when Chitta strutted through the port. He was a policeman today! He wished he wore a uniform so everyone knew, but nobody gave him a second glance. He was just a young boy cluttering up the place.

Dock workers were heading home. Some chatted between themselves, others drifted silently, heads down and dragging their feet, obviously exhausted. Chitta fingered the money in his pocket, resolving to make sure he never ended up like some of these men, breaking their backs like worker ants for nothing but a bowl of slop at the end of the day. He'd already made a start for a successful future, using a bus instead of taking a taxi as Niket wanted, and pocketing the money he'd saved. Niket would never know. He might even pay him a bonus if he found a clue that led to finding the criminal who'd locked the English girl in the freezer.

Uncle Ajeet would be proud, he thought. Ajeet was obsessed with education, saying it was vital if any of the family were going to get ahead. Ajeet had taught nearly all of them not only how to read and write, but also how to do mathematics in their head too. He was clever, old Ajeet, and his eyes would gleam at all the opportunities that would open to the family should Chitta become a Police Constable one day.

The Customs office was closing when he got there. Perfect. He trotted inside and went and found his cousin. Rajani was five years older than him and had a badly scarred face from a kitchen accident that meant she probably wouldn't get married. Today she wore a sari with a green and red floral pattern and a pair of yellow plastic sandals. Her hair was tied into a tight bun at the nape of her neck. She knew how much he wanted to be a policeman, and when he promised her five per cent of his first year's salary when he made constable, she immediately pushed her trolley to one side.

'The information will be on the computer,' she said. 'But I'm not allowed access.' Her look was sly. She wanted to increase her percentage but he wasn't having it and gave an exaggerated snort. He'd hovered around Niket for long enough to have gleaned his username and password. He didn't doubt Rajani could gain access if she wanted and said so.

'All right then,' she relented. 'But keep a lookout, and if someone comes, whistle or shout.'

To look innocent in case anyone suddenly appeared, Chitta plucked a mop from Rajani's bucket and began mopping the floor; cleaners were invisible. But nobody came. Everything remained silent. He'd barely mopped a quarter of the corridor when Rajani reappeared. Talk about a quick worker.

'This charity,' she told him, 'they use Bagai Golden Transport to collect their containers from the dock. If I were you, I'd go and see them.'

First thing the next morning, Chitta was at the transport offices. Even though Niket had given him enough cash for a bribe, it took a while before one of the drivers took him seriously. The driver was fat and sweaty, his hair greasy. He wore a T-shirt with a Coca-Cola logo on it and a tatty pair of black trousers that were heavily frayed at the bottom. Every minute he didn't work, he complained to Chitta, he lost money, but when he saw the roll of notes clasped in Chitta's hand, he paused.

'Who are you working for?'

'It's confidential.' Chitta drew himself tall.

'What do you want to know?' The man's eyes were fastened greedily on the money.

Chitta asked his questions. The driver told him to wait. He went into the office and returned a few minutes later, nodding. 'One of our drivers says he took a couple of containers of theirs from the port recently, straight to the dump. He dropped them off and came back to collect them once they'd been emptied.'

'Can I talk to him?'

'No.' The man held out his hand, clicking his fingers impatiently. Reluctantly, Chitta handed over the money. 'Now bugger off,' the man said.

Chitta headed for the dump, which was swarming with Chennai's hungry combing through the open waste landfill. Urchins and rag-pickers scoured the garbage for recyclable items to sell to scrap dealers. He stopped one raggedy young boy, who wore a pair of faded red shorts rolled over at the waist to stop them falling down. Chitta showed him a little money. 'I want to know about Recycling For Charity,' he said.

'What about them?'

'You know them?' He felt a hop of excitement.

'They've been here the past couple of weeks.' The boy waved towards the main road. 'Dropping stuff off.'

Chitta began walking in the direction of the road. The boy tagged alongside. 'What sort of stuff?' Chitta asked.

'Computers, monitors, mobile phones. The usual.'

They passed a group of men with strips of ripped material tied over their mouths. Flies buzzed in clouds around them. Scrawny, flea-bitten dogs scavenged alongside brown kites and rats. The stinking mess fell away as they approached an area with a handful of shipping containers and hordes of children working to salvage precious metals from old computers and monitors.

'So it's not really a charity then,' Chitta said. 'If it ends up here.'

The boy shrugged. 'You know what it's like.'

'Yes,' Chitta agreed. Even he knew India was the world's biggest dumping ground.

He watched a truck making its way slowly across the dirty terrain, hauling a single container.

'They dump bodies too,' the boy said.

Chitta froze. 'What?'

The boy took a step back, suddenly fearful. 'I shouldn't have said anything.'

'It's OK.' Chitta forced himself to relax. 'I'm not the police. How could I be? I'm far too young and stupid.' He laughed. The boy laughed too.

Chitta pretended to be absorbed in watching the container being opened.

'How many bodies?' Chitta asked.

'One came in last week. It was in a freezer. All wet and slippery. Its flesh slid off the bones like soup. It was disgusting.'

'What happened to it?'

'We dumped it.' He gestured over his shoulder. 'We dumped all three of them.'

CHAPTER TWENTY-NINE

Thursday 29 November, 1.35 a.m.

Lucy should have been in bed, asleep, but sleep seldom came easily, especially without Nate's sonorous breathing next to her. Which was why she was wrapped in her duvet on the sofa in front of the TV, laptop to hand. She'd cried twice tonight, and resolved that was enough. She had to stop wallowing in her aloneness, stop remembering the late-night movies they used to watch together, the pizzas they'd shared, and get on with living.

Stop being pathetic, Davies.

The TV was showing a re-run of one of her favourite sci-fi thrillers, *In Time*, and she was half-watching it, munching her way through a family-sized bag of Maltesers – chocolate being the ultimate cure for loneliness. At the same time she was surfing the Internet for anything that sounded similar to Bella's case, nationally or internationally, cross-referenced with anything to do with handcuffs, recycling charities and, just to make things really complicated, bipolar disorders.

Think, Davies.

Handcuffs. Police issue. Taser. Police issue?

Bella's attacker would have had to have got close enough to her to have used the taser. What if he wasn't working alone? What if there were two of them?

She was immersed in a report about serial killer teams and just about jumped out of her skin when her mobile rang. Lunging for the coffee table, she managed to knock over the standard lamp and send everything else flying. Her phone continued to ring from somewhere on the floor, its tone muffled.

'Shit, shit . . .'

Scrambling off the sofa, she dived on to her hands and knees. Her phone peeked out from beneath a paperback of Sudoku puzzles. She pounced on it.

'Hello?'

'Is this Constable Lucy Davies of the English police?' a boy asked.

Blue quivered in her mind, edged with green.

'Yes it is. Is that Junior Constable Chitta?'

'Oh, yes. It is me. How are you?'

'Very well, thank you.' Despite wearing a pair of thick socks, sweat pants and fleece, Lucy grabbed the duvet and pulled it around her. The flat was fucking *freezing*.

'Constable Davies.' He sounded solemn. 'I am needing to be telling you I am having much success with your queries. Inspector Chakyar is to be ringing your superiors but I am making sure I am contacting you directly.'

'Great.' She bent down and picked up her watch to see it was 2 a.m. Seven thirty in the morning in Chennai. 'And your news?' she asked.

'Ah, yes. We are finding three bodies here. All from this charity you were asking after. All from England.'

Lucy was so gobsmacked she sat down on the sofa with a plop. 'What?'

'Three bodies are being shipped to our country from your country. They are all being very badly broken . . .'

'Broken?' she interjected.

'Their bones are being broken. Their teeth also. Very bad thing. We are having a major investigation into this matter –'

'Chitta,' she interrupted urgently. 'Were any of the bodies wearing handcuffs?'

'Oh, yes. All three victims.'

Her whole body fizzed as though she'd been thrown into an electrical thunderstorm. 'Where?'

'On their wrists.' His voice was faintly puzzled as if to say, *where else?*

'Left or right?'

'Left,' he said decisively.

'Where are the bodies?'

'They are going into the morgue.'

'Where were they before then?'

Lucy continued firing questions until she believed she had a reasonable picture. It appeared that Constable Niket – for whatever reason – had handed over the investigation to his cleaner.

His *cleaner*, for God's sakes. Not that Chitta said as much, but she wasn't stupid and from the story he told of talking to the truck driver and the rag-picking boy on the dump, he'd been working alone.

'Are the victims all women?' she asked.

'No,' he replied. 'Two men. One woman.'

He went on to say that the RFC offices had been impounded, everyone connected with the charity arrested, and that Inspector Chakyar was arranging for them to be interrogated extensively.

'We'll have to repatriate the bodies,' she told Chitta. 'See if we can identify them over here.'

'I will be mentioning this to the Inspector,' he said importantly. 'We will be needing to be getting these permissions and arranging this as soon as possible.'

She had momentarily forgotten she was talking to a boy. 'Can I speak to Senior Constable Niket?'

'It is not being possible, I am sorry.' He paused, and when he spoke, he sounded uncertain. 'He must not be known to be in touch with you.'

Baffled, Lucy tried to work out what he meant.

'You want to keep our phone conversation confidential?' she guessed.

'Yes,' he said, obviously relieved. 'Inspector Chakyar was angry that I was pretending to be a police officer and he will be even more angry if he knows I am telephoning you directly but I wanted you, Madam Constable Davies, to know what is happening here in Chennai.'

She felt a rush of gratitude to Chitta. 'I owe you.'

'I will be remembering your kindness.' She heard the smile in his voice.

Three bodies. Two men, one woman. What did it mean? Had they stumbled upon a criminal gang torturing and murdering people and then disposing of them? The bodies had all been found in freezers. Shipped by the same charity. Her mind jumped to the *Raipur*, the ship that Bella's container had been booked on to. When was she due to sail? Frantically Lucy tried to remember what Lewis Cunningham of Weald Logistics had told her. The ship had been delayed because of repairs. Wasn't she due to sail this week?

She dived for her phone. Rang Lewis Cunningham on his mobile. He answered sounding bleary. 'Who is it?'

'Constable Davies. I need to know when the *Raipur* is sailing.'

'Jesus,' he said. 'It's the middle of the night. Can't this wait until –?'

'No. How long will it take you to get the information to me?'

'Are you serious?'

'How long?'

He sighed. 'OK. I'll go and switch my computer on.'

She heard fumbling noises and a clunk.

'Any luck?' she said.

'Hang on, will you?'

Lucy kept the line open while he switched on lights and booted up his computer. She didn't want him pausing to get coffee. While she waited she peeked outside to see what the weather was like. For a moment she couldn't believe it. It had *snowed* last night. Not much, but her car was frozen solid and the roads would be as slippery as hell.

Finally, Lewis Cunningham said, 'Her repairs are complete. She's due to sail tomorrow.'

'When?'

'Er, no. Sorry, I mean today. 8 a.m.'

Lucy didn't waste any more time talking and hung up. Redialled. 'It's me, Lucy.'

A husky voice answered. 'Hi, Lucy.' Hearing Mac say her name made something inside her weaken.

'Three bodies have been found in Chennai, all dumped by RFC. We have to get to Liverpool and stop the *Raipur* from sailing at eight o'clock. We have to check her cargo. Make sure there isn't another body on board. It's only 130 miles or so to Liverpool. We could be there by 6 a.m.

'Three bodies plus Bella,' Lucy went on. 'Not that she's a body, but she might have been, making it four. What if there's another body in a freezer on board the *Raipur*? We need to know if RFC have any containers on board. Even if they haven't, we still need to search the ship. Our killer might be using another charity, another company.' Her mind leaped. 'He might have killed even more people. We should alert the Liverpool police. Start searching immediately.'

Silence.

'Mac? Are you there?'

'I'll meet you at the station in ten.'

She was about to hang up when she remembered the snow. 'Wait!' she yelled into the phone.

'What?' He sounded alarmed.

'Snow outside. Icy roads. Cold.'

'Oh. Thanks.'

It didn't take long to fire up the Merseyside Police and it was still dark when they arrived at the docks. Although everyone appeared to have rugged up – lots of scarves and woolly hats – people still stamped their feet in the snow, clapping their gloved hands together, trying to keep warm. Steam rose from their nostrils and mouths, lit white by the floodlights. It was just past 7 a.m. but it felt like the middle of the night. Dark, and bitterly cold.

'We don't want anybody entering or leaving while we're conducting the search.' The Detective Chief Superintendent's voice was a surprising foghorn and at odds with his narrow shoulders and whippet-thin stature. 'We want this done *absolutely* by the book. No fuck-ups, please.'

The metal gates were swung open and each team coalesced and began to undertake their specific role. Lucy's was to tag along with Mac and the DCS and try not to be overly *lively* or act stupidly in any way. This was her ticket home. She had to concentrate. Show herself at her best. She could almost smell the apricot pastry she used to buy for breakfast at the Tube station on her way to work, taste the steamy cappuccino . . .

'Lucy.'

It was Mac looking at her expectantly. She shot to his side. He pointed to a white Land Cruiser. 'Our ride.'

She tried not to beam as she hopped in the back. She didn't want to appear shallow but tagging along with the top dogs certainly had its benefits, like not having to walk across acres of freezing docks but being driven in a luxury heated vehicle with two Customs officers and the harbour master.

They passed a ship that had been loading until the police arrived. Containers waited on the dock, the derricks unmoving. A couple of minutes later the car started to slow.

'Here she is,' the harbour master announced.

Lucy craned forward to see a container ship with a two-storey block, painted white, and two derricks. Tears of corrosion streaked from the windows making the vessel look shabby and unkempt. Containers were already stacked on deck. A handful of uniformed police stood with a group of Indian men to one side of the gangway. The crew. They wore scuffed, dirty trousers and oil-stained jackets.

Lucy climbed out of the car. As she approached, the men's eyes slid her way. They didn't look at her directly, but she could feel their gazes probing past her uniform and latching on to her breasts, her waist and legs. *Perverts*, she thought.

The DCS had already ascertained from the ship's paperwork that there was an RFC container on board. Lucy followed him and Mac up the gantry. It began to snow. Soft flakes drifted and settled on their heads and shoulders. Most containers were marked in Hindi but then she saw two standing side-by-side, stamped with English lettering: *RFC – Recycling For Charity.*

Two uniforms set to work removing the steel locking bar with a pair of metal band-saws.

Lucy watched the DCS and a sergeant move inside the container. Nobody moved. Nobody spoke. She didn't realise she was holding her breath until she heard the DCS suddenly call, 'We've got a body. Male, in his twenties. Dreadlocks. Tattoos on his neck and arms. Badly mutilated. Handcuffs on his left wrist.' His voice wavered a fraction and Lucy knew he would be battling with the horror she'd experienced when she'd discovered Bella.

She felt a hand gripping her arm. Saw it was Mac.

'Well done,' he said.

She'd expected to feel triumphant but instead she experienced a wave of sorrow. She wished they'd found the man alive.

CHAPTER THIRTY

Thursday 29 November, 7.32 a.m.

Dan looked out of the kitchen window. The sky was dark, low with clouds. Snow covered the ground. Aimee was going to go crazy when she awoke. He'd better make sure he helped her make some kind of snowman after breakfast or she wouldn't speak to him for a month.

He hadn't slept particularly well last night. He'd dreamed about the woman with the tumbles of raven hair. Her touch was gentle, her joy genuine, but he couldn't relax as he couldn't stop searching while trying not to let her know. Her perfume followed him as he rose to consciousness; wood sage and sea salt. Was she real? If so, why did she create such disquiet in him? Perhaps he'd catch sight of her at a university reunion one day, or bump into her at a party given by friends. He'd like to know what hold she had over his unconscious mind.

Across the valley he saw a tiny cluster of yellow lights that belonged to a hamlet of three cottages and a sheep farm. Had an amnesia drug been used on him? If so, why hadn't he been told? And what about Jenny? Ever since she'd made that call, telling that man about Stella's death and then lying about it, he'd found it almost impossible to look at her and probably wouldn't be able to until he'd sorted this mess out. He didn't want to confront her yet, though. A deep instinct he couldn't fathom told him to hoard as much information as possible first. Knowledge was power. Knowledge brought understanding.

He thought of Grace, her face shadowed by grief and a deep anxiety that she tried to hide. Whether it was connected to the anguish of losing her mother he wasn't sure but, from the way she was burrowing through Stella's things, she was obviously searching for something. When he'd told her about the team of four men coming into her mother's house under the guise of carpet cleaners, her face had blanched.

'I called the police,' he told her. 'They came and checked them out. They told me the men were legitimate, but they weren't.' He went on to tell her about their van giving him the slip.

'Are you sure?' Her voice was faint.

'Yes.'

'Who were they?'

'I don't know, sorry.'

He'd asked Grace for DCA & Co.'s address but she hadn't been able to remember it, just that it was in Mayfair somewhere, and when he'd pressed her she'd closed down on him, obviously unable to think about anything but getting the locks changed in case the men returned.

He'd left her to it, thinking that he'd find DCA & Co. now he knew which area of London they resided in, but no. Nothing. It was as though the company didn't exist.

He'd called Dr Orvis Fatik from his car but the psychiatrist's phone was switched to voicemail. Dan said, 'Call me. It's urgent.'

He then rang his father. 'Don't go anywhere. I'm coming to see you.'

'Now?' His father sounded taken aback. 'I've got golf at two.'

'Cancel it.'

Before his father could protest, he hung up. Eased into the outside lane of the dual carriageway and pressured the accelerator. His father might know something, be able to fill in some blanks. Dad knew Jenny, knew Luke, and had known his old work colleagues. He might have known Stella, and be able to shed some light on what Grace had told him.

His father lived in a ground floor apartment a block from the seafront in Weston-super-Mare with a small garden and a greenhouse where he grew tomatoes and chillies. Dan's mother had died ten years ago, and his father had sold the family house soon afterwards. He never remarried. He continued to work as a security specialist with the Royal Marines until retirement. Since then, he'd done some consultancy work and played golf. If he'd ever had the occasional girlfriend, he never told Dan, and Dan never asked.

He was doing the *Telegraph* crossword when Dan arrived.

'Keeps my mind from going gaga,' he said, slapping the newspaper down. 'What do you do to keep your mind fit?'

Dan was going to make a flip comment about amnesia drugs but at that moment, his phone rang. Dr Orvis.

Dan said, 'I need to see you. I'll be there in –' He checked his watch and did the calculations – 'just over two hours.'

'I'm sorry, Dan, but I'm in Edinburgh today. I'm back tomorrow, late morning, but I have wall-to-wall clients and can't see you until –'

'Tomorrow, midday.'

'Dan, I can't change –'

'Midday,' Dan repeated. He hung up and set the phone to silent.

His father raised his eyebrows. 'You're seem a little on the tense side. Is everything all right?'

Dan walked across the sitting room. Stood with his back to the faux Georgian oak fireplace. He looked at his father, the silver hair tightly cropped, military style, his steady blue gaze.

Dan said, 'I've recently learned that an amnesia drug may have been used on me after Luke was killed.'

He could count on one hand the amount of times he'd shocked his father. Now was one of them. He watched his father open and close his mouth, momentarily lost for words.

'What?'

'It was for my own good, apparently.'

'An *amnesia* drug?' His father looked appalled. 'I've never heard of such a thing.'

Something inside Dan relaxed at his father's obvious horror. He didn't think he could have borne it if Dad had known all along, and hidden it from him.

'Are you serious?' his father's eyes were wide.

'Yes.'

'Good God.' He looked even more horrified. 'How is something like that even *possible*?'

Dan ran his father through what Grace had told him.

'Good God,' his father said again. 'I thought you'd lost your mind because of poor Luke . . . You couldn't cope with what happened, that he died on your watch . . . but now you're saying you suspect your memory may have been interfered with artificially?'

'Yes.'

His father lowered his voice, as though he was concerned they might be overheard. 'Are you sure about this? And the person who told you? Are they reliable?'

Dan nodded. On the drive here, the information had seeped through the landscape of his memory, uncovering odd images and a strange feeling of belonging, as though he'd been reunited with a long-lost sister. Stella.

'You saw me in hospital?' Dan asked.

'Yes.' His father looked away.

'That bad, huh?' Dan gave a twisted smile.

'You were helpless and screwed up and when you lost the memory of what happened . . .' His father wouldn't meet his eye. 'Well, you may not like to hear it, but it was a blessing.'

Dan considered Jenny. He'd relied on her for his memories, taking everything she said as absolute truth, but now his confidence had been shaken his cautious nature dictated that he'd better start double-checking every fact, every detail of his history.

'Which hospital?' he asked.

'Mile End sent you to Croughton Royal near Regent's Park. You were there for two months.' He studied Dan carefully. 'Who told you about the amnesia drug?'

'A friend. Someone from my past, who I couldn't remember.'

'Who?'

'Stella Reavey. Do you know her?'

A strange guilelessness entered his father's expression. He shook his head. 'Sorry,' he said.

Dan added, 'She worked for a company called DCA & Co.'

The guileless look remained.

'Why did she tell you?' his father asked. 'Why now?'

'She wanted me to do something for her.'

'What, exactly?'

Loan myself to her for a couple of days. Pretend my memory was coming back. Help her find Cedric.

'She never said,' he lied. 'She died of a heart attack last week.'

His father looked shocked. 'Are you serious?'

'Yes.'

Small silence while his father gazed outside. Then he seemed to shake himself and said, 'How about if I make a pot of tea?'

Dan ran a hand down his face. 'Tea sounds good.' Once mugs had been filled, they settled back down in the living room. Dan said, 'Dad, how did Luke die?'

His father frowned. 'You already know this.'

'I'd like to hear it again.'

'Are you sure?' He looked doubtful.

'Yes.'

He sighed, took a gulp of tea. Turned his gaze outside, as though it might make the tale easier to tell. 'You were in Brick Lane with Luke, visiting the market. Jenny was tired, and had stayed at home with Aimee. Nobody knows how you got separated from Luke . . .'

His father told the same story that Dan knew. He wasn't sure if he was comforted by this or not. When his father had finished they sat in silence for a while. Dan could hear the faint sound of a TV coming from the flat above, some canned laughter.

'What job did I have in London?' Dan asked.

'You've already asked me these things,' he said slowly, carefully.

Dan met his eye. 'I'd like to hear them again.'

'You were a civil servant.'

'In Immigration.'

'That's correct.'

'Can you remember the names of anyone I worked with?'

'Joe,' he said promptly. 'And the lovely Savannah.'

'Anyone else?'

His father appeared to think. 'Ellis,' he said. 'I can't remember their surnames. Why?' He gave Dan a sharpened look. 'Are you planning on having another reunion?'

Dan had met Joe, Ellis and Savannah a year after his breakdown. Jenny had been desperately anxious that it might cause him to relapse into psychosis once more but Orvis encouraged him to go in case it helped a memory to break through. They'd met at what apparently used to be their favourite drinking hole where they'd hang out Friday evenings, mulling over the events of the week.

The pub felt warm and the lighting was muted, making it difficult to see into the corners and make out people's features. When he entered, he looked at the pictures on the walls – photographs of London in the last century – and then he moved from room to room, ending up pushing open a door marked *Private* and finding a comfortable snug with several armchairs and a private bar.

'Hey, you remember!' Ellis said, looking pleased. Apparently they used the room occasionally when one of them had a birthday or special celebration. Except Dan didn't remember. It was merely one of the moments where his memory came to a junction and allowed him the knowledge of the room, but not when he was last there, or who he'd been with.

He'd done a lot of vacuous smiling that day, and nodding. Smiling and nodding to avoid saying something stupid as well as to try to cover his inability to remember anything about them. Joe, late thirties, fit and strong-looking, lighthearted, with a repertoire of jokes, mostly centred on current affairs. Ellis the same age, but more intense and less quick to rise to laughter. Savannah, twenties, cute with a slender body and bubbly personality. Her honey-brown hair was pulled back in a ponytail, and she wore a figure-hugging black dress over long black leather boots. The men were dressed in plain office garb, grey trousers, jackets, neutral ties.

'I bought you a Guinness,' said Joe. 'Your favourite.'

Except it wasn't any more. He preferred real ale.

'Thanks,' he said, feeling awkward.

They told him stories about other colleagues, but he found it hard to keep interested in people he didn't remember.

'What was I like to work with?' he asked.

'Full on,' said Savannah.

'Energetic, enthusiastic,' said Ellis. He thought a bit more and added, 'dedicated.'

'You were exhausting.' Savannah smiled. 'But the newbies looked up to you.'

'Did I enjoy my work?'

They all laughed. 'You complained like the rest of us,' said Joe with a smile. 'Long hours, not enough pay. The usual stuff. But yes, you loved it.'

They told him he'd had an investigative job, looking into asylum seekers' claims as well as checking immigration references and declarations. Lots of paperwork.

Savannah looked at him, her pretty green eyes concerned and kind. 'Do you think you'll ever get your memory back?'

He looked away. 'I don't know.'

'Can't you remember *anything* about us or your job?'

He shook his head. 'Sorry.'

'But why can you remember your wife and family and not us?' she pressed. 'I don't get it.'

'I don't either.' His tension began to rise beneath her questioning.

'What about skills you learned at work?' She was leaning forward as though willing him to find an answer. 'The courses you went on? Are they lost too? Like –'

'Savannah.' It was Joe. He was shaking his head.

Savannah sank back. 'Sorry.' The word was sullen. 'I only wanted to know why he can remember everything but *us*.'

An uncomfortable silence fell. Dan tried not to appear too eager to leave, but he was desperate to get away from their obvious disappointment. None of them had been in touch since, except Savannah, who hadn't been able to leave the subject of his memory loss alone and had ambushed him six months later in Chepstow where he was shopping at the farmers' market. It had been in the middle of summer. Men in shorts and women in loose summer dresses. Stalls with striped awnings selling everything from preserves to crafts and pet food.

She'd pretended it was an accidental meeting, and he would have believed her if it hadn't been for the way she'd caught her lower lip between her teeth after she'd spoken, sparking a quicksilver memory. It was her tell when she fibbed. He was sure of it.

She looked at his shopping bags. 'Let me guess,' she said. 'Cheese. Bread. A homemade cake of some sort.'

'Anyone could have guessed that.'

'OK. Guess what I would have bought.' She eyed him expectantly.

'Fresh veg. Lots of fresh fruit. Eggs.'

Her face fell. 'No, no and no. All far too healthy for me. I'm a chocoholic and pizza addict.'

'I'm addicted to bliny,' he admitted.

She gave a wan smile. 'I know. You used to bring tons of them back . . . It's not like we don't have pancakes here but you were convinced they never tasted the same.'

'Back from where?' he asked.

'Er . . .' She moved aside for a couple carrying a man-sized pot plant between them. 'Russia. You loved it out there.'

'Russia?' he repeated blankly.

'Jenny wasn't quite as enthusiastic,' she said. 'I don't think she likes snow. How is she?'

'Very well, thank you.'

'She likes living out here?' She made it sound as though they'd moved to the Outer Hebrides.

'Loves it.'

'And you?' Her expression was open and curious.

'Yes.'

'What made you move here?'

'We thought it would be good to make a new start of it.' He repeated what he'd been saying for the past eighteen months. 'After everything that happened before.'

Someone made to push past him for the stall behind, and he moved sideways. Savannah moved with him, stepping close. She was frowning as she said, 'Don't you remember *anything* of Luke's death?'

He shook his head. 'I'm not sure I'd want to even if I could.'

'And you and Jenny are OK?'

'What do you mean?' He was genuinely puzzled.

She looked at him searchingly, her face sombre. 'You're different, you know.'

'So people have said.' Caution rose inside him.

'I mean you're still you, but something fundamental has changed.'

He blinked. 'Like what?'

For the first time, she looked away. Nibbled her lip. 'Sorry. I shouldn't be sticking my nose into things that aren't really my business.'

She looked so crestfallen that he couldn't help it, he smiled.

She smiled back, obviously relieved that he hadn't been offended by anything she'd said, and something about the lightness of her expression triggered a memory. For no reason he could think of, as he looked at her, he thought he could smell cigarette smoke.

'You smoke, right?' he asked.

It was as though a light had been switched on inside her. 'You *do* remember!' she said.

'No, I don't.' He hastened to disabuse her. 'It's just occasionally I get a sense of something, that's all. It's not a real memory. Did I ever smoke?'

'Never.' She wrinkled her nose. 'You always gave me a hard time about it and –'

She swallowed her words when Jenny appeared, expression tight.

'Hi, Jenny,' she said cheerfully.

'Savannah.' Jenny's tone was curt.

The two women surveyed one another. Jenny was as tense as a bowstring but Savannah looked as relaxed and tranquil as a cat sprawled in the sun.

'What are you doing here?' Jenny asked.

'Dirty weekend,' Savannah said.

'Don't let us keep you.'

Savannah smiled slowly, her green eyes glowing. 'I won't,' she purred and then she reached up and pressed a kiss against Dan's cheek. 'Bye,' she said huskily. And walked away, hips swinging sinuously.

'Christ almighty,' said Jenny, watching her go. 'That woman is the *end*.'

Dan had found the situation amusing and not a little flattering but he didn't say so to his wife.

Now, he said to his father, 'I never told you, but Savannah came and saw me in Chepstow not long after we moved, but Jenny saw her off.'

'She came and saw me too,' his father admitted.

'What?' Dan was startled.

'She wanted to know if you'd ever get your memory back. She was a good friend to you.' His father looked sad. 'She was missing you.'

Dan sat quietly for a moment, drinking his tea.

'Does the name Cedric mean anything to you?' Dan asked.

'No.' His father frowned at him. 'Why? Should it?'

Dan said nothing.

'What's going on, son? Does Jenny know you're asking all these questions?'

The TV upstairs was suddenly switched off. Silence.

'Tread carefully,' his father warned. 'She's had a tough time of it, poor girl. She didn't just lose Luke that day, she lost you too. Try not to destroy what she's worked so hard to build. She's only just started to smile again.'

Long silence.

Dan cleared his throat. 'I need you to do something for me.'

'Anything. Just say the word.'

'Don't tell Jenny what we've talked about.' He got to his feet. 'Not under any circumstances.'

Alarm filled his father's eyes. 'Why ever not?'

Dan spouted some bullshit about not worrying her needlessly but inside he longed to shout the truth:

Because I don't trust her anymore.

CHAPTER THIRTY-ONE

'Dan.'

He didn't turn from the window but continued gazing outside. The sky had lightened from dull black to dark grey and the clouds were even lower. He guessed it might snow later.

'Good morning,' Jenny added tentatively.

He heard her cross the kitchen. He moved aside, so he didn't have to be near her when she put on the kettle.

'That's it,' she said. Her voice was tight. 'I've had enough of this crap.'

He briefly closed his eyes. *Here it comes.*

'If you don't tell me what's going on, I am going to scream, OK? I will wake up Aimee and we can have this out in front of her, or we can do it now while she's still asleep.'

Not liking either option, he decided to make his escape and started for the door.

'If you leave,' she bit out, 'I am going to empty every cupboard and smash every glass, every bit of chinaware on the floor. I've had enough, OK? Enough!'

To his surprise, he heard her voice waver. He glanced over his shoulder. She wore sleeping shorts beneath a skinny-ribbed top with spaghetti straps. She'd flung on his dressing gown, an acknowledgement that it was colder than usual, but her feet were bare. Her fists were clenched at her sides and she was biting her lip, trying to control her tears. Immediately, he began to melt, feeling protective, wanting to stop her pain and he faltered, torn between mistrust and love.

'And don't think because I'm tearful I'm not angry,' she choked, 'because I am. You can't keep giving me the cold shoulder. You can't shut me out, Dan. Not again. I won't let you.'

'When have I shut you out?' he asked.

'You used to do it all the time.' A tear escaped and fell down her cheek but she didn't brush it away. 'And that was OK, because that was before . . .'

Before Luke's death.

'. . . but now you're doing it when everything's OK and I don't understand. Where were you yesterday? Why won't you tell me what you're doing, where you're going? Why the sudden secrecy?'

'If you really want to know . . .' He saw her eyes flare with anticipation and felt something shrink inside. 'I went and saw Dad.'

She blinked. 'Oh.'

She hadn't expected that. He wondered where she thought he'd been.

'He sends his love,' Dan added, like he usually did.

'He's OK?'

'Hale and hearty as ever.'

Long silence.

He said, 'I'm going to build a snowman with Aimee. Then I'm going to see Dr Orvis.'

Jenny frowned.

'Don't worry, I'll pay him myself,' Dan assured her. Jenny's parents had footed Dan's extensive medical bills until he'd been discharged from hospital, and at over a hundred pounds a pop, Dr Orvis wasn't cheap. 'I know he's expensive,' he started to say, but Jenny cut him off.

'It's not that.' She shook her head. 'Why do you need to see him? I thought all that had finished.'

'It has. But I want to check a couple of things.'

He saw her apprehension rise. 'Like what?'

'Like whether I'll get any more of my memory back,' he improvised. 'Seeing Stella Reavey made me realise how much I've lost. I want to know the person I used to be. But I can't. I thought seeing her might prompt me to remember something, anything, but she was like a stranger. I want to know the chances of regaining more memories of that time. Like our life in London. You know, things about our friends, maybe even some of Luke . . .'

As he watched, she visibly relaxed. Her fists unclenched and her shoulders dropped. Her release of tension was so obvious that for a moment he wondered if she was doing it on purpose.

'Oh, Dan,' she said. Just two words but they were heartfelt, a combination of sorrow and empathy.

His mouth twisted. 'Yeah,' he said. 'Stupid, I know.'

She came and stood before him. She didn't touch him. If she had, he might have taken a step back, recoiled. He marvelled at how well she knew him. Holding his eyes, she said simply, 'I love you.'

He looked at her and even though he felt her words resonate, and knew she meant them, he couldn't help thinking: *But what about the man you spoke to about me? The one you told Stella was dead?*

Normally he'd say, 'I love you too,' but today he said, 'I know.'

He saw the hurt in her eyes, but he couldn't do anything about it. He said, 'I'll go and wake Aimee now.'

The snowman was pretty pathetic, half mud, half snow, and the size of a wellington boot, but Aimee was thrilled with it. She'd used mismatched shirt buttons for eyes, the tip of a carrot for a nose and put one of her doll's caps jauntily on top. After they'd drunk mugs of hot chocolate in the kitchen, Dan washed up the mugs and told her he had to go, and that he might not be back until after the weekend.

He saw her thinking this over more deeply than usual.

'What's up, hunny bunny?'

'Does this mean you won't be visiting Luke's grave with us?'

For a moment he was flummoxed. He'd completely forgotten they were due in London on Sunday.

'No, it doesn't,' he said. 'I'll meet you and Mummy there. Afterwards we can –'

'Go ice skating!' She leaped up and started play-skating around the kitchen. 'Whoosh, whoosh!'

Jenny came into the kitchen carrying a basket of laundry beneath one arm. She was smiling. 'What's this racket, then?'

'Daddy's taking me ice skating!'

Jenny raised her eyebrows at Dan.

'After visiting Luke's grave,' he said, 'I thought we could go ice skating in South Kensington afterwards.'

Jenny looked at him. Her eyes turned soft. 'I thought you'd forgotten.'

He felt a moment's guilt but swept on. 'I've got two race-day experiences, tomorrow and Saturday.' Which had been true until he'd cancelled them yesterday, but he went on to lie smoothly. 'I'll stay at my usual B & B near Goodwood tonight and drive up to London first thing Sunday morning. I'll meet you at the cemetery. Drive us all back later.'

Normally Jenny would kiss him goodbye, but she obviously sensed his emotional reserve and kept her distance. 'Say hi to Orvis for me.'

He wondered why he should do that when to his knowledge she'd never met him, but bit his tongue. As he drove away, he glanced in his rear-view mirror to see her standing forlornly at the kitchen window, her hand tentatively raised.

The route to Orvis's office was so familiar that Dan barely noticed the journey passing. He listened to the news with half an ear. Apparently the body of a naked man had been found locked in a freezer on board a ship due to sail to Chennai. The man's identity had yet to be confirmed. The reporter said the police had linked the murder to the Bella Frances assault case in Stockton-on-Tees, which surprised Dan. He'd have expected the next victim to be a woman. The fact the killer was using containers and shipping the bodies abroad intrigued him; it seemed overly complicated and fraught with risks. British ports, Customs in particular, were known for being stringent. They had scanners and tried to ensure all cargo leaving and entering the country was legitimate, and matched the documents supplied. No doubt both cases were keeping PC Plod occupied.

Parking outside the familiar converted barn, he climbed into the frosty air, grabbing his jacket and scarf. The temperature hadn't climbed above freezing and although it was cloudy it wasn't snowing yet. There were three cars on the gravel driveway, two of which he recognised from previous visits – the Jaguar belonging to Dr Orvis Fatik, the BMW to his wife. A red Vauxhall sedan was parked in a designated area to the right, indicating it belonged to one of the doctor's patients.

He walked round the side of the house for the orangery – Orvis's office – a beautiful light and airy space overlooking a long lawn and several sweeping beech trees. The orangery was accessible from the main house but the doctor liked his patients to come directly to his office through the garden so as not to disturb his family.

As he approached, he saw Orvis sitting with a small dark-haired woman. When Orvis caught sight of Dan, he nodded and held up a hand, indicating for Dan to remain outside. He said something to the woman and came to the door, opened it and stepped outside, closed it behind him. He was wearing a colourful Indian-print jacket over a plain beige shirt, and caramel trousers that were several shades lighter than his skin. Small and neat with quick gestures and vibrantly coloured clothes, he had always reminded Dan of a kingfisher.

'Dan,' he said in a low, gentle voice. 'I left several messages for you.'

'I know.'

Orvis's calm presence didn't falter. He said, 'Since it's obviously urgent, I can fit you in for twenty minutes when my current client leaves.'

'Thank you.'

Dan turned and headed back to his car. Nerves strumming, he scrolled through his contacts list until he found Savannah's mobile number. Dialled. He wanted to ask her what she knew of his breakdown. When they'd met at the pub, and afterwards in Chepstow, they hadn't spoken of it.

He waited for the ring tone, but instead a woman's voice intoned, *this number is no longer in service.*

Dan tried his next colleague, Ellis. *This number is no longer in service.*

Spine tingling, he rang Joe. *This number is no longer in service.*

He jumped when a footstep crunched on gravel. The dark-haired woman didn't look at him as she climbed into her Vauxhall and drove away. Dutifully, Dan parked in her empty space. Headed back to the orangery. Inside it was warm, thanks to underfloor heating and a massive radiator lining one of the walls. At one end stood a desk and two filing cabinets – the doctor's work space; at the other two armchairs and a low table upon which stood a bowl full of coloured marbles.

As usual, Orvis shook his hand and gestured for him to take a seat. Dan opted to stand. Orvis did the same, mirroring Dan's stance. Dan wondered if the psychiatrist did it deliberately to put him at ease or if he did it without thinking.

'How have you been?' Orvis asked. His brown eyes held Dan's, concerned.

'Could be better,' Dan said. 'I've just learned that an amnesia drug might have been used on me. I may not have lost my memory due to a breakdown but because of a *drug*.'

Although his expression didn't change, something in Orvis's eyes turned strangely guileless. It reminded Dan of his father and he felt a lurch of cold terror. Was his father lying to him? In a rush, he recalled what Stella had said in the supermarket.

Your identity, your past, is a lie. Your entire family has been lying to you.

'Was an amnesia drug used on me?' Dan asked.

Orvis looked out of the window at a blackbird hopping across his lawn, foraging for worms.

'Was it?' Dan persisted.

He looked back at Dan and gave a sigh. He nodded. 'Yes.'

CHAPTER THIRTY-TWO

Dan felt as though he was in an express lift that had just had its cables cut.

'Why wasn't I told?'

'It was thought it would make things easier for you.' Orvis moved across the room to his desk, picked up a slender green folder, flipped it open and pulled out some stapled sheets of A4 paper. 'I didn't agree, but it was what was eventually decided by the leading psychiatrist at Croughton Royal.'

'Is it common practice to use a drug on someone without their knowledge?' Dan's tone hardened. 'What was I, a guinea pig or something?'

Orvis walked over and passed Dan the paper. It was headed: *Patient Agreement to Treatment.* Words flashed before Dan's eyes. *Statement of health professional: I have explained the procedure to the patient along with the aftercare provided, in particular I have explained the intended benefits . . . I have discussed the benefits and risks . . .* It was signed by Dr Stuart Winter.

Dan knew Stuart. He'd been his psychiatrist in hospital but he couldn't remember signing this document with him.

Dan turned to the next page. *Statement of patient: I agree to the procedure and aftercare described on this form. I have been told about available alternative treatments* . . . His signature was at the bottom. It was unmistakable and his stomach turned over when he saw it had the extra, almost unnoticeable pressure at the bottom of the t in Forrester, which he'd perfected over the years so he could tell in an instant whether his signature was genuine.

Dan scratched his throat, using the casual gesture to cover how disturbed he felt. 'OK. So I agreed to the treatment.'

'It probably saved your sanity.'

'Did my wife know?'

Orvis shook his head slightly. 'I don't know. I've never met her or spoken to her.'

'What about Dr Winter?'

Again, Orvis shook his head. 'I never spoke to him either.'

'Is that usual?'

'Normally when a patient is referred to me I like to discuss their case history, what treatment they've already undertaken, but this time . . .' He paused as he crossed the room to take back the consent form. 'I was refused.'

'Why?'

'I wasn't given a reason.'

Dan frowned. 'Why did you take me on?'

'Because I'm a psychiatrist.' Orvis tucked the form back into the file. 'Your case epitomised everything that fascinated me about the field. Psychology, social science, medicine, neuroscience. As well as that, I truly hoped to help return you to a satisfying and fulfilling life.'

'You thought of me as a lab rat.'

'Absolutely not.' Orvis looked offended.

'Was it legal?' Dan asked. 'I mean the drug as well as the treatment.'

'It's in the research phase but yes, your treatment and the use of the drug on you was entirely legal.'

'Do you know what my job was before I was given the drug?'

'You were a civil servant. In Immigration.' He went on to say nothing that Dan hadn't heard before.

'And what do you know about my son's death?'

'That it nearly killed you.'

'That's not what I meant.'

'I know.' Dr Orvis turned and faced Dan, unflappable as always. 'Now, my next patient is due any minute, so if you wouldn't mind –'

'I've been told Luke didn't die in a hit-and-run. Apparently he died in my arms, but he didn't die on Brick Lane as I believed.'

Orvis closed his eyes for a moment as if to collect his thoughts. 'It's best if you go now.'

Dan went and stood close to Orvis. Looked down at him. He said, 'What do you know about Luke's death?'

Orvis swallowed. 'You have a powerful presence, did you know?'

Dan just looked at him.

'I only know what happened to Luke from reading your notes.' Orvis turned and walked to the door and put his hand on the handle. 'That you got separated in the market, and that he stepped into the road and was hit by a van.'

Dan picked up the folder but all it contained was the consent form and a handful of NHS referral documents. His file must be held on computer.

'I'm sorry, Dan.' Orvis's tone was gentle. 'But you must go now.'

As if to accentuate his point, a man appeared at the orangery door. Nervous looking, with wire-rimmed glasses and slicked-back hair. Pale skin. Bitten nails. Dry, flaky skin.

Dan opened the door, brushed past him and walked out of sight. Mindful of Jenny's reaction after he'd told her of Stella's death, he quickly retraced his steps to spy on the orangery. He wanted to see how Orvis acted now he'd left. If he did nothing more than treat his next client, then he could probably relax. But if he sent an email or made a phone call, Dan would like to know to whom, and whether it was to do with his visit.

The man with bitten nails was already slouching in one of the armchairs. Orvis was at his computer but then he rose and said something, it seemed to be an apology as the man gave a seemingly careless shrug and began biting his nails. Orvis picked up the phone from his desk and, while checking his computer screen, punched in a number. Then he closed the lid of his computer and walked into the main house, head ducked and already concentrating on his phone call.

Dan sped across the lawn to the orangery. Ignoring the startled stare of Orvis's client, he slipped across the room to Orvis's computer and raised the lid. The screen lit up a welcome but when it demanded a passcode he let the lid drop and followed Orvis.

Carefully he opened the door into the main house. No hinges squeaked, no creaking wood. Soundlessly, he stepped inside and closed the door behind him. He stood motionless. Against the light of the room behind him, the interior immediately felt dark and gloomy. A standard lamp was lit at one end of a large sitting room. Antique rugs, over-stuffed sofas and an oil painting of what looked like a Scottish mountain gave the room a countrified air. Orvis stood in front of a large stone fireplace. He had his back to Dan. He was talking on the phone.

'No, he didn't appear to remember anything . . . Nothing . . . Absolutely. No, he's gone . . . Yes, he might return . . . because someone told him his son didn't die in a hit-and-run . . .'

Short silence.

'No, he didn't say who . . . Yes, certainly. If he returns I'll call. Of course.'

He hung up and at the same time Dan strode across the room.

Orvis spun round, mouth slackening in shock.

'Who was that?' Dan demanded.

Orvis snapped his mouth shut but didn't say anything. Dan held out his hand for the phone. Orvis passed it over. When Dan checked the number last dialled, a prickly sensation crept over the back of his neck. It was the same number Jenny had called. Holding Orvis's eyes, he pressed re-dial. It rang four times before it was answered, but nobody said anything. Dan pushed the phone next to Orvis's face. He mouthed, *say hello.*

'Hello?' Orvis said. His voice was high with tension.

Dan pushed the phone against Orvis's face once more. *Again*, he urged.

'It's me. Dr Orvis Fatik.' His eyes remained fixed on Dan. 'Sorry to call you back.'

Dan nodded his approval at the doctor's improvisation.

'What is it?' a man said. 'Is something wrong?'

Mid-English accent, mid-level pitch, nothing distinctive.

'What is it?' the man said again.

Dan took back the phone. He said, 'Why did my wife ring you?'

Immediately, the man hung up. Dan handed the phone back to Orvis. 'Who was that?'

He looked away. Swallowed. He said, 'I don't know.'

Dan looked at him.

Orvis swallowed again. 'You have to believe me. I don't know. I swear it. After you were discharged from hospital, Dr Winter told me to ring this number should you ever start questioning your past, including your son's death.'

'Who. Was. It.' Dan's voice was a whisper.

'I swear on my daughter's life . . .' He glanced at a silver-framed photograph of a laughing five-year-old girl. 'I don't know. But . . .'

Dan waited.

'He calls himself Cedric. He says he's from the pharmaceutical company that is researching the amnesia drug. He wants to know if the memory-blocking remains successful.'

Dan's body went cold.

'Cedric?'

'I don't think it's his real name. He's interested in you because you're a living case study, I suppose. He believes the amnesia drug could be invaluable in treating patients with post-traumatic stress. I think he'd like to sell it to the military.'

Dan thought this over. 'Does he pay you for information on me?'

'No!' Orvis recoiled. 'Absolutely not. My sessions with you are one hundred per cent confidential.'

'So what's in it for you?'

Orvis closed his eyes briefly. 'He sends me information, sometimes results, from other psychiatrists who are treating their patients with the same drug. It's experimental, but they all sign a consent form. Like you.'

Dan looked at him. 'And you said I wasn't a lab rat.'

Orvis wouldn't meet Dan's eye.

'How many times have you spoken to him?' Dan asked.

'Several times during the first year of your treatment, but when it appeared your memories had been successfully deleted, we didn't speak any more.' He took a shaky breath. 'We kept in touch by email until last week when he telephoned. He suspected you might come and see me. He wanted to know immediately if you did.'

Dan looked away, thinking. Was he nothing but a guinea pig? If Cedric sold such a drug to the military it could bring in big money, *massive* money.

'What's the name of the drug company?'

'PepsBeevers.'

The same company Grace had mentioned, that funded a brain and neurological research institute near London.

'Do you know Stella Reavey?' Dan asked.

'Who?' Orvis looked blank.

'What about DCA & Co.?'

Orvis shook his head. 'Sorry. Neither name means anything.'

Dan thought fast. 'I want copies of Cedric's emails, and yours to him.'

Orvis sucked in his breath but didn't protest. Dan shadowed him back to his office. Orvis's patient was chewing the other hand but otherwise didn't appear to have moved.

'Sorry about this,' Orvis said to him. 'I'll be with you in a minute.'

The man gave one of his shrugs, giving Dan the impression he wouldn't have cared if he left at the end of an hour without saying a word to his doctor.

Orvis restarted his computer and even although he tried to block Dan's view, Dan saw him punch in his password – GALAXY32 – before he accessed his emails. He went through various folders until he pointed out one titled Dan Forrester. 'They're in there.'

Dan said, 'Send the whole file to me.'

When Orvis's email came through, Dan checked the folder. 'Do you have any other numbers for Cedric? Email addresses?'

'No.'

'Where's my file?' Dan asked. 'The one with all my notes?'

Orvis gave him a pained look.

'Email it to me,' Dan told him. 'Now.'

'You may not like what you read,' he warned.

'Just do it.'

Dan left when he'd received the second email on his phone. He'd read everything later. Back in his car, he began to prioritise what he needed to do. Talk to Dr Stuart Winter and check that everything Orvis had said was true. Track down Cedric. Confront Jenny.

But first, he needed to see Grace Reavey.

CHAPTER THIRTY-THREE

Thursday 29 November, 3.10 p.m.

Grace had taken Dan's demonstration with the umbrella stand to heart, and looked beneath every rubbish bin, the underside of every drawer and the ceiling of every cupboard, but no bank statement or Post-it note covered with bank codes sprang out. She yawned, tears collecting in the corners of her eyes. Without the comforting presence of Ross last night, she hadn't slept much. Every creak in the house, every car that drove past had woken her.

She'd had the locks changed but it hadn't helped. She couldn't stop thinking about the men Dan said he'd seen entering her mother's house while she'd been at the funeral. They had to be after the money Sirius Thiele wanted. She felt oddly grateful they had waited until she'd left the house before they'd searched, and hadn't confronted her. Not like Sirius.

My client has given us until the end of the week.

She felt a desperate urge to run away. To put as much distance between her and Sirius Thiele as possible. But she knew she would just be putting things off, and that despite her almost crippling fear she had to face up, hold firm, so she could go back to her life and normality.

Time was running out. She had to get to her mother's office and see if there were any clues there. She was looking around, wondering where else to search, when the doorbell rang.

Her nerves balled into fists of fear. What if Sirius was early? Grace crept to the front door. Peeked through the fish-eye. Relief made her feel dizzy. It was Dan Forrester. She opened the door.

He looked over her shoulder. 'Still at it, I see.'

Something about him had changed. There was an energy crackling around him she hadn't seen before. Holding the door open, she invited him inside.

'You seem better,' she said.

He blinked.

'Stronger,' she added. Taller as well, she thought, but didn't say it. He was also better-looking than she'd initially thought, with a strong, angular face and clear grey eyes. She closed the door behind him. Saw him gazing around.

'What are you looking for?' he asked.

She could feel herself stiffen.

'Sorry,' he said. 'I know it's none of my business but sometimes I can't help myself. I'm incurably nosy.' He gave a small, rather rueful smile.

It was the first time she'd seen him smile and despite her anxiety, she felt her heart lift.

'I can't tell you,' she said. 'Because I'm not quite sure myself. But it's important. *Really* important.' She was horrified to hear her voice tremble and was glad when Dan didn't comment but became immediately businesslike.

'Size?'

She thought of CDs, memory sticks, and then a suitcase stuffed with fifty-pound notes. 'It could be a disc, a memory card or ... I don't know.' She shrugged helplessly. 'I'm looking for information, I guess, but Mum doesn't keep things in files or folders; everything's on her computer but I don't have her password.'

Dan began prowling around the room. He looked up at the ceiling, down at the floor. Checked behind the curtains. Ran his fingers along the track gliders. He said, 'What did your mother do?'

'She was a translator and interpreter.'

'Where in Mayfair was she based?'

Dan had worked with her mother. She didn't have a problem telling him. 'Upper Brook Street. I can't remember the number offhand. I've never been there. If I was in London Mum and I would meet up for lunch somewhere in the area, but never at the office. She liked to get out. Have a break.'

Methodically, he felt the hem of each curtain. Moved to each corner of the room, testing the edges of the carpet.

'What does DCA & Co. do?' he asked.

'Political risk analysis.'

'Which means?' He picked a cushion off the sofa and squeezed it with both hands before checking the stitching.

'Looking at a company or investment and giving impartial advice. They sent Mum to Belarus once, to look at a company which manufactured trucks and tractors. A client of theirs was thinking of setting up a joint stock company with them.'

'She spoke Russian?'

'French, German, Spanish and Farsi too.'

'Clever woman.'

'She said that once you'd learned a couple of languages, the rest came easily.'

Dan pulled out the sofa cushions and ran his fingers along the stitching. 'How long has she worked for DCA?'

'Five years or so, I guess.'

'What did she do before?'

'She worked for the civil service.'

'As an interpreter and translator?'

'Yes.'

'Which department?'

'Immigration.'

He put down the sofa cushion. His gaze turned distant as he placed his hand on his belly. It was a strange gesture and Grace wondered what he was thinking. He said, 'I used to work in the same department, apparently.'

'Do you speak any languages?' Grace asked.

He frowned. 'I don't think so.'

Her mobile started to ring on the hall table. 'Excuse me,' Grace said. She headed outside, leaving Dan upending the sofa. She hadn't even thought of checking inside cushions and curtain hems. She picked up her phone to see it was a landline number, but not one she recognised.

'Hello?'

'Hi,' a woman said. 'This is Constable Lucy Davies from the Stockton police. Is that Dr Grace Reavey?'

'Yes it is.' Grace leaned against the wall and lowered her head to concentrate. 'How can I help?'

'It's about a patient of yours who went missing. Apparently you requested notification should we have any news.'

'Jamie,' Grace breathed. 'You've found him?'

'Yes.' There was a short pause, and then she added, 'I'm sorry.'

Grace closed her eyes. Oh, no. Not Jamie, she thought. Jamie who had pruned her apple tree and roses, mowed her lawn. Jamie who wore big leather boots and never tied the laces, who loved dogs, who wanted a Labrador puppy but wouldn't get one until he'd climbed Mount Kilimanjaro and launched his prostate cancer awareness project into the stratosphere. She managed to keep her tone level as she said, 'He's dead?'

'Yes.'

'Jamie . . .' She couldn't help it. Tears rose and she battled to control them.

'I'm sorry,' Constable Davies said again.

'Me too.' Grace wiped her eyes. 'I'm not normally so emotional, but . . . my mother. She died last week.'

'Oh, no.' Constable Davies sounded shocked. 'I'm so sorry.'

'You weren't to know.' Grace took a deep breath, felt some control return. 'How did he die?'

'Faris MacDonald – my DI – and I are coming down to Hampshire later today. Would it be possible to see you, perhaps tomorrow morning? We're talking to everyone who knew him, trying to get a picture of what happened.'

The fact the policewoman hadn't answered her question made Grace's trepidation rise. Something bad had happened to Jamie.

She looked along the hallway at a stack of paperback books precariously balanced next to some photograph albums. 'I'm not actually his GP,' she said. 'You really need to speak to Dr Smith.'

'Oh.' The policewoman sounded surprised. 'I didn't realise. I'll call Dr Smith right away, but it would still be good to meet you, since you knew Jamie.'

'Tomorrow's not very good for me, I'm afraid. I'm at my mother's house in Tring. Sorting things out.'

The brief silence from the constable made Grace oddly nervous, but then PC Davies said, 'When will you be back in Hampshire?'

'Not until next week.'

'Perhaps I could come and see you in Tring?'

A chill swept over Grace. She didn't want Sirius finding out she'd seen a police officer. Hurriedly she said, 'I'll be at the surgery first thing on Monday. I can see you then if you let reception know.'

'Not before then?'

'It's not possible, sorry.' Grace was firm.

'OK,' the constable agreed grudgingly. 'I'll see you Monday.'

Grace hung up. She felt shaky as she moved back to the sitting room. Dan was squatting next to the upended sofa. He'd pulled back the hessian, exposing the spring base, and was reaching deep inside. 'I've found something,' he murmured.

Grace joined him on the floor as he extracted a padded A5 envelope and passed it to her. She turned it over in her hands, only half-aware of it because her mind wasn't on the envelope. It was on Jamie Hudson, who liked chocolate brownies and wanted to learn how to cook so he could make them for his children; he'd wanted four but he wasn't going to have any now, because he was dead.

Dan said, 'Do you want me to leave you while you open it?'

A tear slid down her cheek.

'Grace.' His voice was gentle. 'What is it?'

'A friend of mine. He died.'

Dan held out a hand. She put her palm in his and felt his grip, warm and strong. 'I'm sorry.'

'Me too.' Her smile was wobbly. 'I really liked him.'

He gave her hand a little shake, then stood up. 'Brandy, or tea?'

'Tea. Thanks.'

She heard him put on the kettle, then the sound of cupboards and drawers opening, the chink of mugs, the snap of the fridge door. She took a deep breath. Closed her eyes. Visualised Jamie and his dreadlocked brown hair, his cheerful blue eyes. 'I'm sorry,' she whispered. 'I'm so sorry, Jamie.'

She took another deep breath and opened her eyes. Felt herself steady. 'Say hi to Mum for me,' she murmured. 'And hi to Simon too.'

Grace finally turned her attention to the envelope. No address, no label. The flap was stuck down with Scotch tape and looked as though it had already been opened once or twice before. Inside was a stack of used US dollar bills: hundreds, fifties and twenties. Around two thousand dollars in cash. And a British passport that had a fairly recent photograph of her mother. All the details were correct. Age, nationality, place of birth. Except for her name. Instead of Stella Victoria Reavey, it said Denise Anne Gabriel.

She didn't know what to think, so she didn't. With her mother's death, then Jamie's, and now this, her brain seemed to have stopped functioning. She just stared at the name until dots appeared in front of her eyes.

Dan came and hunkered beside her. Holding the passport in one hand, she took the mug proffered with the other and took a sip.

'OK?' he asked.

'Not really,' she replied. She passed him the passport.

'Hmm,' he said when he had a look.

Numbly, Grace picked up the money. Flicked through the notes. There wasn't enough here for Sirius.

Dan returned the passport, got to his feet. Mug in hand, he began prowling the room again. 'Mind if I go next door? Keep looking?'

She didn't reply but opened the passport again. The photograph was recent; her mother had layered her hair in the summer. Her guess was confirmed when she saw the passport had been issued in August. She stared at her mother's image. What was going on? Why did her mother have another name? Which one was real? Stella Reavey or Denise Gabriel? Her mother's maiden name had been Cobb. Grace didn't know anyone with the surname Gabriel. Numbly, she finished her tea. From time to time she could hear Dan moving around the house but she had no idea of time passing. When Dan came and squatted in front of her, he said, 'Come and see.'

Upstairs, behind her mother's bed, he'd pulled the skirting board free to expose an extensive hidey-hole.

'I had a quick look,' he said. 'But I didn't touch anything.'

Grace ducked down and pulled out another envelope. This one contained yet another British passport and a driving license. They showed her mother in the photographs, but they were in the name of Denise Anne Gabriel. Grace pulled out several supermarket carrier bags which held more cash. Wodges of it in US dollar bills and British sterling. She flicked through a stack, trying to work out how much was there.

'I'd say around £30,000 all up,' Dan said, obviously reading her mind.

She handed him the passport. He had a quick look before returning it to her.

Grace said, 'Why?'

'For a quick getaway.'

She looked at him blankly.

'Cash is untraceable,' he added.

She watched him turn a piece of skirting board over in his hands and study it closely. He ran his fingers over the edges, looking thoughtful, but he didn't say anything.

Grace felt as if her stomach had been taken out, leaving a great gaping hole. She mustn't stop and think about it but keep going, carry on until she found the answers. Knowledge would give her the power to get through this, even if it baffled and blindsided her.

She wriggled on to her stomach and checked the hidey-hole in case she'd missed anything. Tucked almost out of sight was another carrier bag of cash – this one with a couple of thousand euros. It also contained what appeared to be a legal document. Sinking onto her heels, Grace saw that it was a deed to a house in the British Virgin Islands.

Ocean View, Nail Bay.

Clutching the deed, Grace scrambled to her feet and on weakening legs, pattered downstairs. Dan followed. He stood watching while she picked up her phone and opened her emails. She liked the fact that he didn't ask questions and didn't interrupt. She scrolled to her mother's last message to her. The list of sort codes and account numbers, all incomplete. One account was held at the First Caribbean International Bank (Cayman) Ltd in Tortola, British Virgin Islands.

She closed her email, feeling oddly and peculiarly calm. Shock, she supposed, because if she didn't know her mother, she might be tempted to think Dan was right, that her mother wanted a quick, untraceable getaway to the British Virgin Islands with Sirius Thiele's large amount of money. She remembered what she'd said to Sirius Thiele in the car park outside the pub at her mother's wake. *She's not that sort of person.*

And Sirius Thiele's response: *Perhaps you didn't know her as well as you thought.*

Part of her insisted there had to be a rational explanation, that her mother would rather die than do something illegal, but the other part inside Grace cowered, small and scared, sensing her entire history was being re-written.

Don't think about it, she told herself. *Not until later, when it's digestible.*

In a rush, she remembered her mother ringing her last Friday evening, almost begging to see her. What if Mum had been going to tell her she was emigrating in a hurry and taking on a new identity? But what about her health? Maybe Mum was going to emigrate after the operation? Or was she going to have the operation abroad? But *why?*

'Anything make sense?' Dan asked.

Grace looked into his eyes. She wanted to share what she'd found with him, but she couldn't shake her mother's final email to her.

Trust no one.

'Not really,' she admitted.

'Do you think you might find some answers where she worked?'

'Perhaps.'

'I'd like to see her offices,' Dan said. 'Because it's also where I may have worked. Do you think we could go together?'

Grace was torn. He'd been Mum's friend. He'd tried to save her life. She chewed the inside of her lip, undecided.

'I'll go on my own if you'd rather do the same,' Dan said. 'I just need the street number.'

Grace checked her mobile before ringing her mother's office.

'DCA,' a man answered briskly.

'Hi, it's Grace Reavey here,' she said. 'Can I speak to Joe, please?'

'Before I put you through,' the man said, 'can I say how very sorry I am about Stella. We're missing her terribly here.'

'Thank you.'

'I'll get Joe for you.'

A small click, then Joe picked up the phone.

'Hey, Grace. How are you bearing up?'

'OK, thanks,' she lied. She wasn't going to share the litany of grief or the terrifying trauma of Sirius Thiele. 'Look, I'm really sorry, but I've forgotten your address. I want to see Mum's office if that's OK, and –'

'When were you thinking of coming? I'll make sure I'm here.'

'Er . . .' Her mind scrambled to work out when to visit. 'How about tomorrow morning? Would that be OK?'

She looked at Dan, who nodded.

'Say, ten o'clock?' she added.

'Fine by me.' His voice was warm. 'I know it's not in the greatest of circumstances, but it'll be nice to see you.'

'I know you're in Upper Brook Street,' Grace said, 'but which number?'

'Thirty-three, but it's not obvious. Look for a black door with a video interphone. There's a pot plant on the top step.'

'Is it OK if I bring someone with me?'

'Ross?'

'No. An old friend of my mother's.'

'Who?' His voice turned sharp.

'Dan Forrester. Apparently he and Mum used to work together.'

'Good grief,' Joe said. 'I used to work with Dan too. How on earth do you know him?'

'Mum contacted him recently.'

'Did she indeed?' he said, obviously interested. 'Well, I'm sure he'll tell me all about it tomorrow. It will be good to see him again.'

'Thanks, Joe.'

'No problem. I'll look forward to seeing you both at ten.'

CHAPTER THIRTY-FOUR

When Dan heard Joe Talbot worked with Stella at DCA, he felt like a kid in a playground who'd been left out of a game. If he could kick his faulty memory into working properly, he would. Funny how he couldn't remember Stella or Joe but could tell you, in minute detail, about the pattern of brown speckles on the belly of the spaniel puppy he'd been given as a boy. He couldn't remember his old work colleagues but there were faces from his childhood that he knew as surely as if he'd created them himself.

Although he didn't expect to find anything more, Dan spent another hour searching the remainder of Stella's house. He'd been surprised to find Stella's main stash behind the skirting board because the wood had been marked from where it had last been pried open, and not painted over afterwards, making it easier to spot, making him wonder if she'd wanted it to be found.

Had the men posing as R.V. Cleaners discovered Stella's stash? If so, why had they left it alone? Perhaps nobody had found her stash, and Stella had been careless by not painting over the jimmy marks on the wood, but he didn't think that would happen. From what he knew of Stella, she was careful, methodical and precise, and he guessed she'd no more leave her hidey-hole with a mark than hack off her own hand with a bread knife.

When he said goodbye to Grace she was emptying the contents of the kitchen cupboards into boxes. She'd rolled the sleeves of her sweater to her elbows and tied her hair back with a strip of red ribbon that looked as though it came from the carton of gift-wrapping lying in the hallway.

'I've got to go,' he said.

She pushed back a lock of hair. 'I can't thank you enough for your help. I would never have found that stuff without you.'

'You might wish I'd never found it,' he said.

She shook her head. 'I needed to know. Where shall we meet tomorrow? Do you want to come here and we travel down together?'

'I'll meet you in London,' he said.

'At DCA?'

'Yes. Can I have your mobile number?'

They each put the other's number into their phones.

'Do you need help with the money?' Dan asked. 'Carrying it to the bank or anything?'

'No, but thanks. You've been great.'

'Just shout if you need me, OK? I'm happy to help.'

She saw him out. A stray curl had escaped and if she'd been Jenny he would have tucked it tenderly behind her ear, but she wasn't his wife and although he felt protective of her, it wasn't the time or place. As he stepped along the path, he heard her close the door behind him, then bolt it. He wondered what she'd do with the cash, and guessed she'd keep it until she knew more of what was going on.

Slipping into his car, Dan opened his road map. Normally he'd use his satnav to guide him but he didn't want to leave a trail should anyone check – like Jenny or Cedric – so he was using good old-fashioned methods to get him from A to B. He would visit DCA with Grace as planned tomorrow but he wanted to check the place out first. Anything to try and keep one step ahead of the game.

As he eased on to the A41 it started to sleet. The road was wet and Dan automatically left more space between himself and the car in front. He could see why Stella had chosen to live in Tring. It was less than forty miles to Mayfair and most of it on a dual carriageway.

Thankfully he was going against the commuter traffic streaming out of London and he made it to a Mayfair car park just before five o'clock. He couldn't have timed it better to see who left DCA's offices at the end of the day, but when he browsed his way inconspicuously along Upper Brook Street – pausing to look into shop windows and check his surroundings – he couldn't immediately find number thirty-three. Eventually he worked out that DCA was probably housed in the narrow red-brick brick building with bars on the lower windows and an anonymous looking matt-black door with a video entry system. No number, no nameplate.

Dan continued to browse. At ten minutes past five, he saw a young woman leave the building. She wore a form-fitting black skirt and a pair of sensible black shoes beneath a thick red woollen jacket and cream scarf. A small red handbag was slung over one shoulder. She walked briskly west then turned north up Park Street, maybe heading for Marble Arch Tube station.

Out of nowhere he felt his chest tighten and his breathing constrict. What if the woman in his recurring dreams worked here? He couldn't shake the thought and when the door next opened he was so caught up in the anticipation of seeing a slender figure with tumbles of raven hair walking out that he started to sweat. In fact, the next figure to emerge was an older man in a suit and raincoat who peered into the drab, dark sky, looking weary.

She doesn't exist, Dan told himself. *Stop being ridiculous.*

Nobody exited for another twelve minutes, when two men in their thirties appeared. Both wore suits. They were talking, intense and animated. One was blond, the other had sandy hair and pale eyes. A mole sat on his right cheekbone, another on his chin. His nose was narrow, and he had a slightly receding chin and a small mouth.

Every cell in Dan's body tensed.

It was the man from R.V. Cleaners. Dan melted behind a delivery van. The men strode east, towards Grosvenor Square. Dan was about to step out, intending to follow them, when to his shock he heard someone say his name.

'Dan?'

The hairs on the back of his neck rose. He thought he recognised the voice.

'Dan Forrester!' the man called, sounding delighted. 'It *is* you!'

Just as Dan began to turn towards the voice, he saw the sandy-haired man and his colleague vanish around the corner, and then he came face to face with Joe Talbot.

'You're early,' Joe said. 'I wasn't expecting you and Grace until tomorrow.'

Dan wanted to follow the men but didn't want to alert Joe. They all worked in the same office. What was going on? Joe didn't seem to notice Dan's reticence. He was grinning from ear to ear.

'So, you couldn't wait until tomorrow to case the joint,' said Joe.

Not liking being read so easily, Dan didn't answer.

Joe nodded at the anonymous black door. 'Sorry it's all a bit cloak and dagger, but that's how we like it. Do you want to come inside? Or shall we hit the pub?' He looked at his watch. 'Definitely time for a drink. I'm gasping. It's been one hell of a week.'

Dan took the hint. 'A drink would be great,' he agreed.

'Come on, then.' Joe began walking east but soon switched south towards Shepherd's Market, and down a quaint, narrow street lined with intimate little restaurants and chic boutiques that to Dan felt oddly familiar.

'Did I work for DCA?' Dan asked.

'No.' Joe shook his head. 'It was only set up six years ago.'

'How long have you worked there?'

'Ohhh . . .' Joe pulled up his collar as he mulled this over. The wind was icy, blowing from the north and wet with sleet. 'It's coming up to four years now.'

'What is it you do?'

'I'm an analyst. I try to judge the political forecast for investors. Today I'd say don't invest in China. Tomorrow I might tell you to set up an engineering firm in Myanmar. Here, after you.' He opened the door to a village-style Victorian pub.

Dan never liked going through a door first and held back. ‘No, after you. Please.’

His gesture seemed to amuse Joe, but he led the way inside without any objection. ‘What would you like?’ he asked, winding his way to the bar. Dark painted walls and green glazed tiles. Stuffed birds on the walls, animal horns and porcelain figures. It was warm, noisy and crowded and smelled of old wood and spilled beer. Dan felt immediately at home and wondered if he’d been here before. ‘Your usual?’ called Joe.

‘Actually, a pint of some kind of winter ale would be good.’

The beer was excellent and although he liked the pub and the cheerful atmosphere, he couldn’t relax. He said, ‘Do Savannah and Ellis work with you?’

‘Not any more. Savannah’s in Brussels doing something for NATO and Ellis moved to work for Customs.’

‘Their phone numbers don’t work anymore,’ said Dan. ‘Neither does yours.’

Joe blinked. ‘You tried to call us?’

‘This morning.’

‘I know mine changed, but I didn’t realise the others’ had too.’ He shrugged, seeming to make little of it. ‘It’s been nearly four years since we were all in the same room together.’ He studied Dan. ‘It wasn’t a great reunion, was it?’

‘No,’ Dan admitted.

‘I’m sorry it didn’t go better.’

Encouraged by Joe’s easy companionship Dan said, ‘Me too.’

‘I think it was the shock of seeing you the same as normal – looking the same, sounding the same – but unable to interact with us.' He looked sad. 'We were all really good friends. We'd go on the piss together, spend nights at each other's places and cook one another greasy breakfasts in the morning, but you couldn't remember us, or any of our jokes.'

'Sorry.'

'No,' Joe sighed. 'We got it wrong, that's all. We shouldn't have bugged you into seeing us.'

'I'm pleased you did,' said Dan, unsure if he was telling the truth or not but glad to lie to an old friend, even if he couldn't remember him.

'So, tell me,' said Joe. 'Grace said Stella contacted you recently. What was that about?'

They both leaned back to let a young couple squeeze past, heading for the Thai restaurant upstairs.

Not wanting to give anything away, Dan merely said, 'We used to be friends.'

'Well, yes.' Joe looked baffled. 'But why didn't she mention it to me? I would have loved to have seen you again. I've missed you, you old bugger.'

'Sorry.' The word felt inadequate so he added, 'I guess I'd have missed you too, if I could remember you.'

Joe looked at him for a second, and then he burst out laughing. It was so genuine and spontaneous that Dan was caught in the moment, and suddenly he found the humour in what he'd said and began to laugh too. Joe punched his arm. 'God, it's good to see you.'

'I guess it's good to see you too,' said Dan. 'But I'm not sure how good because –'

'You can't remember me!' Joe began laughing so hard, he staggered slightly, almost spilling his beer which made him laugh even more. People glanced at them and smiled at two friends having a beer, having a laugh. Dan felt a stab of real sorrow that he couldn't remember Joe.

'Joe,' said Dan. 'Who else works at DCA? I thought I recognised someone earlier.'

Joe blinked. Slowly, he put down his empty glass. 'Like who?'

Dan described the sandy-haired man who had entered Stella's house, along with his colleague.

Joe was frowning. 'The fair-haired guy is Toby James but I don't know the other one. We have a lot of people coming and going, so I'm not surprised. Shall I ask Toby for you?'

'That would be great.' Dan drank some more beer. 'Another thing. I don't suppose a Denise Anne Gabriel works with you?'

Joe gave a sudden lurch, spilling his beer. He swung round. 'Hey,' he admonished someone behind him before returning to Dan. 'Sorry. You were saying?'

'Denise Gabriel. Do you know her?'

Joe pushed out his lower lip as he shook his head. 'No. Sorry.'

Dan drank his beer, wondering how to approach the next subject, and quickly decided a head-on approach would be best. 'Sorry to keep asking you questions,' he said. 'But I have another one . . .'

'God, don't worry about it.' Joe flapped a hand. 'Happy to help. Go ahead.'

'It's about my son, Luke.'

Immediately Joe's eyes became wary.

'I didn't ask you about him when we last met. I didn't think to, or maybe I didn't want to. But I want to talk about him now. I want to know how he died.'

'Christ, Dan.' Joe grimaced. 'You already know. Why torment yourself any further?'

Dan just looked at him.

'OK, OK.' Joe flung up his hands. 'He was hit by a van off Brick Lane. You went insane because you blamed yourself. There, does that make you feel any better?'

Dan considered what Stella had said to him. *Your identity, your past, is a lie.* Was Joe lying too?

'Tell me about my job in Immigration,' Dan said. 'What I did day to day. Who I worked with, who I spoke to.'

Joe groaned. 'If I'm going to bore us both to death, then it's your round.'

Dan bought them both another pint and drank while listening to an extensive inventory of what sounded like an incredibly tedious job of paperwork, form-filling and reference-checking. He'd had a secretary – a rarity nowadays – called Katy that he'd shared with Stella. He'd travelled to work by Tube and took his hour-long lunch break at one o'clock except he usually ate his sandwich at his desk to ensure a prompt departure by 6 p.m. He'd been promoted several times, and was up to head the department. Then Luke died and everything went pear-shaped.

'Did I do any fieldwork with Stella?' Dan asked.

'What?' Joe looked at him blankly.

'Did we do any work outside the office?'

'Not that I know of. You could have, though. It's not like we were in each other's pockets. Why, did she say something to you?'

Dan hesitated. He was struggling to gather any information from Joe that he didn't already know. Although he was reluctant to give anything away, he thought if he offered something it might prompt his supposed old friend into revealing a fresh tit-bit.

He turned his glass in his hands. 'Apparently she suspected an amnesia drug had been used on me.'

Joe looked stunned. 'You're kidding.'

Dan took a sip of beer. 'No.'

Joe's mouth opened and closed. 'Jesus Christ. I thought you lost your memory due to the shock of seeing your son die.'

'That's what everyone thought.'

'It's true? That a drug was used on you?'

Dan shrugged.

'Jesus,' Joe said again. 'Who the hell makes such a thing?'

PepsBeevers, thought Dan, but didn't say so. Instead, he offered Joe another drink.

Joe turned his wrist to look at his watch. 'Sod it. It's later than I thought. Buddy, I've got to go. Laura will go nuts if I don't pick up Noah on time.'

Laura. The name conjured up a vision of vintage velvet and gypsy earrings.

'She's still the Gypsy Queen?' Dan said. For some reason, the name popped into his head.

'Shit.' Joe stared. 'You remember my ex-wife?'

'Am I right?' Dan felt a surge of hope. Maybe talking to an old friend had worked some magic. Maybe his memory wasn't totally wrecked. 'Her name's the Gypsy Queen?'

'That's what you used to call her.' Joe pulled a face. 'Not me.'

'Say hi from me.'

They parted outside, but although Joe said he was looking forward to seeing him again the next day, eyes wide, his whole body expressing friendliness, Dan's spine tingled. He had the peculiar sensation that by mentioning Joe's ex-wife he'd made some sort of gaffe, and when Joe rang the next day saying that he was sorry, he couldn't see him and Grace after all – an urgent meeting had cropped up in Amsterdam – Dan was frustrated but not surprised.

CHAPTER THIRTY-FIVE

Thursday 29 November, 7.20 p.m.

Lucy sat in the hospital, holding Bella's hand as she told the girl about her call to Dr Grace Reavey. 'It's the thing I hate most about my job,' she admitted, 'telling people someone they know has died. Dr Reavey seemed really fond of Jamie. I'm seeing her on Monday as she might shed some light on why you were both taken.'

Lucy checked her watch, thinking it was probably time to head for the station, when Bella suddenly gripped her hand. Lucy gave a startled yelp of shock. She leapt to her feet, looked down at the girl.

'Bella?'

The girl's eyes were shut, her mouth slack.

Lucy shot into the corridor and grabbed the first nurse she came to.

'Bella just moved.' Lucy spoke fast. 'She grabbed my hand!'

She was glad the nurse didn't hang around but headed briskly for Bella's room where she checked her reflexes and pupil size.

'Is she going to wake up?' Lucy asked.

'Not yet I'm afraid.'

The nurse took a blood sample. 'Now, Bella, there's going to be a small prick in your arm . . .' When the needle pierced Bella's skin, the girl grunted. 'That's a good sign.' The nurse smiled. 'She felt that, and let me know it.'

'When will she be conscious?'

'It's a long, slow process I'm afraid. She had no motor response yesterday but today she felt the injection. When she's ready, then maybe she'll surface. It could be days yet but it's looking really positive.'

After the nurse had left, Lucy picked up Bella's chart and had a look. The continuing assessment record didn't look great to Lucy's eye, with an overall score of four out of fifteen today, but it was at least an improvement on yesterday's score of three. 'Attagirl,' she told Bella. 'You're up a point. Let's make it another point tomorrow, OK?'

When she stepped outside it was into icy, driving rain. Christ, it was cold. She dropped her overnight bag at her feet and snapped open her brolly. She'd packed haphazardly on her return from Merseyside, having been told she was accompanying Mac south later in the day, but her mind hadn't been on the job and she hoped she hadn't forgotten anything vital. As long as she had a spare pair of undies, her toothbrush and her computer and chargers, she should be OK. At the last moment, she'd tossed her Swiss Army Knife inside her handbag along with a packet of toffees. She didn't want to get caught without a corkscrew or a sugar hit when the going got tough.

She yawned and shivered. It had been a long, exhausting day helping to kick off an investigation to find a serial killer.

Thrilling and horrifying in equal measure. It could be the biggest case of her life but only because four people had been brutally murdered.

When Mac finally arrived Lucy flung her bag in the boot and jumped into the passenger seat, shoved her brolly by her feet.

'I thought I was supposed to be driving,' she said.

'We'll swap after we've filled up.' Mac increased the wiper speed a notch. Traffic was heavy, the lights from oncoming cars shimmering in the wet. Lucy closed her eyes briefly against the glare.

'You can sleep if you want,' said Mac. 'It's been a long day.'

Her eyes snapped open. 'I'm not tired.'

He winced again. 'Christ, Lucy. You don't have to bite my head off.'

She turned her head away. She hadn't meant to be harsh. Did her continual battle to conform mean she might be bipolar? She'd looked up bipolar on the Internet but aside from the sleeplessness and bouts of wild energy (and the odd couple of days when she struggled to get out of bed, but never more than once or twice a year) she had absolutely nothing in common with any of the people diagnosed with the disorder. She wasn't crazy. She didn't cut herself, twitch, rant (well, only occasionally, but didn't everyone?), abuse drugs or alcohol (again, occasionally, but didn't everyone?), suffer from suicidal thoughts, poor concentration, poor judgement, or have difficulty making decisions. If she did, she'd have been thrown out of the force a long time ago. You couldn't have a PC failing in those particular areas, surely. She was, she decided, pretty normal aside from her insomnia and somewhat volatile temper.

'Sorry,' she muttered.

He shot her a look. 'Will you bite my head off again if I ask why you never took any of my calls?'

She groaned inside. They were back to that old chestnut. 'Please,' she said. 'Just leave it, would you?'

'God help me, I wish I could,' he sighed. 'But I can't.'

Feeling cornered, she turned aggressive. 'Why not? It was just sex for Chrissakes.'

He looked at her again. 'Are you sure about that?'

'Look. I was horny. You were there, OK? Get over it.'

'We spent five days buddied-up on that course. We got to know each other, trust each other, before we . . . er –'

'Fucked,' she supplied helpfully.

He frowned. 'So tell me, our walks along the beach were . . . what?'

Hot sun scorching her salt-encrusted shoulders, sand beneath her feet, between her toes, wet hair from her swim and his skin is as cold as marble from the sea and his arm is around her waist and hers is around his, she comes up to his chest and fits neatly against him like a jigsaw piece slotting into place – very odd, never thought of that before – and they're walking side by side and she looks at his feet and is amazed. He has lovely feet. She's never met a man who hasn't got ugly feet.

'A nice way to get some fresh air,' she said, keeping her gaze firmly ahead. She couldn't look at him with those memories crowding her mind.

'Fresh air?' He sounded incredulous. 'We made love like we were the last people on earth, Lucy, in case you forgot. We spent every minute together. For almost a week you were mine, with me one hundred per cent, and the next minute you'd gone. Vanished. Kaput.'

She remembered going home that night. Nate wanting to kiss her. She hadn't been able to bear him touching her – she'd found it hard not to recoil – and when he'd wanted to make love the next morning a scream had been in the back of her mind *no no no*. But she hadn't stopped him – she'd never stopped him, she'd had no reason to – and afterwards she'd shut herself in the bathroom and cried.

Mac said quietly, 'I thought we had something really good between us.'

She decided not to talk any more. It only seemed to encourage him.

'Why won't you admit it, Lucy?'

Because you're my DI. Because I don't want to lose my colleagues' respect. Because I don't want to risk getting transferred again. It won't be you who gets moved should our relationship go tits up, it'll be me, and next time I might end up even further from London, like the Shetland Isles.

She gazed through the windscreen. The traffic had eased slightly since they'd joined the M1 south, ribbons of cars heading home at the end of the day. She reached forward and switched on the radio. Turned up the volume. Out of the corner of her eye, she saw Mac heave an exaggerated sigh. God alone knew what the next few days were going to be like working closely with him, but she knew she mustn't let down her guard. She mustn't drink any alcohol when he was around, and above all, she had to maintain her distance and NOT LOOK AT HIS MOUTH.

When they arrived at their hotel – a bland and characterless block reserved by the Basingstoke Police – Lucy's eyes were burning from three hours of night driving and attempting to keep her mental distance from Mac. She couldn't stop yawning. As Mac checked them in, she stood a good yard from him and the instant she was given her key card she walked off with a muttered 'see ya'.

Since she hadn't slept the previous night, Lucy thought she'd better give the bed a go. Stripping off, she curled in the middle, pulled the duvet up over her ears and closed her eyes. She felt tired enough to sleep through the night, but she was jerked awake after four hours. She wasn't sure what had woken her but she was sweating, trembling slightly, the tendrils of her dream still gripping her.

Wembley Stadium.

The massive crowd, eerily silent.

The dread inside her building inexorably, until she couldn't control herself and she had to flee for her life.

She sat on the edge of the bed and ran a hand over her head, scrubbed her face. Weird, how that experience had stayed with her.

Walking into the bathroom, she switched on the shower and stepped beneath the jets of hot water, wishing she could soap away the memory. Anything to dispel the sickening sensation of fear that remained.

She'd read somewhere that the unconscious mind introduced people to one's dreams because of how they made you feel. So when she dreamed of her mother, which she did from time to time, her unconscious could have created her to generate a feeling of being loved and secure. Quite what the concert dream meant – aside from fear – Lucy couldn't think, but she wished it would go away. She didn't like being reminded that she'd suffered some kind of breakdown and it invariably made her start her day feeling vulnerable and oddly shaky.

Breakfast wasn't until seven so she made herself a cup of tea and soon she was hunched over her laptop, her brain on fire.

The handcuffs were the clue, she was certain.

Why else leave them on the bodies?

He'd chosen handcuffs because they wouldn't rot or get lost. They were a permanent sign, remaining even when the bodies decomposed; something impossible to remove from the skeletons without a key.

He wants them noticed.

Why?

She picked up her mobile, dithering. Could she claim a phone call to India? She checked the time to see it was 8.30 in the morning in Chennai. Before she could talk herself out of it, she dialled.

'Namaste,' a boy's brisk voice answered.

'Chitta?' she said.

'Madam Constable Lucy!' Chitta's cheerful voice greeted her.

She liked Chitta enormously, and he'd proved himself to be exceptional in his investigative work, but she couldn't get around the fact he was the office cleaner. Why wasn't Niket answering his phone?

'Hi Chitta,' she responded. 'Look, I don't want to insult you because you've done a fantastic job, but I was wondering if I could speak to Niket.'

'I am sorry,' he said regretfully, 'but this is not being possible.'

'Could you tell me why?'

'It is a simple matter,' he told her. 'Senior Constable Niket is being suspended.'

Something prickled at the back of her neck. 'Why?'

Silence.

Was Niket involved somehow? Was that why he'd been so reluctant to help her?

'Chitta?' she prompted.

He gave a groan. 'I cannot be telling you this, much as I would like to be imparting what I know, because Inspector Chakyar will be tearing my head off and kicking it down the street for the dogs to eat if I breathe even a word . . .'

'OK, OK.' She got the message. 'Can I talk to the Inspector maybe?'

Another groan. 'I cannot be interrupting him, Constable Lucy. He has told me I must not be intruding upon him unless it is a matter of life and death and if it is not, I must to be taking him a message and giving it to him quietly, and without speaking.'

Lucy nibbled her lip. 'Maybe you can talk to me about the case?'

'Of course.' He sounded pleased. 'How can I be helping you?'

'Have you found out who dumped the bodies?'

'Oh, yes. The truck driver is doing this. The first time he is finding a body in his container, he is speaking to the charity but they are not wanting to be reporting this thing so they are paying the driver to dispose of it. This is what is happening each time, you see.'

He gave her the names of the driver and the charity personnel who had admitted to covering up the bodies' disposal. According to Chitta, they'd been terrified not just of the chaos that would ensue but in case they were accused of the victims' murders.

'Why do you think the victims were wearing handcuffs?' she asked him.

'I am thinking of this nearly all of the time,' Chitta admitted. 'But I cannot be finding any solution to this matter. Perhaps it is like a . . . how do you say it? A calling card?'

Lucy rubbed her eyes with her fingers. 'You could be right. But why handcuffs?'

Chitta dropped his voice to a whisper. 'Perhaps the killer is being a police officer.'

Please God, no.

'Perhaps,' she told the boy, 'he is using them as a decoy.'

'Perhaps,' he agreed, but he sounded doubtful.

They talked a little more, but it soon appeared there was little more she could learn. After a protracted farewell, she hung up.

Cross-legged on her bed, back against the wall, she studied Jamie's photograph. Young, energetic, not bad-looking. Dreadlocks, tattoos. Something was vaguely familiar about him but she couldn't think what. His hoodie, maybe. She saw enough of those in her job.

Mac met her at the hotel reception and drove them to Jamie's, which was a cutesy cottage with a vegetable patch and roses around the front door. Inside it wasn't tidy, but it wasn't a complete disaster. No dirt or grime, just a comfortable sort of messiness that Lucy rather liked; wellies toppled over in the porch, socks and gardener's gloves jumbled with handfuls of junk mail on the hall table, old TV guides stacked in corners and every windowsill covered with a general detritus of used envelopes, seed packets, Sellotape and screwdrivers.

Jamie's girlfriend sat on a saggy, homely sofa alongside her mother. Gemma was pale, her face blotchy from crying. She wore Ugg boots beneath a suede skirt and flowery top. Lots of bangles and earrings. A silver nose ring. Long brown hair. The poor girl looked as though she hadn't stopped crying since she'd heard the news.

'Please, have a seat,' her mother told them. 'I'll get us some tea. OK, Gemma?'

Gemma gave a nod.

Lucy settled herself on a tattered and squashy leather footstool opposite Gemma while Mac took an armchair next to the fireplace. Leaning forward a little, resting his hands on his knees, he said, 'I'm sorry, Gemma, but we're going to have to ask you some questions.' He reiterated the fact that Jamie and Bella could have been killed by the same person, which is why they were there, but Gemma didn't say anything or ask any questions.

'When did you last see Jamie?'

The girl stuffed her knuckles against her mouth. Tears fell. 'S-sorry,' she managed.

'That's OK,' Lucy assured her. 'Take your time.'

Gemma struggled to regain control. Her mother came in with a tray of mugs and a plate of chocolate Hobnob biscuits which normally Lucy loved, but she'd lost her appetite the second she stepped into this room steeped in sorrow and pain. Mac obviously didn't feel like eating either – they both stuck to tea.

'A-at the pub,' Gemma said. 'Last Thursday.'

'What time did you leave the pub?' Mac asked gently.

'J-just after nine.'

He nodded. They already knew the answers to these questions but they'd agreed to start with the easy ones. 'Who else was in the pub with you?'

Mac led Gemma through the evening but they didn't learn anything new. Jamie had left the pub after Gemma, around ten o'clock, but he never came home. Eventually Lucy shifted forward slightly, glancing at Mac to confirm it was OK for her to ask a question. He gave her a small nod.

'Was there anything that had bothered him more than usual recently?' Lucy asked. 'Especially during the days leading up to his disappearance?'

Gemma frowned, taking her time answering. 'The only thing was that he started getting headaches. Otherwise, I can't think of anything.'

Since headaches could be related to stress, Lucy asked, 'When did his headaches start?'

'Oh, a few weeks back, but they had got better recently.'

Lucy said, 'Can you think of anything that might have triggered them? A particular event that might have made him feel stressed?'

Gemma shook her head. 'No. Sorry.'

Not like Lucy's headaches, which had started almost the day Baz had fired her. She was obviously less stressed now since they'd virtually vanished over the last few days.

Mac took over, asking whether Gemma had heard of RFC or had any contact with Weald Logistics or the shipping industry, but they had no luck. Finally, Mac stood up. He asked, 'Would you mind if we had a look around the cottage, checked Jamie's things?'

Gemma scrunched her tissue between her fingers and shook her head. Mac said to Lucy, 'I'll check upstairs if you do down here.'

Lucy left Gemma and her mother in the sitting room and walked into the kitchen. Pale winter sunshine filtered through the windows and lit up more junk mail and various items that hadn't been put away. The washing up was done, the tea towels hung over the oven door handle. A computer sat on the kitchen table. Lucy grinned. Mac had taken upstairs because he'd guessed that's where Jamie would have kept his computer but he'd guessed wrong.

She checked the cupboards which were surprisingly neat inside. Lots of cereal packets and cans of baked beans. Rice and pasta. Some miso soup and tofu, *yuck*.

Quietly, Lucy picked up the phone and dialled 1471. Made a note of the last number called in her notebook. She searched the kitchen drawers, again finding nothing out of place until she came across what she considered the junk drawer, which was a clutter of receipts, shopping lists and old phone messages scribbled on an assortment of pieces of paper. She pocketed all the phone numbers to check later, pausing at a note written on a lined piece of paper, torn from an A5 pad.

Talk to Dr Grace about this?

Dr Grace Reavey, Lucy assumed. The woman who'd asked to be contacted should any information surface about Jamie's disappearance. Lucy turned the piece of paper over to see a list of names scribbled messily on the other side.

Justin Millebar-Cole

Alan Densley

Mary Perkins

Me

The 'Me' she took to mean Jamie but then all thought stopped as she read the fifth name.

Bella Frances

Her mind was still trying to absorb the words as she read the next name.

Tim Atherton

But it was the last name on the list that made her heart stop.

PC Lucy Davies.

CHAPTER THIRTY-SIX

Friday 30 November, 9.20 a.m.

Lucy still had the list in her hand when Mac came into the kitchen.

'What is it?' he asked.

She looked at him, feeling numb with shock.

'Nothing,' she said. She stuck her hand with the list behind her back.

He stared at her.

She stood there for barely ten seconds, but it could have been an hour.

Her brain was burning.

What was her name doing on a list containing two people who'd been brutally assaulted? The only link she could think of was between herself and Bella – the Zidazapine. But Lucy wasn't bipolar. Was she? Was that the link? If it was, how could she stop it coming out, becoming public knowledge? She couldn't. She would have to leave the police.

Her thoughts whistled past like the wind. Dark blue, blue, flashes of silver, blue, blue, blue. The colours of her uniform.

If she pocketed the list and went off-grid, investigated on her own and the drug wasn't the link and the killer tracked her down – murdered her ... *not a great result.* And if the police found out she'd withheld a potential lead, she could be fired. *Not great either.*

However, if she shared the list there was every chance they'd find the killer and even though she may lose her job, she'd still be alive.

Her thoughts focused on a pinpoint.

Alive, or dead?

'Lucy?' Mac's eyes went to her hand still behind her back, then returned to her. 'What is it?' he repeated.

Alive or dead alive or dead alive or dead?

She pictured her mother at her funeral (black suit borrowed from her friend Jodie whose father had died recently, big fake pearl earrings, black court shoes), her father, freshly flown in from Australia (short-sleeved shirt, weird tan-coloured trousers), her friends (lots of deep black along with a lot of bling) and her work colleagues. She could see Baz shaking his head at her stupidity.

Even though she'd decided to share the information and hopefully find the killer before he found her, it still took an immense amount of willpower to answer Mac. She had to work her mouth before speaking. 'I found this.' She brought out the list. Her voice was hoarse. 'In there.' She gestured at the junk drawer. Delicately she held up the list, between her forefinger and thumb. It would have to be bagged and checked for fingerprints.

Mac bent forward and read it.

'You're kidding,' he said. His eyes flew to hers. 'What the hell's your name doing there?'

'I have no idea.'

Her first lie.

He brought an evidence bag from his pocket. Carefully, she dropped the piece of paper inside and watched him seal it. His expression was dark as he looked at her. He said, 'Are you OK?'

No, she thought, but she gave a nod. 'We should get . . .' Her throat rasped, forcing her to clear it. She tried again. 'We should get these names checked against the bodies from India.'

'Yes,' he said. He peered at the list through the transparent plastic. 'Do you know any of these people?'

'Just Bella and Jamie. And Dr Grace Reavey, whose name is on the other side. And only because of the case.' She gestured at the baggie. 'May I?'

He passed it over. She took it next door and showed it to Gemma and her mum. 'Whose handwriting is this?'

'Jamie's,' Gemma said.

It was the first time she'd seen the list, Gemma added. She didn't know anyone on it. Yes, she'd heard of Bella Frances because of the TV and radio appeals but she'd never met her and, as far as she knew, neither had Jamie. Gemma assumed – like Lucy and Mac – that the 'me' on the list was Jamie. The childlike loops were definitely his writing. The list had been relatively near the top of the junk drawer, meaning it had been written fairly recently.

Lucy returned to the kitchen and handed the bagged list back to Mac. 'Christ.' He ran a hand down his face. 'I don't suppose there's another PC Lucy Davies in the UK, is there?'

'I'll check.' But as she brought out her phone Mac held up a hand.

He said, 'I'll do it.'

She listened as he spoke to his deputy DS back in Stockton, and asked her to call him as soon as she had the information. After he'd hung up, they stood silently in the kitchen for a moment. Then Mac said, 'We're going to have to take this place apart.'

It didn't take long before Mac let the CSI team loose on the cottage. It was going to be a tortuous job bagging and labelling every piece of paper, every list and receipt, but Lucy didn't hesitate to get stuck in with the team. Common sense told her she couldn't be the only PC Lucy Davies in the UK since her name was fairly common, but when Mac told her the only other Lucy Davies in the police force was a DI in Northern Ireland, who spelled her name Davis, Lucy still felt a small piece of hope inside her shatter.

'Sorry,' Mac said.

Lucy rang Dr Grace Reavey. She wanted to know if the GP had anything to do with the list of names or whether Jamie's note about her could be dismissed.

'Hello?' Dr Reavey sounded hesitant, almost nervous.

'Hi. It's PC Davies here. About Jamie Hudson?'

'Oh, yes.' The woman exhaled as though relieved. 'I'm seeing you on Monday.'

'Things have changed.' Lucy was curt. 'I need to see you today.'

'I'm sorry, but that's not possible.'

'It can't wait.' Aware that phones could be hacked and that most electronic equipment was less than secure, Lucy didn't want to say any more.

'I'm not his GP,' Grace Reavey snapped. 'How many times do I have to say it to you people? You need to see Dr Smith.'

Lucy's instincts quivered at the doctor's switch in mood. Her mother had recently died which meant she was probably under immense stress, but even so. Was there something else going on here? Something to do with Jamie?

'I'll do that,' Lucy said. 'But I still need to see you.'

She heard the woman murmur something that sounded like *God, give me strength*, but wearily, as though Lucy's request was the final straw.

'I can come to Tring,' said Lucy, forcing the issue.

'No.' The word was bitten out. 'I'll see you at the surgery tomorrow morning. Eight o'clock.'

Lucy was opening her mouth to say she would have preferred to see her sooner but Dr Reavey hung up.

Towards the end of the day, freezing fog descended. Lucy stood outside watching the team disperse, her breath steaming and forming great clouds in front of her face. Mac came to stand beside her. He said, 'The coroner has confirmed the IDs of the bodies repatriated from India. He used dental records, so there's no doubt. All three victims were British. All were reported missing.'

She latched on to the words *dental records*.

'They still had their teeth?'

'Two victims had their top row of teeth pulled out. The other had their bottom teeth removed.'

She wasn't sure what to think about that right now and filed it for later.

Mac added, 'All three vanished in the third week of October.'

The same week she'd started at Stockton Police.

She looked into his face, his sombre expression. 'Oh, God.' Her knees suddenly felt weak.

His voice was steady as he spoke. 'They are: Justin Millebar-Cole, Alan Densley and Mary Perkins.'

The first three names on the list.

'Fuck,' she said.

She felt oddly shivery and strange. Her mind was filled with purple and red. *What the hell was going on?*

'I'm not sure if you can stay on the investigation,' Mac said.

The colours in her mind were abruptly drowned in tidal waves of sheer white. The shivery sensation abruptly vanished. Her mind cleared. She swung round to face him, her fists balled at her sides.

'Wait, wait.' His hands shot into the air as though she'd pointed a gun at him. 'Don't overreact, I'm just thinking –'

'Don't think,' she snapped. 'OK? You need me on this. There's a reason I'm on the list, we just have to find what it is, and then we'll find the killer and . . . ' She halted abruptly. She said, 'Tim Atherton. He's the only person on the list we don't know about. Where is he?'

'There are over two hundred Tim Athertons in the UK,' Mac said. 'We've already begun tracing each one. We have to find the right guy before the killer does.' He ran a hand over his face. 'I'm going to head back to base later tonight.'

'Can I stay?' Lucy asked. 'Just for a day or so. I have some ideas I want to follow up.'

'Keep the local SIO informed,' he told her. 'And try not to go anywhere alone, OK?'

She nodded.

'Before I go, however . . .' His voice was grave.

Alarm speared her. 'What?'

'I need to question you.'

For a moment her brain stalled, unable to think what he meant, but then she remembered she was on the same list as Bella and four murder victims. She was the only person on the list that wasn't dead, comatose or unknown.

'You might be able to give us the link,' he said.

They used one of the interview rooms in the Basingstoke Police Station. Whitewashed walls, no window, a single Formica table and three plastic chairs bolted to the floor. A camera was set high in one corner. With a feeling of disbelief, she watched Mac pull out his notebook and a pen. *She shouldn't be here.*

Mac looked at her. 'You OK?'

'Sure,' she lied.

He looked at her.

She swallowed. 'I'll be fine once we get started. It's just a bit . . . weird. That's all.'

He looked at her a moment longer, then said, 'There's a pub opposite. Shall we do this over a drink? They can come and grab us if they need to.'

She'd promised not to mix Mac and alcohol, but since it wasn't every day she found herself on a list of murder victims, she said, 'Good idea.'

On their way out, they ducked into the major incident room to tell the SIO where they were going. The place was bustling, everyone running at full tilt with a serial killer having struck in their jurisdiction. The frenetic atmosphere lifted Lucy's spirits and by the time she was settled in one of the corners of the White Hart Inn, a pint of Doom Bar for Mac and half a pint of Thatcher's cider for her, she thought she was ready. However, when Mac started to take her through her recent and somewhat stormy history, she realised she'd made a mistake.

'So it was Magellan who fired you,' he said. 'For making him look stupid.'

'Unofficially,' she confirmed. 'But it was Baz who did his dirty work.'

'Anyone else who resents you?'

She sighed. 'Sergeant Paul Logan.'

'Why?' Mac asked.

'I made him look a little stupid too.'

Mac raised his eyebrows enquiringly.

She said, 'I was called to a shoplifting incident at a department store. When I walked into the back room where the shoplifter was being held, I came face to face with Paul. He was in civvies, and for a moment I was confused . . . but then I realised he was the shoplifter.'

Silence.

'I take it you didn't drop the charges,' Mac said.

'I couldn't.'

Mac waited.

She said, 'If he'd lashed out at someone, say, lost his temper for a good reason, I might have turned a blind eye. But shoplifting is dishonest. He made a *choice* to steal.'

Mac took a sip of beer. 'Anyone else?'

She raised her eyes to the ceiling. 'Commander Duckham.'

'Yes?'

'One night, we arrested two boys stealing a car. Me and another officer. One of the boys was the son of the Commander. I went to the Commander's house and woke him up to tell him what had happened. He thought I was telling him I'd let his son off, but I wasn't. I was telling him his son was in the lock-up and that he'd better get his arse down there.'

'Oh, dear,' said Mac. 'Any more?'

She twisted her hands in her lap. 'I upset Karen Milton.'

'What happened?'

'I told her that her baby reminded me of a Shar Pei dog.'

'Not one of those hideously wrinkly ones?'

'I thought I was being nice,' she said glumly. 'I mean Shar Peis are cute, aren't they?'

He gave a choked snort.

Lucy didn't think it was particularly funny. She'd liked Karen, wouldn't have minded having her as a friend, but Karen didn't like her much. *Too abrasive*, she'd told Baz.

Mac turned serious. He said, 'I hate to say this, but we have to put your life under the microscope and this involves looking at your Met colleagues.'

'Yes.' Her stomach hollowed but she knew it had to be done. God alone knew what they'd say about her when they learned she was on a killer's hit list.

CHAPTER THIRTY-SEVEN

Friday 30 November, 6.30 p.m.

Grace put her mother's computer and cash, spare passports and driving licence in a small leather holdall she'd found in the cupboard under the stairs and placed it with her bag in the hall. She'd tidied the house as much as she could after Dan had left yesterday, but it still looked as though a tornado had blown through. Her mother had been so *neat*. She'd hate what Grace had done to her house, but perhaps if her mother had been honest with her in the first place she wouldn't have had to tear the place apart.

She paused for a moment, aware she was already beginning to look back on her life before her mother died as a time of blissful innocence. Or was it ignorance? Everything was skewed, making her feel as though she was looking at life through a prism. Grace picked up the holdall. She should have been in London this morning to see Joe with Dan, but Joe had cancelled last night, saying he had an urgent meeting he had to go to in Amsterdam but could they make it Monday? She'd tried to persuade Joe he didn't have to be there but when he made it clear her visit would be awkward without him, if not impossible, she found herself almost begging to see her mother's office over the weekend. *I have a deadline!* she wanted to scream, and some of her fear and frustration must have transferred itself to Joe because finally he'd relented, agreeing to see her the next day. She texted Dan to let him know.

At least she'd managed to put off that policewoman from coming to Tring. She was dreading meeting her and . . .

Her thoughts abruptly jammed as the pay-as-you-go mobile on the hall table started to ring. The phone Sirius Thiele had left with her. Her heart began pounding so hard that her chest hurt. She put down the holdall and carefully picked up the phone. 'Hello?'

'Hello, Grace.'

His voice was conversational, as though he was a friend ringing for a chat.

Her hands began to sweat.

'Have you found the money yet?' he asked.

'I've . . .' Her voice quavered. She cleared her throat and tried to steady herself. 'I've found some. But I –'

'How much?'

'Fifty-five thousand pounds.' She hastily rounded it upwards in the hope that it would be adequate.

'It's a start, I suppose, but certainly nowhere near enough.'

'Please, I'm doing my best to –'

'Hold on. I have someone who wants to say hello.'

Brief silence.

'Hello?' It was Martin. He sounded exhausted.

Her head went completely light.

'Martin?' she said. 'I thought you were in Norway.'

'That's what I've told people,' he said.

'Has he kidnapped you?' Her voice was high.

'No, he hasn't,' Martin said wearily. 'Look, Grace. Just get his money, would you? Then he'll go away. Get out of our lives.'

'How did he find out about Simon?' she suddenly demanded with a spurt of fury. '*How*?'

'He heard we'd fallen out. He wanted to know why. I would never have told him except he threatened to –'

Martin's words were snatched away. Sirius Thiele returned to the line.

'When will you have the money?'

'Please,' she said. 'I swear I don't know –'

'Those are five words my client does not want to hear.'

'Please, I –'

'My client isn't known for his patience, but . . .'

Silence. Her heart continued to pound.

'I'll try and persuade him to stretch things until Monday. Meantime, make sure our arrangement remains confidential.'

Click.

He'd gone.

She hung up and stood shaking, gazing at the burglar alarm panel but without seeing it. She had a reprieve. She had the weekend in which to make this mess go away. Could she do it? Keep the truth hidden? Carry on with her life as before? She couldn't lose her job, she realised. It was part of her nature, her spirit, her whole being. And what about Ross? She had to keep him out of this at all cost. She couldn't have him harmed. She loved him deeply, irrevocably. If he moved to Scotland, she would too. If he wanted to move to Bolivia, she would join him. A happy lightness entered her soul for a moment. She was meant to be with him, and he with her. They were good together, really good, and they would make Scotland work. All she had to do was find her mother's sodding money, and get Sirius Thiele out of her life, forever.

When she arrived home, it felt as though she'd been away for three weeks, not three days. A small clutter of mail sat inside the front door, including two DHL notices. *We tried to deliver a package . . . We tried to re-deliver your package . . .* She shoved both notices inside her handbag for when she was next in Basingstoke. She wasn't expecting anything in particular, and since the last parcel she'd collected from DHL turned out to be nothing but a set of low-energy bulbs she'd bought off the Internet, she didn't consider it a priority.

She put her mother's computer on the kitchen table, and then made herself a cup of tea and drank it while she considered where to hide the contents of the holdall. By the time she'd finished the tea, she knew there was no hidey-hole in the house that someone like Dan couldn't find. So she decided on an age-old fallback.

Bury it.

But first she needed bin bags. Air-tight freezer bags to keep everything from the elements. Air-tight food containers. A spade. Simple.

Fortunately, her cottage backed on to a small coppice of beech trees, so finding somewhere private wasn't a problem. Nor was it overlooked. But digging a hole took more of an effort than she'd expected. Despite the soft, mulchy ground it was almost dark by the time she finished and she was sweating heavily. She raked over some twigs and leaves and stood back. She'd check in the morning, but she reckoned it would be hard to tell there was something buried there.

Inside, she saw she'd missed a call from Dan. She rang him back.

He said, 'Thanks for the text.'

'Can you make it tomorrow?'

'Hopefully, yes. But if not, I want you to keep your eyes out for one of the guys who entered your mother's home while you were at her funeral.'

Grace blinked. 'You think someone from her work broke in?'

'Someone connected, yes. I saw him leaving DCA yesterday.' He went on to vividly describe a man with sandy hair and pale eyes. A mole on his right cheekbone, another on his chin. Narrow, slightly skewed nose. Small earlobes. By the time Dan finished his description she felt as though she could paint a picture of the man.

'What if I see him?' she asked.

'Text me, ring me, get me there at all costs. I want to know what he does, where he goes. I'm convinced he's the link that will explain what's going on. Why Stella had those passports and money. Why she contacted me in the first place.'

Pretty important, then.

Then he said, 'Anything new?'

She wasn't sure why, but she told him about PC Lucy Davies wanting to see her urgently about Jamie's death. 'I think something really bad happened to him but she won't say anything over the phone.'

'If I can help, let me know.'

'Thanks.'

Grace slept fitfully that night, disturbed by dreams of Sirius and her mother, and when she checked her appearance in the mirror she wasn't surprised to see a pale reflection of her usual self with drawn skin and bloodshot eyes. Before she went to the surgery, she checked the site where she'd buried her mother's things. In daylight, the ground definitely looked as though it had been disturbed. Grace raked a few more leaves over the ground, along with some twigs and a moss-laden branch. There, now it was perfect. Nobody would suspect a thing.

At 7 a.m. she was the first one into work so she disabled the alarm and switched on the coffee machine. Booted up her computer. She'd asked their receptionist to deal with anything that needed attention while she was away, or forward it to one of the partners, so there wasn't much outstanding. A chickenpox outbreak at one of the schools. A statutory sick note to attend to. She found comfort immersing herself in everyday, ordinary things and when the front door bell rang, she jumped.

Eight o'clock.

Grace opened the front door to a lithe, energetic-looking young woman in jeans and boots and a leather jacket lined with sheepskin.

'Dr Reavey?' she said. She showed Grace her warrant card. 'I'm Lucy Davies.'

'Grace.'

They shook. Lucy's grip was much stronger than Grace's and made her feel oddly weak and insubstantial. She gestured Lucy inside.

'I'm sorry about your mother,' said Lucy, following Grace down the hall. 'It's tough when a parent dies.'

Something in her tone made Grace turn. 'You lost someone?'

'Sort of.' The policewoman gave a wry smile. 'My dad ran away when I was ten. It was like he died. Mum never remarried.'

'My father died when I was a baby,' Grace admitted. 'My mother didn't remarry either.'

Both women appraised one another.

'I guess we're living proof that you don't necessarily need a father to do OK,' Lucy said. She gave Grace a quick smile.

'I guess so,' Grace agreed. She smiled back.

In her office, she offered Lucy coffee but the policewoman declined, settling herself straight away on the chair next to Grace's desk. She was focused and intent, making it obvious that she didn't want to be deflected.

Feeling oddly nervous, Grace sat down. 'How can I help?'

'I need you to tell me about Jamie. As much as you can, no matter how small the detail. Anything could be important.' She took a breath. 'I'm sorry to have to tell you that he was murdered in a particularly brutal way. We want to find his killer.'

Dear God. Poor Jamie.

She looked at Lucy. Lively, deep brown eyes met hers. Lucy said, 'How about I start with some questions, OK?'

'Sure.'

They covered Jamie's family and relationships before turning to his medical history. Standard stuff, Grace guessed.

'Was he on any medication?' Lucy asked. She was looking at her notebook, appearing to be ticking off a set list of questions.

Grace brought up Jamie's file. She'd had a quick look earlier and now she felt the same small shock beneath her breastbone. She may be a GP but she'd had no clue about Jamie's medical history. She'd simply seen him as a vibrant young man, not bipolar, proving how things could work really well for patients if they sought help at the right time and took the right advice.

'Jamie was taking a drug called Zidazapine.'

'He *what?*'

If Grace had stabbed the policewoman with an electric cattle prod she couldn't have had a more startled response.

'Jamie was bipolar,' Grace said. 'Severe mood swings.'

The policewoman was still staring at her. 'You're kidding,' she said.

'No.' She checked the notes again. 'He's actually bipolar 1 and is, apparently, pretty much symptom-free. But he still needed medication.'

The policewoman's gaze turned distant. Eventually she said, 'Why wasn't this mentioned on Jamie's missing person's report?' Her tone was calm but there was an underlying tension that made Grace anxious.

'I don't know,' Grace replied, her tone indicating she shouldn't have to know either. 'But it might be an idea to talk to the officer who spoke to me when Jamie went missing. Is his name on the report?'

Lucy's attention narrowed. 'Why?'

'He was in a hurry. He wanted to know if Jamie was vulnerable or not, and although I said he probably *wasn't* vulnerable, I'm not sure if he really took on board my insistence that he speak to Dr Smith, let alone get another doctor to check his file . . .'

'Are you suggesting this officer didn't do his job properly?'

Grace swallowed. 'All I'm saying is that he was in a hurry. He didn't seem particularly worried about Jamie either. He told me he'd probably return home by the weekend.'

Lucy squeezed her eyes shut briefly. She gritted her teeth and Grace sensed she was battling an urge to scream.

Wanting to help, Grace added, 'But I wouldn't say that being bipolar made Jamie particularly vulnerable. Especially if he was taking that particular drug. He'd still be low risk.'

'That's not the point,' said Lucy. Her tone was strangled. 'We should have known this right from the start. Why didn't *you* know?' Lucy was accusing. 'You're a GP. You say you knew Jamie.'

'Not as a patient,' Grace reminded her. 'There was no reason for Dr Smith to tell me Jamie's medical condition, just as if you were my patient I wouldn't tell Dr Smith that you were suffering from, say, diabetes. We don't discuss individual cases unless it's necessary, for example, if there's another partner in the practice who may have a special interest in a particular field, or we feel we need help with a particular patient.'

Her explanation didn't seem to appease Lucy who appeared to be struggling to keep her temper. Several seconds ticked past before the policewoman took a breath and exhaled, obviously trying to calm herself. 'How do you diagnose bipolar disorder?' she asked.

Grace glanced outside to see a lone blackbird perched on a branch, its plumage puffed against the cold. 'There's no definitive medical test, which makes an immediate diagnosis problematic. There are several conditions – both physical and psychiatric – which can present symptoms that can be confused with those relating to bipolar disorder.'

'It's easy to misdiagnose?' For some reason Lucy seemed to brighten.

'It's a complicated issue,' Grace said carefully.

'How did Dr Smith diagnose Jamie?'

Grace read through the notes. 'After a period of depression, followed by a manic phase, Dr Smith sent him to a psychiatrist to review Jamie's history and his mood swings, among other things.'

'What things?'

Grace spread her hands. 'Personality changes and lifestyle habits. Detailed questions would have been asked about reasoning, memory, his ability to express himself and maintain relationships. Mood swings from day to day or moment to moment don't necessarily indicate bipolar.'

Lucy's attention sharpened. 'What do you mean?'

'OK. Let's say Jamie had hypomanic episodes when he was exceptionally energetic and animated, needed only three hours' sleep instead of his usual eight, spent more money than he safely should and spoke faster than usual. This behaviour was noticeably different from his own *stable* mood, yet there are energetic, animated people who need little sleep, spend a lot and talk fast who don't have bipolar disorder. Which is why Jamie needed to be fully assessed using specific criteria.'

'Such as?' The policewoman was leaning forward, expression intent.

Grace checked the screen. 'Jamie filled out a mood questionnaire to help guide the psychiatrist's clinical interview when he assessed Jamie's mood symptoms. Changes in sleep, energy, thinking, speech and behaviour were monitored closely. In addition, blood and urine tests helped to rule out other causes of symptoms.'

Lucy stared at her. 'Would a GP be able to diagnose someone bipolar without all these checks?'

'I wouldn't recommend it.'

'Christ.' The word was muttered. Then Lucy said, 'Sorry,' but she didn't look sorry. Her cheeks were flushed, her eyes glittering. She was, Grace realised with a stab of alarm, furious.

'I know some people think we're becoming a prescription culture,' Grace said, wanting to alleviate Lucy's mood. 'I also know some GPs view such drugs as harmless and prescribe them far too easily, but in Jamie's case the Zidazapine suited him really well. His appears to be a classic example of successful diagnosis and treatment.'

A door banged and Grace glanced up, surprised to see it was past 8.30, when the surgery officially opened. She'd been so absorbed with Lucy that she hadn't heard the staff arrive, nor the first handful of patients, but now she could hear people chatting, the phone in reception ringing.

Lucy cleared her throat. Brought out a piece of paper. A photocopy. To Grace's relief, the policewoman seemed to have regained her composure. Lucy said, 'There's another reason why I wanted to see you.'

Grace nodded but didn't say anything.

'You see,' Lucy said, 'this piece of paper links Jamie's murder and Bella Frances's vicious attack to three more murders.'

'Three?' A feather of frigid breath trailed down Grace's spine. 'Are you talking about a serial killer?'

The policewoman held Grace's eyes.

'Yes,' she said. 'And your name is on the same piece of paper as the victims. We need to know why.'

CHAPTER THIRTY-EIGHT

Grace couldn't stop staring at the photocopy Lucy had shown her.

Jamie's handwriting.

Talk to Dr Grace about this?

'He wanted to talk to me about a friend of his going missing,' she told Lucy. 'It didn't cross my mind that it might be Bella Frances. I don't think the policeman filling in Jamie's missing person's report gave it a second's thought either.'

Lucy's eyes gleamed. 'What else?'

'He said he'd only met her once, but she was really nice. That's it, I'm afraid.'

Lucy made a note in her notebook while Grace looked at the photocopy once more. 'Why is *your* name there?' she asked again, unable to get her head around it.

Instead of replying *I don't know* for the second time, Lucy abruptly shook her head.

Grace read the names again. Turned the piece of paper to re-read Jamie's six-word sentence. 'Just because he's written that on the other side doesn't mean I'm involved. It might have been the only piece of paper to hand, and it's not connected. He could have been writing about something else.'

'You could be right. But we can't discount it immediately . . .' Lucy trailed off and fiddled with her pen. The distant expression had returned, indicating that she was deep in thought. Grace pushed away the paper and sat back in her chair, finding the silence a relief after the past hour's revelations.

Finally, Lucy straightened and Grace's heart sank when she started going through everything again. When was Jamie diagnosed bipolar? (Six years ago.) What were his symptoms? (Manic episodes leading to excessive grandiosity.) How long had he been on Zidazapine? (Four years.) Did he belong to a bipolar support group? (No.) Did he have any enemies? (Not that she knew.) How long had Grace been in the village? (Six months.) Was she an expert on bipolar disorder? (No more than any other GP.) By the time Lucy put away her notebook, it was nearing ten o'clock and Grace felt as though she'd been through an old-fashioned mangle; emotionally flattened and wrung out.

She walked Lucy outside. 'You'll keep me informed?'

Lucy nodded and thanked her for her time. Grace watched her patter quickly down the steps and disappear around the corner. Hoping the cold air might help steady her, Grace stood quietly until she spotted a car draw up and saw one of her least favourite patients – a particularly disagreeable hypochondriac – clamber out, forcing her to scurry back inside.

She spent the rest of the morning trying to regain some sort of equilibrium. Opening her surgery helped, and when she finally caught the train for London, she was feeling much better.

The fact that Jamie had written her name on the back of that piece of paper had to be a coincidence. He'd written the note thinking about his prostate awareness campaign, which had nothing to do with a list of murder victims. But why on earth did Jamie have this list? Why was Lucy's name on it? Her mind scuttled from side to side and it was only when she alighted at Waterloo that she remembered she'd forgotten to pick up her DHL package. She'd have to do it on her return.

When she reached Mayfair she was early, but she didn't wait for Dan. She had no time to waste. She pressed the button beneath the video intercom, and half a minute later Joe opened the matt-black door. Immediately he said, 'I'm sorry, but it's just you today.'

'Dan can't come?' She was surprised. He hadn't said anything to her.

A guarded look came into his eyes. 'I had to put him off.'

'How come?'

'It's just that . . .' He looked up and down the street. When he returned his gaze to her his jaw had tensed. He seemed to have come to a decision. 'Not everybody got on with Dan. I thought it politic to keep it simple today.'

'Oh,' she said, but she could see his point. Dan wasn't everyone's cup of tea – he could be exceptionally taciturn and aloof – but she was sorry he wasn't here. He'd really wanted to see where her mother used to work.

From the narrow exterior of the building Grace had expected cramped rooms and poky corridors but it was surprisingly spacious inside, made light by pale walls and lots of chrome and glass fittings. A sleek and glossy environment that exuded modernity and style and immediately reminded Grace of her mother's shoes.

He showed her into a roomy office with a bow window and two armchairs set next to a low coffee table. A man with wispy hair and rumpled trousers and jacket rose from behind a desk. He said, 'Hello, Grace.'

'Hello.' She recognised him from her mother's funeral. Philip Denton, her mother's boss.

'I know I should be at home on a Saturday morning.' He spread his hands ruefully. 'But when Joe said you were coming in, I thought I'd do a bit of work so that I'd be here to see you. How are you bearing up?'

'Not too bad,' she said.

He came round the desk and offered her one of the armchairs. 'Can we get you a coffee?' he asked.

'Thanks, but I don't want to take up your time. I'm only here to see my mother's office. I've never been here before and just wanted to . . . see it,' she finished lamely.

'I understand.' Denton came to stand beside Grace. Cleared his throat. 'Thank you, Joe. I shall take Grace to Stella's office.'

Joe was looking at Denton and, for an instant, a look of dislike passed across his face. He said, 'It's OK. I'll show her.'

'No.' Denton's tone was firm. 'I know you have a lot of work to do.'

Joe hesitated.

'I'll look after Grace,' Denton insisted.

With reluctant steps, Joe walked outside.

Quietly, Denton said, 'Joe tells me you're in touch with Dan Forrester.'

'Yes.'

'Poor Dan,' Denton said. 'Losing his son like that. You know he went quite mad?'

'So Mum said.'

'Did she tell you he lost his memory?'

'Yes.'

'Good.' He nodded. 'Now, a quiet word about Dan. I advise you to be careful.' Denton cocked his head as though listening and then said quietly, 'Has Dan mentioned your mother's money?'

It was so far from what she'd expected him to say, that for a moment she stared at him in surprise. 'What money?'

'It's just that I know Stella had a tidy nest egg and knowing Dan . . . well, it wouldn't be unlike him to come sniffing around.'

She opened and closed her mouth. 'But he couldn't remember my mother.'

'Is that what he said?' Denton studied her keenly.

No. It was what Mum said.

'Look,' Denton continued in a low voice. 'I just wanted to warn you to be careful. And keep an eye on Joe too. He's blinded by his friendship with Dan, as was your mother. OK?'

'OK.' Her voice was weak. Desperately she tried to rally herself and bring her ragged thoughts into a coherent stream. She said, 'How do you know about my mother's money?'

'I helped advise her on investments from time to time. She invested wisely over the years and did very well.' He appraised Grace openly. 'You will be quite a rich young lady, I think.'

She was about to ask him, wisely or unwisely, where he thought the money was, when his eyes flicked to the door and back. Footsteps padded past the open doorway.

Denton said, 'Now. To show you Stella's office.'

His face had closed, his manner becoming businesslike. Without waiting for her to respond, he gestured for her to walk before him and into the corridor. Her breathing was tight, her nerves tingling. He knew about her mother's money. *A tidy nest egg . . .*

Her mother's office was decorated in more chrome and glass, rich maroon carpet and matching maroon blinds. Two easy chairs and a view of the street outside. A pen pot and note-book stood on the desk along with a single framed photograph of Grace astride a pony when she was little. She was beaming into the camera. The pony, Butterpat, looked as bored as only a twenty-year-old riding stable pony could. Grace lay a hand on the barren desk top.

'Didn't Mum have a computer?'

'Of course.'

'Would you mind if I had a look at it?'

Denton frowned. 'May I ask why? It's just that we have some extremely sensitive information that –'

He stopped speaking when a dark-haired man stuck his head around the door. He said, 'Philip . . .' and stopped when he saw Grace. His eyes rounded. 'Shit. Sorry. I didn't realise . . .'

'Hell's teeth, man . . .' Denton's face twisted.

The man's head immediately vanished. Denton strode after him. Grace could hear his hiss from where she stood. 'Didn't you get my message?' He was irate.

'Well, yes. But Clipper said it would be OK because –'

'Christ. Don't tell me he's here too.'

'Er . . .' The man's voice shrank. 'He's waiting for me outside. We needed –'

'Don't say another word. I want you both out of here, *now.*'

A door slammed.

Silence.

Grace went to the window to see the dark-haired man appear on the pavement. The set of his shoulders was taut, his footsteps brusque and angry. She watched him cross the road and just as he started to turn into the next road, he was joined by another man, fit-looking, in his late twenties. Clipper, she assumed. Her heart gave a bump when she took in his sandy hair . . .

She was too far away to see Clipper's features but she'd bet it was the man Dan had asked her to look out for.

The man who'd searched her mother's house while she'd been at her funeral.

When the two men vanished around the corner, Grace stood paralysed, her thoughts buzzing feverishly like flies caught in a jam jar.

Fingers trembling, she pulled out her phone and dialled Dan's number.

CHAPTER THIRTY-NINE

Saturday 1 December, 10.35 a.m.

When Joe cancelled, Dan immediately made an appointment to see Stuart Winter, his consultant psychiatrist, making his way to the Croughton Royal Hospital near Regent's Park. He stood in the waiting room, looking outside at the café opposite with its burgundy awning and steamy windows. *Breakfasts, hot meals, salads, cappuccino, espresso.* He could remember ducking across the road occasionally and having a coffee there, sitting and looking back across at the hospital. He'd been allowed to meet Jenny in the café from time to time, when he was 'getting better'.

It felt good remembering the Pay-Less shop on the corner, the Jobcentre and the newsagents. He felt less vulnerable, as though not everything in his past was a lie. His father said he'd spent two months in hospital, of which he could only remember a fortnight. Those two weeks had been taken up with seeing Stuart every day. He'd used the gym and read a lot, something he couldn't remember having time to do since he was a kid. Dan had no bad memories of the place. It was warm and comfortable, and felt more like a hotel than an acute mental hospital with its spacious double bedrooms and en-suites, TV and coffee machine.

While he waited, Dan considered Dr Orvis. He'd read most of what the psychologist had sent him by email, including the notes written after each session. He hadn't found it as uncomfortable as Orvis predicted, probably because he was scanning the documents for clues into Luke's death and anything that might lead him to Cedric. Words like *excessively controlled* and *ordered, constrained* and *unemotional* didn't bother him, they were all part of who he was. But he didn't like Orvis's discourse on Jenny for moving them to Wales.

She is more controlling than him, perhaps. According to Dr Winter she didn't discuss the move with him, she just went ahead and Dan let her. Why? He liked his home in London very much. He doesn't say so, but it is obvious to me he isn't particularly taken with Wales. Why didn't he fight to stay?

That particular paragraph made uneasy reading because although Dan couldn't remember discussing the move with his wife, Jenny told him they had and that they'd both agreed it would be good for them. What else had she hidden from him?

Although he couldn't hear anything, he sensed someone approaching. He turned and a few seconds later, a man entered the room. Short and stocky, wavy dark hair, blue trousers and white shirt beneath a casual blue-checked jacket. No tie. An expressive face that lit up when he saw Dan.

'Dan,' he said.

Dan couldn't help it, he smiled. He liked Stuart. He could remember him clearly, the mental health 'work' they'd done together to get him in the right mental space to leave hospital and re-start his life after his breakdown.

'Stuart.'

They shook hands.

'Please . . .' Stuart gestured at one of the chairs. Dan took one, and the psychiatrist took the other, not quite opposite Dan but not quite alongside either, creating a relaxed and comfortable non-interrogative atmosphere.

'Orvis Fatik telephoned me,' Stuart said. 'You scared him.'

That's one thing Dan liked about Stuart. He didn't beat around the bush.

'He deserved it.'

Stuart Winter raised his eyebrows enquiringly, and Dan filled him in, giving him a heavily edited version of events but including most of what had been said during his scene with Dr Orvis. He finished by saying, 'It appears I've been a lab rat.'

Stuart frowned. 'I think you're being a bit harsh. I mean, you left here in a reasonable state but you still needed a lot of work to stabilise things, and help you come to terms with what happened.'

'What did happen?' Dan's gaze sharpened.

'I don't think we'll gain anything by going over old ground,' said Stuart.

'I can only remember being here for two weeks: why?'

'That's because of the amnesia drug. You were actually here for six weeks. You spent a fortnight at the Bethlem Royal but when it was decided you'd be treated privately, you were transferred here.'

'Who decided?'

'Your employer.'

Dan frowned. 'I don't understand. I thought it was down to Jenny's parents. I mean, they paid the bills.' He held Stuart's eyes. 'Didn't they?'

Stuart shook his head. 'No.'

Dan stared. 'Jenny lied to me?'

'I don't know what your wife said to you about the billing situation,' Stuart said carefully. 'All I know is that your medical bills were picked up by your employer and . . .'

He trailed off as Dan reached into his pocket and bought out his phone, which was buzzing. 'Sorry,' he said, and when he saw it was Grace, he added, 'I wouldn't normally . . . but I have to take this.'

Stuart nodded.

'Grace,' Dan said.

'Oh, thank God.' She sounded stressed, brittle. 'Dan, look, I'm in Mum's office and I've just seen the man who you told me about. The man with the sandy hair. He's called Clipper and –'

'Follow him,' Dan snapped.

'But I'm looking for my mother's –'

'He's the *link*, Grace. Don't lose him.'

'But –'

'You can go back to what you were doing later. *Follow him!*'

Brief silence.

'OK.' Her voice firmed, became decisive. 'I'm going after him.'

'Stay on –'

He'd been going to say *Stay on the line*, but she'd hung up.

Energy flooded him. He was already halfway through the door when he spoke to Stuart. 'I'll ring you later.'

'Later . . .' Stuart's voice floated after him as he ran along the corridor.

CHAPTER FORTY

Grace hesitated, not through indecision but through the realisation that she was about to do something she'd never before contemplated, something that could be dangerous. *Mum! How could you do this to me?!* Overcoming any compulsion toward good manners, Grace rocketed out of the offices of DCA & Co. without saying anything to Joe or Philip Denton.

No time.

She'd make an excuse later, like she'd been overcome with emotion, and that she was embarrassed to be seen crying. Something along those lines would do. Philip Denton's warning about Dan didn't make a dent in her urgency. This wasn't about Dan, it was about the man who had tricked his way into her mother's home. There had to be a connection between Clipper and her mother's money. A connection that might bring her answers.

Handbag bouncing wildly against her hip, she ran across the road, dodging between a man walking a dachshund and a couple gazing into a shop window. More people browsed, moving in and out of cafés, walking, chatting.

Grace jogged to the corner where she'd seen the men vanish. Peered along Davies Street. She couldn't see them. Since they'd appeared to walk south, she headed that way too. Each time she came to a cross street, she looked left and right but had no luck. She had to pray they'd stayed on the same street. She ran faster, her shoes clattering, her breath steaming in the cold air. She dodged and weaved between pedestrians, craning her neck, trying to look ahead and then –

There!

Immediately she stopped running. Two men, one dark-haired, one sandy. Both wore dark winter puffa jackets over jeans and trainers. They were a hundred yards or so ahead of her, striding out. They appeared oblivious to her frantically racing behind them. She was breathing hard as she settled into a brisk walk, following them around Berkeley Square and south into Green Park. The wind picked up, biting her face and neck, but she was warm from her run and barely felt it.

She couldn't believe what she was doing. *Following two men.* A sense of disbelief descended. How had it come to this?

People walked across the winter-withered grass, hunched against the cold. Most people wore hats and gloves. When they left the park the streets were quiet and Grace fell back a little, petrified one of the men would turn his head and look over his shoulder and see her and . . . what? Run away? Shout? Attack her?

Her phone had rung a few times, and when it rang again, she yanked it out.

'Where are you?' Dan asked.

'Just off Buckingham Gate but I'm not sure exactly which street.'

'Stay on the line. I'm in a taxi, barely a minute away.'

Grace kept walking. The men were still shoulder-to-shoulder, talking intently.

'Where's Clipper?' Dan asked.

'Not far ahead of me. He's with another man.' She told him about Philip Denton and his fury. 'I don't think he wanted me to see Clipper and his friend. He doesn't seem to like you much, either,' she added.

Dan didn't comment. Just said, 'Tell me the next street you come to.'

'Great Peter Street,' she said.

Silence for a short while. Then he said, 'Grace, I can see you . . .'

She heard him saying urgently *pull over*, then, to her: 'I'm in the black cab . . .'

She was aware of the taxi stopping just ahead, the door opening, but her concentration was on the two men because, at that moment, Clipper touched his companion on the arm and peeled away.

'Dan.' Her voice was urgent. 'They're separating.'

Both men vanished at the crossing ahead, Clipper turning left, Dark Hair right.

Dan pounded to her side. 'You think they saw you?'

'I haven't been hiding from them.'

'OK. They haven't clocked me yet so I'll take Clipper. You take the other guy. Keep your phone on and keep talking to me.'

He ran for the crossroads. Grace ran after him. Both of them fell into a walk as they turned after their individual quarry. Grace could feel her heart pounding, her adrenaline ticking fast as she continued alone, but when she glanced at Dan, he looked as relaxed as though he was out for nothing but a winter's stroll.

She could see the dark-haired man was on the phone. He'd dropped his pace so Grace pulled back. He remained on the phone. So did Grace. He continued ambling, meandering south-west.

'Clipper's cleaning,' said Dan. 'Trying to see if he's being followed. I'm hoping he's just looking for you and that he won't spot me . . .'

'My guy seems to be in no hurry. Out having a ramble . . .'

They kept in touch for the next ten minutes, until Grace said, 'My guy's gone into Tate Britain.'

'Clipper is . . . he's doubling back . . .'

Everything went quiet.

'Clipper's on a mission,' said Dan. 'He thinks he's lost you. Your guy is the red herring.'

'What should I do?'

'Stay where you are . . .'

Grace hovered inside the gallery's entrance, near an information desk, but couldn't see her target. People came and went, kids, grandparents and young couples chilling out on a Saturday afternoon. The minutes ticked past.

'Grace,' Dan said. There was something odd about his voice.

'What?'

'Clipper's gone to ground,' he told her.

'Where?'

He gave her directions. It wasn't far.

She found him standing on the corner of Millbank and Horseferry Road, seemingly oblivious to the traffic roaring past. He was staring at an impressive stone building decorated with statues. It had started to snow and flakes had caught in his hair and settled on his shoulders. His face was pale. He didn't turn or greet her as she approached, just said, 'He's in there.'

She looked at the entrance and noted the closed-circuit TV camera, which felt as though it was directed straight at them.

'MI5's headquarters,' he said.

He took a deep breath and added, 'I think it's where I used to work.'

CHAPTER FORTY-ONE

As Dan stood, snow clinging to his eyelashes, his mouth, images flew at him. Joe Talbot's pleasure at seeing him. His old colleagues' discomfort at the reunion. His father's odd guilelessness when it came to discussing Dan's old job. Grace's shock when he'd upended the umbrella stand and found her mother's front door key. Stella standing in the supermarket gazing at him, her expression amused.

You knew I was watching you but you didn't give anything away. I guess it shows that our training sticks with us even if we don't realise it.

Dan felt his mind open as more pieces fell into place. He now knew why he was so private. Why he hated being made the centre of attention. Abruptly, he recalled the R. V. Carpet Cleaners' van. The way the van had driven when he'd followed it, like professionals. Had they been MI5? Were they old colleagues of his?

He used to work for MI5.

He could feel the shock of it, the strangeness, a sense of disbelief – *had he really been in a firefight with Stella?* – but these sensations paled beneath the sensation of liberation. Somehow, somewhere inside him, he knew it was true. Now he knew why he'd wept when Stella died. How he'd found her hiding places. Why he watched the news avidly, why he got his kicks out of driving hard and fast, searching for an adrenaline buzz.

Stella's voice: *Because it's the most exciting thing you could find to do.*

He said, 'Your mother worked here too.'

'Oh, God.' Grace's voice was faint. He turned to look at her. She was staring at the building. She'd gone white. 'I really don't want to hear this.'

'It explains why she had those passports and money. Why she contacted me in the first place.' He still hadn't told Grace about Cedric and wondered if he should.

'So what's DCA & Co.?' Grace asked. She was hugging herself but whether from shock or cold – maybe both – he couldn't tell.

'What it says it is. An intelligence and advisory firm. My guess is it's staffed by ex-service personnel.'

'Oh, God,' Grace moaned again. 'I don't believe this.'

'Hey.' He was surprised to find himself smiling. 'At least we're the good guys.'

She shot him a look of disbelief. 'Are you sure about that?'

He thought for a moment then brought out his phone. He saw he had a text message from Jenny. He read it dispassionately, his feelings locked down tight. He didn't respond but dialled another number.

'Sorry about earlier,' he said when Stuart answered.

'No problem. Everything all right?'

'Yes and no.'

'Can I help?'

'Yes. I'm standing outside the edifice where I believe I used to work. I'll give you a couple of clues. It overlooks the river and is a stone's throw from the Home Office.'

'Ah. I was wondering when you'd find out.'

'Tell me.'

'I was going to, earlier. But then you rushed –'

'Stuart. Tell me.'

'OK. You worked in Immigration, as you already know. As a civil servant. But it was more than that.'

Dan waited.

'You worked for the Security Service. MI5 to be precise.'

Dan let the knowledge settle in his heart like a wild animal returning to its nest.

'Who knew?' Dan said.

'Close family and your employer only.'

'Close family being?'

'Your wife and your father.'

'Not my old school buddy, Matt?' Dan asked.

'No.'

'Dr Orvis?' Dan said.

'No. But I can't discount the fact he might have guessed. I can assure you that aside from our financial director, I'm the only person at both hospitals who knew.'

'Why didn't you tell me before?' Dan asked.

'I wanted to.' Stuart Winter sighed. 'But I was told that under no circumstances should you know. Not unless it was absolutely vital.'

'And now?'

'When I heard from Orvis on Thursday, I rang a number I was given after you were discharged. I spoke to someone called Bernard. He used to be your employer. He agreed the circumstances dictated it was time for you to know the truth.'

'His number?'

Stuart recited a London landline number.

Dan said, 'What about Cedric?'

'Who?' Stuart sounded genuinely puzzled.

Dan repeated the name.

'I don't know anyone called Cedric. Sorry.'

'What about Stella Reavey?' He felt Grace's gaze fix on him, intent.

Stuart said, 'Stella visited you practically every day, along with another work colleague, Joe Talbot. They were desperately worried about you and when you lost your memory of them, they were both very upset.'

There was a long pause.

Stuart added, 'You do realise that if we hadn't administered it, you wouldn't be functioning very well, if at all.'

'So Orvis said.' Dan's voice was curt. He resented having to be reminded of how ill he'd been when he couldn't remember anything about it.

'Sorry, Dan.' Stuart was instantly apologetic.

A brief silence.

Stuart said cautiously, 'Is there anything else I can help with?'

'No,' Dan said, then he added, 'Thanks.' And he meant not just for the number, but for the man's honesty and Stuart seemed to know this, because he said quietly, 'Keep safe, Dan.'

Dan ended the call but didn't put away his phone. Aware Grace was watching him, he dialled another number. He said, 'I know where I used to work.'

'Oh, really?' His father sounded as blandly interested as though Dan had just announced he'd booked his summer holiday. He wondered if he'd inherited his father's ability to dissemble so flawlessly or if it was something he'd learned over the years. Nature or nurture? He couldn't tell, but it appeared both of them were masters at the art.

'I'll give you a clue,' said Dan. His voice was tight. 'It's next to Lambeth Bridge.'

'Ah,' said his father.

'Why didn't you tell me?'

Short pause.

'They asked me not to.' His father sighed. 'The doctors too. They thought it would do you more harm than good.'

Dan's grip on the phone tightened so hard he wondered why it didn't crack in half.

'Look,' his father said. 'This is better done face-to-face, don't you think? When can you come down?'

A white-hot poker of anger speared Dan's heart, driven by betrayal and heated with deceit.

He hung up without replying.

Ragged images, barely formed, moved at the periphery of his consciousness.

Dr Orvis's voice: *Each memory has an emotional core.*

Even if he had no memory of a place he could still find himself drawn to it without knowing why. Now he stared at the imposing building that was Thames House North. The urge to walk inside, hear his footsteps on the lobby stone floor, greet the security guards before slipping his smart pass into the barrier and stepping into one of the security capsules was so strong he felt he could fall to his knees and scream.

He wanted to immerse himself in the intense atmosphere. Hear the computer keyboards clicking, the phones ringing, join in with the everyday banter.

He wanted to go to work.

Impossible. Even he knew that, but it didn't stop him wanting, *longing* to reconnect with the person he'd once been.

'Dan?' Grace was watching him anxiously.

'It's confirmed. Your mother and I used to work here. Joe too.'

Grace's eyes went to the imposing building. 'For how long?'

'I don't know.'

She looked back at him. Her expression was wary, almost fearful. She licked her lips. Glanced at Thames House North, then over his shoulder, over the river and up and down Millbank. She said, 'There's something you need to know. About Mum.'

He waited. The snow was falling harder now, beginning to settle on the road.

She closed her eyes briefly and clenched her fists. Quietly, she said, 'Do you know someone called Sirius Thiele?'

He was going to say no, but then he paused. The sound of the name *Sirius* had caused a strange feeling to climb inside him, reminding him of being at home and wanting to close the curtains in case someone was watching. Disquieting, slightly repulsive. Odd. He couldn't explain it so he gave her his stock response when he was in doubt. 'I don't think so. Why?'

CHAPTER FORTY-TWO

Saturday 1 December, 3.40 p.m.

After leaving Grace Reavey's surgery, Lucy returned to Basingstoke cop shop feeling dazed. Reality seemed to be unravelling: it was as though someone had taken the end of a thread on a sweater and pulled until the stitches slipped, undoing the seam and leaving the garment gaping, useless.

Three people on Jamie's list had been diagnosed as bipolar.

Bella, Jamie and herself.

It couldn't be a coincidence that each of them had been prescribed the same drug, could it? She remembered her instructor at the Training School. In his thirties, bespectacled, concave chest, his nerdy looks belied a sharp analytical mind. Now, his voice echoed in her memory.

There are no coincidences in police work.

She popped out of the station to grab some lunch and get some fresh air – it was stifling inside – and now she was hurrying back. It was when she paused on the pavement, waiting for a taxi to pass, that she noticed him, the man who'd been in the queue behind her at the sandwich bar. Narrow-shouldered with short brown hair, a dark padded jacket, jeans and boots. She wouldn't have noticed him if he hadn't stepped out in front of a delivery lorry, forcing it to slow.

She didn't think anything of it until five minutes later, when she saw him walking ahead of her. He'd put on a beanie. He paused at a shop window and as she overtook him, he fell into step behind her. For a moment she thought he was an undercover cop returning to the station, but as she turned her head slightly to see him better, she found him staring at her, intent, his eyes seeming to burn with an inner flame.

She'd surprised him, because the second their eyes met, he almost seemed to flinch. Then he snatched his gaze from hers and scurried down a side street. Vanished.

Something cold touched her spine.

'Shit,' she whispered.

Hastily she pattered up the station steps and pushed past the handful of reporters loitering.

'Do you work here?' one asked eagerly.

'Do you know anything about the Cargo Killer?' another demanded.

It hadn't taken them long to find a nickname for the killer, she thought. She said, 'Nope, sorry. I just want to report a lost dog.'

Immediately they lost interest.

Even though the police hadn't released the fact that there were three bodies being repatriated from India that were linked to Bella's attack and Jamie's murder, they were still circling like sharks in bloody water. God alone knew what they'd do when all *that* came out.

Inside the station, Lucy peered through the window but the man in the padded jacket wasn't there.

Was she being paranoid?

Shivering, she went and grabbed a cup of coffee before immersing herself in the comforting commotion of the beat office. A couple of officers greeted her – they'd met at an earlier briefing – before turning back to whatever they'd been doing. They were busy, preoccupied. No one was watching as she went to the first empty desk and opened the top drawer. Nothing. She moved to the next. Her mind sparkled. A set of handcuffs as well as a key. She swiped the key and stuffed it in her front pocket. She didn't want to get kidnapped and handcuffed and not have a key to hand.

She saw the whiteboard already had notes about her and the other victims. Things were moving fast. She checked outside a couple of times, but she didn't see the man again. Paranoid or not, it was a reminder for her to be vigilant. She made a note of the man on a colleague's computer but when she came to describe him, she had woefully little to go on. Forties? Medium-brown hair, mid-build, mid-height. She could be describing half the male population.

She spoke to one of the constables. 'Where can I find Constable Glebe?'

'Over there.' He pointed out a young, florid-faced man sitting in front of a computer screen. Overweight, thinning blond hair, fleshy lips, eyebrows so fair they were hardly visible. She studied his features so she'd know him again: Constable Glebe had been the officer attending Jamie's missing person investigation and, if she got out of this alive, she was going to report him, not just for being slack in not ringing Dr Smith when he should have, but for putting her life in danger. If he'd done his job properly they might have found the killer by now. *Stupid bastard.*

Before she stepped outside, she checked to see if the man in the padded jacket was there.

Nobody.

She slipped through the front doors, senses alert. Past the journos. The air was piercingly cold and a thin layer of fresh snow lay all around. Lucy hurried down the steps, careful not to slip, and began walking along the street. She faced the traffic to make it difficult for a car to pull up and bundle her in.

Better to be paranoid than dead.

Away from the station, her mind reignited. She had to investigate the bipolar angle on the quiet. She couldn't risk anyone at work finding out what Dr Mike Adamson had said. She couldn't risk her career but she didn't want to risk her life either. If a killer really was on her trail, she had to find out who he was and stop him. Preferably from a place of safety.

She passed a Victorian house offering bed and breakfast. Three stars, free wi-fi and free off-road parking. Lucy paused by the driveway to ring Mac.

'Missing me already?' he asked cheerfully.

'Like a skewer in my ear.'

He snorted. 'So, what's up?'

'I'm going underground,' she told him. 'I'm going to find somewhere anonymous to stay and rent a car. I'll put everything on expenses and –'

'Hang on a minute, Lucy, you can't just –'

'I'll make sure I stay somewhere cheap and rent a wreck so you won't get hauled over hot coals later. I'm going to get a pay-as-you-go phone so he can't track me.'

'No,' he said firmly. 'If you're going to go anywhere, it should be back here.'

A flash of red seared across her vision. 'You'll regret saying that when my body's found beaten to a pulp with a fucking handcuff clamped to my wrist.'

Silence.

'Point taken,' he sighed. 'But I don't like you going it alone. What if he finds you? What if you disappear like the others? We won't know where you are or where to look.'

'OK. I'll tell you, but if you tell a single soul I will reach down your throat and pull your testicles out through your mouth.'

'Christ. You sure know how to engender a feeling of trust, don't you?'

'Do you agree?'

Another silence, then he said, 'What about Nate? Will he know where you are?'

She bit her lip. She didn't want to tell him, but since he'd find out soon enough that Nate was now her ex-boyfriend, she thought she'd better come clean.

'No, he won't,' she said. 'We split up.'

'When?' His voice was sharp.

'Before I was transferred to Stockton.'

Brief silence.

'Lucy, we still need to check him out. You understand?'

'Not you,' she said. 'I want Howard to do it.'

'OK,' he agreed.

'Can you hang on a second?' She checked her calendar on her phone. 'Nate was with me, or at work, just about every day through October,' she told him. 'Except for the weekend of the thirteenth, when he visited his parents.'

'He'll be cleared pretty quickly, then.'

Which meant the subject of Dr Mike prescribing her Zidazapine probably wouldn't come up. Phew.

A car pulled up just ahead of her. A man sat in the driver's seat. Immediately every nerve in her body tightened but when the passenger door opened to disgorge an elderly woman, Lucy exhaled.

'Look,' she said. 'I'll be much safer on my own if nobody knows where I am.'

'OK. But only if you swear to ring in three times a day and if I ring you and you miss my call, you ring me back as soon as humanly possible. Agreed?'

'Yup,' she said, her tone brightening in relief. For a moment she'd doubted she'd get his consent. 'There, that wasn't so bad, was it?'

'Christ almighty,' he said despairingly and hung up without another word.

After she'd bought a phone, Lucy texted Mac with the number. Then she texted her mother to let her know she'd be off the radar for a while. She would have loved to have gone to Southfield and hidden in comfort, but she didn't want to bring the killer to her mother's door.

Lucy reached a hairdresser's and paused, glanced in the window. Her pulse rose when she saw a man in a long coat and hat on the other side of the road, walking slowly. Narrow shoulders, short brown hair. Was it the same man? He didn't seem interested in her, but the second she moved away his pace lifted.

Lucy extended her stride. The man kept up.

Checking the street names around her, Lucy rang for a taxi. It didn't take long before it arrived and as she drove away she saw the man was still walking. Was it a ruse to make her think he wasn't following her?

She collected her bag from her hotel and took another taxi to the next town east, Aldershot. She tried to keep track of the cars behind them but it was difficult, so she took another taxi from Aldershot to Horley, which was even further east and in West Sussex. It cost a fortune, but since it was her life at stake she wasn't going to quibble.

Horley was the stepping-off point for Gatwick Airport and the area was stuffed with hotels and B & Bs. People came and went every day. A strange face wouldn't be unusual. She could move around the area without being noticed. It was, in her view, the perfect place to hide.

She got the taxi to drop her off on Victoria Road, beside a row of restaurants offering Indian baltis, pizzas, charcoal grills and Chinese takeaways. She was hungry but didn't want to eat. She looked into the sky. A soft pearlescent cloud held a strangely green tint, suggesting there was more snow to come.

The B & B she chose was small but clean and offered early departures and full English breakfast. While her computer booted up she washed her underclothes and set them to dry. Then she made herself a cup of coffee in a ridiculously small cup – she much preferred big mugs – before settling on the bed with her laptop and phone. Here, she could work without interruption. Centre herself. Her mind was tearing ahead and she galloped after it as hard as she could. She would find the Cargo Killer and lock him up. Simple. Nothing could stop her.

Her priority, however, was to find the Tim Atherton on Jamie's list and warn him. She started by texting Mac and asking him to email her the contact details for each Tim Atherton in the UK. All two hundred of them.

Why? he asked. *We're already ringing them.*

I have another angle.

Which is?

Just send them over, OK?

She could picture him rolling his eyes but within ten minutes the list came through. Immediately, Lucy began ringing Tim Athertons around the country, trying to ascertain which of them were bipolar. She said she'd got their number from a local bipolar support group, were they interested in setting up a British Foundation? She got two strikes in the first twenty minutes and sent their names to Mac saying, *These could be in the line of fire. Warn them.*

What angle are you working?

Just do it, would you?!!!

She didn't like it when he didn't respond straight away so she sent another email. *I'm serious. They're dangerously at risk. I'll explain later. Please, trust me on this? I know what I'm doing. OK?*

OK.

She could almost hear his long-suffering sigh from where she sat.

Not everyone answered their phone and if it clicked to their messaging service she hung up and marked the name to try later. It was a hard slog but she didn't stop.

She sat cross-legged on her bed, making notes, punching numbers into her cheap throwaway phone, brain racing, hopping up to make herself more coffee, scrawling hasty pen marks on the list of names. She was in her element, fuelled by an immense fear of being beaten to death by some crazy murderer and having her body dumped in a container and shipped off to India.

Darkness fell. She continued calling. Her stomach was growling but she didn't want to waste time eating. She had to find the right Tim Atherton and save him.

On her sixty-second call, a man – he sounded energetic, slightly irritated, she put him in his thirties and probably wearing a nicely-cut suit by the confidence in his voice – said snappily, 'Is this to do with the symposium last month?'

Lucy's attention sharpened into a pinprick. She stopped moving. Concentrated completely on his voice. 'Which one are you referring to?'

'I'm sorry, what did you say your name was?' Suspicion laced his voice. She could hear something rattling in the background, but couldn't work out what it was.

'Carol Wilson.' The name popped into her head, unbidden and from who-knew-where.

'Well, Carol. What did you say you wanted?'

'The name of the symposium would be good. I'd like to recommend it –'

'How did you get my name?' he snapped.

The fact that Tim Atherton – Tim 62 as she thought of him – hadn't immediately denied he was bipolar, had her fizzing with so much excitement that she felt she would burst if she couldn't ask the question burning, flaming red at the forefront of her mind. Desperately she tried to control herself. She said, 'We're conducting a survey about Zidazapine. You are taking it, right?'

'None of your fucking business,' he said, and hung up.

She rang him back but unsurprisingly, he didn't answer. She looked up his address. 10 Stanley Gardens, Notting Hill.

Heart thumping, Lucy looked up bipolar symposiums held around the country last month but came up with a big fat zero. There was one in Brisbane, Australia, and another in Barcelona, Spain, but in the UK? Zilch. She extended her search to find one held in Manchester in July, which couldn't be termed *last month* by any means.

She didn't think she could hold on to this information any longer. She'd already held on to the fact that Jamie was bipolar for far too long. She had to share this with the team and get Tim 62 pulled in. Dread descended. She could deny she was bipolar but someone on the team would dig around until they found Dr Mike. That's what cops did, even to other cops. They dug and scratched and dug some more until they found what they wanted. The damage would be done. Everyone would know. Even if she went to a dozen psychiatrists and each diagnosed her normal, it would still leave a permanent stain on her character.

And what if, God forbid, she *was* actually bipolar?

She closed her eyes.

But what if Tim 62 was in danger right now? The Cargo Killer approaching him this very second?

She had no choice.

Lucy picked up the phone and rang Mac.

'Get Tim 62 pulled off the streets,' she told him. 'I think he could be next.'

CHAPTER FORTY-THREE

Saturday 1 December, 9.10 p.m.

When Tim Atherton's phone rang again, he switched it to silent. He didn't want to talk to that woman again. He didn't know what survey she was conducting but he hated having a stranger know his medical history.

He was puzzled how she came to get his number. Virtually nobody knew he was bipolar so how come Carol whatever-her-name-was, had found out? Had someone slipped up? Or maybe she'd done it by cyber-theft, wormed her way into his therapist's files, or even his GP's computer.

Pulling his suitcase close, he brushed his Oyster card over the ticket barrier and stepped through, yawning. After a week of business meetings in Hong Kong he was knackered. All he wanted was to pour himself a drink, collapse on the sofa and watch TV. It was Sunday tomorrow and he planned to lie in before heading out to see his girlfriend, Mia.

He felt his phone buzz. What did that woman want? His mind moved to consider targeted sales lists, where people's names were sold to various companies so they could start a round of cold calling. Dear God, was there now a public list of people taking Zidazapine doing the rounds? He didn't want his past exposed because since he'd started taking the drug he'd reinvented himself. Back in Oxford, where he'd been a student, he was known as the Nut Job, a lunatic who was perpetually drunk until one day, without thinking and on a blind impulse, he slashed his arm with a pocket knife so hard he hit the bone. He was locked up in a psychiatric ward after that. But then he was put on Zidazapine. The drug had levelled him out and turned him almost 'normal'. So normal in fact, he'd lost his uni friends who labelled him boring when they no longer had someone to laugh at. When he'd moved to London five years ago, he'd stopped seeing anyone from his past. He'd shed the crazy skin for a city suit, a smartphone, and an annual bonus that paid for his holidays to Tuscany, Bordeaux, the Seychelles.

Tim lifted his suitcase up the Tube steps and strode along Pembridge Road. It was past ten and against the dark sky the shop lights burned brightly, glittering with tinsel and baubles. Patches of snow lay on the ground giving it a festive air and despite his anger at the cold caller he felt a wave of contentment. He was spending Christmas with his parents and sisters. Mia was coming too. They'd drink eggnog at midnight and open their presents with glasses of champagne when Mum and Dad returned from church.

Soon the bustle of the main streets fell away. A taxi drove past but otherwise it was quiet. Warm lights glowed from behind curtains and drapes, everybody tucked up inside, keeping warm. Tim was thinking about Christmas lunch and wondering how much red wine he should bring down when his phone rang again. *Unknown caller.* Jesus Christ, not again. Anger rising, he answered it.

'Now look,' he said, 'if you think you can fuck me around –'

'Sir, *sir*.' It was a man speaking.

'God, sorry,' Tim was apologetic. 'I thought you were someone else.'

'This is DI William Niles from the Notting Hill Police. Am I speaking with Tim Atherton?'

A prickle of unease flashed across his skin. Immediate thoughts of speeding tickets (he was a point from losing his licence) followed by motorway accidents, firearm accidents (his father went pheasant shooting during the season) and household accidents (had Mia set fire to her flat?) flashed across his mind.

'Yes, I'm Tim Atherton.'

'Please may I ask where you are, sir?'

'Er . . . I'm walking home.'

'Ten Stanley Gardens,' the policeman said. 'We sent a car to your abode just now, but you were obviously out.'

Tim blinked, but he didn't slow his pace. He'd rather do this in the warmth of his flat with a glass of wine to hand. It was freezing out here and his cheeks felt as though they were being flayed by razor blades.

'Is there any chance you could make your way to a police station? Right away?'

'What?' The police station was at the end of Ladbroke Grove, ten minutes away. His home, thirty seconds away.

'If you'd rather I sent a car to collect you, that can be arranged. Where exactly are you?'

Suspicion arose. 'Why?'

'I'd rather explain it in person, but please rest assured you've done nothing wrong . . .'

The policeman was still talking as Tim turned into his street. Immediately his eyes went to the man standing on his doorstep, pressing the bell. He didn't recognise him.

'Sir, are you on your way to the station? It is extremely urgent we see you.'

'Er . . .' He slowed at the insistence in the man's voice.

'Sir, I don't want to alarm you but we have reason to believe someone is out to harm you.'

At that, Tim stopped. 'What?'

The man on his doorstep turned and when his eyes fell upon Tim, he gave him a little wave. Odd. He'd never seen the man before. The man pattered down the steps and began walking towards him, expression light, as though he was delighted to see him. Perhaps he was a friend of a friend or he'd met him at a party . . .

'Sir, please do not allow anyone to approach you. Not until we have spoken. Do you understand, sir?'

A rush of disbelief. 'What?'

'You could be in grave danger. Please come to the police station. It is extremely urgent.'

Tim stared at the man approaching. He took a step back. The man's face broke into a happy smile.

'There's a man,' Tim said into the phone. He felt as though he was sliding into some sort of living nightmare. 'A stranger. He's walking towards me like he knows me . . .'

'Where are you?'

'Outside my flat.'

'We're on our way. Stay on the phone!'

Tim heard the policeman shouting for a car and that was when he knew it was real, he was in danger. He didn't know why, but it seemed to be true.

'Hello, Tim,' said the man.

Tim ran.

CHAPTER FORTY-FOUR

Tim didn't get far. He'd barely turned and taken four steps when he felt tight rings travelling up each leg. It was like having a rubber ring dog toy rolling up and disappearing into his groin, and then the sensation was totally eclipsed by the most indescribable agonising pain.

Cramp, burns, stabbing, scalding, cold, all at once.

The muscles in his legs locked.

Pain on the surface of his skin and pain deep in his legs as though his muscles were being ripped apart.

His body stiffened like a board.

His ankles, calves, knees and thighs were tearing, splitting –

He was screaming. *Help, help, help!*

But he didn't make a sound.

And then it stopped.

His legs turned to jelly and he collapsed to the ground.

The pain was instantly gone. There was no ache, no dull throb, no tenderness. It was just a memory, overlaid with the shock of what had happened.

'Get up,' the man said.

'Jesus Christ.' He began to tremble. His face was in the snow. Cold and wet. An odd comfort. No pain, thank God. No pain.

'I'll do it again if you don't *get up*.'

Putting his hands on the ground – slushy, gritty snow – Tim stumbled upright. Part of him was amazed he could function.

'Walk to the van.' The man pointed at a white van barely twenty yards away.

Tim didn't move. The police were coming. They were just around the corner.

'Move.'

Tim looked frantically around the street. Nobody was there but lights were on so people were at home . . . He took a deep breath and opened his mouth to yell –

A blast of pain.

Tim collapsed to the ground. He was screaming, shouting, begging, but his throat wouldn't work. He didn't make a sound.

The pain stopped.

Saliva ran out of his mouth into the snow.

Tim lay there, panting. *Please God let the police come soon. Please God . . .*

The man stepped close. Tim's eyes were open and he was looking at the man's ankle and he was about to lunge and grab it and topple the man over when the man moved swiftly and –

Something slammed into the side of his head.

The world exploded with light.

Darkness flooded in, but he fought it.

He could hear a squawking sound nearby and realised it was coming from his phone lying on the ground. He tried to form words but he couldn't move his lips. A second later, the man hit him again.

Everything turned black.

CHAPTER FORTY-FIVE

Saturday 1 December, 11.35 p.m.

When Mac told Lucy that Tim 62 had been snatched barely two minutes before the Notting Hill police arrived, she'd wanted to bend double and shout out her fury and frustration, but she held it inside. She hadn't wanted the B & B owners to remember her. She packed fast and walked to the railway station, catching the 9.59 train to Blackfriars.

She hadn't had the guts to tell Mac about the bipolar angle. When he'd asked why she was so convinced Tim 62 was the next victim, she'd opened her mouth but nothing had come out.

'Lucy,' he said urgently. 'I need *something* to tell the local force. What have you got?'

And God help her, she'd lied.

'They all met at a symposium,' she said. After all, hadn't Tim mentioned a symposium last month?

'What sort?'

'London,' she added wildly. 'They met in London.'

'But what type of –'

'You're wasting time!' Her voice rose. 'Get him pulled, Mac! Trust me, OK? I'll fill you in on everything once he's safe!'

'Promise?'

'Yes!'

She'd hung up, hands shaking, and when Mac had texted her to say the local boys were on the case, she'd almost wept with relief. But she hadn't been quick enough. She hadn't saved Tim.

Where was he now? Was he being beaten to a pulp in the Cargo Killer's torture chamber? His fingers and toes snapped in two, his teeth being pulled out?

She tried to put herself in the killer's mind. All the Recycling For Charity outlets were under observation. They hadn't found a torture room at any of these locations, so where did he take his victims? They had no clues, *nothing*, from Jamie's body, that could point them in a particular direction. The killer was fiendishly clever and careful but she couldn't wait for him to trip up. If Jamie's list was definitive, she was the last potential victim still walking the streets.

She turned her attention to PepsBeevers, which was based near Slough. All its employees were associates of academic departments, devoting their research efforts to programmes that, the website told her, advanced the knowledge of the function and structure of the brain and its relation to behaviour. It was where Zidazapine had, apparently, been invented, along with a wide array of other medications that helped control a variety of behavioural disorders and psychological symptoms.

PepsBeevers were at the cutting edge of brain research and Lucy resolved to interview them as soon as she could.

The second she stepped off the train she felt a rush of belonging. She was home. A moment of exhilaration followed. She *would* find the killer. She *would* return to live in London. Her burst of optimism remained until she walked out of Notting Hill Gate Tube station. Even though common sense told her the killer was long gone, she couldn't stop looking over her shoulder and around the area. She arrived at Stanley Gardens out of breath and jumpy.

Tim 62 lived in the top floor flat. Eighty-five stairs and no lift, and views stretching over a garden and half a dozen tall trees, laced white with snow, to Ladbroke Grove and beyond. It would have been beautiful if Lucy had looked at it properly, but she was absorbed in searching the place for a clue, *anything* that might lead her to Tim 62 and the killer.

Thanks to Mac, the investigating team were ready for her, along with DI William Niles.

'He didn't have any idea he was in danger,' Niles said. 'I was just getting through to him that the situation was serious, when it all blew up.'

'Anything left at the scene?'

'Nothing.'

'Hmmm,' she said, looking around. Two uniforms were also searching the place. 'If Tim had a suitcase, it means he took that as well as Tim's phone.'

It had been Niles who'd rung Tim's parents. They'd told him their son had rung them from Heathrow, just after he'd flown in from overseas to tell them their godson had just won an important business contract out there.

'Witnesses?' Lucy asked.

'Nobody yet. We're going to canvass the neighbourhood.'

'There's something about the killer that makes people trust him,' said Lucy. 'Lets him get close enough to snatch them.'

'He won't be wearing a hoodie, then,' said Niles.

'No,' Lucy agreed. 'More like a suit.' Or a uniform, she thought, but kept this to herself. 'Did you find a computer?'

'No.' Niles was sorting through the contents of the hall side table. Lots of loose change, receipts and old train tickets. Tim's dumping drawer when he came home. 'He's got superfast broadband so he'll have one, but it's not here. We're assuming it's with him.'

She left Niles in the hall and walked quickly through the apartment. Neat, organised, no dust or dirt that she could see which meant Tim probably had a cleaner. The bedroom was tucked beneath the eaves of the building giving it a rustic air. King-sized bed, armchair, bare clotheshorse. A photograph of him and, she assumed, his girlfriend on top of the chest of drawers. She studied Tim. Mid-thirties, brown curly hair, chunky build. He and the girlfriend were smiling as they sat at a restaurant table overlooking a harbour filled with sailboats – it looked like Cornwall.

Lucy opened a bedside drawer to see it stuffed with detritus – tissues, watches, sunglasses, an old alarm clock – before heading for the bathroom. White and blue tiles with a nautical motif and big fluffy white towels. She opened the medicine cabinet. Her gaze went straight to the second shelf and the distinctive pink and blue flashes on the side of two boxes. Zidazapine.

A cold feeling spread through her chest. She'd run out of time. She had to come clean with Mac now there was evidence that three of the people on Jamie's list were taking the same drug. The killer could be a doctor or dentist, a brain research scientist, a surgeon or psychologist, a pharmacist . . .

Her fingers felt stiff as she shut the cabinet door. She knew she should text Mac to let him know, but still she hesitated. *In a minute*, she told herself.

She walked to the kitchen. Lots of granite and shiny chrome. The counter tops were bare except for a coffee machine and sugar bowl. The fridge had no food, just some orange juice and out-of-date milk, a bottle of white wine. Nothing seemed out of place.

She knew she was procrastinating. Putting things off. But she couldn't help it. She was hoping against hope that something might turn up. *Like what? You don't believe in miracles.*

The spare room had been converted into a study and was a glorious mess that the cleaner obviously didn't bother trying to tidy. Or perhaps they weren't allowed in here. There seemed to be three major piles of litter. Lucy started on the nearest and had a flip through. Old envelopes, funny cards from Mia, some light aviation magazines, invoices, more receipts, and although she read the words – ASDA, WHSmith, National Trust – her mind was on the Zidazapine.

'Found anything yet?' Niles stuck his head around the door.

She rubbed the spot between her eyes with her fingertips. 'No.'

'Who would have contact with so many disparate people?' He shook his head. 'It's not possible. My bet is that the only person the victims know is the abductor,' he said.

Lucy couldn't meet his eyes and busied herself with the next pile of litter. Now was the time to go into the bathroom and open the cabinet door and bring out a blister pack of Zidazapine and tell Niles. Tell Mac. She couldn't keep quiet any more. She felt sick. She wanted to cry. She took a deep breath and braced herself to turn around and –

Then she saw it.

A name that leaped out at her. Printed on a receipt.

Slowly, she picked it up.

Boots UK Limited.

Using his Visa card, Tim had bought a pack of travel tissues, a packet of Nurofen, one apple juice and a chicken and mayo sandwich, but this wasn't what had sent a shower of orange sparks through her mind.

It was the store's address and the date.

'You've found something,' Niles said. His tone lifted in excitement. 'What is it?'

She said, 'Do you have his girlfriend's address?'

'Yes.'

'I need to see her. Now.'

Mia Dray lived with another young woman in a maisonette near Earls Court. Tall and supple, she had blue eyes and a short red bob that was currently a tangled mess. Her tracksuit was crumpled but despite her bewilderment, she managed to maintain her self-possession and asked her flatmate to make coffee for them all.

'The thirteenth of October?' Mia repeated.

Lucy had persuaded Niles not to tell Mia her boyfriend had been abducted until she'd asked her questions, explaining that Mia might get hysterical and they couldn't waste the time calming her. Niles had agreed.

'Saturday,' added Lucy.

'Why on earth –'

'Please, Mia,' Lucy said. 'I know this is unsettling, but we urgently need to know what Tim was doing that day.'

Giving her a look that said *How the hell should I know?* Mia said, 'I'll check my diary.'

'Thank you.'

Mia switched on her phone. Had a look. 'Oh,' she said, her face clearing. 'I went to a wedding, an old school friend of mine. It was held at Lucknam Park in Wiltshire – just gorgeous.'

'And Tim? Was he with you?'

'No. He was invited but since he didn't know anyone – except for me of course – he made some excuse, which was a shame as he would have actually had a really good time. They had a great live band and –'

Lucy held up a hand to halt the woman's prattle. Jesus, what was she on? You would think she was talking to a pair of socialites, not two plain-clothed cops in the middle of the night. 'So what did Tim do while you were at the wedding?'

Mia looked at her blankly. 'I have absolutely no idea.'

'Perhaps he texted you that day?' Lucy suggested. 'That might give you a clue.'

'Hey, good idea.' Mia picked up her phone and scrolled through her messages while the flatmate delivered mugs of coffee. 'What date did you say?'

Trying to keep control of her frustration, Lucy repeated herself.

'Yup. Here it is. I texted him a photo of me in my outfit . . . then some stuff about weddings, I was winding him up and . . . oh, yes.' Her eyebrows arched. 'He went to a concert that evening. He sent me a photo.'

'Can I see?' Lucy asked.

'It's not very good.' Mia squinted at it. 'It's a bit blurry.'

'Please.' Lucy held out her hand.

Mia passed over the phone.

The photograph showed lights blazing, silhouettes of crowds and, in the distance, a giant dragon. She checked the time and date. Checked again.

The world seemed to turn one-dimensional, black and white. Hot then cold. A long hiss of breath streamed from her lips.

She could feel her terror, her whole being paralysed with dread and then all sense fleeing as she bolted outside.

It wasn't just the Zidazapine. *It was the concert.*

CHAPTER FORTY-SIX

Sunday 2 December, 10.00 a.m.

Dan began walking along the central avenue of the cemetery, looking for his wife and daughter. A cold, keening wind whipped around the little chapel and, in the distance, he could hear church bells pealing for the morning service.

Despite the cold there were several people about and he had to remind himself that it was perfectly normal for them to be here, paying their respects. He didn't feel reassured. The nape of his neck began to hum ominously.

He noticed a man standing next to a family mausoleum. Dark trousers, leather coat, maroon scarf. He was leaning against the railings, smoking a cigarette. The man looked out of place and although he didn't look directly at Dan as he passed, Dan was convinced he was watching him.

Dan tried to tell himself the man was another mourner, but it didn't work. Ever since Grace had told him about Sirius Thiele, and that apparently Stella owed his client a huge amount of money, he'd been on edge. Stella had wanted him to find Cedric. Did Stella owe Cedric this money? Although he couldn't remember Sirius, an instinct told him to steer well clear; his name brought up dangerous, dark feelings.

He'd called the number Stuart Winter had given him for the man called Bernard, without success. He let it ring and ring, waiting for an answering service to kick in, and when it didn't, allowed it to ring out. He'd go back to Stuart tomorrow and ask him more about his hospital stay as well as Bernard but in the meantime, he had to get through today.

Then he spotted Aimee and his heart lifted. He increased his stride. He noticed the man by the mausoleum hadn't moved but his head had turned. He was definitely watching him.

'Daddy!'

He hunkered down, hoping as always she wouldn't decide to change the way she greeted him. His heart flipped when she broke into a run for him, happily leaping into his embrace, wrapping her arms round his neck and whacking him in the back with her pink plastic handbag and the ever-present Neddy. He buried his face in her neck, inhaling her scent – fruity shampoo, chocolate, something slightly musty that he couldn't identify – and closed his eyes.

Keep her safe, keep her safe . . .

'It took us ages to get here,' she babbled against his cheek. 'I coloured in my flower fairies book but one was really difficult and Mummy had to help me. She used pink when I wanted yellow but it was OK in the end, wasn't it, Mummy?'

Aimee wriggled out of Dan's arms. 'Tara and Sally and me are going to catch fairies later. Tara's got a butterfly net. I think we should dress like fairies so we won't frighten them away. Can I have a fairy dress? And some fairy slippers . . .'

Dan's eyes went to Jenny. She was wearing her expensive little black dress and delicate tights beneath a dark grey cashmere coat. Glinting through curtains of blond hair were the pearl and white gold earrings she told him he'd bought her in Venice on their fifth wedding anniversary. Another memory lost forever. In her hands she held a simple bouquet of paperwhite narcissi tied with satin ribbon. She stood tall and slim and elegant and he didn't think she'd ever looked more beautiful or more unreachable.

Slowly he rose to his feet. The man by the mausoleum continued to watch.

Jenny said, 'Hi.'

'Hi.'

Neither made any move to go to the other. Aimee looked up at them. Dan said, 'Sweetheart, why don't you lead the way? You can remember where Luke's grave is, right?'

With Neddy dangling, Aimee spun on her heels and started walking for the western part of the cemetery. Dan followed behind with Jenny, feeling each step. She said, 'I'm sorry.'

Inside him something tightened. 'What for?'

'For lying to you.'

'About what?'

Her hand lifted, fluttering like a pale bird. 'The job you used to do.'

Bile rose, born from treachery. She'd been talking behind his back. As she'd obviously been doing for the past five years.

'Who have you spoken to?' he asked. He had to modulate his voice carefully. He didn't want her to know how deeply his feelings ran.

'Your father.'

Blood pulsed behind his eyes. 'You didn't see fit to speak to me about it?'

'He rang me,' she said, protesting. 'What was I supposed to do? Not take his call?'

'You could have rung me after you'd spoken to him. Seen how I was. I'd just learned who I used to work for . . .' He could feel emotion constricting his throat so he took a deep breath and exhaled, trying to regulate his anger. 'Or did you think I'd take it all in my stride? Finding out that my father and wife knew about my real job all along but lied about it to me all these years . . .'

She put a hand on his arm. 'Dan, it's not like that.'

'Then tell me, what is it like?' His voice was like frozen gravel. He didn't take his eyes off Aimee.

Jenny seemed to be struggling for the right words to say. Then she took a deep breath.

'That job . . . I hated it.'

He turned his head at the passion in her voice but she was staring straight ahead. Her fists were clenched.

'It took up every minute of your life. You worked every hour God sent you and then when you were at home all you thought about was work, work, work, but you couldn't talk about it because it was classified. Restricted. On a need-to-know basis. Your wife didn't *need to know*.'

He was surprised at the bitterness in her voice. 'Jen,' he started, but she spoke over him.

'I felt left out and isolated. And when you went undercover . . . my God. It was even worse. No communication for weeks on end.

Not knowing if you were dead or alive. Then you'd come home unshaven and exhausted, usually underweight and stressed out.' She sighed. 'But you were alive. Animated. You loved it. You loved *every minute* of that *fucking* job.'

She suddenly stopped and turned to him. She had tears shining in her eyes. 'I couldn't ask you to leave because I knew you'd choose your job over me. Do you know how that made me feel?'

The tears spilled down her cheeks but she didn't brush them away.

'And then Luke died. You went crazy, blaming yourself. Seeing you locked up like that, you have no idea what it was like. Aimee was just a baby . . . I was at the end of my tether and when you were given that amnesia drug it was as though God had heard every prayer I'd ever spoken. I'd lost Luke but gained a husband. You were there, at my side, supporting me for the first time. We were a normal couple, trying to come to terms with the loss of our son. We started doing normal things. Shopping together. Going to the movies. I didn't lie awake at night worrying about you getting shot at or poisoned or gassed . . .'

It was only then that she seemed to realise Dan had stopped walking. She turned and looked at him through her tears.

The low hum turned into a loud buzzing. It spread from his neck through his chest and stomach and down his arms.

He didn't realise he was shaking.

'You knew about the amnesia drug?'

She came and stood in front of him. She raised her chin. 'Yes.'

He fought the urge to shout at her. He knew if he did, he'd never be able to stop.

'Your parents,' he choked. 'They didn't pay for the treatment, either. That was picked up by my employer.'

'Yes.'

'Why didn't you *tell me?*'

'I was advised not to.'

'Who by?'

'Dr Stuart Winter.'

Aimee trotted back to hold Jenny's hand. 'Don't be sad, Mummy. Luke's in heaven. He's really happy there.'

'Yes, sweetie.'

Jenny gave Aimee the flowers before bringing out a tissue and wiping her eyes. They allowed Aimee to lead them to Luke's grave. Dan followed. There were too many thoughts running through his head, too many emotions, so he pushed everything aside and concentrated on his daughter, the way her hair had started to escape her ponytail, the smudge of mud on Neddy's hind leg.

He watched Aimee place the narcissi on the grave. As he did every year, he stared at the simple monolith headstone and tried to summon up a picture of his son, but all he could visualise were the photographs dotted around the house: Luke on his shoulders, Luke on a see-saw, Luke swinging between him and Jenny, bright blond hair gleaming in the sun. He had no true memories of his boy. Just the odd flash that occasionally broke the surface like the flick of a fish's tail.

Jenny withdrew a piece of paper from her pocket and read out a poem. Aimee fidgeted. Dan kept an eye on Mausoleum Man. When she'd finished reading, Jenny held out her hands to Dan and Aimee. Normally they'd hold hands as they walked out of the cemetery, but this time Dan turned away. She took Aimee's hand, lifting her chin once more and looking dead ahead. He fell in beside her. He said quietly, 'Since we're being so honest with one another, who's the man you rang from our landline last Friday?' He added the time and then recited the mobile number.

'Aimee,' Jenny said, 'do you want to run ahead? Show us the way out?'

'No.' Dan stopped Aimee. He'd seen Mausoleum Man leave the railings. He was walking behind them. Tailing them. He wanted Aimee kept close.

'What, you need your daughter to adjudicate?' Jenny's tone was uncharacteristically acidic and this time he let his temper flare.

'No,' he snapped. 'I want to keep her safe. There are things going on that might put her at risk.'

Jenny stopped in her tracks. Turned to face him. 'Please, not again, Dan.' She sounded weary.

'What?'

'Your paranoia.'

He decided not to mention Mausoleum Man, who had also paused. When they began to approach Fulham Road, Mausoleum Man brought out his phone.

Dan leaned over to Jenny. He spoke softly, so Aimee wouldn't hear. He said, 'Who rang you?'

'Bernard.' The word was spoken with a sigh, as though she was exhausted.

He blinked. 'You've been talking to my old employer about me?'

'He kept in touch after your breakdown. Not much, just the occasional call to make sure you were OK.'

'Who's Cedric?'

'Who?' Jenny glanced at him, the tiny kink between her eyes indicating she was genuinely puzzled, but he wasn't taken in by it any more. His wife was a champion liar.

He shrugged as though it didn't matter, aware that Aimee was watching them warily. As they passed the chapel, nearing the exit, Dan glanced back to see if Mausoleum Man was following. He'd stopped.

Dan didn't see the other men until they stepped on to Fulham Road.

One was standing on the opposite pavement, beneath a plane tree. The other stood to the right, at a bus stop. Both were looking straight at him. They didn't look away when he looked back.

'Aimee, Jenny. Step behind me.'

Something in his tone made them do as he asked without questioning.

The buzzing through his body increased. He considered turning around and walking back through the cemetery, but then a vehicle began to approach, began to slow down.

A blue van.

A small blue panel van.

What felt like a bolt of electricity ran through his body.

Automatically he looked at the number plate. Although nobody had been able to identify the van that had run Luke down, the witness had said the van was blue . . .

The two men were checking the street. Eyeing the cars driving past, the smattering of pedestrians.

They were lookouts.

'Daddy?' Aimee said at the same time as Jenny said, 'Dan? Is everything all right?'

The van pulled up five yards away, next to the pavement. Close enough but not too close to be threatening. The passenger door opened and a blue suede high-heeled shoe appeared below a shapely leg.

For a second his heart faltered and even though he knew it wasn't possible, he longed for it to be Stella.

'Dan,' the woman called as she climbed out of the van. Savannah. The driver of the van opened his door and climbed out as well. Ellis.

His old work colleagues.

'Join us?' Savannah said.

'Who are the guys?' Dan nodded at the lookouts.

'Safekeeping.'

He arched his eyebrows.

Savannah said, 'They'll keep an eye on Jenny and Aimee until you get back to them. That OK with you, Jenny? You remember Greg and Jonathan, don't you?'

Jenny gave a curt nod.

Dan's gaze was locked on Savannah even though he spoke to Jenny and Aimee. 'I have to go.'

Aimee's voice trembled. 'But what about ice skating? You promised!'

'It's work, sorry.'

'Can't I come with you?' Her face scrunched up. 'Pleeeease?'

'Not this time.'

Jenny looked at Dan and then at Savannah. She didn't say anything. Her face was sad. 'Goodbye,' she said.

She sounded as though it was forever.

CHAPTER FORTY-SEVEN

Savannah sat in the middle of the front seat, flanked by Ellis driving on one side and Dan on the other.

Savannah said, 'Greg and Jonathan will stay with Jenny and Aimee until we call them off.'

Anxiety nipped his belly. 'Who are your guys protecting my family from?'

'It's just a precaution.' She turned her head to look at him. Her expression was as bright and alert as a cat on the hunt. 'They're not at risk. But we thought you might not come with us unless we played it like that.'

True. The fact that Jenny knew Greg and Jonathan and had been happy to have them around, had convinced him it was OK to leave his wife and daughter with them.

Ellis slipped through an amber light as they drove through South Kensington, around the pedestrian precinct lined with cafés and flower stalls, and past the huge facade of the Victoria and Albert Museum.

Dan looked at Savannah, 'I thought you were in Brussels working with NATO.'

She laughed. 'Is that what Joe told you?'

'And that Ellis moved to work with Customs.'

Ellis rolled his eyes. 'Typical Joe, winding me up. Just because I brought that carpet back from Afghanistan without declaring it.'

'And I hate Brussels,' Savannah added, pulling a face. 'Apart from Vincent's, of course, which serves the best steak on the planet.'

Which made Joe a champion liar too. He wondered what else his old buddy had hidden from him.

They joined Brompton Road, passing Harrods and turning right at the next set of traffic lights, towards Hyde Park Corner. Dan resisted the urge to ask where they were going. They would either tell him, or he'd find out when they got there, but he had the sneaking suspicion the journey wasn't going to last much longer.

'Sorry about the vehicle,' Savannah said. 'Can you believe we had to go out and hire it? We were told by those-who-know-best to use every psychological trick to make sure you came with us.'

It had worked, but he wasn't going to admit it.

'Do you work where I think you work?' Dan asked.

'Yup.' Her eyes twinkled at him. 'Where you used to work too.'

'Thames House North?'

'Yup.'

'In the Immigration Department?'

'Sort of.' Ellis chuckled. 'I mean we deal with a lot of people who come from overseas, if that's what you mean.'

It wasn't, but Dan fell quiet. They were now driving through the depths of Mayfair, and when Ellis parked three streets from

DCA & Co., Dan wasn't surprised. He followed them across the pavement and down some steps to a basement door with no number or nameplate. Savannah knocked. The door was opened by an upright, middle-aged man in dark trousers, white shirt and a waistcoat. He looked like a waiter.

'Hello, sir,' he greeted Ellis. 'Ma'am.' This to Savannah.

'Hi, Mick,' Savannah said. 'You remember Dan?'

'Of course.' He inclined his head before opening the door for them.

Inside was an intimate private bar. There were booths and armchairs and sporting photographs on the walls – motorsport as well as horse racing and golf. The room was empty. Not particularly surprising, Dan thought, considering it was 11.30 on Sunday morning.

'This is the Gray Room,' Savannah told Dan. 'We can talk privately here without anyone listening in.' She stepped lightly across the room, leading Dan to a booth with more sporting pictures. No windows. A man sat on the right side of the booth. 'This is Bernard.'

Dan studied him with interest. Fifties, sparse grey hair neatly trimmed; pale, soft-looking skin; nicely cut jacket; blue tie. He looked very smart for a Sunday, making Dan wonder if he'd been to church.

'Bernard Gilpin,' the man introduced himself. He held Dan's eyes as though waiting for a reaction but Dan didn't recognise him. He did, however, know the name. Bernard Gilpin was the head of the Security Service, reporting directly to the Home Secretary. He was the DG, the Director General of MI5.

Bernard said, 'Welcome back.'

Dan didn't know how to respond, so he kept quiet. His heart was thudding, his senses tingling.

'Please, do sit down.'

Dan slid into the booth.

Bernard glanced at Savannah and Ellis. He didn't say anything, but Savannah said, 'We'll wait in the car.'

After they'd left, Mick asked if they'd like coffee. 'Black for you, sir,' he said to Bernard. Then he turned to Dan saying, 'Your usual, sir? White, no sugar?'

Dan nodded, shifting slightly on his seat, uncomfortable that Mick knew him and how he liked his coffee, whereas he knew nothing about Mick. When Mick left, he said, 'Did I come here a lot, or does Mick just have an exceptional memory?'

'Both.'

Bernard didn't fill in the silence that followed. He seemed happy to sit and wait for their coffee without saying anything. It was, Dan thought, oddly refreshing in a world filled with people who, the second they sat down in a bar, brought out their phones. Bernard obviously liked having time to reflect, to think about things. Which was probably a good thing considering his job.

Mick returned after only a couple of minutes and set down two large cups before leaving the room. Bernard took a sip of coffee. So did Dan. The coffee was good and strong, freshly ground.

Bernard put down his cup. 'Stuart Winter has told me you know about the amnesia drug.'

'Yes.'

'And that we paid for your rehabilitation.'

Dan locked his gaze with Bernard's. 'Whose idea was it to erase my memories?'

Bernard looked straight back. 'Mine.'

All at once, Dan understood.

He closed his eyes briefly. 'You wanted to stop a crazy man remembering crucial, top secret information.'

Bernard nodded.

'One hell of a way to do it.' He was careful to keep his tone neutral.

'You didn't argue.' Bernard took a sip of coffee and set his cup back in the saucer.

'Who else knew, aside from Jenny?'

'No one.' Bernard took another sip of coffee. 'I'm sorry if you've felt as though we've been going behind your back, but we were trying to keep you stable. We didn't want to tip you back into the abyss.'

The truth fluttered in his lungs like caged birds waiting to break free.

'You told Dr Orvis your name was Cedric,' Dan said.

'I wanted to keep an eye on you.'

'Pretending to be a psychiatrist?'

A look of amusement crossed Bernard's face. 'I'm not sure if I succeeded that well, but he seemed to appreciate the titbits of experimental medical information I dribbled his way. We're looking at treating soldiers with the amnesia drug, you know. Could be invaluable. But in truth, I used the name because I wanted to stir things up a little.'

Talk about an understatement.

'So,' said Bernard. 'I expect you want to know about your past.'

Another understatement.

'Yes.'

'Very well. Just after you left university, you applied for a job with us on the Internet . . .'

Dan listened to a sparse account of his Security Service CV. Where he'd worked – mostly London; what training he'd received – high-speed defensive driving, weapons, close hand-to-hand combat. And although Bernard filled in a few gaps, he said he couldn't discuss anything in detail, and certainly not any past missions, because not only was everything confidential but Dan no longer worked for MI5.

'I can, however, discuss your last job,' Bernard added. 'Which brings me to why you're here today.'

He pushed his coffee cup aside. Dan did the same.

'Stella approached you.'

'Yes.'

'She wanted you to find Cedric.'

'That's what she said.'

Bernard nodded.

They sat in silence for a minute or so, oddly companionable. Then Bernard said, 'Cedric is a code name for a particular thorn in our side. An informant. A profiteer. The last job you did was with me and Stella. We were trying to find Cedric just before your son was killed. Just the three of us, on the quiet. But when you were hospitalised, Cedric went to ground. He vanished completely. When a year went by with no new intel we honestly began to believe you'd scared him into giving up his nefarious ways. We put Cedric's file aside. Stella moved to DCA. Years passed.

'We heard nothing about Cedric until recently, when something came up that alerted us that he'd resurfaced and –'

'What something?'

'– even though Stella was with DCA she agreed to work secretly with me again, to try to find him.'

Bernard spoke straight over Dan as though he hadn't been interrupted, compelling Dan to make a mental note not to interrupt again if he could help it.

'Five years ago you were closing in on Cedric, breathing down his neck. You were *so close* to finding him . . .' Bernard sighed. 'It was Stella's idea to bring you in and pretend your memory was returning, to draw him out.'

'She wanted to use me as bait.'

'Yes.' Bernard's eyes flicked to the door then back. 'And I have to add that neither Stella nor I knew whether Cedric was a man or a woman. So don't be deceived by the name.'

Dan said, 'Do Savannah and Ellis know this?'

'No. Nobody does, except you and me. And I want it to stay that way.'

Dan looked at him.

Bernard put his hands on the table, the shadows beneath his eyes deepening and making him appear ten years older. 'We had a suspicion Cedric might be one of our own.'

Both men turned their heads when they heard voices. Dan checked his watch to see it was now past midday. People coming in for a drink.

'Did Stella mention how Luke died?' Bernard said.

'She said . . .' Dan took a deep breath. 'That he didn't die in a hit-and-run. Yes, he died in my arms, but he didn't die on Brick Lane as I'd been told.'

'Correct.'

Dan opened and closed his mouth. 'How did he die?' His voice was hoarse.

'We don't know,' Bernard said calmly.

Dan felt the anger building in his chest and tried to push it away. 'So how do you know he *didn't* get killed in a hit-and-run?'

'Because Caliber told us.' He paused, as though he had all the time in the world. Dan had to resist the urge to reach across the table and put his hands around the man's neck and squeeze the information out of him.

Bernard said, 'Caliber was the code name for one of your agents. Khaalid Rahim. You ran him.'

Bernard went on to say that Khaalid came to England in a wave of refugees from Ethiopia in the 1980s. He'd survived civil war, droughts and famine, and arrived with no family and no money. Although he wasn't a young man at thirty-five, he was a quick learner and was soon fluent in English. He started translating for clan members but before long he was fully employed as a teacher. He was a devout Muslim, and became a devoted family man with four children and seven grandchildren. He loved

England and the opportunities it had given him, and even though it didn't always make him popular, he was known for giving critics of his adopted country short shrift and terrorists that threatened his country even shorter shrift.

'He walked into Ealing Police Station six years ago,' Bernard told Dan, 'and told the duty sergeant that a hardline terrorist group linked to al-Qaida was recruiting and raising money in his community to buy a weapon that would ensure the insurgents won the civil war in Somalia.'

Bernard leaned forward. 'The fear in intelligence circles wasn't just that they could return to this country on UK passports with the expertise and motivation to launch terror attacks; it was the thought of them getting their hands on the weapon that was being talked about. Code name GABRIEL.'

Dan raised his eyebrows to appear mildly curious and try to cover the frisson that ran through him. The passports he'd discovered in Stella's hidey-holes had shown the name Denise Anne Gabriel.

'Gabriel,' Bernard continued, 'was in the prototype stage, top secret. QinetiQ developed it for us.'

Dan knew that QinetiQ was a British company and one of the world's leading defence technology and research experts.

'One of their brightest young sparks had the idea for Gabriel and when QinetiQ brought it to us we immediately saw its potential. The British government funded Gabriel's development in the strictest secrecy. We wanted to know how a bunch of Somali insurgents knew about it, so we got you to run Khaalid to try to get more information. It was Khaalid who gave us the name Cedric.'

A low buzz of conversation rose. More people had obviously entered the bar.

'We sent you undercover to meet with an illegal arms dealer, Besnik Kolcei, who had links to the Somalis. You were closing in on Cedric when Luke died.'

Something in his tone made Dan stare. His mouth turned dry. 'You think Cedric was responsible for my son's death?'

'I didn't say that.' Bernard wouldn't meet his eye.

'What about Khaalid? Did he know how Luke died?'

'We don't know. Immediately after you were hospitalised, he was stabbed to death on his way home from the shops.' He kept his gaze averted. 'We suspect Cedric told Besnik that you and Khaalid were working for MI5.'

Dan felt as though lightning was playing over his skin as another flash of understanding seared inside his consciousness.

Bernard had erased his memories because he hadn't wanted his officer going rogue, wanting revenge.

'What alerted you to Cedric's return?' he asked.

'We heard from an unimpeachable source that Cedric had attended a public demonstration of Gabriel recently, and that he was touting the weapon on the illegal arms market, trying to drum up business by selling to the highest bidder. Intel gathered told us it wasn't just military organisations lining up to buy Gabriel, but various terrorist groups as well.' Bernard's lips tightened briefly. 'Gabriel isn't a prototype any more. It's a fully functioning weapon. Cedric has managed to gain access to the technology. The bidding was fierce, apparently.' Bernard's eyes rested on Dan's. 'Daesh won.'

Dan's stomach twisted. 'IS,' he said

'I prefer to call them Daesh.' Bernard's tone was hard. 'I don't want to confer any legitimacy on IS.'

Dan knew the group hated the word Daesh, which was similar to another Arabic word – das – which meant 'to trample down' or 'crush'. The group had reportedly threatened to cut out the tongues of anyone who used it in public.

'Imagine,' Bernard said. 'If Daesh get their hands on Gabriel. They will have the upper hand in any engagement. They will be able to expand their so-called caliphate almost effortlessly, and move anywhere in the world without being challenged. It's a game-changer. We have to prevent Gabriel's handover. Which, my source tells me, is the day after tomorrow. Tuesday. We don't know exactly where, unfortunately, but we can be sure that Gabriel will leave the country on that day.'

The stakes couldn't be much higher, Dan thought.

Bernard's gaze intensified. 'We need to know if Besnik is the broker between Cedric and Daesh. And if so, where the handover is to take place. If you go to Besnik pretending your memory is coming back, it's my bet you'll flush out Cedric. Then we'll have him, and prevent the handover.'

'You know where Besnik is?'

This time Bernard looked at him. 'I know you have your own agenda here, but I need your absolute assurance that you won't do anything stupid before you get the information we need.'

'I'm not sure if I can promise anything,' Dan said.

Bernard studied him for a few moments. 'You're all I've got Dan. Please don't mess it up.'

Dan remained silent.

Bernard sighed. 'I will trust you to do the right thing.'

Still Dan didn't say anything.

'You'll need some leverage with Besnik,' Bernard said. He passed Dan an envelope. 'His ex-wife came to us over a year ago. You might find some of what she says useful.'

Dan pocketed the envelope.

'Savannah and Ellis will take you. They've already been briefed.'

When Dan slid out of the booth with Bernard, he spotted Joe Talbot drinking a pint at the bar. He was talking to a dishevelled-looking man in his fifties.

'That's Philip Denton,' Bernard said when he saw Dan looking. 'An old colleague of mine. Brilliant mind. He set up DCA & Co. six years ago. I train up the best officers and then he pinches them.' He chuckled without rancour. 'Including Stella and Joe. Now, I shall join them for a drink,' and at the same time his body language changed subtly, encouraging Dan to step away. 'Savannah and Ellis will give you my contact details. Keep me informed as to how you get on, would you? An hourly update would be ideal.'

He'd been firmly and expertly dismissed. Bernard moved away but as Dan made for the door, Joe put down his pint and came across. He punched Dan lightly on the shoulder. 'Can I buy you a drink? Then you can fill me in on what God has been filling your ears with.'

'Sorry.' Dan's eyes went to Bernard who was watching them. 'I've got to go.'

'Next time.' Joe glanced at Bernard before turning back to Dan. He studied him seriously for a moment. 'Be careful, OK?'

'Sure.'

As soon as he stepped outside, Ellis started the van and drove it over. Dan climbed inside.

'How'd it go?' Savannah looked at him in bright curiosity.

'OK.' What else was he supposed to say? If Bernard was to be believed, Savannah or Ellis could be Cedric. He added, 'Thanks,' not wanting to appear curt.

'The boss just texted us. Told us to take you to Besnik.'

'Address?'

She rattled off an address in Isleworth.

'Thanks.' He put his hand on the door handle. 'I'll take it from here.'

'Hey, Dan.' She put a hand on his arm. 'We're here to help, OK?'

He looked at her. 'I need to do this my own way, OK?'

She dropped her hand. 'At least put our numbers into your phone. You never know when you might need us.'

He complied silently.

'Ring us any time,' Ellis added. His expression was sombre. 'I'm serious, Dan. We may not know what's going on, but that's nothing new in our game. Just holler, OK?'

Dan gave a nod and climbed out of the van. Walked to Park Lane car park. In his car he opened the envelope Bernard had given him. Took out a USB stick and put it in the car's music player. Then he drove to Isleworth.

CHAPTER FORTY-EIGHT

Sunday 2 December, 2.15 p.m.

Tim Atherton's consciousness crawled awake. He was lying in the corner of a windowless brick room. Vaguely he registered the concrete floor, bare walls with cracked and peeling paint. Two beams of light shone down from a pair of industrial-sized metal lamps hanging from the ceiling. To one side stood a table holding several items. He couldn't see what they were. A plastic apron hung from the back of the door.

He struggled to his knees. His head was thick and muzzy, his mouth sour.

What was going on?

He remembered the man coming for him. The taser. The police calling him, urging him to go to a police station. Why hadn't he listened to them from the start? Why had he insisted on going home? He ran a hand over his face. He was trembling.

The air in the room was fetid and reeking and his bile rose. The temperature was cool, but he could feel the sweat forming on his forehead, beginning to pool at the base of his spine. He clambered up. Put a hand on the wall to steady himself. The bricks felt tacky and he took his hand away, repulsed, and that was when he saw the blood.

Great dried pools of it on the floor. Splashes up the walls. Runnels of old blood poured into a drain. What looked suspiciously like old vomit lay in one corner. Dried piss was everywhere.

His stomach rolled, sending a wave of nausea over him.

He stumbled for the door. When he saw the plastic apron was blood-stained, splattered with yellow and brown gunk that he couldn't identify, he gagged.

Trembling, terrified, he tried the door. Locked.

He looked back at the room. A ten-litre plastic jerrycan stood on the table. He went and opened the lid. It was full of water. He walked to the bucket set in one corner. Piss and faeces clung to the sides.

A moan started in his throat. Gradually it built until he began to scream. He leaped at the door and crashed his fists against it, shouting at the top of his voice.

Let me out!

But nobody came.

CHAPTER FORTY-NINE

Sunday 2 December, 2.45 p.m.

Lucy tucked up in a café, keeping warm while she collated a report for Mac. Now she had a legitimate excuse to be tied to the victims – she'd attended the same concert – she decided to come clean about the bipolar angle. The relief at not having to lie any more was indescribable and, suddenly, her appetite kicked in. She ordered a full English breakfast and was tucking into her second slice of fried bread when Mac rang.

He said, 'Bella's awake. She's asking for you.'

For a moment she was so stunned, she was lost for words.

'She woke up this morning,' Mac went on. 'I went and saw her but she won't talk to anyone in authority except you. She was pretty hysterical about it. She says she doesn't trust anyone else.'

Mentally, Lucy punched the air. Yes!

'How soon can you get here?' Mac asked.

Lucy put down her fork. Made a wild calculation. 'Give me three hours.'

When Lucy arrived at the hospital she was wired on coffee and chocolate, not a great combination for conducting a calm interview with a newly awakened coma patient.

It was icy cold and already dark as she walked for the hospital entrance; dirty snow lay heaped at the bases of streetlights. Pulling up her collar, Lucy checked her messages to see she had one from her mother, nothing urgent, just telling her she'd bumped into one of Lucy's old school friends at the pub. She started texting back.

She jumped when a man walked past her. She hadn't heard him approaching. The police officer in her did a quick scan. Long coat (dark wool, expensive-looking), his shoes (polished leather, also expensive), dark hair slightly thinning on top, long face and dark eyes, brown leather gloves. He strode for the revolving door without glancing round.

She flinched again when her phone beeped, making her swear off caffeine for the rest of the day. It was only Mac, texting to say he was running late, and that she should start the interview without him, get the preliminaries over with. He'd be there within the next fifteen minutes.

Lucy entered Bella's room to see the same greetings cards arranged on the windowsill. Same plastic jug of water on the table, same box of tissues and stuffed teddy bear on the bedside table. Everything was the same except that, instead of lying supine and motionless in the bed, Bella was sitting upright.

Her parents sat on chairs next to their daughter. Bella's hair was freshly washed, falling in waves over her shoulders, her eyes vivid blue in a face as white as milk. Despite her pallor and hollow cheeks, she was still a pretty girl and although she had been deeply traumatised she greeted Lucy with surprising energy. 'Hello, Lucy,' she said. Her words were oddly muffled and she covered her mouth as she spoke.

Lucy's stomach lurched sickeningly. She'd forgotten Bella had no teeth. The implants were due to come later.

'Hi,' she said. 'Are you OK to talk? I know you're probably exhausted, but we've got to act fast. You know he has another victim? Tim Atherton?'

Bella nodded. 'Yes.' She glanced at her parents. 'I heard yesterday. They didn't say his name, just that he'd abducted a young man. I thought it was my brother. I think that's why I woke up. Because I wanted to help Patrick.'

'Wow,' said Lucy. 'Talk about the power of the mind. That's fantastic. I'm hoping you can help Tim by remembering every little detail of your attack. Everything about the man who took you.' Lucy looked at Bella's parents. 'Would you mind giving us some time? My DI's on his way over. I saw there was a coffee machine along the corridor . . .'

They took the hint. They both kissed their daughter, obviously reluctant to leave her, but unable to protest with another victim's life at stake. Lucy settled in one of the chairs they'd vacated. Brought out her notebook. At that moment the door cracked open and when the man saw Lucy, he immediately said, 'Sorry, wrong room,' and vanished.

An invisible spider scurried across Lucy's neck.

He wore a doctor's coat but she recognised the long face and dark eyes. It was the same man who'd walked past her in the hospital car park, with the quiet footsteps.

'Do you know that doctor?' she asked Bella.

'I didn't see him.' Bella looked startled. 'Sorry.'

If it wasn't for the warning scurry Lucy would have thought no more about the man, but something about his sudden withdrawal made her go to the door and look along the corridor. He was walking briskly away.

'Excuse me!' she called.

He didn't look round. He increased his pace.

'Hey!' she called.

Still he didn't turn.

Lucy broke into a run after him. The corridor streamed by, doors and pastel pictures and wheelchairs.

Oddly, the man didn't seem to take any notice of her running, clattering behind him.

She was closing in, maybe twenty yards away.

And then he rounded the end of the corridor and disappeared.

Lucy tore to the corner, her shoes skidding on the floor as she veered after him, but when she got there, he was nowhere to be seen. He'd gone.

CHAPTER FIFTY

'We have to put a guard on her door,' Lucy told Mac.

'Yes,' he agreed.

When Lucy had described the man to Bella, the girl's skin had turned bone white. Although she hadn't seen him, from Lucy's description Bella was convinced it was the same man who'd kidnapped her.

'I'll get the police artist over,' Mac said. 'They'll talk to Bella first, then you.'

Normally they'd try and use a CCTV picture but the system had been disabled, showing the killer was highly organised.

Mac passed her a styrofoam cup of tea. She held it in both hands as she sipped, still shaken that she'd looked the killer in the eye, still furious that she hadn't caught the man. She'd raced down the corridor he'd taken, opening doors, looking left and right when another corridor appeared, running to the main exits, checking the fire escapes, but she hadn't seen him again.

Police were swarming through and around the hospital but Lucy didn't hold out much hope of them finding the killer. He'd had nearly seven minutes to flee the building. You could go a long way in that time.

'He's one of us.' Lucy gazed outside, not seeing the fog or the street lights burning like shrouded glow-worms. 'He has to be. Otherwise how did he know Bella was awake? The press don't know yet, do they?'

'No,' Mac confirmed.

'Why didn't he attack me?' she said. 'I'm on the list. I don't get it.' She closed her eyes. 'Fuck,' she said. 'I can't believe I got that close to him . . .'

Mac reached across and gripped her hand. His skin was warm and the delicious shock of it made her pause.

'You scared him off,' he told her quietly. 'Good job, Constable.'

He held on to her hand tightly, as though he wanted to warm her. It felt great. Better than great, but she shouldn't be holding hands with her DI, so she pulled free.

'We have to talk to Bella,' she said.

'Yes,' he agreed.

Bella had been moved to another part of the hospital, not just for her safety, but so forensics could check the door handle to her room in the faintest hope the Cargo Killer might have left a speck of DNA behind.

Bella was huddled in bed. A staff nurse sat at her side, talking softly.

'Are you OK?' Bella asked Lucy. Her eyes were anxious.

'Absolutely OK, thanks. You?'

'Th-thank you.' Bella started to cry. 'You saved my life. Again.' When Lucy leaned down, Bella wrapped her arms around her neck. Lucy held the girl tightly as she cried. She could feel Mac's eyes on her back as she comforted Bella, stroking the girl's back gently and murmuring soothing noises into her hair. She waited until Bella regained some control before pulling back and peering into her face.

'OK?' Lucy asked.

'OK,' said Bella.

Lucy led the interview. To start with Bella was fearful, finding it hard to communicate the pain and terror she'd suffered, but as she talked her voice gained strength. To Lucy's frustration, Bella couldn't seem to add anything new to the picture they'd built of her abduction. They'd already guessed the killer had to be exceptionally persuasive and believable when approaching his victims, and he'd acted no differently with Bella when he'd pretended to be a friend of her parents.

'He said Dad had had a car accident and that Mum had asked him to collect me and take me to the hospital. He said we'd met last year, at Mum and Dad's. He knew the name of our dog, when my birthday was. I thought I kind of remembered him. He was so *believable*.' Her face spasmed. 'I can't believe I fell for it.'

'You mustn't blame yourself,' Lucy soothed her. 'He's obviously a master of deception.'

Bella said she had been tasered before she'd been given an injection which had knocked her out. She'd woken in a room with no windows. It had a concrete floor, bare walls with cracked and peeling paint. Two large metal lamps hung from the ceiling. There was a table, and on the back of the door hung a plastic apron.

'I was only awake a couple of minutes,' Bella said. She started to tremble. Fear rose.

Lucy held her hand. 'You're safe now. He can't hurt you again. We won't let him.'

Bella took a breath. She continued to tremble, but she'd taken control of her terror. She said, 'I tried the door but there was no lock, not even a door handle. I was crying, hysterical, when he came in. He said he was sorry, that he hadn't wanted to scare me. He injected me again. Knocked me out.'

Bella had next awoken in the container, thirsty, battered, broken and bleeding. She couldn't remember anything in between. She couldn't remember being tortured.

'Nothing?' Lucy was baffled.

'No. Sorry.'

Lucy glanced at Mac. He raised his shoulders slightly, also confounded. Perhaps Bella had blanked out her actual torture? She'd been hiding in a coma for the past two weeks, possibly because she'd been unable to process what had happened, so a period of voluntary memory loss couldn't be discounted. Or had her attacker anaesthetised her purposely? Beaten her while she was unconscious? But why? What sort of pathological situation was he acting out?

Lucy asked Bella for as many details of the room as she could remember. Sounds of traffic or aircraft, cooking smells, but she couldn't give them anything except it felt damp and cold. *A basement*, thought Lucy.

Eventually Lucy moved on to the At Risk concert.

'Tim Atherton went to the same performance,' Lucy said.

'Yeah,' Bella sighed. 'Normally I wouldn't have gone, except it was a freebie, all expenses up to London paid for, a five-star hotel, cocktails, food, the lot.'

'Who paid?'

'The drug company.'

'PepsBeevers?'

'Yeah. They wanted us to take part in their symposium on the Saturday. None of us wanted to go. I mean who wants to be stared at because of their medical condition? But when they offered us all a free weekend in London . . . well, it was a no-brainer.'

'Tell me about the symposium.'

'They wanted us to talk to their reps and marketing guys, whoever, show them we could live normally thanks to the drug. They made an in-house video of us. We were interviewed about how we were before we took the drug, how we were afterwards, that sort of stuff. They were going to quote us in their company magazines and stuff. Endorsements.'

Which was why the symposium hadn't been advertised. It had been for PepsBeevers personnel only.

'Who else was with you?'

'Jamie and Justin. Mary. Tim. Me . . .' she frowned. 'There was another guy, I can't remember his name.'

'Alan Densley?' Lucy offered the name of one of the victims whose body had been repatriated from India.

'Yeah, that's right. Alan. He wasn't a fan of At Risk but he said he'd do anything for a free weekend.' She sighed. 'Their photographer came with us to the concert but it all went wrong when we fled the arena, scared witless . . .'

'You were all taking Zidazapine at the time?'

'Yes. That was the point. To show us living normally thanks to the drug. Ha-ha. Talk about a major backfire with all of us convinced we were about to die, running outside as though our lives depended on it.' Bella picked at her bedcover. 'We all went home after that. We tried to forget about it, except for Jamie.'

'Jamie?'

'He was fit-looking, very cute, but boy he became a pain in the bum.'

Lucy's attention sharpened. 'How come?'

'Because I was doing a Bachelor of Science course in Sport and Exercise, he thought I had an interest in medicine. Which I do, but he was way off the charts with his theories of what happened at the concert.'

'What did he think happened?'

'He was convinced an EMW had been used.'

Lucy blinked. 'A what?'

'Electromagnetic Weapon.' Bella raised her eyes to the ceiling, letting Lucy know what she thought of *that*. 'He said our freaking out was due to an EMW being used. What a load of bollocks.'

Lucy was frowning as her mind shone pink and yellow, fighting to understand. She said, 'Tell me more about what Jamie thought.'

'Well, to start with we all got headaches after the concert, which convinced him we'd been part of a massive experiment. He was one of those wackos, you know, certain that his headache was caused by microwaves. He'd spout stuff about secret projects and invisible murders and suicide and that "they" will be killing more people soon.'

'Who are "they"?'

'He called them the black government. He'd rattle on about the UK military using EMWs in the belief they're non-lethal but Jamie said they kill you slowly by causing nerve damage, cancers, mental collapse . . . He was paranoid. He'd ring me at odd times, using public phone boxes and telling me about it. It was creepy. I thought of changing my number but it was such a hassle . . .'

'He thought the At Risk concert was an experiment?' Lucy backtracked. 'Into what, exactly?'

'Mass mind control. Brainwashing. Cybernetic warfare, mind invasion. You name it, he thought we were part of it. He believed that when the crowd fell silent, an EMW was used, and that when we bolted, another type of EMW was brought into play. Or something like that. Half the time I didn't really listen. He wanted us to go to the police and report what had happened. Go public with his theories. He was convinced he was being followed, that we'd been spotted on CCTV at the concert and that "they" knew who we were. I don't know what the others thought, but I wasn't interested. He was sweet, a nice guy, but he was nuts. I'd hang up as soon as I could.'

Mind whirling, Lucy eventually wound up the interview and took a seat in the corridor, brought out her phone. Accessed the Internet and looked up EMWs. She scanned the first paragraph she came to and said, 'Bloody hell.'

'What is it?' Mac dropped into the seat next to her.

'An EMW is a radiation weapon,' Lucy said, reading from Wikipedia. 'A type of directed energy that delivers heat, mechanical or electrical energy to a target to cause various, sometimes very subtle, effects. They can be used against humans, electronic equipment and military targets generally, depending on the technology.'

She continued to read out loud. Her skin began to crawl.

'When used against humans, electromagnetic weapons can have dramatic effects, such as an intense burning sensation or more subtle effects such as the creation – at a distance – of a sense of anxiety or dread or confusion in an individual or a group of people . . .'

She trailed off, reliving her overwhelming feeling of fear at the concert. What if she hadn't had a breakdown after all? What if an EMW really had been used? Her fingers began to tingle. She forced herself to keep reading.

'Military advantages of such weapons are that the individual or group of people won't know that they are being targeted. That with specialised antennas the effects can be focused on either an individual or a large area such as a city or country.'

Or focused to freeze 85,000 people in a stadium.

Lucy was gazing at the screen, her mind a churning tunnel of orange. She didn't know what the orange meant. Shock? Disbelief?

Words tumbled across her vision. *Influence an enemy force or population to flee rather than stand and fight by imposing on them a sense of impending disaster . . . an ability to impose a feeling of overwhelming drowsiness on an already weary enemy force . . . capability to persuade, indirectly, the close comrades of an enemy soldier that the soldier is mentally unsound . . .*

'Did you also run from the concert?' Mac asked.

'No,' she lied smoothly. 'I saw a group of people bolt outside and went to investigate.'

Mac gave a nod. Looked at her phone. 'Anything else?'

'It's suggested that law enforcement officials could covertly influence protestors to disband without the demonstrators being aware they were being coerced.'

'Let's order one tomorrow.' Mac yawned. She looked at him properly for the first time to see the dark circles under his eyes, his hair standing on end, his clothes rumpled. He was working every hour he could to solve this case, and it showed.

She said, 'I want to talk to PepsBeevers.'

'Well, yes,' he said, frowning, 'but you can't seriously think a weapon was used at the concert?'

She felt a rush of energy.

'Only one way to find out.'

CHAPTER FIFTY-ONE

Sunday 2 December, 10.35 p.m.

Bella was fast asleep. She'd drunk some hot chocolate after the police artist had gone and although she'd been 'asleep' for days she felt shattered. Barely able to keep her eyes open. Her parents had let her doze but the second they left to go home, she'd curled onto her side and fallen into a deep sleep, comforted immeasurably by the uniformed policeman they'd posted outside her door.

She wasn't sure why she woke up. She could hear a distant siren and the hum of the air-conditioning system. She didn't move. She closed her eyes again.

And then he was there.

A gloved hand over her mouth.

A sharp prick on her thigh.

She screamed but it was muffled. She kicked out with all her might, twisting around and reaching to scratch his face, dig her fingers into his eyes. She fought with every ounce of her strength but to her horror it started to ebb. A floating sensation began to drift like a cloud across her mind.

No! she shouted. *Please!*

'I'm sorry.' His voice was gentle. 'You weren't meant to feel anything. You weren't meant to know what was happening. I didn't give you enough ketamine. I'm sorry you suffered. Truly I am.'

She continued to fight, using her hands, her feet.

She would not give in.

The cloud thickened.

A sense of detachment set in. The space behind her eyes began to change. It became deeper and darker then became split by a single red twisting band that folded in on itself, then it pulsed with light and exploded. She was thrown outside of herself and into another level of reality.

She was a child again. It was Christmas and she was filled with simple joy. Then she was kissing her first boyfriend at the arcade. Finishing her GCSEs. Going to her grandmother's funeral. Sadness, excitement, anxiety. Each scene was filled with intense emotion.

'There,' he murmured. 'That's better, isn't it?'

Bella marvelled at the beauty of her life, the dozens of personalities and experiences spinning through her consciousness.

She was extraordinary.

Life was incredible.

Bella died as she was telling her brother Patrick not to let down her tyres again.

CHAPTER FIFTY-TWO

Monday 3 December, 8.40 a.m.

As Dan drove, he listened to the recording Bernard had given him. A meeting between Bernard and Besnik's wife, Nicola. Dan didn't know where they'd met, or whether Nicola had known she was being taped by the Security Service, but from the tone of the conversation, he guessed she knew the score.

The thing is, she said quietly, calmly, *that I want my life back.*

Her accent was pure English, educated, upper-class. Not what he'd expected.

Besnik and I, we're divorced, right? But you wouldn't know it. He won't let me change my name. He won't let me return to Norfolk. He won't let me change my car, my TV, my deodorant without his permission. He decides where the kids go to school and where they spend their holidays. We live in separate houses, have lived apart for over three years, but he still controls my every move.

Emigrate. Bernard's voice.

You think I haven't thought of that? She gave a bitter laugh.

Long silence.

Dan heard her take a breath. *I want him out of my life.*

How?

If I tell you, how do I know you won't tell Besnik?

It had taken Bernard a long time to reassure her that her secret was safe with him and him alone. And now it was Dan's secret too.

As he neared Isleworth, aircraft roared overhead, coming to land at Heathrow. The roads were busy with trucks hauling freight to and from the airport, delivering mail, transporting consumer goods. Nicola had told Bernard that although Besnik owned a multi-million pound mansion in Kensington and another in the south of France, he preferred to spend most of his time in his office.

It shows who he really is, she'd said. *Where he comes from. If I'd seen the place before we got married, I would have probably changed my mind.*

He slowed as he approached Besnik's. A high wire-mesh fence enclosed a fly-tipped sprawl of rubble, tyres, broken bicycles, mattresses, electricals and furniture. Where the soil showed through, it was black with oil. He took in the signs on the gate. *Goods for export to be in working order prior to storage. No waste on the premises.* Another said: *Vehicle disposal and recycling with integrity.* A third stated: *We take your rubbish for nothing.* It looked as though you could dispose of anything you wanted at Besnik's junkyard.

Dan's pulse echoed in his head, an ache building behind his eyes.

Beyond the meshed gate, metal shipping containers were arranged in a haphazard row. A mountain of wrecked cars rose from a sea of rusted appliances. Two muscular Rottweilers stood behind the gate. Massive shoulders and meaty jaws. They wore no collars. They stood with their muzzles pushed through the bars, watching him drive past.

He hadn't appeared to have been followed, but he still scouted the area. He didn't see anything to worry him. He didn't like the fact that Savannah and Ellis knew he was visiting Besnik. It smacked of collusion. Being set up. The sooner he got in and out of here, the better.

Dan drove to a Portakabin. Another sign: *Site Office.*

There was a large paved area with a truck parked next to a loading dock. He drove past then did a U-turn and parked opposite. Switched off the ignition. Breathed in and tried to centre himself. The man who killed his son might be here, which meant the answers he'd been searching for might also be here.

He climbed outside and into the still, cold air. He could feel the webbed knife holster scratching against his ankle, the combat knife sheath inflexible at his waist. The covert Kevlar vest felt bulky beneath his shirt, but to his critical eye in the army surplus store that morning, it hadn't appeared particularly obvious. Sadly the store hadn't had anything that resembled a gun, or he'd have bought that as well. Even a replica weapon or a kids' toy could gain him a couple of precious seconds. If they took the weapons from him, he had a concealed double-edged spear-point knife on his silver keychain. Useful in a tight pinch, but not if they had guns.

He walked across the street and to the site office door. Knocked.

'Yeah,' said a voice on the other side. 'Who is it?'

'A friend of Besnik's.'

'Name?'

'Dan Forrester.'

Silence.

Dan could hear the man's voice. It sounded as though he was on the phone. Seconds later, he returned.

'What do you want?'

'Tell him I want to talk about his status as a British citizen, which is currently in jeopardy.'

The man disappeared briefly. Then Dan heard a bolt being slammed back, and the door opened to reveal a thick-necked young man, no more than twenty, with a buzz cut and pink-rimmed piggy eyes the colour of water.

Dan stepped inside. Stood waiting while Piggy Eyes re-bolted the door. Another man appeared. Around the same age as Dan, he wore black jeans, a black shirt open at the neck and a sharply tailored jacket. 'Hey, man,' he said, looking wary. 'How's it going?' His Albanian accent was soft, indicating he'd been in the UK for a while. He kept his distance, looking at Dan as though faced with a wild animal that might respond unpredictably, maybe suddenly cross the room and bite him.

Dan said, 'Hi.'

The man stared. His jaw softened. 'You're fucking kidding me. You don't remember me?'

Dan took the sensible option, and remained silent.

'Holy shit.' The man's eyes bulged. 'It's true, isn't it? You don't fucking remember.'

Dan shrugged.

'Shit, man.' The man came over and studied him as though he was an interesting species of insect. 'I heard you got some sort of treatment that wiped your memory but I didn't think it was true. Jesus Christ.' He was shaking his head. 'Fucking with your head, that sucks, man.'

'Yes,' Dan agreed. 'It sucks.'

The man studied him some more. 'I'm Jacks.'

'Hi, Jacks.'

'So what the fuck are you doing here?' He looked around. 'I mean, I know you can't remember, but hell . . .' He stared at him, incredulous.

'I want to see Besnik,' Dan said.

'So he said.' Jacks glanced away, looking uneasy. 'Don't take offence, but I've got to check you.'

He came over to frisk Dan. The second he put his hands below Dan's jacket he said, 'No vest, man. Take it off.'

Dan did as he said. Handed it over.

'This is unreal.' Jacks was shaking his head in disbelief. 'You fucked us over and you don't even fucking remember?'

Dan wanted to say *you fucked me over too* but held his tongue.

Jacks finished frisking him quickly and professionally. He found both knives but not the concealed knife in his keychain. Not that professional after all.

'I'll give them back when you come out,' he said, and vanished.

Piggy Eyes jerked a fleshy thumb over his shoulder and at another door that led directly into the yard. 'The boss is out the back.'

Dan looked through the window to see a two-storey brick building. It was difficult to tell if it had been built before the rubbish arrived, or if the rubbish had simply been dumped around it.

Dan said, 'What about the dogs?'

'You've been here before, you don't have to worry. They've memories like elephants.'

'Clever dogs.' Dan forced a chuckle. 'What if they don't know you?'

The piggy eyes narrowed. 'Whaddya mean?'

'I haven't been here in a while. Are you sure they'll remember me?'

'You nervous of them?' He gave a surprisingly high-pitched laugh.

'Just cautious.'

Piggy Eyes shrugged carelessly as though to say *Your lookout*, and went and sat down at a cheap Formica table. Pushed aside a couple of dirty coffee mugs and picked up a car magazine. Flicked it open.

Dan took the hint.

Muscles tense, he moved into the yard. Casually, he put his hand in his pocket. Unscrewed the cap on his keychain and extracted the knife. Started walking. He looked straight ahead at the building. The two steps leading to the door. He had to remain calm. Pretend he'd been here a hundred times before. He stepped over a puddle shimmering with oil. Passed a crushed motorcycle and a stack of broken skateboards. A battered mobility scooter. Several split water butts. He'd only gone a handful of paces when he heard a low growl.

He didn't look around. Kept walking.

Paws pattered behind him, splashing through puddles.

The growl increased.

Dan crushed the urge to run. Kept walking.

Out of the corner of his eye he saw both dogs keeping pace with him. One held its head low, its lips curled back, showing rows of strong white teeth. The other was snuffling the air, trying to identify his scent.

Dan didn't look at the dogs. He showed no interest in them. Continued walking.

One of the dogs made a little dart towards him. He didn't react. It did it again, and when it darted the third time, the other dog joined in. They were preparing to test him with some fast and small bites on his legs.

Sweat trickled down Dan's back. He concentrated on keeping his pace steady.

Only twenty yards to go.

He felt a nudge on his calf from one of the dogs' muzzles. He ignored it.

Another nudge.

He kept walking. Only ten yards to go.

As soon as his feet touched the bottom step, the dogs stopped. Dan turned and looked at them. Heads cocked, they looked back, tongues lolling. He realised their stumpy tails were ticking from side to side. Tick-tock. A slow wag.

'I wouldn't let them fool you.' A voice spoke behind him. Heavily accented Albanian. 'A kid came over the fence last month looking to steal something and ended up in hospital having his face rebuilt.'

'They're handsome creatures,' Dan said, knowing dog owners were invariably proud of their dogs. 'Very strong.'

'They have a bite pressure of two thousand pounds per square inch.'

'Impressive.'

'Please, come inside.'

The man bore a striking resemblance to his dogs. He was short and powerful with a wide head and powerful jaw. His hair was thick and brown, his lips fleshy. He was handsome in a muscular, bull-like fashion. He studied Dan with interest through cold grey eyes. He said, 'You don't remember me, do you?'

'Besnik Kolcei,' said Dan.

'Yes, that's me. But you can't *remember*, can you?'

'Who told you that? Jacks?'

Besnik turned and walked away, not looking back.

Dan's chest tightened. *Had this man killed his son?* He had no memory of the man and no subconscious instinct either. Not a single thing to help guide him.

'What are you waiting for?' Besnik called out. 'The red carpet?'

Sheathing his miniature knife, Dan followed him through a hall and into a room filled with rows of metal shelves overflowing with items. There were china figurines, tools, penholders, pewter mugs, trophies, stereo speakers, books. Besnik walked through a door at the far end, passing a flight of stone steps leading to a basement. As Dan passed, he heard a man screaming. All the hairs rose on his body. He said, 'What's that noise?'

Besnik paused to listen. Then he brought out a phone. He spoke into it as he walked.

'Shut our guest up. He's making a row.'

Dan tasted acid in his mouth.

He swallowed hard.

He mustn't forget why he was here. He had to keep his focus. He could do something about the man screaming later.

He followed Besnik to the rear of the building and up a flight of stairs. He glanced outside, expecting to see the dogs, maybe one of Besnik's thugs, but instead he spotted a small, lithe figure slipping between two shipping crates. It was only a glimpse, but the lightness of step reminded him of Savannah.

On the second floor Besnik opened a door and showed Dan inside. Deep green carpet, dark wood desk and chairs, gilt-edged pictures on the walls, it felt like a club room if it hadn't been for the two goons with thick necks and swollen knuckles standing to one side. While Besnik moved to sit behind his desk, Dan went to the windows, looking for the slight figure outside but didn't see anybody. He glanced round to see the goons had taken up position in front of the door. To keep him in or stop others from entering, he couldn't tell.

He heard the click of a lighter as Besnik lit a cigarette. 'What do you want, Mr Forrester?'

'It's about Gabriel.'

Besnik's eyes narrowed.

'I want to know where the handover is going to take place tomorrow. To your Daesh buyers.'

For a moment Besnik stared. Then he gave a sharp bark of laughter. 'You haven't changed, have you? Still got balls the size of watermelons.'

'I also want to know who Cedric is.'

Besnik laughed harder but there was no humour in the sound. 'You cannot be serious.' He looked over at his goons. 'He lost his memory and now he thinks he is a comedian.'

The goons looked straight ahead. They didn't respond.

'In return for this information,' Dan said, 'I will allow you to retain your British citizenship.'

Besnik stilled.

'What do you mean?'

'I mean that when the Home Office finds out about your past deals with a Russian arms broker in an attempt to win arms contracts from Assad's regime in Syria, they won't be best pleased. They will revoke your citizenship and you will have to leave the country, permanently.'

'Lies,' Besnik said with a flick of the hand.

'I've already spoken to Imad Mansoor. He's willing to testify.'

Besnik stared.

'He'll be a star witness in the case,' Dan continued conversationally. 'His documents note that a key part of his income came from you wanting to secure a deal to supply cluster weapons to Bashar al-Assad.'

Besnik leaned back, seemingly expansive and confident, but his eyes began flickering fast, indicating he was thinking about how to respond. Leaning forward once more, he tapped a length of ash into the ashtray on his desk. He said, 'Mansoor is dispensable.'

'Oh, how predictable.' Dan curved his mouth into a smile. 'Which is why we brought him over here first, before you could get to him.' Dan was bluffing, but Besnik couldn't be sure he wasn't telling the truth.

A long silence followed, during which Dan looked at Besnik and the Albanian arms dealer looked back.

'I think you've been talking to Nicola,' said Besnik.

Dan said, 'Who?' He injected his tone with uncertainty.

Again, Besnik considered Dan. 'Nicola is my darling wife and mother of my children.'

He'd said wife, not ex-wife. Dan didn't remark on it. Just said, 'I didn't know you were married.'

Another long silence during which Besnik smoked his cigarette.

'I'm not sure I can trust you, Dan Forrester, or anything you say. You're a slippery customer who has already cost my organisation dearly. I think you have another agenda. Tell me, why are you really here?'

'I think you already know.'

'But if you don't remember what happened, why does it matter?'

Dan walked to the desk. He put his hands flat on its surface and leaned across. 'Because you killed my son.'

CHAPTER FIFTY-THREE

'Ah,' said Besnik.' He lit another cigarette and exhaled, watching Dan carefully. 'Now we get to it. Who told you?'

Dan ignored him. 'You killed him to warn others like me to leave you alone.'

'Correct.' The grey eyes held his without remorse.

'You tortured my boy.' This time, Dan's voice shook.

'And I forced you to watch every second. Is this what you want to hear?'

A pain started behind Dan's eyes. He remembered the post-mortem report. *Luke Forrester. Three years old. Died of multiple wounds . . . A broken back, a three-inch gash on his forehead, a seven-inch gash in his scalp, a skull fracture, brain swelling, a lacerated liver and fractured pelvis and broken leg.*

Dan made himself breathe.

'It sent you mad.' Besnik gave a slow smile. 'And since then, I haven't seen a single one of your little grey men.' The smile broadened. His voice was laced with triumph. 'MI5. Gutless, spineless, ready to run away at the first opportunity.'

Dan laughed.

'Something is funny?'

'Oh, dear.' Dan shook his head. 'You really believe that? You really think we'd leave a *cope muti* like you alone?' The Albanian tripped off his tongue easily. Piece of shit. 'Someone's been telling you porkies, because I had drinks with the Director General earlier and he told me he has two people in place and has had since I left the Service. How do you think I found you?'

'You lie. I know all my men. They are family. None are traitors.'

Dan leaned back and folded his arms. Raised his eyebrows. 'I'd think a bit more carefully about where your team came from originally, if I were you.'

'They are all Albanian.' Besnik flicked his hand arrogantly. 'Loyal to me.'

'And all Albanians have no interest in protecting themselves with the authorities and making a shit-load of money on the side, am I right?'

Besnik smoked his cigarette in silence, watching him. Then he crushed his cigarette out. He said, 'Perhaps we can come to an arrangement.'

'I know,' Dan said as if he'd just had a brilliant idea, 'you tell me the details of Gabriel's handover, who Cedric is, and I won't kill you.'

'Mr Forrester.' Besnik sighed as though bored. 'I think you should be careful how you proceed. You have your wife and daughter to think about, and –'

It was the mention of Aimee that did it. One moment Dan was standing there, calm, controlled, the next a red cloud descended over him, sending his blood pressure through the roof. Pure rage scorched into every cell of his body. Blindly, driven by a primal fury he never knew he had, he launched himself across the desk. He piled into Besnik so hard the man toppled off his chair and crashed to the floor. Dan went with him. Besnik twisted, slamming his fist against the side of Dan's face, making Dan's ears ring but it didn't stop him from bringing his head back and ramming his forehead as hard as he could straight into Besnik's face.

Gristle and bone crunched. Blood sprayed.

Dan brought his head back again, wanting to pulverise Besnik's face, smash it into pieces, but his arms were grabbed and yanked behind his back and he was being hauled upright. He jerked aside, breaking free briefly to punch one man in the face. The man reeled back and as Dan brought up his knee to ram it into his groin, the other man slammed him aside, sending him sprawling.

The same man kicked him in the stomach. The breath rushed out of him and he curled up on the floor, wheezing, desperately trying to draw breath. As he fought to haul oxygen into his lungs, he tried to reach for his little hidden knife, but another kick in the side of his head immobilised him. He felt his face dig into the carpet briefly as he was turned onto his back.

Besnik staggered to his feet, clutching his nose, coughing blood.

'You fuck,' he said. His voice was fragmented.

Dan lay quietly, riding the pain.

Then Besnik nodded at his goons.

The first kick caught him high in the ribs. He rolled into a foetal position, trying to protect his stomach, his organs, his groin.

The second kick crushed his kidneys, making him cry out. The two men continued to kick him. Besnik joined in.

A kick caught him on the back of his skull. He felt a wave of nausea pass through him and then he vomited. He tried to raise his head away from the mess but couldn't.

The men grunted with the effort of kicking him again and again.

Dan didn't see the kick which smashed into the side of his head. The impact caused stars to explode behind his eyes. A deep ringing vibrated through his head and into his body.

The two men grabbed his wrists. He was aware of being dragged across the floor, head lolling. He faded in and out of consciousness as he was lugged down one set of stairs, and then another. A cool earthy smell. The basement.

He heard banging in the distance. A man shouting.

The sound of bolts being pulled back.

More shouting, but the voices suddenly vanished, as though someone had punched the mute button.

He was on the floor and looking at an industrial-sized lamp dangling from the ceiling. A man's face came into view. Eyes wide, panicky. He was saying something but Dan couldn't hear through the pain. He closed his eyes.

The pain went away.

CHAPTER FIFTY-FOUR

Tim didn't know the man they dumped in his cell, or what he'd done, but he hoped he wasn't going to suffer the same fate. The man was a mess. His face was already starting to swell and bruise. His eyes were puffy, his knuckles bleeding. His jacket was torn and covered in vomit. Blood was spattered everywhere.

Tim felt a moment's admiration for the guy. He'd obviously put up a fight.

He squatted next to him and did his best to make him more comfortable. The thugs hadn't cared how the man had fallen when they'd dropped him and now Tim cautiously adjusted the man's limbs so they wouldn't stiffen into awkward positions. He wasn't a doctor but he knew he had to be careful, in case anything was broken. He was grateful the man was unconscious; he didn't want to cause him any more pain.

When he moved the man's leg, twisted at a painful angle, Tim felt something in the man's pocket. He had a quick delve and brought out a car key, attached to a key chain holding what looked like a couple of house keys. His spirits rose. If he escaped he could press the unlock button on the car key and hopefully the car lights would blink so he could identify the right vehicle and he'd jump in and drive away.

But first, he had to get out of this room.

The door was bolted from the outside.

No handle on the inside. No lock.

No windows.

No way of breaking out unless he had a stick of dynamite. He let out a shout of frustration. In desperation he brought out the keys hoping they might inspire him. If he had a month or two, he could dig his way through the door. He fiddled with the silver keychain to find it had a screw cap.

He unscrewed the top.

To his amazement he pulled out a knife.

Tim assessed the miniature weapon. Stainless steel, the blade had a double-edged spear point with a plain edge.

He turned it from side to side. He could do some serious damage with this if he hit the right part of an assailant's body, like an eye or throat.

He'd been so absorbed with the knife that it was only when a man called out that he realised someone was approaching. Hurriedly, he secreted the knife back into its sheath and pocketed the keys.

The bolts clanged back and two thugs stepped inside. The same men who'd dumped the unconscious man inside the room earlier.

One of the men jerked his head at him. 'Come.'

Tim didn't wait to be asked again.

Anything to get out of this room.

One man walked ahead of him, the other behind, boxing him in as they walked down the corridor. They marched him up the stairs and through a room filled with junk. He looked through the windows to see a scrapyard outside. Then they were crossing a hall. A door was on his left, leading outside. He took a deep breath and made a rush for the door but the man ahead of him simply put out a hand and grabbed his collar and punched him in the side of the head. Stars exploded. He collapsed as though his legs were made of rubber.

He was dragged across the hall and into a room. The door slammed shut. He heard a lock click into place.

Head muzzy, he struggled up.

He was in a storage room. Boxes of files, envelopes, electrical leads, old fax machines, typewriters. Things were looking up. They obviously thought he was of such little threat they were prepared to lock him up with a variety of items he could use against them. But he wasn't harmless. He'd happily smash a typewriter over the thugs' heads until their brains leaked on to the floor. He was a survivor. He'd show them.

Tim looked at the door.

His eyes widened.

More good news.

It had a keyhole.

He brought out the key chain and its concealed knife and set to work.

CHAPTER FIFTY-FIVE

Monday 3 December, 8.45 a.m.

Grace had spent Sunday at home with Ross. She hadn't been able to put him off any longer. When he'd arrived he'd taken one horrified look at her and demanded to know what was wrong.

So she told him about her mother's past, who she used to work for, but nothing else. Nothing about Sirius Thiele, or that the deadline was tomorrow, or that Martin would be in immense danger if she missed it. And she certainly didn't mention anything about the possibility of her secret being exposed. She wasn't going to say a word about that until she was well and truly pushed against the wire.

Ross was almost as shaken as she'd been by the fact that her mother had lied to her for so long. Why hadn't Mum trusted her? Or had she been protecting her? She was aware her mother couldn't tell anyone she worked for the Security Service, but she was her *daughter.* Yes, some things now made sense, why her mother was always so reticent when talking about her work, why Grace had never been to her office, but it didn't make her feel any better.

She felt deceived and cheated and if her mother had been there, she would have been tempted to slap her. Anger and hurt and fear intermingled, along with a deep distress that she couldn't continue her search for the money because Ross was there. When she told him she wasn't feeling well, Ross tucked her up on the sofa with a duvet and the TV guide while he brought little treats to tempt her appetite.

She wasn't ill, but she was tired, every synapse and cell in her body fatigued. She'd only buried her mother a week ago, and in that time she'd been threatened by a man she'd never met before, tailed another man through the streets of London and discovered that her mother used to work for MI5. And to top all this off was the small fact that her name had been written on the reverse side of a list of victims targeted by the Cargo Killer.

No wonder she was shattered.

But being compelled to spend a day alternately napping and watching old movies, being tended by the man she loved, seemed to have helped, because when she awoke on Monday, she felt more energised and able to cope. She would get through this. After all, she had an MI5 officer for a mother, which meant she should have inherited some of her traits, like strength, confidence and resilience. She wasn't sure she was as brave as her mother, though, but she'd do her best.

When she kissed Ross goodbye, he'd looked relieved.

'I was worried,' he admitted. 'I've never seen you so low.'

'No thanks to Mum.' Her tone was dry.

'She was only guarding you. Personally, I think she was an amazing woman. Being a spook suited her.' He smiled and gave her a kiss and a hug. 'I'll see you in a couple of days. Ring me if you need me any sooner.'

As he walked out, he glanced at the hall table. 'Grace . . .' His tone was fondly exasperated.

'OK, OK.' She grabbed her car keys. Ross was always convinced an arbitrary car thief was going to open the front door and steal them. 'I'll hide them in the kitchen.'

'You don't have to do that, just keep them out of sight. That's all.' But she still put them in the kitchen. Which made him smile and kiss her again.

'Love you,' he said.

'I love you too.'

She drove the long way to work so she could drop into the DHL office and retrieve her package, which turned out to be a single, flat plastic envelope. She tossed it on to the passenger seat and opened it once she was settled at her desk.

Inside the DHL envelope was another envelope. Unmarked, brown, A4.

Inside was a single piece of A4 paper.

For a moment, she was bewildered when she saw what appeared to be a list of typed random numbers. Then she saw the word 'Butterpat', and her skin tingled.

Butterpat had been the first pony she'd ridden when she was a little girl. He'd been a palomino. He'd belonged to the Walters Riding School in Tring and her mother used to cut carrots and apples into easy-feeding bite sizes for him. He'd been gentle and placid and they'd both adored him.

Grace studied the numbers. It took her befuddled brain a couple of minutes to sort through them but when she had, the tingling sensation intensified. She brought out her phone and checked her mother's emails before accessing the Internet, then the site of the First Caribbean International Bank (Cayman) Ltd in Tortola, British Virgin Islands, where she was asked for her mother's IB number.

She didn't merge the numbers from the list to her mother's email correctly first time, or the next, but on the third try suddenly the screen changed and she was asked for a password.

She typed in the word *Butterpat.*

Amazingly, the page changed and she was logged into her mother's accounts.

She'd done it. She'd logged in.

But who had sent the codes? Grace looked at the DHL envelope again to see it had come from a central London address. Mr Smith. She Googled the postcode, SW3 6QB. The Royal Brompton Hospital, Chelsea, appeared in the centre of the map, but the postcode could relate to any of the streets around.

She returned to the screen showing her mother's accounts. Stared at it for a moment. Her mother had two accounts. Grace asked for the balance on both.

The first appeared to be a current account, with a healthy balance of just over $5,000. The second was a savings account and when Grace opened it, she had to check the amount twice to make sure she hadn't misread it.

Too many zeroes, she thought. Then: *Oh my God, oh my God.*

She closed her eyes briefly. Took a breath. Checked again, but the figures remained the same. Her mother was worth *millions.*

'Fuck.'

A patient walking past her open door turned his head and stared at her. She hadn't realised she'd left the door open. Nor that she'd spoken aloud.

'Sorry,' she said.

She'd found Sirius's money.

What should she do? Ring him straight away? Wait until she'd spoken to Dan?

Ring him immediately, she decided. Prevent him from forcing Martin to report her to the authorities. She wanted him off her back. Out of her life.

She brought out his pay-as-you-go phone from her handbag. Fingers trembling, she dialled the only number there. Walked to the door and closed it.

'Grace,' he said. With that one word, he conveyed pleasure and delight at hearing from her.

'I've found it. At least I think I have.'

Please God he doesn't want more.

'How much?' he asked.

Someone knocked on her door and before she could say a word, the same patient who'd walked past earlier stuck his head around the door. 'The Gents?' he asked. He was holding an empty sample pot.

'Two doors down on the left,' she told him.

'Who was that?' Sirius's voice was sharp.

'I'm at work.'

'At the surgery.' It wasn't a question but a statement.

She didn't answer but went and stood with her back against the door to prevent anyone else barging in. 'Mr Thiele,' she said. It was the first time she'd used his name and it felt strange, dangerous.

'Sirius, please.'

'Sirius.' Unseeingly, she stared through the window. 'How much did my mother owe your client?'

Brief silence.

When he told her, she closed her eyes in relief. She said, 'In that case, I can repay her debt.'

'I will email you my client's instructions as soon as I obtain them. If you could respond immediately upon receipt, it would be appreciated.'

CHAPTER FIFTY-SIX

Monday 3 December, 8.56 a.m.

When Mac told Lucy that Bella had been murdered, she'd felt as though a horse had kicked her in the diaphragm. The breath rushed out of her. She felt a wave of nausea.

'How?'

'An overdose of ketamine.'

'But she had a guard outside! Where the fuck was he?!'

'The last thing he remembers was looking at a Detective Chief Superintendent's ID.'

'The Cargo Killer impersonated a *cop*?' She didn't wait for Mac to respond. 'Fucksake! We told *everyone* to be on the lookout for someone in a disguise! We *knew* he was clever! That we had to be alert for *anything*!' Rage tore through her like burning white-hot lava. 'I hope you've fired them. The cop who let Bella down.'

'Yes. He's been suspended.'

'Too fucking late.' She slammed down the phone. Then she burst into tears.

She cried and cursed her way down the M1. Bella, Bella. If it was the last thing Lucy did, she'd track down the killer, get the girl justice. She hated him with every ounce of her being. Hated his softened footsteps, his long face and dark eyes. She was aware her hate was also fear-driven and that she was, deep down, terrified. A toxic combination.

Lucy's fear and hate continued to simmer just below the surface as she skirted London and headed for Reading. She was driving too fast but she didn't slow down. She had no time to lose.

Tim Atherton's life was at stake.

When she spotted a discreet green and white sign on the left-hand side of the road – PepsBeevers – she swung on to a private drive. Dripping beech trees slumped low on either side. The sky was an unbroken slate canvas, the roads puddled with broken ice and inky water. She rolled her shoulders, trying to release them from the tension of the journey. She felt as though she'd driven from one end of the country to the other thanks to being forced to use her own crappy car.

Mac hadn't been able to justify her using a pool car. Not only were they in short supply, but the Officer in Overall Command hadn't been convinced by the connection between Jamie's paranoid ramblings about electromagnetic weapons and Zidazapine. He had, however, apparently told the Basingstoke Police to investigate PepsBeevers.

'I'm going anyway,' she told Mac.

He'd looked as though he was thinking about arguing and then said, 'Usual rules apply, OK?'

Which meant ringing him three times a day. She could live with that.

She didn't slow for the speed bumps. The Basingstoke cops were due at PepsBeevers any time now and she wanted to beat them to it.

The road broadened and the trees fell away. A large modern complex loomed into view. Neatly trimmed lawns dusted with wet snow. Frozen water fountains and ice-rimmed potted shrubs decorated the entrance.

A security guard took her details and directed her to a parking spot which had a little placard marked *Director*. As she jogged for the front door she scanned the vehicles: *No cop cars. Good.*

Lucy hastened to the receptionist who, according to her name tag, was called Holly. 'I have an appointment with Richard James Smith.'

'Yes. He's expecting you. I'll show you to his office.'

Lucy's mind was a smooth blue as she signed in and followed Holly on a two-minute journey involving a lift, two corridors and a hallway.

All very efficient.

Which made her wonder about her appointment. Initially, she'd asked to see the Chief Executive (always start at the top) and when he wasn't available had been given his deputy. But then the deputy had rung and suggested she meet with their Research Director. The deputy would be available if she wanted to see him too, but Richard was, apparently, the man she should be speaking to. Oddly, she didn't feel as though she was being palmed off, probably because she hadn't been phoned by anyone's secretary but by the men themselves.

Richard James Smith was a harassed-looking man in his early forties. Blue trousers, blue jacket over a white shirt and a tie with little green dogs all over it that his wife or child had no doubt given him.

'I heard this morning,' he said. 'On the news. It's true? That Bella was murdered?'

'Yes.'

His mouth crumpled. 'Oh, no.'

'I'm sorry.'

'How awful. She was a lovely girl. I met her at a symposium we held in October. I can't believe it.'

Lucy made soothing noises, giving him time to collect himself.

'I'm sorry,' she said again. 'I know it's unsettling, but I need to ask some questions.'

'Of course.' He offered her tea and coffee, which she declined. He directed Lucy to a chair. He took the other chair behind his desk. 'Some police officers from Basingstoke are coming later this morning,' he said. 'I don't want to make waves, but could I ask why two visits are necessary?'

'Jamie Hudson was local to Basingstoke,' she said. 'Whereas Bella was killed in Stockton. And since I'm with the Stockton police . . .'

'Oh, I see.'

He blinked, obviously still baffled, but she didn't say anything further. She didn't have time. She ploughed on.

'Bella was taking a drug of yours. Zidazapine.'

'That's right.' He looked at her expectantly.

'Tell me about it.'

She listened to a litany of pharmacological details, and then the drugs' heroic actions on gazillions of patients who, according to him, hadn't had a life before its existence.

'As therapy continues, the initial sedative effect disappears,' he told her. 'But the effect continues, modifying delusions, hallucinations and confusion while keeping the patient calm and in control. It has also proved to be immensely effective in helping patients cope with their fear of crowds, and agoraphobia.'

Which led nicely to her first question.

'Then why did six people taking Zidazapine run out of the stadium at a concert recently, crazed with fear?'

He looked away, then back. He sighed. 'You know about the At Risk concert at Wembley?'

'Yes.'

'We can't explain it. None of the patients had displayed any psychotic behaviour while on the drug before. Then suddenly . . .' Another sigh. 'We had such high hopes and overnight we had to cancel our overseas sales plans and go back to doing more research.'

Lucy leaned forward. Concentrated her senses on him. 'Someone told me that an electromagnetic weapon could have had that kind of effect on them. There's been a rumour one was used at the concert. What do you make of that?'

He stared at her for a moment before giving a slightly embarrassed laugh. 'I'd say you were, er . . . well . . . it sounds more like something from a science fiction novel.'

He obviously thought she was barmy and it took several minutes of her precious time to convince him otherwise.

'You're serious.' He blinked several times.

'One hundred per cent.'

'Good grief. I'm not sure what to think. I suppose it's possible that Zidazapine interferes with electromagnetic waves, but –' He suddenly leaned forward, excitement lighting his eyes – 'if this actually happened, then it would mean Zidazapine could be acquitted. All six patients were taking Zidazapine over a sustained period, which could have initiated an interaction of some sort when the electromagnetic waves were introduced . . . But we haven't done any research in this area. We haven't even considered it, not knowing of this before.' His eyes continued to gleam. 'Do you have any evidence that anything like that happened at the concert?'

'No.'

He looked momentarily crestfallen.

Lucy gazed at him, her mind buzzing. What if a weapon *had* been used? Why? What did it mean? She felt deeply frustrated that she hadn't found a new avenue of investigation. Only one question hadn't been answered.

'May I ask why the chief executive passed me to his deputy who then passed me on to see you?'

'Oh.' He frowned. 'It was because we had someone from the authorities visit us recently. We thought it might be connected. We were trying to save you time, you see, but they wanted to discuss an amnesia drug we're currently conducting trials with. Nothing to do with Zidazapine or poor Bella.'

Her antennae were quivering.

'Who were they?'

'Oh, sorry.' He blinked. 'She was from the Security Service. She came and saw me two weeks ago. Stella Reavey.'

CHAPTER FIFTY-SEVEN

Monday 3 December, 9.00 a.m.

Grace tried to concentrate on what her patient was saying.

'There's a lump in my throat, Doctor,' the woman whined. 'Sometimes, but not always, it's really difficult to swallow. Food doesn't stick, but I'm afraid it might.'

Grace examined her. Healthy as a horse. Not that she said as such but the woman got the drift.

'Can't I have an X-ray?' she pleaded.

Grace frowned. 'Why don't you tell me why you think you need one?'

'Well, since you ask, what made me come and see you was that I saw that programme on throat cancer last night . . .'

When Sirius's phone rang, she was almost glad. Ross was right. She wanted a change from the Worried Well. She wanted real patients with real problems.

Heart thudding, she answered the phone. She heard him say, 'Grace.' His voice was warm and intimate.

'Please, wait a minute. I'm with a patient.' With a self-control that amazed her, she put the phone down on her desk and turned back to her patient. After reassuring the woman that she wasn't going to drop dead of throat cancer before the week was out, and that *no* it wasn't necessary for her to have an X-ray or a CAT scan or whatever else she thought she needed, she ushered her back into reception and then picked up the phone.

'Yes?' she said.

'My client wants me to witness and check the transfer,' said Sirius. 'I will be at your surgery at 10.30.'

'No.' Grace was horrified. 'I'll be at home.'

Small silence.

She gave him her address. He repeated it back. 'Ten thirty,' he said again, always impeccably polite.

CHAPTER FIFTY-EIGHT

Monday 3 December, 9.50 a.m.

Lucy drove as fast as she dared to Basingstoke. She didn't want to risk getting a speeding ticket but she also couldn't bear trundling bang on the 30mph speed limit on a three-lane road almost free of traffic. It didn't matter that she was a cop with a mission. The law was still the law. She'd tried to call Grace three times, and it was only when she tried for the fourth time that she got through.

'Who is it?' Grace sounded nervous.

'PC Lucy Davies. I'm on my way to see you. It's urgent.'

'Not today,' she said quickly. 'I'm very busy, sorry.'

'It's to do with your mother.'

'What about her?' Grace's voice turned wary.

'I'd rather wait until I see you.'

'Tomorrow,' Grace said. 'Please, come tomorrow.'

Lucy hung up without saying anything. Sorry, sister, she thought. You've been hiding something from me and I'm going to find out what it is. I'm on my way and nothing is going to stop me, not even . . .

She saw the speed camera too late and although she rammed her foot on the brake the camera went off, flashing in her rear-view mirror. She glanced at her speedo. She was now doing thirty, which meant she'd been doing, what? Forty? Fifty? She already had six points on her licence . . . shit, shit, shit. If the Cargo Killer didn't get her first, she might have to kill herself if she lost her licence.

CHAPTER FIFTY-NINE

Monday 3 December, 10.00 a.m.

Unable to give her patients even two per cent of her attention, Grace cancelled her surgery, telling reception she had an emergency at home. 'Burst water pipe,' she said. The receptionist gave her what could only be called an old-fashioned look that said *Yeah, right.* Grace didn't bother lying any further. She'd been pretty unreliable since her mother died but once she'd got rid of Sirius, she would get her life back.

Sirius arrived at her cottage promptly, looking neat and businesslike. He carried a laptop under one arm. He said, 'I won't take up much of your time.'

Mouth dry, she led him into the kitchen, where she'd set her own laptop on the scrubbed oak table, ready to go. He put his machine next to it, switched it on.

He looked around as his computer booted up. 'You have a nice home.'

She decided against saying anything. She didn't want to make small talk with him. She wanted him *out of here, out of her life.*

He tapped a password into his laptop. He didn't take off his gloves. Looking at the screen, he said, 'Why didn't you want me at the surgery? Why here, at your home?'

She stared at the side of his head. He had a tiny white scar shaped like a crescent just below his ear. She said, 'I didn't want you near my patients.'

He turned his head to look at her. Twin shiny black pebbles, appraising. 'But you would have been safer, with people around.'

She already knew she was potentially in more danger by meeting him on her own, but it still didn't stop the bolt of terror that shot through her. Had his client told him to kill her once she'd transferred the money?

He didn't seem to need a response. He turned back to his laptop and tapped his keyboard. A window opened. He typed in another password.

'I don't know if that makes you brave,' he said, 'or stupid.'

Unsure how to respond, she kept quiet.

'What do you think?' he asked. He sounded genuinely interested.

'Both,' she managed.

He nodded. 'You're probably right.'

More taps on his keyboard.

Grace watched him, then gathered her courage. She said, 'You never said why my mother owed your client this money.'

He glanced at her as though deliberating whether to answer her or not. Then he said, 'She sold my client a defective product. This product only partially worked during a recent demonstration, rendering it useless. My client wanted his money back.'

'What product?'

'I'm not at liberty to say.' He turned back to his computer. 'If you wouldn't mind transferring the money now.'

As he'd said, it didn't take long. When he was satisfied that the correct amount had gone into the correct account, he said, 'Thank you,' and shut down his computer. Just after he closed the lid, he paused and glanced at the window as though he'd heard something outside.

He said, 'Are you expecting someone?'

'No.' Grace licked her lips. 'I promise. Nobody.'

He went to the window. Drew back the curtain. 'Well,' he said. He sounded happily surprised. 'Look who it is.'

Grace was at the far side of the kitchen and couldn't see but she desperately hoped Ross hadn't decided to come down from London and surprise her. She started to panic. He'd gone to work but he might still be worried about her and decided to return and –

'I shall answer the door,' said Sirius decisively.

CHAPTER SIXTY

Monday 3 December, 10.35 a.m.

Forcing herself to keep her speed down, Lucy managed to arrive at Ellisfield without setting off another speed camera. She'd initially driven to Grace's surgery but apparently the doctor had gone home. The receptionist had made it clear that Grace was shirking until Lucy showed her warrant card, at which point the woman shut up.

Now, Lucy tucked her car behind what she assumed was Grace's hatchback. There was another car there, a big grey sedan, which she assumed belonged to the boyfriend.

Lucy walked up Grace's front path, made out of hand-cut stone and edged with lavender and herbs – thyme, sage and rosemary – all pruned back for winter. She knocked at the door. She wasn't looking directly at the door when it opened, she was looking at the roses climbing the wall and wondering what kind of flowers to send to Bella's funeral.

'Lucy,' he said.

It was like being thrown against an electric fence. Her entire body fizzed. All the hairs over her skin stood upright.

It was the man from the hospital. The same long face and dark eyes. The man who'd abducted and then murdered Bella.

The Cargo Killer.

'Please,' he said. 'Come in.'

At his side stood Grace, her eyes filled with fear.

'If you run, I will catch you.' He stepped back, forcing Grace to move with him as he opened the door wide. He had her wrist imprisoned in what looked like an iron grip.

Lucy's mind rioted cherry and crimson.

'No,' she said.

He held out his other hand. 'Give me your handbag.'

Lucy didn't move.

'Be nice,' he said, as though he was talking to a recalcitrant child. 'I don't want to harm the doctor. But I will have to if you don't do as I say.'

Every instinct told her not to give him her bag, which contained her warrant card, her phone, car keys and address.

'What do you want?' she asked. She was glad her voice was steady and didn't betray how hard her heart was hammering.

'I want you and Grace to sit on her sofa while I drive away. Grace and I have completed our business, so there is no reason for us to see one another again.'

Grace's eyes were fixed on Lucy, pleading, desperate. *Please, do as he says.*

'Come, Lucy.' He beckoned at her handbag. 'I promise I won't do you any harm.'

'Like hell.' She managed to produce some heat into her tone even though she was cold with terror. 'You killed Bella. You killed all those people. Don't tell me you won't hurt us.'

'I have no interest in hurting either of you. It is not in my remit.'

Lucy stared. 'What do you mean, not your remit?'

A tiny smile curved his mouth.

'That's for you to work out.'

'This is a *job* for you?' she said.

He gestured at her handbag again. 'Please,' he said.

'Who's your employer?' she demanded. 'Who pays you?'

'If I told you that, I'd never work in the industry again. Now, look –'

'Why did you torture and cuff them?'

He studied her, as though he was considering whether to answer her or not. 'Why do you think?' He appeared genuinely curious.

Her mind crackled and burned with showers of fireworks.

'As a distraction,' she said. 'But if that were the case, wouldn't you have ensured the victims were found? It was only by the remotest chance I found Bella, then Jamie.'

'But you did find them, didn't you?' He surveyed her calmly.

'You're not saying you tortured them as some kind of back-up plan?' Disbelief mingled with horror.

He nodded, looking pleased, like a teacher with a clever pupil. 'British ports are notoriously stringent and although I agree it would have been simpler not to torture and cuff them, I'm a cautious man and experience has taught me always to be one step ahead. It would have worked nicely without you, Lucy, but as it is, here you are and I have been found out.'

'You tortured them while they were unconscious,' she said in sudden realisation.

'I saw no point in causing them unnecessary anguish.'

'But Bella –'

'An error.' His mouth puckered slightly. 'For which I am truly sorry.'

A bird chittered briefly and his eyes snapped to the sound then straight back. 'Now, look, I admire your courage and dogmatism but time is pressing. Please pass me your bag or I shall break the doctor's wrist.'

In two quick movements he'd gripped Grace's right hand and lower arm.

'Throw it to the ground,' he said. He'd dropped any pretense of friendliness. 'Or I will snap it. And when I've broken it I will break the other.'

His grip tightened, putting strain on Grace's joint.

Grace's skin turned waxy. She gave a moan.

Lucy's mouth turned as dry as cotton. She dropped her handbag to the ground.

'Step back,' he told Lucy.

She did as he said.

'And again.'

When she was at what he obviously considered a safe distance, he swiftly picked up her bag. Then he turned and angled Grace inside her cottage, making her stand by the hall window.

'Lucy,' he said. 'Come inside, please.'

Lucy hesitated.

He gripped Grace's arm once again. 'I will break it,' he warned.

Desperately playing for time, looking for an opportunity – she wasn't sure what – but longing for a miracle like he tripped and knocked his head on the floor and she'd jump on him and tie him up . . .

'Today,' he snapped. 'Not tomorrow.'

Her inner self was screaming. *Whatever you do don't go in!*

Her mouth was dry, her heart thumping.

She couldn't see she had any other option.

She spun round.

And ran.

She heard a grunt behind her. She'd surprised him. *Good.*

Her feet flew over the ground. She arrowed straight for the shelter of beech trees at the end of the lawn.

Fight him, Grace! Give me a chance!

She kept her gaze on the trees. Focused on running. Her legs pummelling, her arms pumping, straining for every ounce of speed.

She heard Grace scream, *Lucy!*

Panic scalded her blood.

She tried to run faster.

But when she felt tight rings travelling up each leg and starting to concertina into her groin, she knew it was over.

CHAPTER SIXTY-ONE

Monday 3 December, 10.40 a.m.

'Dan. *Dan*. For Chrissakes, wake up.'

Dan groaned. Waves of pain washed along every nerve, making him feel dizzy and sick.

'Come *on*. We can't sit around all bloody day. Make an effort, would you?'

Dan struggled to open an eye. It felt swollen and hot. He squinted to see a man squatting next to him. Joe Talbot.

'Thank Christ.' Joe ran a hand over his face. 'I thought you were never going to come round. Look, we've got to get moving. We don't have much time.'

Dan rolled his head to look at the room. He had to work his mouth to gather enough saliva to speak. 'Where's the guy who was in here with me?'

'What guy?'

They'd obviously taken him away. Dan struggled to rise. Tried to fight down the nausea. 'How did you get in?'

Joe rose and went to the table. Came back with a plastic jerrycan of water.

'I don't understand,' Dan said. His thoughts were sluggish and sticky, like glue. 'What are you doing here?'

'I followed you, OK? I was worried about you. And not without cause, either. You're a mess.'

Joe helped Dan drink then put the water back.

'I know you'll kill me when you hear,' Joe said, 'but I put a tracker on your car. I did it ages ago. I didn't know who to trust and when Stella died I wanted to keep an eye on you. You were blundering around like a bloody buffalo, sending shockwaves through MI5 like you wouldn't believe . . .'

Dan took a clumsy inventory of his body. Tried to check to see if he had any broken bones or fractures. He found plenty of tender spots and a swelling the size and shape of a pigeon's egg forming behind his right ear – painful but hopefully it wouldn't kill him. His right eye was swollen almost completely shut and his lips were split.

'It's like the past has come back to bite us on the arse all over again,' Joe said. 'You getting in the shit with Besnik. I can't believe you came here. What were you thinking?'

When he'd ascertained he was at least superficially OK, Dan rolled over and began levering himself upright, pausing each time a wave of dizziness threatened to knock him down. Joe came and helped.

'You OK to walk outside? Run if you have to?'

Dan gave him a lopsided smile. 'Just like old times, eh?'

'Old times.' Joe smiled in return but it was brief and filled with tension. He reached past his jacket and brought out a Walther P5 Compact pistol from a holster. Semi-automatic. A shell in the chamber, hammer cocked. Ready to go.

Joe led the way while Dan hobbled behind.

Along the basement corridor. Up a narrow staircase. Dan had to pause at the top, put a hand on the wall until a surge of nausea had passed.

Pistol gripped in both hands, Joe walked through the room filled with shelves and clutter. Along the hall. Through the door and down two steps. Dan looked around. Couldn't see anyone. Where were Besnik and his men?

'OK?' Joe asked. His voice was taut.

'Yup.'

They started walking for the Portakabin. Past the crushed motorcycle, the stack of broken skateboards and battered mobility scooter. When they neared the Portakabin, the dogs appeared. Trotted over, expressions curious. Dan tried not to tense, but it was hard when being followed by two creatures that weighed over two hundred pounds between them.

They sniffed Dan. Then they sniffed Joe. They made little darts at Joe's legs. Bumped him with their noses. A precursor to an attack?

Then they were safely inside the Portakabin. His relief intensified when he saw it was empty.

'Where's Jacks?' Dan asked. 'The other guy?'

Joe didn't answer. He went to the door and opened it. Peered out. 'My car's over there.' With his left hand he brought out a car key, beeped it open. 'Go. I'll cover you.'

Dan was moving through the door when he heard a woman shout, 'Joe! Stop!'

Dan jerked his head round. Snapshots streamed before his eyes: Savannah crouched in the Portakabin doorway, aiming a pistol at Joe; Joe swinging his gun to aim it at her; Besnik and his men running across the yard for the Portakabin; the dogs running alongside, alert and expectant.

'Joe, drop it!' she yelled.

Dan couldn't tell who fired first.

The shots were flat and sharp in the enclosed space.

Crack! Crack!

Savannah dived for the floor. Joe fired twice then spun and pushed Dan outside. 'GO!' he yelled.

Dan ran across the street. Adrenaline cauterised every bruise, every wound. He felt no pain. He yanked open the passenger door and dived inside. Three more gunshots: then it fell quiet. No shouts. Nothing.

Joe piled in beside him. Started the car, rammed it into gear and accelerated hard up the street.

Dan looked over his shoulder to see Besnik and his goons erupt from the Portakabin and stop to stand in the road, staring after them.

'Shit,' said Joe. He was trembling. 'That was close. She came out of nowhere. I didn't even know she was there. Shit.'

Dan didn't say anything. His heart and stomach felt as though they'd been wrapped in barbed wire. Savannah, Savannah, Savannah. Her name echoed inside his head.

'I'd better ring the DG,' said Joe. 'Tell him what happened.'

Dan gazed outside, feeling numb.

Joe dialled a number from his dashboard display. When Joe greeted Bernard, Dan could only hear one side of the conversation and belatedly saw that Joe wore an earpiece. 'I just had to rescue Dan,' Joe said. 'Besnik had him in a cell in a basement, beaten to shit. Yeah, yeah. He's here.'

He looked at Dan to corroborate this. When Dan didn't respond, he pressed a button on his steering wheel.

'Dan?' said Bernard. 'Are you all right?'

'Yeah, I'm OK.'

'What happened?'

'I had a chat to Besnik. He didn't like what I had to say so things got a bit heated.'

'And Joe got you out?'

'Yes.' He closed his eyes. 'Savannah tried to stop him.'

Silence.

'Savannah?' The DG's voice was distant.

'Yes.'

Another silence.

'Put me back to Joe,' said Bernard briskly.

Joe pressed the button once more. 'Yeah . . . Yes, that's right. Savannah. Yes, I know I don't work for you . . . No, I didn't tell you because you would have stopped me. Er . . .' He flicked a look at Dan. 'I tracked him. Yes, but . . .'

He paused for a moment. 'Yes, of course. Yes, sir. Absolutely, sir.' Finally, he hung up. 'Jesus, you'd think he'd say thank you for once in his life. What the hell was Savannah doing there? Jesus Christ. What a fuck-up.'

A wave of weakness crashed over Dan and he closed his eyes. Despite the pain riding his body, the waves of darkness lapping against his consciousness, something was niggling him. Something to do with the dogs. Their nudges. The thought rose like drifting seaweed in the ocean of his mind but then Joe spoke, and it vanished.

'You need a doctor,' said Joe. 'I'll take you to A & E. And relax, OK? You're safe now.'

'I know a doctor,' Dan said. 'I'd rather see her than go to hospital.'

'Where is she?'

'Near Basingstoke.'

CHAPTER SIXTY-TWO

Monday 3 December, 10.53 a.m.

Lucy and Grace knelt together on the floor. They were in the hall and handcuffed to the radiator pipe.

One small mercy: the Cargo Killer hadn't broken Grace's wrist.

'Sorry,' said Lucy.

'No, no.' Grace's mouth was trembling but she was making a valiant effort not to cry. 'I'm sorry I couldn't stop him. He was so *strong*.'

After he'd handcuffed them, Sirius vanished through a doorway. Lucy could hear him moving around but couldn't work out what he might be doing.

She looked around for a phone but couldn't see one. She was about to ask Grace when he reappeared with a big leather shoulder bag, which she assumed belonged to Grace. He pulled out the hall drawer and withdrew various sets of keys, put them in the bag. Then he picked up Lucy's handbag and walked outside.

The second he disappeared, Lucy plunged her free hand into her jeans pocket. Grabbed the handcuff key she'd swiped from

Basingstoke Police Station. She was shaking so much it took two tries to release the cuffs but then they were free and she was springing to her feet.

'Phone!' she hissed.

Grace scrambled up, looking around nervously. 'He's gone?' Her face was a mixture of fear and hope.

'Phone!' Lucy almost screamed.

Grace seemed to wake up. She vanished next door briefly. 'He's taken both handsets. He's got my mobile too.'

'Your car keys,' Lucy said. 'Do you have a spare set?'

Grace looked blank.

'I can't let him get away,' Lucy said urgently. 'He's the Cargo Killer, Grace! He's killed five people! I need another set of *keys*!'

Grace opened and closed her mouth. She seemed to be having trouble taking it all in.

'KEYS!'

Her shout galvanised Grace. She rushed away, got the spare set from the kitchen and shoved them at Lucy. 'Here.'

Lucy grabbed them. She said, 'You've got to come with me. I'll drop you at a phone. To ring the police.'

Grace hesitated a second. Then she said, 'OK.'

They both pelted out of the cottage.

The grey sedan was gone. Lucy cursed herself that she hadn't made a note of the number plate when she'd first arrived. *Idiot.*

They piled into Grace's car. Lucy started the engine. Picked reverse. Looked in the rear-view mirror.

She said, 'There might be a small bump.'

She already knew she couldn't get out without ramming her own car. She'd left it in gear as usual, in case the car slipped or her handbrake broke, and it would take a good shove to shift it aside.

Before Grace could take the time to grasp the situation, Lucy released the handbrake and pressed on the accelerator until she felt the metal between the two cars kiss.

'What the . . .'

Alarmed, Grace started to turn in her seat.

Lucy pressed the accelerator harder. Gravel spun as she turned the wheel, trying to nudge her car aside. She only needed a few inches. Spinning the steering wheel, she drove forward a fraction. Then back, with a CLANG! and screech of metal.

'Lucy!' Grace protested.

'I can't let him get away.'

Lucy drove forward again, and rammed her car harder this time. BANG! Her car shuddered and slewed a little to one side. It was just enough. Lucy spun the steering wheel and squeezed the hatchback past her Corsa's fender. Rammed the car into first and rocketed along the lane after the Cargo Killer.

'I'll pay for the damage,' Lucy panted. 'I'll get a loan, I'll sort it, I promise.'

'I'm insured,' said Grace.

'But not with me driving.'

Grace turned to look at her. 'Who says you're driving?'

Lucy's heart was hammering, sweat pouring over her skin. She couldn't believe he hadn't killed her. She was on the list. Why had he let her live?

It's not in my remit.

A flash of yellow seared her synapses as she raced the car along the lane. A picture rose of her gasping, doubled over having run from Wembley Stadium. A young man – his face indistinct and blurred in her memory – came up to her and asked if she was OK. He'd used her name, reading it from her epaulettes. What if the young man had been Jamie?

Paranoid, suspicious Jamie had guessed from her behaviour that she'd also been on Zidazapine, which is why he'd put her on his list. But aside from Dr Mike Adamson, nobody knew she'd taken the drug.

The Cargo Killer wasn't after her.

He'd wanted to kill the six Zidazapine patients who'd attended the symposium.

Lucy tore down another narrow, muddy lane, then another. She couldn't lose him. She barely paused at the crossroads ahead. She heard Grace gasp but it didn't stop her from pressing the accelerator.

'What's his name?' Lucy demanded. 'How do you know him?'

'He's called Sirius Thiele. My mother owed his client a lot of money. Are you sure he's the Cargo Killer?'

'Yes.'

'Dear God.' Her voice was faint. 'Sirius killed Jamie. Why?'

Lucy quickly ran Grace through the story. When she'd finished, neither woman spoke again until his grey sedan came into view. Lucy immediately eased off, keeping well back but not too far away in case he took a sudden turn off the road. She said, 'He may well spot us, and if he speeds up, it could be too dangerous to follow him. I've done some driver training but no high-speed pursuits.'

'I understand.'

But he didn't seem to see them and if he did, thought Grace's commonplace silver hatchback belonged to just another member of the general public. He continued at the same sedate pace along the country lane, slowing for a horse-rider as though he had all the time in the world, and indicating left well before he came to the T-junction on to the A339.

'Where's a phone box around here?' said Lucy, frustrated to be surrounded by nothing but wet fields and dripping woodland.

'Farleigh Wallop, but it's behind us. Besides . . .' Grace paused before adding, 'what am I going to tell them? That the last time I saw you, you were driving north for Basingstoke? It's not going to help them much, is it?'

'They can put out an APB on his number plate.'

'What if it's false?' Grace said.

'That's the sort of thing I'm supposed to say.' Lucy's voice was tight.

'What if he sees you dropping me off?' Grace added. 'We mustn't let him know that we're here.'

'It's dangerous for you to be with me, following him . . .'

'What if while you're dropping me off, he turns off the road and you lose him?'

'Are you always this argumentative?' Lucy said.

'He killed Jamie.' Grace's voice wobbled. 'I wouldn't forgive myself if we lost him. My mother wouldn't forgive me either.'

Lucy dithered, torn between keeping Grace safe and potentially losing the Cargo Killer.

'The first time I saw him,' said Grace, 'was at my mother's wake two weeks ago . . .'

Lucy couldn't resist listening to the extraordinary story unfold and put all thoughts of ejecting Grace from the car aside for the moment. Sirius Thiele. Lucy had a name. She would get her promotion. She would return to London in that Blaze of Glory.

When Sirius joined the motorway towards London, Lucy carefully dropped back, hiding the hatchback from his view as much as she could. She was glad he didn't speed but stuck to the limit. 70 mph. Gradually her heartbeat settled. Grace talked about Dan Forrester, his ruined memory, and that he and her mother used to work for MI5.

'Why did your mother owe his client so much money?' Lucy asked.

'Apparently she sold him a defective product. It only partially worked during a recent demonstration, so he wanted his money back.'

Lucy's hands gripped the steering wheel so tightly her knuckles bleached white. She barely saw the traffic around her as she tried to bring the threads together into a cohesive form.

The minutes ticked past.

Her mind was snatching at words and phrases, trying to make sense of evidence and events. She was on the cusp of understanding, on the brink of bringing it all together.

Lucy could feel Grace watching her but she didn't say anything. She was recalling her conversation with Richard James

Smith. And that was when another pin of comprehension dropped into the machine of everything she knew.

What if Stella's *defective product* was an electromagnetic weapon that had been demonstrated at the concert? Eighty-five thousand happy, arm-waving people falling as still and silent as zombies for no apparent reason. Except for six people who had fled, all of whom had been taking Zidazapine. What if all six of them needed to be silenced because they hadn't reacted like the rest of the crowd? Because they'd run away, they'd shown that Zidazapine could be a possible antidote, thus making the weapon useless.

Lucy's mind continued to whirl as they crossed the M25 and passed Sunbury at a sedate 65mph. Traffic had thickened now they were entering the outskirts of London.

What about Sirius? She stared ahead as she recalled what he'd said. *It would have been simpler not to torture and cuff them, I agree, but experience has taught me always to be one step ahead.*

Sirius had created a smokescreen in case one or more of the victims were found, ensuring the police would be misled into believing they were after a crazy serial killer rather than a professional assassin working for someone demonstrating an EMW. Which was, she guessed, why Stella Reavey – from the Security Service – had been involved.

The motorway turned into a dual carriageway, past Hanworth and Twickenham, busy with trucks. Aircraft roared overhead, lumbering west as they headed for Heathrow. Ahead, Lucy saw Sirius had put on his indicator and was turning left towards Isleworth.

CHAPTER SIXTY-THREE

Monday 3 December, 11.05 a.m.

Being in the car had lulled Dan to sleep. He hadn't wanted to drift off, he had too many questions – like where Besnik and his goons had taken the man who'd been screaming – but a dark wave lapped at the corner of his consciousness and although he'd tried his hardest, he hadn't been able to stop it from flooding his mind.

He awoke with a thundering headache. His body had started to stiffen and he knew it would take some serious medication to make any kind of dent in the pain. He took in the fact that he was still in Joe's car, but it wasn't moving.

His eyes were gummed together and he had to force them open.

Blearily, he looked through the windscreen.

He forgot all about his pain. He forgot about the blood all over his clothes, the vomit in his hair.

Besnik stood dead ahead, looking at him, arms crossed. His goons were on either side.

He was back at the junkyard.

Joe said, 'Sorry, pal. It's all over now.'

Dan tried to think past the pain. He felt more tired than he had in his life. Utterly spent. He felt stupid that he hadn't seen it before.

Wearily, Dan said, 'It was all about showing the DG that you'd rescued me, wasn't it.'

'Clever boy,' said Joe. Pocketing his car key, he climbed out of the car. Bent down to add, 'And thanks to you, he swallowed it.'

Dan watched as his old friend, his colleague, informant and profiteer – code name Cedric – went and spoke to Besnik. The goons came over and opened Dan's door.

'Out,' said one, jerking a thumb at him.

Dan struggled to get out of the car. He made it look worse than it was but Joe called, 'He's playing it up. Just get him inside, would you?'

They grabbed him and marched him back to the Portakabin. The first thing he saw was Savannah, lying motionless on the floor. She was sprawled at an angle, one arm flung wide. Her eyes were shut, her face as white as paper. Blood seeped from her jacket onto the synthetic carpet. Dan sank to her side. Pressed his fingers against her throat. He tried not to react when he felt a faint pulse.

Besnik walked past him without a glance. Headed into the yard. Joe came and stood over Dan.

'Why?' asked Dan. He was looking at Savannah as he spoke. His question meant to cover everything but the main one burning was, *why did you betray me, get my son tortured and killed?*

When Joe didn't answer, Dan looked up to see him looking at him. Joe said, 'You just don't remember, do you?' He looked regretful.

'Why?' Dan said again. 'Please. I want to know.'

'Look, I've been trading with Besnik for years. Everything nice and tidy until you came along, Stella's little protégé who could do no wrong.'

'You got Luke killed,' Dan said hoarsely.

'You probably won't believe me, but I didn't know what Besnik planned on doing. I thought he was going to torture you, throw you back at MI5 unable to walk without a walking frame or eat without a feeding tube, but he went that one step further. Clever. Because it worked. Nobody wanted to risk their families by going undercover against Besnik again, which made things a lot easier for me, I have to admit.'

Dan's breathing constricted.

'Didn't you think of Jenny? Luke's death just about killed her.'

Joe smiled. 'Oh, the lovely Jenny. The stunningly beautiful arrogant Jenny who always looked at me like I was something she'd scraped off the bottom of her shoe. The lovely Jenny who needed comforting when her husband went mad, but even then she wouldn't fuck me. I would have done anything to have fucked your wife, you know. So you'd know first-hand what it feels like to be a cuckold.'

Dan stared.

'You and Laura were at it like rabbits for over a year.' Joe's face twisted. 'Everyone knew about it but me. People dropped hints but I refused to believe them. Can you imagine the humiliation? My best friend and work colleague, fucking my wife?'

Laura. So the woman from his dreams wasn't a figment of his imagination. She was a real person. Having an affair with his best friend's wife explained the anxiety that dogged his subconscious.

Savannah's voice: *You're different, you know . . . you're still you, but something fundamental has changed.*

Like he was no longer sleeping with his colleague's wife.

'But Luke,' Dan protested. 'He was just a *boy*.'

Joe didn't appear to hear. He turned to one of the goons. 'Tie him up. Get the container ready.'

There seemed no point trying to fight the two thugs but Dan gave it his best shot. He surged to his feet. One of them slammed against him, driving a fist into Dan's stomach. For a terrifying moment, Dan couldn't breathe. And then his legs were kicked out from under him. As he fell and struck the floor, his breath returned in a rush. Spasms of pain surged through his body and made him groan.

He felt a narrow band of plastic tighten on his left wrist. He was dragged to Savannah. His right wrist tied to her left.

Dazed, Dan watched Joe cross the Portakabin and open the door. A man Dan recognised stepped inside. Fifties, with a long face and dark eyes. Winter coat, leather gloves. He'd seen him outside Stella's house all those days ago, wearing a camel coat. He held a laptop in one hand. He looked at Savannah and Dan incuriously.

'You're late,' Joe told the man.

'I don't like to speed,' the man said calmly.

'Jesus, Sirius. We're on a timetable here and you're worried about getting caught on camera?'

'Correct.' Sirius put his laptop on the table and opened the lid, booted it up. 'The transaction went smoothly. Would you like to check?'

'OK.' Joe ran a hand over his head. He brought out his phone. Tapped and looked, tapped and looked again. 'Excellent,' he said.

'Indeed,' said Sirius. 'While I am here, I would like our account settled.'

Joe blinked. 'What, now?'

Sirius turned to his laptop. 'I'd like to be paid half in US dollars, half in sterling.'

'Can't we do this another time?' Joe indicated Dan and Savannah. 'As you can see, I'm somewhat preoccupied.'

Sirius simply looked at Joe. Joe fidgeted.

'OK,' Joe relented. 'Let's do it.'

Dan watched as Joe and Sirius completed their transaction. When Sirius closed the lid of his laptop, Joe reached out a hand to shake with Sirius, but Sirius ignored him. He simply picked up his computer and walked outside without a word.

Dan waited for one of the men to go to the door and push the bolts back into place, but they didn't. A small part of his spirit lifted at their carelessness. If he could free himself from Savannah, he could be through that door in a trice.

'Jesus.' Joe rubbed his face. 'That guy gets worse every time I see him.'

'Who is he?' asked Dan.

Joe looked across. 'You really don't have a clue, do you?'

'He doesn't seem to like you much.'

'Sirius doesn't like anyone much.' Joe put his phone away. 'I guess he doesn't have to, considering his job. He's a cleaner. Freelance. He's the best there is. Costs a fortune but he gets the job done. You should know that. You used him enough.'

Joe glanced through the window as though to watch Sirius leave. He craned his neck sharply. Stared for a few seconds. Then his whole body tensed. He said, 'Jesus Christ. What the fuck is Grace Reavey doing here?'

CHAPTER SIXTY-FOUR

When Sirius Thiele pulled up outside a junkyard, Lucy slowed too, turning her head from side to side, taking it all in. Her pulse jumped when she saw a scattering of shipping containers near a loading dock, the notice saying *recycling with integrity.*

Her nerves tightened. Was this where Sirius had disposed of the bodies? What about the torture site? Was it also here?

Sirius pulled to the side of the road, next to what appeared to be the site office and Lucy drove past and kept going, checking her rear-view mirror all the time.

Heart tripping, she drove to the bottom of the street and turned right and out of sight. She quickly drove three sides of the box, checking out the area. Wall-to-wall warehouses and industrial buildings. Everything was quiet. No public phones. Lucy hurriedly returned to check on the grey sedan. Still there.

'I'm going to do another recce,' Lucy told Grace. 'I want to see if the scrapyard is guarded, whether it has CCTV or dogs or razor wire. Then we'll find a phone.'

She retraced her route. Drove up the street from the opposite direction.

She couldn't see any razor wire but there were several CCTV cameras dotted about. She dropped her speed, studying the handful of containers but none were stamped with RCF, Recycling For Charity. She was letting her eyes scan over the rubble of tyres and rusting washing machines, dishwashers, when a man came into view.

He was running like hell.

His mouth was agape, his arms and legs moving like pistons.

Behind him loped two enormous mastiffs.

'Christ,' she said. She veered the car to the kerb.

The man leaped over a stack of computer monitors, stumbling as he landed. The dogs began to close in on him.

Lucy sprang out of the car. Ducked down to Grace.

'Get to a phone,' she said urgently. 'Dial 999. Then ring my boss, Faris MacDonald. GO!'

Lucy tore to the fence. The man spotted her. 'Help!' he gasped.

Lucy froze for a split second. She recognised him from his photographs. Mid-thirties, brown curly hair, chunky build.

Tim Atherton.

He tried to run in her direction but one of the dogs saw him off.

Lucy hooked her fingers into the mesh and began to climb. She glanced over her shoulder to see Grace running down the street full tilt, arms neat at her sides, her legs moving straight and true.

Shit! Why hadn't Grace taken the car?

No time to waste thinking about it. Lucy turned back to the junkyard to see Tim duck around a decaying sofa. He desperately began to climb a stack of balsa wood but one of the dogs snapped at his foot and he overbalanced, came crashing down.

Lucy rattled the fence as hard as she could.

She shouted, 'Dogs! Come!'

To her astonishment, both dogs paused in their attack.

'Come!' she commanded fiercely.

They hesitated. One of them looked back at Tim who was now on the other side of the balsa wood and legging it across the yard.

'Dogs! Come!' she tried again, but this time they ignored her and raced after Tim once more. She had to hope she'd given him enough time to hide.

She clung to the fence, hesitating. Her priority as a police officer was to preserve life. Then to preserve the scene and secure evidence. Should she jump in the car and grab Grace and get help or continue over the fence and try and help Tim Atherton?

A movement out of the corner of her eye made her click her attention back to the Portakabin. Sirius was stepping outside.

Lucy's pulse went into overdrive. She prayed he wouldn't see Grace running away. Grace was fast, but she wasn't out of view yet. Lucy froze. She didn't want to move, bring his attention to her but she may as well have been painted head to toe in Day-Glo yellow because the second his feet hit the pavement, Sirius looked straight at her.

She didn't hesitate.

She clambered up and over the fence as fast as she could, dropping to the other side and racing for cover behind a battered estate car. Her heart was thundering, her skin pouring sweat. She peered around the car's metal flank to see Sirius was in his vehicle, driving past. He was looking dead ahead, as though he hadn't seen her.

She didn't understand it, but she didn't have time to make sense of his behaviour.

Where was Tim Atherton?

And then she heard the barking.

CHAPTER SIXTY-FIVE

Grace had fallen into a rhythm. There was no point in sprinting and then collapsing in a heap, so the second she turned the corner at the bottom of the street, she levelled out her speed. Began looking for help.

More warehouses. More industrial buildings.

She had to head for a residential area. Shops, buses, traffic, people, life. Her heart soared when, ahead, she saw a van cross the street. Then another.

She increased her pace.

When she heard an engine behind her, she paused, looking over her shoulder.

A cry escaped her throat.

It was the grey sedan.

Sirius Thiele was coming after her.

She hadn't wanted to leave Lucy without her car, a quick getaway, but now she wished she'd taken it. *You fool.*

She faced forward. Began to race for the crossroads.

She could hear his engine, a smooth hum. It got closer. And closer.

She began to whimper.

The car passed her, drove ahead. Then pulled over.

Sirius climbed out.

Grace stopped. She stared at him. She felt lightheaded and fought to concentrate.

He held up her and Lucy's handbags.

He said, 'I have fulfilled my previous contract. I am under no obligations to my previous employer. Which is why I would like to return these items.'

No way was Grace going to believe anything he said and he seemed to realise this because he nodded and said, 'I will leave them here.'

In disbelief she watched him place both handbags on the pavement and return to his car. He looked back at her. Black pebbles in a long face. He looked oddly sad. He said quietly, 'You're not stupid. You're brave.'

And then he turned and climbed into his sedan and drove away.

CHAPTER SIXTY-SIX

Dan heard the dogs going berserk. Deep guttural barks that gradually rose in pitch to a hysterical baying.

The plastic tie was cutting into his wrist, his fingers starting to numb, but he didn't move. He lay slumped, motionless, face down, pretending he'd lost consciousness.

He heard Joe say, 'What the . . .'

Then Joe's footsteps crossing the Portakabin.

Brief silence.

'Shit,' he said, then he clicked his fingers twice. 'The prisoner's escaped. You two, with me. Alek, guard this prick.'

Dan counted three pairs of footsteps leaving the Portakabin. As soon as the door clicked shut behind them, Dan took a peek at Alek, the piggy-eyed guard, who appeared riveted to whatever was happening outside.

Surreptitiously Dan pressed his fingers against the underside of Savannah's wrist. Felt her pulse. Thready. It was weakening. If she wasn't hospitalised soon, she'd die.

The thought gave him strength.

He dug in his pocket for his key chain, his little knife.

But it had gone.

CHAPTER SIXTY-SEVEN

Grace ran back to the junkyard, giving directions on her phone. She'd slung Lucy's handbag across her shoulder and now she clutched her voluminous bag against her chest, wishing it wasn't so heavy, so unwieldy.

'I'm approaching the Portakabin now . . .' She was panting hard, struggling to keep up her pace.

'Under no circumstances should you approach the premises,' the policeman told her.

As she ran past the junkyard she could hear dogs barking furiously. Then she heard a *crack!*

Holy crap. It was a gunshot.

Crack, crack!

'Guns,' she gasped. 'They're shooting.'

'I need you to get out of the area,' the officer said.

Where's Lucy?

She could hardly breathe now – her lungs were burning – but her legs somehow kept going and she made it to the Portakabin. Chest heaving, she peered through the window. A thick-necked young man with a buzz cut had his back to her. He seemed to be staring through the window overlooking the yard.

Her eyes went to the figures on the floor. A man and a woman. Tied together. The woman was bleeding and deathly pale.

She was opening her mouth to tell the officer to call an ambulance when the man looked up, straight at her.

'Oh my God.' Her head began to buzz.

'What is it?' the officer demanded urgently.

'It's Dan.' Her voice was faint.

He was a mess. Bruised and bloody, one eye was almost swollen shut and his mouth was also caked in blood, but his one good eye was bright, his expression fierce.

He showed Grace the plastic tie strapping his wrist to the injured woman. Then he made a sawing motion across the tie and raised his eyebrows at her.

Dear God. He wanted her to free him.

No way. She wasn't cut out for this. Her stomach tightened so much she thought she might be sick. She started to back away. She didn't want to die.

Oh for goodness sake, Grace. Her mother's voice. *Stop being so pathetic and help the poor man.*

But I don't want to!

You're much braver than you know. Just do it.

She heard the policeman's squawks as she shoved the phone inside her trouser pocket. Her hands were shaking so hard it took two tries before she managed to open her handbag. A quick search showed there was nothing that would cut him free. Lucy's handbag, however, came up trumps.

A Swiss Army Knife.

Trembling, whimpering under her breath, she put both bags on the ground. Palmed the knife and slipped to the Portakabin door. As quietly as she could, she tried the door handle.

Slowly, it turned.

When it had gone as far as it could, she pushed the door gently.

Surely, it has to be locked. Please make it locked so I can go and hide and wait for the police to arrive.

But it wasn't.

She felt a moan lodge in her throat.

I should wait for the police.

But what if the woman died in the meantime? Or Dan got shot? *How will I live with myself then?*

She was her mother's daughter, she reminded herself. It was time to prove it.

She began to open the door.

CHAPTER SIXTY-EIGHT

The instant Dan saw the door move, he braced himself.

Slowly, it inched open.

Grace's eyes were on Alek, her face taut with fear.

But Alek was absorbed in whatever was happening in the yard.

Grace glanced at Dan. She showed him the distinctive red of a Swiss Army Knife in her palm. Good girl, she'd already opened a blade. He nodded at her, trying to encourage her inside.

She pushed the door open a little more. Then a little more, until the gap was wide enough for her to creep through. But as she took her first step inside, something creaked.

Alek turned.

He stared at Grace.

'Hello,' said Grace. She was so white Dan wondered how she didn't faint.

'Who the fuck are you?' asked Alek. His piggy eyes looked as though they were about to pop from his head.

'I'm Grace,' she repeated. Her voice was thin and reedy.

'Who?'

He began to walk forward and for a moment Dan thought Grace was going to turn around and flee, but instead she sidled into the Portakabin, pulling the door behind her.

'I'm a doctor,' she said.

'What?' Alek looked at her as though she was speaking Martian.

When she took a step towards Dan, Alek said, 'Keep away from them.'

'Why?'

'Just keep away. And keep still, OK?'

He moved across the room and picked up the phone. He never took his eyes off Grace.

'Who are you ringing?' she croaked.

Alek didn't answer. He dialled, and waited. Nobody appeared to answer but he continued to wait.

'I'm sorry,' said Grace, 'but there are two injured people here. I have to help them.'

She moved with surprising decisiveness for Dan.

'No,' Alek interjected. He dropped the phone into the cradle and started for her.

'I'm a doctor,' Grace snapped.

And then she was ducked next to Dan and for a moment he thought she wouldn't be able to cut the tie, she was shaking so badly, but then she put both hands around the body of the knife and jerked the blade upwards, straight through the plastic.

Dan grabbed the knife. Pushed her to one side and lunged for Alek.

Alek narrowed his gaze and raised his fist, striking Dan's shoulder with such force that he was knocked to the floor. Gasping, ignoring his pain, Dan scrambled to his feet and charged Alek, ramming his elbow deep into his kidneys. Before Alek could recover, he rammed him again.

Alek groaned, doubling over, holding his side from the pain in his right kidney. Instantly Dan punched him in his mid-riff, just below his breastbone. Twice. The breath rushed out of him. *Ooof.*

Alek went down slowly, writhing, struggling to breathe. Dan gripped his chin and put the knife against his throat. Alek continued to gasp but he tried to still his body, his gaze riveted on Dan.

'Tell Grace where the plastic cables are. She wants to tie you up, don't you Grace?'

'Box,' Alek choked. 'Under the table.'

Dan heard Grace moving but he didn't turn around. He said, 'What do you know about Gabriel's handover tomorrow?'

'Nothing.' Fear flooded the man's eyes. 'I swear it.'

Dan pushed the knife until it broke the skin. Blood started to trickle down Alek's throat. The man moaned. 'Please. I'm only a guard. I don't know anything about any other stuff.'

Grace returned to stand at their side. She held out a handful of plastic cables. 'Just two,' Dan told her.

He moved Alek to secure one hand to a heating pipe, the other to one of the table struts. The guard was spread-eagled, able to use only a limited amount of force against his bonds.

Dan went to Savannah and, with Grace's help, pulled her into a sitting position. Then he knelt and, bowing before her, let her fall over his shoulder.

'Are you sure you're up to this?' Grace asked anxiously.

'Yup.'

He heaved himself to his knees. Every muscle in his body screamed at him to stop, but he ignored the pain. Shifted his position slightly. Felt Savannah's weight settle on his shoulder.

He rose. A wave of dizziness made him stumble to one side but he fought it. Remained upright.

Walked for the door.

Grace opened it.

They stepped outside. Grace picked two bags off the pavement and followed him up the street.

'A policewoman's gone into the yard,' she said. 'Lucy Davies.' Hastily, she filled him in. 'I also called the police,' she added. 'They should be here any minute.'

'Good.'

The instant they turned the corner and were out of sight, Dan sank to his knees. He said, 'Help her.'

Grace dumped the bags on the ground. Stripped off the woman's jacket and unclipped her holster. Raised the blood-sodden shirt.

'Pass me my phone,' she said urgently. 'It's in the big bag.'

While she put pressure on the woman's wound, checked her vital signs – not great – he upended her bag on the ground. Passed the phone over. She dialed 999. Demanded an ambulance, paramedics, blue lights.

Dan said, 'Stay with her.'

She looked up to see he was already stumbling back to the junkyard.

CHAPTER SIXTY-NINE

Sweat pouring, heart thundering, Lucy crept through the yard.

The dogs continued their hysterical barking.

She slunk past a pile of old shipping pallets. The barking grew louder.

Then she saw them.

Tim Atherton was atop a crushed mini-van. The dogs were leaping at him, jaws snapping, but he stood just out of reach.

Before him stood another man, tall and lean, neatly dressed in dark trousers, white shirt and jacket. He didn't look as though he belonged here. He looked as though he should be in a corporate meeting. He appeared to be talking to Tim but Lucy couldn't hear what he was saying above the barking.

Then Lucy saw a heavy-set man appear. Brown hair, fleshy lips. He wore strips of tape over a nose which looked as though it had been recently broken. His clothes were bloodstained, the skin around his eyes swelling. He was smoking a cigarette. As she watched, he said something to the Suit who brought out a gun, trained it on Tim.

The man with the cigarette walked to a shipping container and opened the door. Then he called the dogs to him. Stood by the container with the dogs at his side.

The Suit spoke to Tim.

Tim shook his head.

The Suit fired his gun.

Crack!

Tim jumped. Began to scramble off the van.

The Suit indicated the container. Tim took a step backwards.

The man sent the dogs for Tim. Tim flung up his hands and yelled. This time she heard him.

'OK, OK!'

The man called off his dogs once more.

Tim walked unsteadily to the container.

Lucy wanted to break up the tableau. Give Tim another chance. She looked around. Grabbed what appeared to be part of an old bicycle pump. Lobbed it as hard as she could away from her.

CLANG.

All three men turned their heads towards the sound.

Lucy immediately crawled away, looking for somewhere safe to hide. She didn't want the dogs to rip her to pieces. She wriggled past a pile of washing machines, heading for a rusting, burned-out Jeep carcass.

She heard a noise behind her and her adrenaline spiked. She raised her body to sprint away from it but hands grabbed her shirt, lifting her by the collar and slamming her against the side of a car.

A bulky man with bulging shoulders stood in front of her, holding her up by her throat. She clutched his hand, gasping but he didn't relax his grip. She felt her feet leave the ground.

His breath smelled of stale onions and cigarettes.

He said something but it was in another language and she didn't understand. Was he Russian? Albanian?

Her legs swung wildly but she couldn't reach him.

Desperately she tried to breathe.

Suddenly, a man silently loomed behind her attacker. He raised his fist and slammed it against her attacker's head.

There was a soft *chock*. Like the sound of an axe hitting wood.

Her attacker's eyes rolled upwards and his mouth opened. He released his grip on her throat.

Her feet met the ground at the same moment the man crumpled into a heap.

Holding her throat, panting, she looked at the man who'd knocked him out. He had a smashed up face, bruised and bloody with one eye almost swollen shut. He held a small rock cupped in his hand.

For a second neither of them spoke. Then she said, 'Who the hell are you?'

CHAPTER SEVENTY

Dan hurried to the container with Lucy on his heels. He'd told her to stay where she was, that the police had been alerted by Grace, but she'd ignored him, wired to the max, convinced Tim Atherton was going to be killed any second.

He couldn't argue with her. He'd seen Besnik and his dogs, heard Joe tell Tim to get into the container.

Once Tim was inside, Joe would shoot him. Seal it up and send it overseas. And if he wasn't careful, he and Lucy would suffer the same fate.

But time was running out for Joe.

The police were on their way.

All Dan and Lucy had to do was disarm Joe. Contain the dogs. Get Besnik and his men to see sense and surrender.

Yeah, right.

They were two goons down. Only another two to go, but where were they? At that moment, he saw Jacks. He was standing next to the container with Besnik. He held a pistol at his side. He was jumpy, obviously waiting for an explanation of the loud 'clang' Lucy had made, but Besnik didn't look too worried. He clearly had more faith in his goons than Jacks did.

Dan turned to Lucy. Outlined his plan.

'No way.' Her eyes were wide with alarm. 'It's suicide. Neither of us have a weapon and besides, you're a mess. You can barely see through one eye it's so swollen.'

He ignored her. Began to move away.

'Dan,' she hissed.

He kept going.

'Dan!'

He ducked down, beginning to track around the yard.

He heard her say *fuck*, but he didn't pause. Keeping low, he continued his progress towards the men and the container. When he'd positioned himself to his satisfaction, he rose. Straightened his shoulders and walked into sight.

All four men – Tim Atherton, Besnik, Joe and Jacks – stared at him.

He said, 'Hi guys. How's it going?'

He kept walking.

Besnik's nose had started to bloat. His face was bruised and he was splattered with blood. He made a growling noise at the back of his throat when he saw Dan. The dogs looked up at him.

'Here, doggy doggy,' called Dan.

The dogs looked at him, tongues lolling. Their tails tick-tocked from side to side at the sound of his voice. A slow wag. They remembered him as they'd remembered Joe. The bumps they'd made with their snouts hadn't been a precursor to an attack. They had been friendly nudges. A dog's way of saying hello, remember me?

'Fucksake.' Joe's face turned white with fury. He swung his pistol round. Trained it on him. But Dan didn't stop walking.

'I thought you should know that the police have been called,' Dan said. 'So before you do anything rash, I'd put your weapons down. You have approximately three minutes before they arrive. I'd use the time wisely. Say, get your affairs in order, or make a run for it.'

Jacks stared. He said, 'Are you messing with us?'

'No.'

In the distance, he heard the faint sound of a siren.

Jacks heard it too. He shook his head, saying, 'Hell, man. You're nothing but trouble.'

'Tim,' said Dan. 'Walk away. Now.'

The man was trembling and shaking. He started to walk unsteadily towards Dan.

Joe turned his pistol to aim at Tim's back.

'You shoot him, you go to jail for life,' Dan warned. He extended his pace. 'You shoot me, you can make up any story you like. They might even believe you.'

'You fuck,' said Joe. He swung his gun back. Aimed it straight between Dan's eyes.

Dan was closing in. Besnik moved towards the container. The dogs moved with him. Joe was ten yards away. Jacks five.

Tim walked past him. Out of sight.

Now, Lucy, he thought.

Jacks was shifting from foot to foot and bringing up his gun.

Now! he yelled in his mind.

He saw Joe's grip tighten on the pistol.

Dan's gut tightened.

Joe was going to shoot him.

'POLICE!' yelled Lucy. 'PUT DOWN YOUR WEAPONS OR WE WILL SHOOT!'

At that, everything went crazy.

CHAPTER SEVENTY-ONE

The second Lucy shouted, Dan exploded into a sprint for Jacks.

Crack!

Joe had been caught by surprise. He'd missed.

Dan was aware of Tim Atherton breaking into a run, disappearing; Besnik taking shelter behind the container door; the dogs vanishing.

Knowing Joe would be aiming for him again, Dan jinked.

Crack!

Joe had missed again.

Jacks tried to turn away but Dan was upon him in a flash. He punched him in the chest, going for his gun. Jacks didn't seem to have the stomach for a fight and virtually gave Dan his weapon.

When Jacks made to run away Dan grabbed him, spun him round, using him as a shield.

Crack!

Joe fired at Dan again. Jacks gave a groan and doubled over. Dan pushed him aside, bringing up his gun. 'Drop it, Joe!'

Jacks staggered away, clutching his stomach.

The two men faced each other.

Besnik stepped from behind the container door. He said to Joe, 'Shoot him.'

Dan shifted his weight and swung his gun in one easy movement. It was so fast that by the time Besnik realised what was happening it was too late.

The bullet hit Besnik in the forehead, just above his right eye. His head snapped back, blood spraying. He toppled backwards, crashed to the ground.

'JOE TALBOT! IF YOU MOVE I WILL SHOOT YOU!'

Joe flinched as Lucy shouted. Hearing his name had distracted him. His attention on Dan wavered.

Lucy's timing was immaculate.

Dan dropped to the ground, rolling to his left at the same time as Joe pulled his trigger.

A sound like a whiplash by Dan's ear as the bullet just missed him.

Still rolling, Dan held Jacks's gun in both hands. In control. As though he'd been doing it all his life. He brought the bead to rest perfectly in the V. He squeezed off his second shot.

The bullet hit Joe in the chest. He staggered to the side. There was a hole above his ribcage, and blood gushed out in waves, flooding his shirt.

His right arm dangled. His fingers opened. He dropped his gun. Slowly he fell to his knees.

Dan walked over. Lifted his gun and pressed it against the side of Joe's head.

'Please,' said Joe. 'No.'

'You killed my son.'

'That was Besnik,' Joe said. He coughed. Blood coated his lips.

'But it was you who betrayed me.'

'Dan!' shouted Lucy.

Gently, he pressured the trigger.

'DAN!' she yelled. 'NO!'

The world seemed to tilt. A flash of blond hair flew at the corner of his vision, followed by a little boy's laughter. Aimee ran after Luke, beaming. Jenny was laughing and crying. Tears of happiness, of loss.

He felt Lucy's hand on his arm.

'Enough, Dan,' she said. Her tone was gentle.

He maintained the pressure on the trigger. He could still hear Luke's laughter.

'Enough,' she repeated.

His son's voice faded.

Silence.

Finally, he nodded. Retracted the pistol.

'Yes,' he said. 'Enough.'

CHAPTER SEVENTY-TWO

Lucy sat on the pavement while police swarmed through the scrapyard. She was shivering. Her skin felt cold.

Grace came and sat next to her.

'You OK?'

Lucy gave a nod. 'Thanks for calling the cavalry.'

'I wish it had been sooner.'

'Me too.'

After Lucy had stopped Dan from shooting Joe Talbot, she'd gone to find Tim Atherton. She'd found him cowering behind the mountain of mashed cars, clutching a crowbar. He'd been so scared, so strung out that it had taken her a good minute to talk him into dropping his weapon and another two to calm him into some semblance of normality. Whatever that was.

When she returned to the scene of the shooting, Dan came over.

He looked at her. He said, 'Thanks.'

'You were going to kill him.'

'Yes.'

Dan stared at her for a long time.

'I'm glad I didn't,' he said.

'Me too,' she agreed. He would have put her in the impossible position of having to decide whether to cover up for him or not. Even though it wouldn't have been her job to investigate the crime scene – which would be undertaken by the local division – she wouldn't have wanted to carry that sort of judgement with her for the rest of her life.

One dead and three seriously wounded. The MI5 officer Savannah Connors was on her way to hospital, along with Joe Talbot and Jacks, who'd been shot in the stomach.

The goon that Dan had knocked unconscious came round to find he was already handcuffed and in police custody. The second goon never materialised. Nobody knew where he'd gone but Lucy guessed he'd legged it the second he'd heard the sirens closing in.

Both dogs had had to be tranquillised before the RSPCA transported them to their animal welfare centre. What would happen to two attack dogs with a dodgy past was anyone's guess. Lucy couldn't imagine who might be brave enough to rehome them.

And Sirius? When Grace told her he'd given her their handbags back, she hadn't known what to make of it. What a peculiar and frightening man. Had he known they were following him? If so, why hadn't he shaken them off? She couldn't work it out. She wondered what made him tick but didn't spend too much time on the subject. Even a professional psychiatrist would have trouble comprehending a professional 'cleaner'.

She'd already checked his sedan's number plate to find the car had been rented from Heathrow Airport to a Mr Robson, on business in the UK from Washington DC. He'd provided a passport and driver's licence but Lucy bet that his ID as well as the address he'd given didn't exist. He'd paid cash, of course.

She watched SOCOs come and go. They wouldn't send in the forensic team until their boss was happy they had everything from the crime scene. Then the pathologist would arrive and finally Besnik Kolcei's remains would be heaved into a body bag and shovelled inside a coroner's van.

She and Grace sat quietly. Lucy wondered who would interview them and hoped they'd be top-tier. She didn't fancy repeating herself ad infinitum – and she didn't hold out much hope since the team had already stuffed up by not keeping her and Grace separate – but who was she to point this out? She was just a PC.

A black Jaguar with darkened windows was stopped by an officer and directed to park further down the street. Two men climbed out. The older one wore a suit, the other running shoes, jeans and a fleece. As they approached, Dan appeared, went over and greeted them. Shook hands. Together they approached the DI in charge of the investigation. Lots of talking. Gesticulating. Finally, the DI flung up his hands and turned away, looking disgusted. The three men started to walk to the Jaguar. Then Dan looked her way. Came over.

He said, 'Nice working with you.'

She gave a nod.

'If you ever need a job, I can have a word with the Director General.' He indicated the older guy climbing into the driver's seat.

Lucy laughed. She hadn't laughed for so long it felt odd, but wildly satisfying.

Her, a spook?

He had to be joking.

CHAPTER SEVENTY-THREE

Lucy returned to Stockton late that night. She staggered off the train exhausted, her mind spinning after a six-hour debrief with the Metropolitan police. She'd thought about staying with her mother overnight but she knew she'd be unbearable, pacing her house trying to pull together the last threads of the case, so she'd caught the Tube straight to Kings Cross Station. She wanted to get back to Stockton – she still had questions that needed answering.

'But what about your car?' Grace said.

'I'll collect it at the weekend.'

'Stay the night,' Grace offered. 'We can share a bottle of wine.'

To Lucy's surprise the GP had embraced her and kissed both her cheeks. 'You're one hell of a woman,' she said.

'You are too.'

On the train, Lucy texted Mac to tell him she'd be at work in the morning. He texted straight back, saying he'd pick her up from the station, what train was she on?

She didn't respond.

When she arrived outside her flat, it was pouring with rain and she was drenched in the eight steps it took to get from the taxi to her front door. She fumbled with her key, cursing when she missed the lock.

'Lucy,' he called.

Her stomach thrilled to hear his voice. Her heart beat faster.

'Lucy,' he called again, urgently.

His footsteps splashed through the rain. He was running.

She turned round. When she saw him, a rush of blood flowed from her heart and through every vein, sending a shiver down her legs.

'God, Lucy. When I heard . . .' He came and stood before her. Rain ran from his hair, down his face. 'Are you OK?'

'Fine, thanks.'

'I've been worried sick.'

She moved her attention to unlocking her front door. Stepping inside, she turned and began closing it behind her.

'Hey.' Mac put out a hand. 'Can't I come in for a moment?'

'No.'

'What if I told you that Joe Talbot had a sister? Eileen Price? And that her husband is on the board of Recycling For Charity?'

She studied him for a moment. And then she made a fatal mistake.

It must have been because she was tired. Because she'd faced a serial killer. Because she'd seen a man die, his head blown apart. She still had rust marks on her clothes from climbing the junkyard fence, specks of blood on her shoes. Her defences were down.

She looked at his mouth.

Remembered what it was like kissing him. Being held by him.

His eyes darkened. He made a low groaning sound. 'Christ,' he said.

In two quick steps he was in the hall. His hands were on her waist. His breathing was ragged.

She was staring at his lips. She thought she would never breathe again unless she kissed him right here, right now.

He bent his head to hers, hesitating for a second as though asking her permission.

No thought. No hesitation.

Her mind was a smooth clear lake.

She reached up and wrapped her arms around his neck and kissed him. Opened her mouth and touched her tongue to his.

He groaned again, deep in his throat.

Then he slammed the front door shut with his foot. In one movement he swept her off her feet and into his arms.

'Which way?' he panted.

She pointed.

He carried her up the stairs. Held her against his chest while she opened her bedroom door. The second they were inside, they began undressing each other, fingers fumbling in their haste and urgency.

The shock of his naked skin against hers made her gasp.

She'd forgotten how good he felt. How they fitted so well together.

He kept saying her name. *Lucy, Lucy, Lucy.*

She didn't say his until he was asleep. And when she whispered it, it was for her alone to hear.

Faris.

CHAPTER SEVENTY-FOUR

Grace attempted to make a lasagne over the weekend. Ross helped by washing up and making helpful comments, like *shouldn't the onion be browned before you add the meat?*

She'd have to do a cookery course, she decided. They couldn't live on takeaways and deli food for ever. Or could they? She still had her mother's £30,000 buried in the back garden which could keep them in chicken curries for a couple of decades.

Ross was more in love with Lone Pine Farm than ever, but Grace was no longer panicking because she knew that no matter where in the world he went, she'd go with him. The relief of knowing this was immense because she didn't have to worry about losing him any more and she could look forward to a whole new surgery of – hopefully – more vigorous patients.

She was taking the pasta out of its container – fresh from the supermarket, she wasn't going to try making that yet – when she heard someone at the door. Dismayed, she glanced at the kitchen clock. Bang on eleven.

'We'll finish it later.' Ross looked at her. 'Are you OK?'

'Yes.'

'I'll hide in the study. Leave you guys to the sitting room. If you need me, shout.'

Grace whipped off her kitchen apron and dragged her fingers through her hair as she walked to the door. Opened it.

'Hello, Grace.'

'Hi, Bernard.'

Despite the fact that she hadn't met her mother's old boss before, he seemed remarkably familiar. Then she realised she'd seen him with Dan outside the junkyard. The same black Jaguar now sat next to her hatchback. A young man was in the driver's seat, looking at them.

'That's Ellis,' said Bernard. 'One of Dan's old colleagues.'

She nodded at Ellis, who nodded back.

'Shall I come in?' asked Bernard.

'Of course.' She felt oddly flustered. 'Can I get you a coffee?'

'No, thank you. But it's kind of you to offer.'

He followed her into the sitting room, where Ross had lit a fire. He took the armchair while Grace took the sofa. Normally she'd tuck her legs beneath her but she was too tense. She leaned forward. 'You wanted to talk to me about Mum?'

'Yes. She wasn't just a colleague of mine, you see. She was a very dear friend. She entrusted me with her life not once, but several times.'

He held her eyes. 'You received the package I sent you? With your mother's bank details?'

Grace blinked. 'You're Mr Smith?'

He smiled.

'About my mother's money . . .' she began.

'She didn't earn it doing anything illicit,' Bernard said. 'But we set it up to make it look as though she had. Cedric – as we code-named Joe Talbot before we knew who he was – would never have bought Gabriel from her if he didn't think she'd crossed the line into criminality.'

He cleared his throat. 'Stella made a mistake, though. She tried to entrap Cedric without telling me, without telling anyone. I could understand why she chose to do it but I couldn't condone it. It was risky and hazardous, and it went terribly wrong. A rather brilliant scientist died.'

Grace continued to watch Bernard carefully but inside something tightened. Her mother's mistake had caused someone's death?

'It was Stella, you see, who demonstrated Gabriel at the Wembley concert, along with two scientists, Peter Miller and Suzie Lui. Stella let it be known through dark circles that she was going to demonstrate the machine but not when or where, but that any interested buyer would see evidence of it in the newspapers on Sunday the fourth of November.

'No buyer knew who Gabriel's seller was, but as Stella hoped, Cedric – Joe – guessed. Joe must have put a tracker on Stella without her knowing. It's our guess the moment he saw the two scientists at Wembley with Stella, he put two and two together and brought in Besnik and his goons to snatch Gabriel after the demonstration. He paid Stella that very evening. Cunning old Cedric seized Gabriel from beneath everyone's noses – Syria, Russia and China had all expressed interest – and put it on the market himself but at a much higher price.'

Inside, Grace was dazed, picking her way through the strands of deceit and seemingly endless machinations. Her mother, the woman she thought she knew, had grown in stature and become flawed as well as heroic, and she found herself suffused with a mixture of astonishment and an immense sense of pride.

'She never told me she was with MI5,' Grace said sadly. If only she'd *known*, she could have supported her mother, but then her mother hadn't really needed supporting, she'd been so self-reliant.

'She wanted to protect you.'

Bernard leaned forward.

'Now, Grace. I actually came to talk about the, ah, money in one of her savings accounts. Nearly all of it is from Joe, when he bought Gabriel from Stella. Which means that the funds held at the First Caribbean Bank don't actually belong to your mother. I'm afraid I need this money moved to a solicitor's account where it will be held until the courts decide what is to be done with it.'

Grace cringed. She said, 'There's not much left. I had to pay Sirius.'

'Ah.' His gaze turned distant. 'The indubitable Sirius.'

Her skin prickled. 'You know him?'

'Personally, I've never met him,' he replied, as though that would answer her question.

'He absolutely terrified me,' she admitted. And Martin, she could have added, but didn't. Martin and Simon were still a secret, and she hoped they would remain as such. When she'd texted Martin and told him Sirius had his money, he'd called her immediately. 'Thank Christ.'

'You told him about Simon,' she said.

'I didn't have a choice. He wanted a lever against you and he threatened me with . . . Oh, God. Grace, it was awful . . .'

'Does anyone else know?' she asked.

'No, no.' He raced to reassure her. 'Jesus, you think I want it made public I didn't report you? It was only him, I swear it. Look, I'm going now. I don't expect to hear from you again, OK? Goodbye.'

He'd hung up and she didn't ring back, dropping any curiosity about how Sirius had pressured the country GP. She honestly didn't want to know. Oddly, she trusted Sirius to keep the secret, but she couldn't put her finger on exactly why. It may have had something to do with the way he'd looked when he'd returned her and Lucy's bags, his long face strangely sad.

You're not stupid. You're brave.

Bernard said, 'Your mother did an exemplary job in trapping Cedric the second time round. Without her plan to involve Dan, we might never have exposed Joe. I saw him in hospital yesterday, before he went into surgery. He was extremely cooperative, in the hope we'd be lenient. We managed to intercept Gabriel before the handover.'

'But isn't the weapon defective?' Grace asked.

'We didn't know this at the time. It is still extremely effective, but yes, we will now be working on a possible antidote, in case another undesirable obtains the technology. It means we will be one step ahead.' His eyes gleamed briefly before dimming into sobriety. 'Stella didn't die in vain, if that's what you're thinking. You can rest assured of that.'

Grace looked into the fire. She shifted her position slightly. Tucked a strand of hair behind her ear. 'What about the house in the British Virgin Islands?' she asked quietly. 'Do you want that as well?'

'What house?'

'It's in Nail Bay. Virgin Gorda.'

He raised his eyebrows. 'I don't know anything about a house in the Caribbean. Are you sure it's your mother's?'

'Yes. The title deeds were sent to me this week.'

'Then you and Ross will be having some nice holidays in the sun.' His expression warmed. 'It's a beautiful place to visit during the English winter.'

Grace thought for a moment, then said, 'Did Philip Denton have anything to do with this?'

'He knew something was up. He tried to put you off teaming up with Dan. He didn't succeed very well, did he?' Bernard gave a sigh. 'Philip isn't wholly popular with us at the moment since he's spending most of his time trying to keep DCA & Co.'s name clear of the whole mess, both here as well as in India. The last thing his company needs is to be tarnished with one of its own going bad.'

Rain pattered against the window. A log shifted on the fire, sending a shower of sparks up the chimney.

'Who searched my mother's house?' she asked. 'While I was at her funeral?'

'That was Joe. He persuaded Philip to check that Stella didn't have anything that might embarrass DCA & Co. in her house. Stella knew Cedric would be suspicious of her, so before your mother demonstrated the machine, she planted evidence that made it look as though she was a double-dealing felon out to feather her nest before she retired.'

'So her passports and money were planted specifically for Cedric, I mean Joe, to find? And then for Philip to find too? So everyone would think Stella was Cedric?'

'Yes.'

'And the sandy-haired man who searched my mother's house? Who Dan and I saw at DCA and followed to MI5?'

'One of mine. I planted him in DCA to give Stella back-up in case she needed it. Philip was furious Clipper was at the Mayfair office at the same time as you because he didn't want anyone to know he'd had your mother's house searched.'

Grace gazed at the rain dribbling down the windowpanes. What a strange world her mother had inhabited. A shadow world where nothing was real and where duplicity and subterfuge were the norm.

'She was one of our best officers,' Bernard said. His face grew sad. 'I miss her very much.'

CHAPTER SEVENTY-FIVE

Lucy's life turned into a blur of extensive debriefs and endless report writing. There were press conferences and media interviews. Endless questions and theorising. She chose to wear her uniform, not so much as a shield but because she felt an odd need to reclaim herself. People kept coming up and congratulating her and her email box was stuffed with laudatory messages, including some from her old colleagues in the Met. Even Magellan wrote one and if he tried to crawl any further up her backside she might have to throw up. He wanted her back on his team, he said. She was invaluable, an exemplary officer. She'd done her time in the boonies. It was time to return to her roots.

She hadn't responded yet. She'd put things on hold. Just for a little while. She wanted to think things over before she responded.

Mac worked hard to get her out on a date, but while she worked in the same station, she refused. He said, 'I'm not going to stop, you know. I won't give up.'

When she told him about the man who'd followed her in Reading, he'd looked away sheepishly. 'I pulled in a favour with

Vice,' he confessed. 'I asked them to keep an eye on you but they didn't do such a great job, did they?'

Lucy hadn't been able to stop her snort of laughter.

She visited Grace. They ate bowls of pasta in the kitchen and drank cheap red wine. Then Lucy asked if Grace could do her a favour.

'Of course.' Grace looked at her curiously.

'It's confidential.'

'OK.'

Lucy took a breath. 'I'd like you to test me to see if I'm bipolar.'

Grace stared. 'What?'

Once Lucy had explained, Grace agreed. No hesitation.

It took less time than she'd expected for Grace to come back to her and when the email pinged in her personal account, marked *Confidential: results*, Lucy went lightheaded.

Grace's message was lengthy and full of explanations, but Lucy's eyes went to the first word in the first sentence. It was all she needed.

NEGATIVE.

Not only was she *not* bipolar, but in a handwritten note Grace said Lucy's ability to see colours in her mind was probably due to a form of grapheme-colour synaesthesia, a neurological phenomenon in which stimulation of one cognitive pathway led to an involuntary experience in another, second pathway. Although very little scientific research had been done in this area, Grace assured her it wasn't anything to worry about. *Celebrate it!* Grace told her. *It sounds fantastic!*

And then there was the small fact she hadn't got any speeding tickets during her chase around the country. Sure, she probably wouldn't have been prosecuted once all was realised, but it was nice not to have the hassle.

The icing on the cake, however, was anonymously setting her old Met colleagues on Dr Mike Adamson, suggesting he might be taking kickbacks from PepsBeevers for some sort of unofficial trial on Zidazapine. The investigation found nothing along those lines but instead exposed the GP as a doctor who advocated doling out antidepressants like chocolate buttons and earning him a certified warning from the General Medical Council.

And what about Nate? She'd barely had the chance to think about him over the past fortnight, proving the adage *out of sight, out of mind* held true, at least for her. He'd rung her last week, ostensibly to see how she was, and when she'd heard his voice on her answerphone, she hadn't broken down and burst into tears. She'd erased his message and it had felt OK. Not great, but OK. Which meant she was OK too. More than OK, if she was honest, because right now she felt as though her life was just starting.

CHAPTER SEVENTY-SIX

Chitta sat at Niket's desk, checking his emails. Niket had told him he was only allowed to do this twice a day and if anything important came up, to let him know immediately.

He glanced at the Inspector's office to make sure he was still talking to Niket. Niket was in the chair opposite his boss, looking relaxed and at ease and nothing like he'd been over the past few weeks. It transpired that Niket had been blackmailed not to investigate the Cargo Killer case – a well-known local gang had threatened to snatch his little sister and pour kerosene down her throat – which was why he'd dragged his feet with the English policewoman.

But when Constable Lucy had brought her bosses and Chakyar into the loop, Niket had done the only thing he could think of. He'd got Chitta to do the investigating on his behalf. Chitta was invisible, someone nobody would look at or take any notice of, and when Chitta discovered the bodies dumped on the rubbish site, Niket went straight to his boss and confessed what had happened.

Inspector Chakyar immediately suspended his Senior Constable, but not for doing anything wrong. It was to keep him and his little sister safe.

Chitta quickly checked for new messages for the third time in ten minutes. He didn't want something important to come in and to be the last to know. He wanted to be at the forefront of the next investigation. Prove himself to Inspector Chakyar, so he would continue to sponsor him, and then he could one day sit the Civil Services Examination so he would be elevated from the state cadre and earn a decent rank along with a decent wage.

His blood fizzed when he spotted an email from Police Constable Lucy Davies. Except she wasn't a PC any more. As he read her message, he saw she was now a detective.

The email had been sent to several police officers, not just Niket. She was still looking for the Cargo Killer. She'd attached a police photo-fit of him. Dark hair thinning on top, long face, dark eyes.

Chitta stared at the picture but he didn't recognise the man. He printed off the photograph and pushed it inside his pocket. He would keep it, just in case the man came to Chennai. You never knew. That was what good detecting was all about. Being ready for that moment when you found the perfect clue to solve the perfect crime.

CHAPTER SEVENTY-SEVEN

Dan didn't return home straight away. He spoke to Aimee twice daily on FaceTime, but after a week had passed he knew he couldn't put it off any longer. He texted Jenny to let her know he was coming.

His father rang as he was driving over the Severn Bridge. Dan wasn't going to answer, but at the last minute relented.

'Hi, Dad.'

'Dan. How are you?'

'OK. Everything OK your end?'

'Yes. Thank you.'

They were unusually stilted, which wasn't surprising after their last meeting.

'You betrayed me.' Dan had laid it on the line. 'I asked you all those questions about Stella, Joe and Ellis, Savannah, and even though I was searching, desperate for the truth, you wouldn't give it to me.'

His father squared his shoulders. 'I was told it could harm you. Bring on a psychosis or something. I had your best interests in mind.'

'Well, next time, I won't bother asking.'

At that, his father had looked away. 'I'm sorry you feel like that.'

Neither had apologised.

'Have you seen Jenny yet?' his father now asked.

Dan was tempted not to reply. Part of him wanted to punish his father but the other part knew it was childish and that it would only hurt everyone in the long run. They had bridges to repair and withholding what was happening between him and Jenny would only make things worse.

He said, 'I'm heading there now.'

'I won't say anything more,' said his father, 'except I'll be thinking of you.'

Jenny was standing at the kitchen window when he arrived. She didn't wave. Neither did he.

He parked. Climbed out and into the wet air that smelled of grass and sheep.

Jenny stepped outside. Her hair was freshly washed and shone like satin. She wore skinny jeans and a stretchy lilac top that clung to her body, showing off her breasts and taut stomach. He couldn't help staring. Despite everything, she still took his breath away.

She looked at his vehicle. She said, 'Where's your car?'

'I swapped it.'

Her mouth opened and closed. 'What?'

'Is Aimee here?'

'She's at her grandmother's.' A look of anxiety crossed her face. 'That's what you wanted, right?'

'Yes.' He walked to the rear of the estate car and opened the door. 'Out you come,' he told her.

The Rottweiler didn't need asking twice. She leaped on to the grass and looked around, tail high, ears stiff.

'Dear God.' Jenny had her hands clapped to her face. 'What's that?'

'My dog.'

'But . . . It's huge.'

'Yes.'

Jenny stared as the dog trotted away. Not far. Just ten yards or so. After the animal had squatted, it tracked the area, never going far, keeping Dan close.

Dan couldn't say why he'd gone to the RSPCA centre. Perhaps it was a form of subconscious closure, or a desire to connect with his past – both dogs had remembered him – but he couldn't get them out of his mind. The moment the male dog saw anyone pass his cage he lunged at them, barking insanely, even at Dan, but when Dan visited the female – who they'd separated and put at the opposite end of the kennels – she ambled over and pushed her nose through the fence, wanting to be stroked. Her tail ticked from side to side in a stumpy, happy wag. When he'd scratched the back of her head with his fingers, she'd closed her eyes and emitted a purr.

'The male dog will be impossible to rehome,' the RSPCA officer told Dan. 'He's too aggressive. And the female . . . Well, she's a lovely creature, great with kids. She only acts aggressively when the male does, but even so I doubt we'll find her a home.' He looked depressed. 'Nobody wants big dogs. Too costly to feed. Both will be put to sleep tomorrow.'

Dan had walked out with the female dog an hour later.

'You can't keep it,' Jenny said. A wild look entered her eyes. 'Who's going to walk it while you're at work? Where will it sleep? Dear God, what about Aimee?'

'Poppy's great with kids. Besides, we won't be staying here, so it won't be a problem.' He began to walk for the house. 'I just wanted to pick up some stuff.'

'What do you mean?' She looked alarmed.

He stopped and turned to look at her. His heart felt as though a knife was being driven through it.

Quietly he said, 'We need some time apart.'

The blood drained from her face. 'No,' she said.

'We both need some space after what's happened.'

'Why?'

'Because I know the truth.'

A shadow slid in the depths of her eyes. 'Which is?'

'That I had an affair with Joe's wife.'

Long silence. He heard the wind shiver across the grass.

'Yes.' Her voice was a whisper.

He waited.

'She was in love with you.' Her voice trembled. 'She wanted you to leave me for her. You were thinking about it.'

The knife twisted in his heart.

Jenny closed her eyes. 'I saw her in the hospital with you. You were such a mess, you couldn't stop pacing the ward, muttering, shouting like a crazy man that Luke's death was all your fault. But when she was there you stopped. You focused on her one hundred per cent. Listened to everything she said.'

Her eyes sparked blue bitter fire. 'I hated her. I hated you.'

'Joe tried to sleep with you.'

She looked away. 'Yes.'

'I shot him.'

Her mouth gaped. 'Because he tried to sleep with me?'

He wanted to say, *no, because he got Luke killed*, but he held his tongue. He'd met with Bernard yesterday, and the DG had told him that Jenny didn't know about Besnik and genuinely believed Luke had been killed in a hit-and-run. Apparently when Besnik had dumped Dan and Luke's broken body on the street, he'd rung MI5 and told them where to find them. Savannah and Ellis had raced to pick them up and when they saw the state they were in, sped them to the nearest A & E. Ellis had made up the hit-and-run story. Dan supposed he'd corroborated. Layer upon layer of lies. And although Jenny may have been duplicitous she didn't deserve to know the reality behind their son's death. That Luke had been beaten to death in front of his father.

'Dan?' she prompted. She was looking aghast.

'He's in hospital.' He didn't want to explain the whole story. If she wanted to find out what had happened between him and Joe, then good luck to her. He wouldn't stop her.

'What about Laura?' Anguish was etched onto her face, her blue eyes burning. 'Are you going to her now?'

'I have no memory of Laura,' he said. Which was true. He went on to tell her about his meeting with Bernard. Bernard had shown him a photograph of Joe's wife, her raven hair and lithe, dancer's body, but no memories emerged. When Dan had pressed him, Bernard had been expressly cautious about Dan's personal history, but he'd intimated that Dan had a talent for befriending women and using pillow talk to access their secrets.

Dan recalled the anxiety he had felt in his dreams, his continual search for something important, and Bernard had looked at him long and hard before he said, 'Do you think you suspected Joe was Cedric? That you thought by getting close to his wife you might find the evidence we needed?'

And that was when the final jigsaw pieces fell into place.

He looked into Bernard's eyes and when he spoke, the truth resonated like a bell inside his heart, his soul. 'Yes,' he said.

Now, he looked at Jenny and she looked back.

'You're serious?' she said. 'You carried on with her all that time because you were using her to *spy* on Joe?'

'Yes.'

'And you think that excuses you?' Jenny's expression was incredulous.

'No.' He took a breath. 'But that was before. This is now. I have to collect my things.'

'No, wait.' A look of panic crossed her face. 'Stay with me. We can work it out.' She stepped forward and instinctively, he stepped back. 'Please, don't go,' she begged.

'I have to,' he said. 'We both need to think about where we go next. What you want from me. Whether I can live with the fact that you lied to me for so long about so many things.' His tone hardened. 'Why did you leave me struggling to find out about my past?'

'Because I love you!' she cried. 'Can't you imagine what it was like for me when you couldn't remember Laura any more? When you couldn't remember that you were thinking of leaving me? My God. Why would I want you to *remember?*'

The pain in his heart spread to his lungs until he had to fight to draw breath. He said, 'I'm sorry.'

He walked into the house. Climbed into the attic and retrieved a suitcase and two holdalls. He packed indiscriminately, unable to concentrate.

When he walked back outside it was to find Poppy sitting in the back of the car, expression expectant. Jenny stood to one side, motionless. Her skin was ashen.

Dan put the suitcase on the back seat and stuffed the holdalls alongside.

Jenny said, 'Where will you go?'

'London,' he said.

'But you can't teach high-performance driving in a city.'

He said, 'I'm not doing that anymore.'

She blinked.

'There's a vacancy with a company in Mayfair.' He closed the car's rear door. 'DCA & Co. They've already said dogs are welcome in the office.'

'Not MI5?' She looked genuinely baffled.

He stared at her. 'You really think they'd take me with my messed-up memory?'

'I guess not,' she whispered.

He walked to the other side of the car and opened the door, climbed inside. 'I'll come and see Aimee at the weekend.'

She nodded.

He drove down the mountain steadily, careful of his new passenger in the back. Trees flashed past. Stretches of moorland. The sky was blue-black in the distance but across the valley fields were bathed in bright sunshine. Rain spattered on his windscreen. A blast of wind rocked the car.

Moods of the countryside. Dark and light. Shade and clarity.

He was driving from a past he now knew. Sorrow and shame. Betrayal and perfidy. Hope and redemption. Liberation, compassion.

He saw it all now. In this moment on the mountain with only a handful of possessions and with his eyes wide open.

He saw it all.

At last.

AUTHOR'S NOTE

This book is a work of fiction. However, the story of Dan Forrester being given an amnesia drug is based on real-life research. On 1 July 2007 I saw an article by the *Telegraph*'s science correspondent Richard Gray, which sparked the idea for this novel. In it, Gray stated, 'Researchers have found they can use drugs to wipe away single, specific memories while leaving other memories intact.'

He went on to write that, 'In a new study, revealed in the *Journal of Psychiatric Research*, psychiatrists at McGill University, in Montreal, and Harvard University, in Boston, used an amnesia drug to "dampen" the memories of trauma victims.'

The researchers used propranolol, a non-selective beta-blocker used to treat hypertension in patients with heart problems.

Browsing the Internet further I came across: http://www.livescience.com/7315-drug-deletes-bad-memories.html

Here I read that 'similar research led by Professor Joseph LeDoux has been carried out at New York University on rats; scientists were able to remove a specific memory from the brains of rats while leaving the rest of the animals' memories intact. An amnesia drug called U0126 was administered'.

Great, I thought. A memory-erasing drug!

But when I looked closer it became clear that most of the research was actually looking at erasing fear from memory. Not quite the same, but who am I to split hairs when creating a story.

I guess it will only be a question of time before fiction becomes fact and an amnesia drug becomes available. In my view the downside of such a drug would be that it could be taken on a whim. Upset after a broken relationship? Pop a pill. Angry at your boss after a bad day? Pop a pill. However, the upside is that severely traumatised victims of crime or war could find a life-saving tool to help them return to a relatively normal life.

Regarding electromagnetic (radiation) weapons, these are very much a reality. Technologies for stimulating the brain and controlling the mind have a dark side that military and intelligence planners have been keen to exploit for decades. Whether or not the UK Government has a non-lethal weapons programme is debatable; however there is a wealth of scientific literature, including official US Government sources showing that such non-lethal weapons capability is being developed in the West. MEDUSA (Mob Excess Deterrent Using Silent Audio) is a directional non-lethal microwave sound weapon that bypasses human ears and eardrums to create an uncomfortably high noise in the skull. MEDUSA is developed by Sierra Nevada Corporation.

BIBLIOGRAPHY

Books

Becker, R., *The Body Electric: Electromagnetism and the Foundation of Life* (New York, 1987).

Begich, N., *Controlling the Human Mind: The Technologies of Political Control or Tools for Peak Performance* (Alaska, 2006).

Begich, N., *Earth Rising II: The Betrayal of Science, Society and the Soul* (Alaska, 2003).

Brodeur, P., *Currents of Death* (New York, 1989).

Duncan, R., *Project Soul Catcher: Secrets of Cyber and Cybernetic Warfare Revealed* (Kempton, Ill., 2010).

Lin, J. C., *Microwave Auditory Effects and Applications* (Springfield, Ill., 1978).

Mind Control Publishing, *The Encyclopedia of Mind-Control: Strategy, Natural and Man Made* (2012).

Owen, S. and Saunders, A., *Bipolar Disorder: The Ultimate Guide* (Oxford, 2008).

Smith, J., *HARRP: The Ultimate Weapon of the Conspiracy* (Kempton, Ill., 1998).

Websites

Bill Christensen, 'New Drug Deletes Bad Memories', *LiveScience*, (published online July 2007) <http://www.livescience.com/7315-drug-deletes-bad-memories.html>

http://www.haarp.alaska.edu/ website of the High Frequency Active Auroral Research Program

Richard Gray, 'Scientists find drug to banish bad memories', *Telegraph*, (published online July 2007) <http://www.telegraph.co.uk/science/science-news/3298988/Scientists-find-drug-to-banish-bad-memories.html>

David Hambling, 'Microwave ray gun controls crowds with noise', *New Scientist*, (published online July 2008) <http://www.newscientist.com/article/dn14250-microwave-ray-gun-controls-crowds-with-noise.html>

Peter Phillips, 'US Electromagnetic Weapons and Human Rights', Mind Justice, (published December 2006) <http://mindjustice.org/censored12-06.htm>

http://www.navysbirprogram.com/NavySearch/Summary/summary.aspx?pk=F5B07D68-1B19-4235-B140-950CE2E19D08

Useful websites on bipolar disorder

Bipolar UK is the national charity dedicated to supporting people affected by bipolar: <www.bipolaruk.org.uk/>

Mind is a mental health charity which provides information on bipolar: <www.mind.org.uk/>

Bipolar Support provides information and support for bipolar patients and their loved ones: <www.bipolarsupport.org/>

ACKNOWLEDGEMENTS

I would like to thank Chief Constable Jacqui Cheer, Cleveland Police, for her generous sanction of my research, and Sergeant Stephen Williams-Reader, Stockton Neighbourhood Police, for giving me such a great tour of his home town and advising me on numerous aspects of policing.

Thanks also to Inspector Kevin Robinson, West Yorkshire Police (retired), for his in-depth insight into police analysis; Paul and Ruth McGrath, Cleveland Police (retired), whose incisive knowledge on police procedure I couldn't have done without; Dr Michael Seed, who I called on for his expertise not just in weaponry but also in biology and pharmacology; Joseph Coventry, whose keen interest in the science behind this story inspired me to write it.

Dr Ashish Bhatia and Dr Rebecca Bhatia have been immensely helpful, sharing what it is like to be a GP and responding to my inquisition with equanimity, as well as coming up with some great creative ideas.

Special thanks are due to Anthony Weale and Dudley Ankerson for a terrific brainstorming session right at the start. Thanks to Juliet Coombe for providing the title. Also to Rachel Legg, practice nurse; Liz Kolovos, defence project negotiator; Susan Opie, critical reader.

Thanks also to the team at Zaffre Publishing for their enthusiasm right from their start, especially my extremely talented editor, Joel Richardson.

I owe a massive thanks to my wonderful agent Rowan Lawton who not only appears to have a boundless store of energy but the invaluable ability to think outside the box.

Lastly, as is customary in such matters, I must declare that any mistakes are mine.

If you enjoyed *Spare Me the Truth*, why not read CJ Carver's CWA Debut Dagger Award winning novel – available now in ebook

BLOOD JUNCTION

Journalist India Kane's trip to the Australian outback takes a horrifying turn when she arrives in the town of Cooinda to find that her best friend Lauren is missing.

Seemingly no one knows what has happened to her, but it's not long before India finds herself arrested for a double murder that she didn't commit, caught up in the dark past of a small town hiding a devastating truth – one that could destroy a family, a friendship, and a nation.

A powerful and compulsive thriller about a woman on the run from a brutal killer, as well as from her own past.

And follow on with the rest of the backlist – also available in ebook . . .

BLACK TIDE

India Kane is back in a dark and dangerous quest for justice.

GONE WITHOUT TRACE

Jay McCaulay is on a trail of murder, corruption and evil that leads to the very heart of London.

BACK WITH VENGEANCE

Jay McCaulay finds herself once again entangled in a web of lies.

THE HONEST ASSASSIN

Jay McCaulay was the only witness to an assassination and is determined to discover the truth.

DEAD HEAT

When the plane Georgia Parish is on crashes, it soon becomes clear that it was no accident.

BENEATH THE SNOW

When a young scientist vanishes in the Alaskan wilderness, her sister joins the search and finds more than she bargained for.